The
Sparrow Sisters

The
Sparrow Sisters

Ellen Herrick

wm

WILLIAM MORROW

An Imprint of HarperCollins*Publishers*

P.S.™ is a trademark of HarperCollins Publishers.

THE SPARROW SISTERS. Copyright © 2015 by Ellen Herrick. All rights reserved. Printed in the United States of America. No part of this book may be used or reproduced in any manner whatsoever without written permission except in the case of brief quotations embodied in critical articles and reviews. For information address HarperCollins Publishers, 195 Broadway, New York, NY 10007.

HarperCollins books may be purchased for educational, business, or sales promotional use. For information please e-mail the Special Markets Department at SPsales@harpercollins.com.

FIRST EDITION

Designed by Diahann Sturge

Library of Congress Cataloging-in-Publication Data has been applied for.

ISBN 978-0-06-238634-2

15 16 17 18 19   OV/RRD   10 9 8 7 6 5 4 3 2 1

For Emma, who dared me

The
Sparrow Sisters

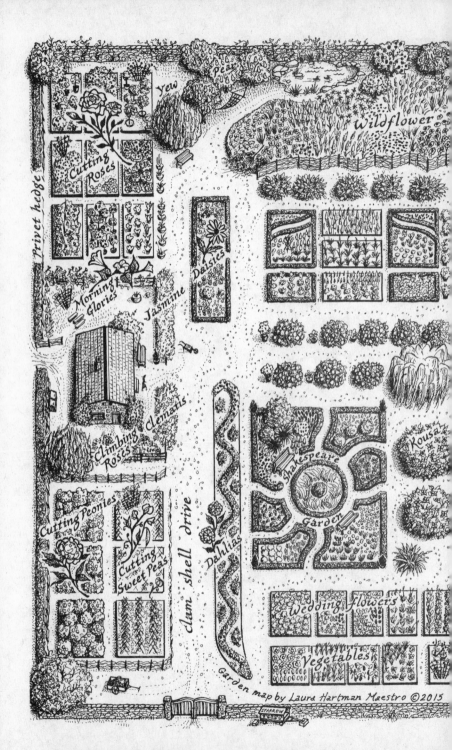

Pear

Yew

Wildflower

Cutting Roses

Privet hedge

Daisies

Morning Glories

Jasmine

Climbing Roses

Clematis

Kousa

Shakespeare Garden

Cutting Peonies

clam shell drive

Dahlias

Cutting Sweet Peas

Wedding Flowers

Vegetables

Garden map by Laura Hartman Maestro ©2015

SPARROW

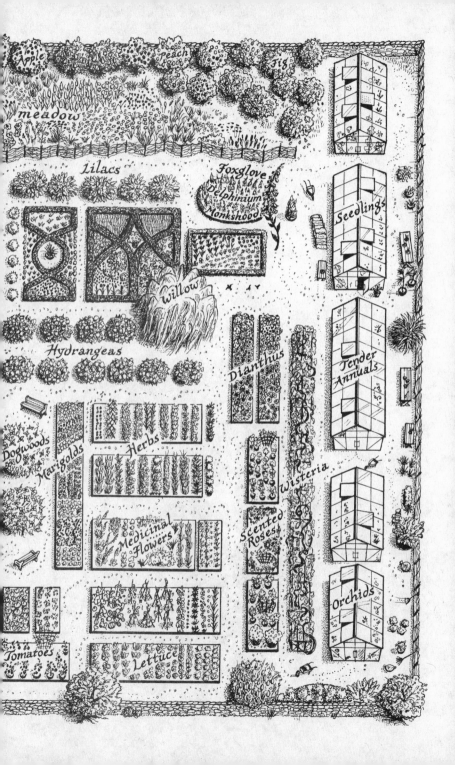

PROLOGUE

*A*ll stories are true. Some of them actually happened."

Three sisters in the third pew nodded sharply in unison as John Hathaway looked out over his congregation; this made him stutter in an otherwise seamless sermon.

Patience Sparrow rocked in the pew until she made her sister Sorrel look away from the altar. Nettie Sparrow leaned in so that she could see both her sisters and smiled when she noticed they were already bent toward each other. Someone's stomach growled. It was Easter Sunday, and the women were ready to bolt. It wasn't that the sermon was dull, or that they already knew how right the Episcopal minister was. Some stories, told enough, became as true as their words. Any of these sisters could tell you that. It's just that they were *hungry*. The three swayed back and resumed their attentive poses.

In the last pew but two, Henry Carlyle sat on the aisle. He was not a regular at the First Episcopal Church on the green. He was too new in town to be a regular anywhere, although he thought the little bakery down the street from his house was so good he might start showing up there every day. The phone in his pocket vibrated against his thigh, and he put his hand over it before the woman next to him got the wrong idea. She'd already shot him several curious glances, and he'd let his heavy, dark forelock fall over his eye to block her out. Henry needed a haircut. The phone buzzed again. He knew it was work; Henry didn't have a friend in Granite Point, not yet anyway. Sampling the churches in town was his sorry attempt at meeting people. He watched the three heads a few pews up from his. He'd seen them laughing, acting up really, their shoulders shaking like naughty kids. A soft snort floated up from the redhead when the blonde in the middle nudged the others. Their behavior seemed so unlikely; one of the women (they were women, he had to acknowledge) had graying hair. Henry knew he'd have to slip out to answer the call, but before he did, he told himself a story about the women: how they couldn't convince their husbands or kids to come to church with them, how they were best friends or neighbors who would pick up their Easter desserts at the bakery after the service. But his story wasn't true because how could he know anything at all about the Sparrow Sisters? The true story would come later.

CHAPTER ONE

Lupin creates a fresh color in the cheek and a cheerful countenance

Once there were four Sparrow Sisters. Everyone called them the Sisters, capitalized, and referred to them as a group, even when just one had come to the post office to collect the mail. "The Sisters are here for their package," the postmistress would say, calling her clerk to the desk. Or, "What do you know, the Sisters are taking the train into the city." All four had left Granite Point over the years on school trips to Boston and for the symphony or the museum, but they always came back; it was home. The only Sparrow sister who did leave town forever did so in the hardest way. The oldest Sparrow, if only by seven minutes, was Marigold, Sorrel's twin. She was the real homebody, the one people still shook their heads over, and she actually left Granite Point just twice; the first time to accompany her father to a meeting with lawyers upon the death of her mother and the last upon her own death, in a smallish wooden box nestled inside an Adams's Hardware bag on the arm of her twin. Sorrel took Marigold to the Outer Beach, past the break north of the seal colony, to scatter her ashes in the Atlantic.

Now there were only three Sparrows left in the house at the top of the hill overlooking the far harbor. Long ago this house that their great-great (and more) grandmother Clarissa Sparrow built had rung with the shouts and laughter of her four sons and the many Sparrow sons that followed. It was made of the timber used to craft the whaling fleet that sailed out from the harbor and into the dark waves. Her husband was a sea captain so fond of his trade that Clarissa chose wood from her father's shipyard with the idea that if George Sparrow loved his boat so much, surely he would be called home to a house made of the very same wood. She'd even built a widow's walk high above the street so that she could watch for him to sail back to her. Eventually, the widow's walk would earn its name several times over.

By the time the Sparrow Sisters lived in the house on Ivy Street, lanes and hedges and other houses had grown up, blocking all but a narrow sliver of the deep blue water of Big Point Bay. Ivy House, as everyone called it, stood tall and white as it had for all those years, home to the last of the Sparrows altogether. The house was beautiful and spare with high ceilings and windows of wavy glass. It was most often filled with the flowers and herbs, vegetables and fruits of the Sparrow Sisters Nursery. Like their mother, Honor Sparrow, dead now for twenty-some years—gone on the very day her youngest daughter, Impatiens, arrived—the sisters all had green thumbs. It was ordained, really. They had each been named after a botanical, mostly flowers, and as their mother kept producing girls, the names became slightly ridiculous. But Honor was a keen gardener and in darkest winter, calling her daughter's names reminded her that spring would come again. For months after her death the older girls hated their names and all they recalled for them. By the time they founded the Sparrow Sisters Nursery, though, each thoroughly embraced their names as the sign they were.

Sorrel, Nettie, and Patience might well have gone on as they were accustomed, planting and reaping, selling the abundance of their labors, cooking for each other and listening to the opera every Saturday afternoon as Sorrel did the ironing, fulfilling the roles of town eccentrics. Although to be fair, Sorrel was not yet forty, hardly biddy material. But then the old town doctor, Eliakim Higgins, retired and set in motion everything that came after. He'd delivered all but one of the girls and cared for each of them on the rare occasions that they fell ill. He had diagnosed Marigold, and overseen her chemotherapy, as pointless as it turned out to be, in the seven months it took her to die. Dr. Higgins was very attached to the sisters, even more so after he'd been unable to save their mother and then Marigold.

But at seventy-six his hands were not as steady nor his eyes so clear. He decided to leave his practice for the creosote-scented air of Arizona. Although there was a group medical practice in Hayward seventeen miles west, Dr. Higgins had always been the town's first choice. Well, he and then Patience Sparrow, whose reputation for curing everyday maladies like cradle cap and insomnia had turned her gift into an unexpected sideline. She was more often paid in eggs and striped bass, hand-knitted sweaters and fresh quahogs, than cash, but still. Her ability was cultivated along with the plants at the Sparrow Sisters Nursery, and it wasn't long after college that Patience decided she would stay in Granite Point and go to work with her sisters. Her degree in botany wasn't the reason the Nursery called to her. It was the Nursery that called her to study. In fact, if the older girls hadn't invested their inheritance and, even more, their hearts, in the land, Patience might well have wandered away and had a very different story indeed.

The Sisters remained close to the doctor (he was, after all, as alone as they were), but after Marigold they were never his patients again. The spring after Dr. Higgins left town, a young doctor straight out of Massachusetts General by way of the army bought the small shingled house and practice on Baker's Way where Dr. Higgins had lived and worked for over forty years. The arrangements were made quietly through a Boston firm, leaving little time for speculation in town and even less for real digging. The young man remained a mystery.

Henry Carlyle moved in quickly, alone, on a cold Wednesday in April. He'd collected few things over the years in medical school and then the service. The neighbors watched Dr. Carlyle, muffled in a dark blue sweater, sleeves pushed up over his elbows as he unloaded the rented van. Movers had already brought all the big stuff, so what Henry now carried into the house was expected: boxes, lamps, two suitcases, and a large duffel. The oddest item was a long single shell and oars. Henry slid it out effortlessly, shouldering the impossibly thin boat before he went back for the oars. His little audience behind their twitching curtains might have wondered where he meant to row—the glacial lake, Frost Fish perhaps, or the still pond down Arey's Lane? But the snoopers were more curious that the tall, broad-shouldered doctor limped, and as the van began to empty, the hitch became more pronounced. By the time Henry Carlyle climbed into the van to return it to the U-Haul in Hayward, he'd begun to wince with every step. His first patients would try to divine how he'd been hurt but, although he was attentive and gentle in his examinations, Dr. Carlyle revealed nothing personal beyond the fact that he was a product of Yale Medical School (class of 1999—the diploma was on his wall).

Henry Carlyle was just a year or so younger than Nettie Sparrow, and on the day she came to see him, she couldn't help but notice the way his dark hair curled behind his ear. There were strands of gray in it that led Nettie to think that while it might be youthful in its length, perhaps it showed he hadn't had things so very easy. She sat on the crinkly paper covering the old leather examination table, the first and likely the only sister to consult Dr. Carlyle. She was a bit of a hypochondriac, but really, who could blame her after Marigold and her parents? Nettie had been fighting a chest cold for weeks, it seemed, so she made an appointment, convinced it was pneumonia. The nurse who doubled as receptionist at the practice had gone to high school with Nettie. Sally Tabor had waggled her eyebrows as she beckoned Nettie closer to the counter. She leaned in to whisper, which wasn't easy given that Sally was heavily pregnant.

"Look out," she said, glancing behind her to be sure her boss wasn't in earshot. "He's as handsome as anything and as chilly as Big Point Bay in January."

Nettie was in mid-giggle when Dr. Carlyle came to the doorway and called her name. She followed him down the hall, her fingers at her lips as she saw his limp. Now, as she sat watching him glance through her chart (a thin file that was proof of both the Sparrow Sisters' hearty constitutions and their mistrust of doctors), she hoped that Sally was wrong about him.

Dr. Carlyle looked straight into Nettie's eyes as he put the file on the table beside her, which made her heart flutter just enough to worry her.

"Nettie, is that short for Annette?" Dr. Carlyle asked.

"It's short for Nettle." Nettie hated the way her voice quavered as she shivered in the office gown. "Stinging nettle tea was the only thing that soothed my mother's hives when she was carrying me."

Henry laughed and then apologized. "That's unusual."

"Yes, well," Nettie said, "All our names are unusual."

Henry took her pulse and temperature, laying a gentle hand against her forehead for a moment. He breathed onto his stethoscope to warm it before he slipped it under her gown. Nettie noted the small courtesy and decided there and then that this Dr. Carlyle was a suitable replacement for Dr. Higgins—not that she would be seeing him again. Just being in his office made her feel traitorous, and she regretted her moment of panic. Or was it rebellion? Patience could smell a doctor a mile off.

After listening to her lungs, Dr. Carlyle determined that she did not have pneumonia but rather a stubborn case of bronchitis and prescribed antibiotics and rest. Nettie left his office in an unreasonably grateful state, prescription in hand, feeling better already. There was only a moment of hesitation when she considered the reaction of the pharmacist. Since Marigold's death none of the Sisters had needed Mr. Howe's services. It had not gone unnoticed. As she waited for her medicine, Nettie knew that his clerk had her ears pricked as she unnecessarily straightened the magazines on the rack next to Nettie.

When Dr. Carlyle brought her chart to Sally, he saw that Nettie had left her jacket on the chair nearest the counter. It actually belonged to her sister Patience, but Nettie was feverish and distracted; she'd grabbed the first thing she saw as she snuck out of Ivy House that morning. He picked it up to give it to his nurse, but the smell of tarragon and thyme and something almost *cool* made him pause and hold it a little closer. Sally eyed him as she took the coat from his hands and signaled the next patient. Henry was already planning what would be the first of many house calls since arriving in a town that seemed absolutely determined to stay trapped in the amber of a time long past. The last patient was dispatched by 5:30 so Henry had just enough time to listen to a filing lecture from Sally before he washed the disinfectant off his hands and face. As Henry picked up the jacket Nettie had left behind, he remembered how his father had always told him that he should start as he meant to continue, so Henry decided that he'd make Nettie Sparrow his first house call. He buttoned his vest and stepped out into the slanting light.

BACK AT THE house Sorrel and Patience settled their sister in her room. Patience brought her white pepper, ginger, and honey mixed into hot water and tied a length of eucalyptus-scented flannel around Nettie's neck. Then she went back to the Nursery. Patience had a talent for healing, but she wasn't much for nursing and certainly not for a sister who chose to bypass her in favor of a stranger.

This is how Dr. Carlyle found Nettie that early evening when he stopped by to check on his patient and return the jacket. Propped up in her bed, a thick eiderdown pulled up to her shoulders, even in the warmth of the house, Nettie was shocked when the tall doctor walked into her room followed by a clearly discombobulated Sorrel.

"Well," he said. "I see someone has their own ideas about medicine." Dr. Carlyle leaned down, his hand on the iron bedpost for balance, and took a deep sniff of Nettie's flannel. "Eucalyptus?" he asked, cocking his head as he inhaled, his long lashes casting his gray eyes in darker shadow. Poor Nettie felt a shiver leap up her neck.

"My sister made this," she stuttered. "And the tea."

Henry picked up the cup and sniffed again. It was an odd smell, sharp from the pepper, soft from the honey.

"Patience has the gift," Sorrel added from the end of the bed. "She's quite popular here in town."

"Popular as in all the boys like her?" The doctor laughed.

"Oh, no," Nettie said. "Patience isn't interested in boys anymore."

Henry laughed again. "All grown up or already taken?"

Sorrel gave a laugh. "Patience is the baby, Dr. Carlyle, and none of us are taken." She blushed and desperately wanted to unsay the last bit. "She has a gift with herbs and plants," she continued. "Everyone comes for her remedies."

Now Henry turned to look at Sorrel. "Remedies?" he said with a frown.

"Oh, yes." Nettie sat up straighter; she had heard the disapproval in the doctor's voice and was already on the defensive. "Patience has inherited an ancestral ability and the recipe book. She has the touch; ask anyone."

Henry Carlyle didn't know whether to be alarmed or just amused that this unseen Sparrow sister had managed to hoodwink an entire town. He was pretty sure that he didn't like it. He might have left with nothing more than a vague feeling of disappointment about how gullible people could be, had Patience not come home just then, the back screen door slamming behind her with a loud clap. Nettie started, and Sorrel escorted the doctor from the room, down the front stairs, away from the kitchen, hoping to get him out of the house before he had a chance to meet their sister. She nearly made it, too. Henry had his hand on the front door when Patience wandered in from the kitchen, her arms full of chamomile. The little flowers brushed her chin with yellow pollen, and her hair had sprung loose from its messy twist.

The sisters had lived in an isolated state for so long that Patience was shocked to see a strange man in her front room. Almost as soon as she felt that shock, Patience was embarrassed, and then she was irked.

"Who is that?" she asked her sister, completely ignoring the man himself. Sorrel spluttered out Henry's name and purpose. She saw the face-off that was setting up and clapped her hands at Patience, an unspoken request for civility from her prickling sister. The entire scene was so unexpected that it brought out the worst in all three players. Henry didn't want to lecture this very pretty woman he'd barely met. He realized she was the snorter in church on Easter, the redhead, and as he stared at her, he became fascinated by the precarious nature of her hairdo. In the last of the sun it appeared like a halo around her head. But, perhaps because he was new to Granite Point and eager to establish his authority, Henry spoke, his voice harder than he meant it to be.

"What's all this I hear about your remedies?" The dismissal was clear and Patience, for the first time in days (a record), turned snappish.

"I beg your pardon?" Patience asked with a bit of a bark. Out of the corner of her eye she saw Sorrel flinch.

The doctor looked at Patience with a mixture of surprise and anger. It was not a pretty look. His brow lowered, and his jaw stood out sharply as he clenched it. As for the object of his irritation, two hectic spots of red bloomed on her cheeks and, to her horror, tears sprang to her eyes, threatening to spill over her burning face.

Sorrel ushered Henry out as she excused her sister's outburst in calming tones. As soon as the door clicked into place, she rounded on Patience.

"How could you be so rude!" she snapped. "Honestly, I think you put all your care, every bit of it, into your remedies."

She stomped out into the back garden, leaving Patience staring at the black-and-white checked floor. A hot tear dropped at her feet. It smelled of chamomile, as did her skin and clothes, but there was nothing soothing in it for Patience. Sorrel lost her temper with her sisters so infrequently that Patience wasn't sure if she was (damn it) crying because of Sorrel's angry words or over the very odd reaction she'd had to Henry Carlyle. Simmering under her anger with Dr. Carlyle was a wholly unexpected tug. If Henry had been captured in that moment,

Patience had been caught too. She would never tell her sisters, but Patience had already noticed Henry, twice. One evening as she walked home from Baker's Way Bakers, Patience had looked up to see him standing at his window. He hadn't seen her in the darkness, but she was able to pick out the slump of his shoulders, his fingertips pressed against the glass. She'd wondered what his story was. Patience had sidled closer to the building across the street so she could look at him for another minute. When she saw him coming out of the post office a week later, she ducked her head and fiddled with her phone.

Patience swiped at her cheeks and pulled her heavy hair back up into a ponytail. "Really," she muttered, "get a grip," and walked down the hall to the kitchen.

The air around her had taken on a sharp, astringent smell, the soft chamomile burned away in a matter of moments. Sorrel smelled it as she gathered laundry from the line; it was so strong even the sheets were imbued. She knew that sometimes Patience's rich interior life, a thing of bright colors, strong scents, and a good deal of swearing, burst forth. The smells that followed her were the most noticeable, and even the town had learned to interpret at least some of the scents that wrapped around the youngest sister. Her graceful surface was often at odds with the force of her emotions. When that happened, everything and everyone around her knew it. Her sisters had gotten used to it: her internal struggles externalized. In fact, they could read Patience as easily as Patience read the people she helped. The three sisters were as tightly entwined as the bittersweet they battled each fall, and as stubborn. If the town ever wondered why they didn't break away—and it did—no one dared to ask them.

All the Sparrow Sisters were naturally beautiful, each in very different ways—except for the twins, of course, who were eerily identical. So even the three who were left in the house had the certain confidence that came with knowing you needn't worry about your looks. They were never self-conscious around the men in town, which made Patience's reaction to Dr. Carlyle all the odder. In fact, as the years passed and neither Sorrel nor Nettie married, everyone stopped bothering about them. A natural New England reserve meant people didn't give in to curiosity often, and really, it was easier to assign them the status of the slightly sad single Sisters than to keep wondering. The girls seemed unconcerned and went about their days, each as lovely in their own way as the flowers they tended. Sorrel's black hair became streaked with premature white, which gave her an exotic air, although the elegance was somewhat ruined by the muddy jeans and shorts she practically lived in. Nettie, on the other hand, had a head of baby-fine blond hair that she wore short, thinking, wrongly, that it would look less child-like. Nettie wouldn't dream of being caught in dirty jeans and was always crisply turned out in khaki capris or a skirt and a white shirt. She considered her legs to be her finest feature. She was not wrong.

Patience was the sole Sparrow redhead, although her hair had deepened from its childhood ginger and was now closer to the color of a chestnut. It was as heavy and glossy as a horse's mane, and she paid absolutely no attention to it or to much else about her appearance, nor did she have to. In the summer her wide-legged linen trousers and cut-off shorts were speckled with dirt and greenery, her camisoles tatty and damp. The broad-brimmed hat she wore to pick was most often dangling from a cord down her back. As a result, the freckles that feathered across her shoulders and chest were the color of caramel and resistant to her own buttermilk lotion (Nettie smoothed it on Patience whenever she could make her stand still). When it was terribly hot, Patience wore the sundresses she'd found packed away in the attic. She knew they were her mother's, and she liked to imagine how happy Honor had been in them.

On the surprisingly warm June day on which Dr. Carlyle threw the Sparrow Sisters into a swivet, Patience was wearing a pair of Sorrel's too-loose shorts rolled down at the waist until her hip bones showed below her tee shirt. She hadn't expected a visitor, and certainly not a stranger, so it wasn't until she went back into the kitchen and caught sight of herself in the French doors to the dining room that Patience realized how undressed she really was. She stared for a minute and then she laughed. *Ha!* she thought. *No wonder he was so unbalanced.*

Patience wasn't vain, but she knew what the sight of her bare midriff could do to a man. It made her laugh again as she pulled the chamomile flowers from their stems. But when she thought about how silly her sisters were, how completely "girly" their behavior had been in front of the doctor, her smile faded. And when she recalled how Henry Carlyle's jaw had hardened as he looked at her, Patience dropped the chamomile into the sink and slapped the cold porcelain, her tears completely dried, as teed off at him as Sorrel had been at her.

OUTSIDE IVY HOUSE, the doctor stood for a full minute before he turned to walk back to his practice. The scent of herbs and grass and damp soil trailed in the air behind him. He turned in a circle trying to focus on the scent, and for the second time that day he sniffed like a rabbit and tried to pinpoint what it was.

When Henry got back to his shingled house on Baker's Way, he wavered in front of the door to the apartment he lived in over the "shop." It was after six, and there was no real reason to go back into the office, but he did so anyway. It was too quiet in his apartment, which struck him as funny, really. The one thing he'd craved in the hospital was quiet. The one thing he didn't have when he was deployed was solitude. Now that he had both, it made him restless. So he unlocked the door and turned on the lights in the office. There were always notes to dictate, charts to catch up on; paperwork was not Henry's strong suit, and he usually left anything to do with organization to the last minute, or to Sally, who he'd inherited from Dr. Higgins. He found a pile of patient files with a yellow sticky on his desk and growled as he toed his chair out.

"Dr. Carlyle, please try to keep up," Sally had written in purple ink. He huffed and deliberately moved them aside so he could put his bag on the desk. Henry opened the old satchel, meaning to restock it with saline, Tylenol, a suture kit. The scent of chamomile slipped out, or at least that's what Henry thought. He snapped the bag shut and crossed to lie down on the exam table. The paper rattled under him as it did under his patients. Not for the first time he wondered what he thought he was doing in this town of fishermen and spinsters, shop-keepers and faith healers.

The smell of cookies replaced the chamomile, and Henry figured that the little store down the street, Baker's Way Bakers, was probably just closing, the last of the stock set aside for dis-count sale in the morning. Henry coughed, certain he could feel the flour on the back of his throat. He gave in to fatigue, a very different kind than that of his residency in Boston. There he'd felt hollowed out by exhaustion, a dark place inside wait-ing to be filled by the desperation and panic of a city hospital. Remembering that, Henry understood, again, why he'd left and why he'd come to Granite Point. He dozed off, slightly hungry for cake, the ache in his leg a nervy hum.

When Henry woke, it was full dark, and a small circle of lamplight puddled on his desk. Sitting up, he had a renewed sense of purpose; maybe it was the half hour of oblivion. Henry had trained himself to sleep quickly and deeply. He grabbed the charts and made his way upstairs, opened a beer, swallowed three aspirin, considered a Vicodin, and sat at the kitchen counter to work. There weren't too many patients yet: Dr. Higgins's practice had begun to wind down before he did, but Henry had high hopes. Already word of his kind manner and good looks had filtered down to the young mothers, their babies swaddled tight even into June, their toddlers already in bathing suits. News traveled fast, no doubt about it; rumors even faster. The women speculated that he'd left heartbreak behind in Boston, and their husbands figured he'd seen too much death in Iraq, too many sick people, accidents, and car wrecks at the hospital. Both were right, although his heart had broken far from Boston.

Hunger drove Henry back outside. He set aside his papers and slipped on the blue sweater. He was more susceptible to the cold since his return. The tree peepers seemed to echo the insistent buzz of pain in his leg. He walked slowly, trying to make his gait as even as possible. He was used to the way people's eyes flicked to his leg when he walked through the hospital or into his own waiting room. But, he realized now, Patience hadn't lowered her gaze, not even for an instant, as she stood with her arms full of damp flowers. Henry stuck his hands in his pockets as he rounded Main Street, glad that the lights of Doyle's were bright.

He took a seat at the bar. Frank Redmond approached, drying his hands on a stained white cloth.

"What'll you have, Doc?" he asked, and Henry snorted.

Frank looked at him, eyebrows raised.

"It's just that you're so welcoming and I just had a run in with . . . I have no idea what." Henry laughed. "Pretty tight, this town."

"Well now," Frank said, already pulling a pint for Henry. "There's some who might take offense at that, coming from an inlander."

"Oh, I'm sorry"—Henry raised his hand—"I only meant that nearly everyone I've met is . . ." He stopped. "Just, I'm sorry."

Frank was chuckling as he watched Henry fumble. "Shit, Henry, I'm just messing with you. Inlander, like that's even a word." He handed Henry a menu and moved off, still smiling.

Henry looked at the menu, not really seeing any of it. He'd have a grilled cheese and leave it at that. What Henry was seeing was Patience: the way her hair stuck to the dampness at her neck, the smudge of dirt over her eyebrow, the spark of anger he'd drawn from her even as he suspected that the last thing he wanted to make her was angry. Henry thought that making her smile would be wonderful, and he felt his own lips twitch.

"So?" Frank was back. "See something you like?"

"Oh yes," said Henry and shook his head to clear it of the springy green scent that seemed to cling to Patience, even in memory.

When his sandwich came, he ate it in silence, listening to the chatter of the locals who were Frank's bread and butter until the summer season got underway. He wiped his mouth and reached for his wallet, shifting on the stool until he had to slide off to keep his balance. He landed harder than he meant to on his bad leg and grimaced, dropping the wallet.

"A quart of the chowder, Frank." Patience stood at the end

of the bar, an old hoodie over her tee shirt. The stretched hem came to the middle of her thighs; she looked naked beneath it, but her dirty boots and slouchy socks dismissed that image with an oddly childish look.

Henry paused, his head just below the bar, his wallet halfway to his hip pocket. *Damn it,* he thought. It felt as if his little reverie had called Patience to Doyle's long before he was ready to see her again.

"How's Nettie?" Frank asked.

"She's better," Patience said shortly.

Frank lowered his voice, and Henry had to strain to hear him. "She went to the new guy, didn't she?"

"Yeah," Patience said. "She gets nervous, you know." She shuffled through some bills as Frank brought the soup.

"No charge, P," Frank said. "I still owe you for Claire's migraines."

"Thanks." Patience shoved all but a couple dollars back into her pocket. "See ya."

"Yup." Frank turned back, and Henry stood up slowly, careful not to look toward the front door as it swung shut behind Patience.

"Where'd you go there?" Frank asked.

"I dropped my wallet," Henry answered and opened it to pay for his dinner. Frank took the money, and Henry asked, "Not on the house for me?"

"When you cure my wife's headaches in the time it takes to make a martini, I'll tear up your bill too."

Henry felt the heat rise up his throat. He put a hand on the bar to stop Frank. "You seriously think her stuff works?"

"I seriously think it does, and so do most of the people in this town." Frank looked at Henry. "What do you know about the Sparrow Sisters?"

"There are three of them," Henry said. He took a last swallow of his beer. "That's all."

"That's true," Frank said and let the name Marigold flit through his head. "And you were hiding from Patience because, what? She doesn't like you?"

That was a question; she sure didn't seem to like him. "I wasn't hiding," Henry said. "How long am I going to be the new guy?" he asked.

"A while," Frank said.

Henry stepped back, preparing to leave, but Frank stopped him.

"You should know that the Sparrow Sisters are something of a legend in Granite Point. Their family history, hell their own story, it's as much a part of this place as the harbor." Frank closed the register. "I'm surprised you've seen one in your office. They aren't much for doctors after Marigold. Dr. Higgins was one thing, but the rest of the medical world, let's just say the Sisters aren't exactly fans." Henry faked a shudder. "I wouldn't want any of them pissed off at me."

"I'll remember that," Henry said. *Too late,* he thought as he walked out and right into Simon Mayo.

"Whoa, there," Simon said as both men grabbed each other's elbows.

As Henry apologized, he gave a slight hop to take the weight off his leg. He watched Simon's eyes travel down.

"So, the city doctor meets the country lawyer," Simon said as he stuck out his hand. "I'm Simon Mayo."

"Henry Carlyle," Henry said as he shook. "The new guy. How do you know me?"

Simon gestured to Henry's face and leg and smiled. "I'm afraid you're already famous."

"Oh" was all Henry could come up with.

"Can I buy you a beer?" Simon asked.

"I've got work to do," Henry replied.

"Another house call to the Sisters?" Simon's voice thinned, and Henry heard the shift.

"No, I'm finished there." Henry shook his head. "How does everybody know everything?"

Simon nodded and smiled again. "Very small town," He said. "I'll let you go, then."

Henry watched him walk into Doyle's. The light spilling around Simon's shoulders and the familiar greetings he got from people in the bar reminded Henry of the extent to which he was under scrutiny in Granite Point. Somehow Henry had ended up in a town with three odd sisters digging around at their nursery, making "remedies" in a cauldron no doubt, and *he* was the curiosity.

Frank had slipped out from behind the bar to watch Simon and Henry through the big window. He reckoned that the new doctor had a lot to learn about the Sisters if he wanted to belong in Granite Point. Frank understood, or at least his wife had taught him, that each sister had a life that held in its smallness all the detail of a much larger tragedy. He'd listened to the story of the Sparrows because Claire had told it to him. If Henry seemed a bit undone by Patience, maybe it was because her story was still unwritten.

CHAPTER TWO

Viola gently stimulates the immunity

Like their mother, the Sisters loved the soil, though it took some years after Honor's death before any of them were willing to be around her beloved plants. But when they were ready, the Sisters made haste. First, they reclaimed Honor's garden, tending the flowers and herbs that spilled over pea gravel paths and dwarf boxwood hedges in the nearly half acre behind the house. The week after Honor died, Thaddeus Sparrow swept through the land in a rage, pulling up every plant and crushing them underfoot as he swore and wept over the loss of his wife. In moments it seemed the garden was gone and four years later, so was their father. For a full year after Thaddeus's death, the Sisters turned their heads as they walked past the screen door off the kitchen. They pretended that the weeds that had crawled in so fast once Thaddeus wrecked the garden were just wildflowers finding their way home. Nettie longed to salvage the cosmos that struggled up through the rampant nutsedge and sow thistle, but she just clasped her hands and looked away.

It was Marigold who took the first step when she gave in and picked some foxtail for the kitchen table. The housekeeper who had moved into the big bedroom at the end of the hall frowned and tossed the spikelets back out the door. "Why don't you grow something pretty," she said. "That garden is nothing but a hazard with all those weeds." The sisters blinked owlishly and considered her idea.They didn't often listen to Mrs. Bartlet (who Patience called Mrs. Batlett as soon as she could talk) but it has to be said that she was often right, as she was this time.

Mrs. Bartlet stayed with the girls until the twins were eighteen. Then she came each weekday and took care that they ate sensible, stodgy food, and that Patience dressed in something other than bedsheet togas and didn't wear her slicker into the shower. She never did understand the murmured language the sisters made up to tell their secrets or the way Marigold could convince her to leave early on summer nights. But she loved them all the same and if any of the girls became mothers, they would remember how Mrs. Bartlet sent them back to the garden and made them safe after all.

In the end, it took the Sisters three seasons to tame the back garden, and when they saw how beautiful it was, they realized that they were indeed their mother's daughters and that their hands thrummed with the same gift. Still, as they looked after Patience and worked at the jobs each had chosen after going to Granite Point College (Marigold at the library, Nettie at the small catering company one town over, and Sorrel in charge of the family finances) the girls felt thwarted. So, when the four acres just off Calumet Landing came up for sale at the start of Patience's freshman year at the very same college, the Sisters needed barely ten minutes of talk before they put an offer on the land. There was money in a trust from their father (the Sparrows had been clever with their cash over some three centuries), and more from their mother's family, and it seemed right and proper that it go into a garden. The flowers, herbs, fruit trees, and vegetables that now lived in orderly plots at the Nursery were Honor's real legacy.

Patience was only seventeen when her sisters started their business, and Marigold had only three years, hands buried deep in the sandy soil, before she failed. Sorrel, who cared for her twin with an almost single-minded devotion in Marigold's last year, left most of the day-to-day work to Nettie and Patience. After classes and on weekends the youngest Sparrow grumped around the Nursery, unwittingly absorbing the knowledge that would eventually define her. Together, the Sparrow Sisters became, if not quite legend in the town of Granite Point, certainly a good story to tell: three sisters, the last of the Sparrows, still living in their childhood home, fingernails rimmed in the now rich soil of the Nursery. Nettie and Sorrel were firmly settled into a life alone, although they would never call themselves anything so dry and hopeless as lonely. Patience was considered young enough to avoid her sisters' fate. After all, Granite Point was hardly a prison; she could leave at any time. It was generally agreed that Patience was just bold enough to do that. Yet, here she was, still.

Nettie and Sorrel didn't wish anything so solitary as they sometimes felt to claim Patience. Neither did they want her heart broken. So they made their lives in Ivy House and the Nursery as full and busy as they could, hoping that if Patience was distracted enough by the lush world they had planted together, she might not want to look beyond the high privet hedges, she might never be in danger of getting hurt. There wasn't much they could do to prevent heartache while Patience made her way through high school, but they needn't have worried. She showed as little interest in the moony boys who left her notes or waited by her locker as she did in actual schoolwork. If her fumbling romantic collision with Sam Parker, her closest friend since grade school was any indication, there wasn't a chance she'd lose her head. Nettie was a little disappointed that she herself couldn't experience the wildness of first love, at least through her sister. Sorrel was only relieved.

The truth was that Sorrel had been in love once. Simon Mayo, the oldest of three very accomplished Mayos, had loved Sorrel Sparrow from the moment he saw her. And that was in first grade. Her black hair was already long, and Honor had plaited it in two thick, glossy ropes that lay across her shoulders like epaulets. Simon, the son of a white-shoe Boston lawyer and as tightly bound by his parents as Sorrel's braids, was undone by the little girl who stood, lunch box under her arm, a wilting Shasta daisy for the teacher in her hand, next to the swings in the schoolyard. She met his stare frankly, and Simon found himself moving away from the noisy crowd of jostling boys to stand next to Sorrel. They would be best friends until Simon came back from his last year in law school with a sporty blond and an engagement announcement. Sorrel had broken Simon's heart, not by falling for someone else but by never falling for him. But, of course, she had loved Simon too. Sorrel never knew how to tell him, and Simon was afraid to tell her. They were both so frightened of losing the other that, through silence, they did.

As for Nettie, she was as light and flyaway as her hair, although she had shown amazing fortitude and focus as she cared for her father in his last year. None of the other girls could bear to see him so reduced by alcohol and grief. They'd all felt robbed of a father when Thaddeus couldn't recover from Honor's death but grateful—later—that he didn't see Marigold's. Each sister felt cheated that they were forced to look out for the younger one, except Patience because she was the one who got all the care. But all the girls blamed him for leaving them to be the last. Only Nettie was able to forgive that as she sat beside his bed waiting for Thaddeus Sparrow to leave as well. And when he did, she made sure his ashes were buried next to his wife at the top of the hill in the cemetery that rolled along Monument Road. She stood alone as Ben Avellar shoveled the last of the dirt into the small grave. She lingered until dark, and Ben stayed too, worried that she was on her own. It wasn't until Nettie had thoroughly soaked his bandanna with her tears that she left, climbing into the old Toyota, heading away leaving a trail of exhaust and a pinch in Ben's throat.

Only Nettie came back the next spring to watch as Thaddeus's headstone was placed next to Honor's. When the sisters brought anemone and alyssum from the Nursery to plant for their mother, Nettie stayed behind to tend the heather she'd dug in that first year after her father's death. It didn't matter how any of the girls felt about either parent now that they were gone. Soon, both gravesites were buried under the woody stems and hardy purple blossoms of Thaddeus's heather. If the girls couldn't forgive him, it seemed that Honor had.

Once the Sisters settled into the Nursery, and the town of Granite Point settled with them, it seemed that each had found a way forward. Everyone knew where they belonged, how they were meant to fit into the town, just exactly where the ground was solid. When Henry Carlisle appeared, it wasn't just Patience who felt the shift.

AFTER HIS DINNER at the bar Henry walked aimlessly, not ready to enter the empty little clapboard house. Unlike the rest of the town, he was confused about the Sisters' place in Granite Point. Henry did not yet appreciate the order of things. He sifted through his visit with the women, his conversation with Frank Redmond, and the manner in which this town made way for Sparrows. He might have been able to dismiss Nettie and Sorrel as a couple of accomplished gardeners, isolated by circumstances, eccentrics even, but he couldn't reject Patience so easily. She was young, she was lovely, and she was still so fresh in his mind that for a minute Henry considered going back to Ivy House and demanding that she tell him why she was so pissed off, as Frank said. When he got back to his house, Henry made straight for the patient records: a long triple row of folders, their tabs marked with colored labels. Marigold Sparrow had a fat one while the folders for Nettie and Sorrel were slimmer. The thinnest was for Patience, only childhood vaccinations. Pulling Marigold's folder onto his lap, Henry had only to read her death certificate to understand why the Sisters were skittish about doctors. He guessed that her end had been painful and hard on her sisters, and Henry felt an unexpected sadness wash over him. When he looked at the dates on each of the folders, including Honor's and Thaddeus's, he began to put together the Sparrow timeline. Looking more closely at Honor's file, Henry saw that she had died in childbirth. With a start he realized that Patience must have been that child. Dr. Higgins kept track of the girls; there were notes in both files covering the death of Thaddeus, the purchase of the Nursery, even the date of Patience's high school graduation, then college—with honors. Perhaps the old doctor hoped that they would reconsider their mistrust and that some new internist would need their records. Out of habit, Henry organized the charts by the Sisters' ages and read them the same way.

What Henry couldn't fully learn from the charts was that Marigold was Sorrel's twin, and was only thirty when she died. Breast cancer took her as quickly and shockingly as the first frost killed the dahlias she had so carefully planted. There was a single mammogram for Sorrel just after the diagnosis, and one for Nettie, but nothing more for either. Henry noted the botanical names for the sisters, but he couldn't quite figure out how Patience fit into that tradition.

In fact, Patience came by her name (and her nature) after her mother's untimely death. Honor had gone into labor prematurely and as she bent over a kitchen chair, sweat already soaking the back of her sundress, she tried to joke with the frightened girls who clustered around her. "Boy, this one is impatient," she said between pants. Nettie, who was so frightened by her mother's pain that she could barely breathe, thought Honor had already named the new baby Impatiens after the small shade-loving flower. When Honor died in the hospital (an embolism, unpredictable, unbelievable), her husband came home alone carrying an impossibly tiny bundle. Nettie held out her arms and said, "Hello, Impatiens." Thaddeus Sparrow looked at Nettie and then at his newest daughter and managed a smile. Marigold always said it was his last.

Impatiens became Patience as she learned to be the youngest of four motherless sisters. She found that she had to wait for nearly everything and that if she fussed, the rest of the girls just called her "Impatience." So, patient she was and Patience she became. It wasn't until her tenth birthday that Patience actually understood her own story. It had now been years since she wrote her given name on a school form, years since she signed it on the papers for the land that became the Sparrow Sisters Nursery. Patience wouldn't have an official part in the Nursery for some time after it started, but she would smell and eat and feel the fruits of her sister's labors. By the time Henry moved to Granite Point, Patience was so deep into the soil that it was as if she had sprung straight from it.

Each Sparrow Sister file came to a sudden halt when Marigold died. And with the exception of a sprained wrist suffered by Sorrel the winter it snowed nearly every day for two straight months, none of the girls had ever returned to Dr. Higgins.

Henry put the files back and took the stairs to his apartment slowly. He suspected that he'd lost the Sisters that evening when he questioned Patience. He wanted them back, not just because he was worried that their stubborn rejection of modern medicine was reckless. No, Henry wasn't that noble. Henry wanted in. He wanted to belong in Granite Point, and it looked like the best way was to convince the influential sisters to join him in the twenty-first century. What Henry wouldn't acknowledge to himself was that he hoped that if Patience found that she liked a shiny new world, she just might like the man who introduced her to it. Of course, that logic was flawed: the Sisters were perfectly comfortable in the current century; they just knew when to plant around it.

CHAPTER THREE

Cowslip is also called Fairy Cups and makes a fine wine

Patience washed out the soup bowls, the steam warm and scented with rosemary, her hands slippery with the dish soap she made herself. She rinsed them before reaching for the beer on the draining board. Patience was peeved. Nettie was feeling better, and that was good, wasn't it? The antibiotics had already begun to clear her chest, leaving Nettie limp with relief. Patience and Sorrel felt better too although Patience begrudged her relief; she didn't like to admit that she'd been a little nervous about Nettie's cough as well. It wasn't that she didn't believe in conventional medicine, she just didn't trust it. And she certainly didn't trust the entirely too attractive Henry Carlyle.

He was snooty and nothing but an old stick, Patience thought. Not old, she corrected herself, and shook her head, just stuffy in his funny linen vest and wrinkled shirt. Really, who wore a vest anymore? And his pants; actually, Patience hadn't noticed his legs at all. That he had made Nettie better was good; that Patience had wanted to tuck his shirttail back in was not.

Nettie hadn't told her sister she had an appointment with the new doctor; she knew Patience would have made her try several unpalatable remedies that might well have worked in time. Nettie absolutely believed in Patience, but she'd felt so shaken by her fever that she hadn't had the time or energy to consult her sister. So Patience was, not unreasonably, feeling a little put out. And that feeling had to assert itself somehow.

Grabbing a chunk of Baker's Way bread, dipping it in the softening butter in the dish on the counter, she took her beer onto the front porch. The light was gone from the sky so Patience flipped on the porch lamp and sat in the creaky swing, pushing it into a sway with her bare foot. She watched old Mrs. Avery walk her equally old beagle down Ivy Street toward the harbor. She laughed as Beanie found enough energy to pull his mistress into the elm he had his eye on. Mrs. Avery looked up at Patience and waved.

"It seems your biscuits are working on Beanie's arthritis," she called out.

"Good," Patience said. Her gifts weren't restricted to the human population in Granite Point. Patience found that at least some of her remedies worked just as well on their pets.

"I guess you've got something for mine?" Mrs. Avery held up a hand crooked by arthritis.

"You know I do," Patience answered. "You only have to ask."

Mrs. Avery shook her head. "I'm seeing that new doctor tomorrow. Wouldn't want him to feel unwelcome."

Patience sat up taller and stilled the swing. *Unwelcome,* she thought, *I'll give you unwelcome.* But all she said was, "I hear he's a bit stiff."

"Really?" Mrs. Avery said, gathering Beanie closer. "I hear he's quite a catch." She smiled and tilted her head toward Patience. "He won't be single long," she warned.

"Thanks for the tip," Patience said with the bite of frost in her voice. "I'll pass it on to my sisters."

Mrs. Avery moved off, and Patience suddenly found the porch too exposed. Her irritation was fizzing around her along with the gnats. Patience stood quickly, sending the swing into the side of the house with a smack. She didn't want to believe that jealousy had any part in the anxiety that gripped her like a cramp. But, to be honest, Patience hadn't been challenged in at least five years, and she didn't like the feeling. She poured the now-warm beer into the sink and went up to see Nettie.

"How are you, Nettie-Pot?" Patience said as she opened the door.

Sorrel was sitting in the chaise by the window, her long legs tucked up. She turned to Patience, her eyes still holding a hint of hardness.

"Oh." Patience stepped back. "You already have a nurse."

"Come on," Sorrel sighed. "Don't be such a bitch." It was not lost on Sorrel these days that she had outlived Marigold by some years now. She'd found herself more and more aware of how fragile everything was and if Nettie needed Dr. Carlyle to keep her healthy, to keep her *here,* Sorrel wasn't complaining. In fact, she found herself tense and watchful, so she lingered as Nettie settled in for the night.

Patience crossed to the bed and lay back, her legs dangling over its foot.

"I am not a bitch, Sorrel. Thanks for your support, though." Her voice dropped. "Ass."

"Heard that," Sorrel said from her spot.

Nettie watched her sisters, her chapped lips pulled down in a frown. Her hair seemed alight in the dim bedroom as if her nerves had shot sparks right out of her head. And she *was* nervous. She knew she'd been caught out by Patience, which unsettled everyone. Now, just being in bed, her pajamas damp with breaking fever, made her a wreck.

"Please don't fight," she said. "This is my fault, I panicked. Henry needn't ever come back."

"Henry?" both sisters said.

"Dr. Carlyle, jeez!" Nettie all but shrieked. "He's just young and cute, you know, like our age. It's weird calling him 'Doctor' after all the years with old Dr. Higgins."

Sorrel leaned back in the chaise and took a long look at Patience.

"What do you think, P?" she asked, their spat forgotten.

"Does young—like us—*Dr.* Carlyle"— she looked at Nettie— "seem like someone to keep tabs on?"

"Well, you guys aren't so young." The Sisters harrumphed. "Kidding," Patience said and patted Nettie's foot under the covers. "He didn't do it for me. His jaw's horribly square, and his eyelashes are way too long for a guy."

"Ha!" Nettie said, pointing at Patience. "You saw the lashes too!"

"Please, no man needs lashes like that." Patience sat up. "And another thing, what was all that stuck-up crap about my remedies?" She slid her voice into a soft growl on the word "remedies." Henry Carlyle's voice had been low and a little rough, as if he hadn't spoken for a while, or had spoken too much. Patience had just the tea for that.

"What did you expect?" Sorrel said. "He doesn't know us, he doesn't know this town." She picked up her cup and headed for the door. "No matter how skilled you are, or how beloved"— and here Sorrel stood to twine her fingers through Patience's hair—"you can't cure everyone. We need Henry Carlyle." Patience brought her own hands up to meet Sorrel's and squeezed.

Once Patience was alone in her room she allowed herself to replay Sorrel's remark. Why did they need Dr. Carlyle? Was someone sick with more than bronchitis? No, she would feel that. Patience shivered and curled into her pillow. Naked, as she always was in bed, she considered digging out a tee shirt, but she was too lazy to get up. She stretched out again, running her legs back and forth along the sheets, trying to work up enough friction to generate some heat.

"Shit!" she said and threw herself onto her stomach. Sleep didn't come for nearly an hour, but Patience willed her body to sink into stillness. She could be patient.

THE LAST MORNING that Nettie spent at home was overcast and humid, heat clinging to the screen door along with the dew. Patience made coffee, pouring it into a heavy mug. She was surprised that Nettie had spent five days in the house, not even once venturing out to the backyard. Nettie almost never spent a whole day, let alone nearly a week, inside, and it worried Patience. Perhaps Nettie was really as delicate as she seemed. Patience looked at the garden, her hand on the screen doorknob but chose instead to leave Ivy House altogether. Walking barefoot down the rumpled sidewalk, elm roots heaving against the red brick, she headed toward Baker's Way Bakers. Even though Patience hadn't a penny in her jeans pockets, she knew Claire Redmond or her daughter Ryder would spot her a muffin.

A full block before she could even see the blue-and-white sign, Patience smelled the shop, and she lifted her chin and closed her eyes. If she had to, Patience could follow the scented wave like a cartoon character floating inches off the sidewalk. She was not alone. Already there was a clump of customers milling around the shop.

Claire was at the counter, and one look at Patience sent her to the ovens. She lifted out a pan of cinnamon muffins. Juggling one to a cutting board, she slathered it with salt-speckled Normandy butter and wrapped it in a piece of parchment paper.

"I'd love to know why you need this, P," she said.

Patience just rolled her eyes. "How are the headaches?" she asked.

"Gone." Claire was beaming. "Now I just have to convince Ryder to come on a college trip and the stress will be gone, too."

"Maybe she just wants to stay here, like me."

Claire's face fell before she could catch it, but Patience just waved and left, the muffin already at her lips, butter shiny on her chin. She stopped at the bench outside and spread the parchment onto her lap. She wedged a chunk into her mouth with a sigh and leaned back, her long legs splayed.

"That looks wonderful," Henry Carlyle said and instantly wanted to suture his lips shut.

Patience sat up and frowned, crumbs still at the corners of her mouth.

"Right, that came out all wrong," Henry said.

Patience snorted. "Yeah, well, you're good at that."

"That's not fair." Henry felt his jaw seize and his voice narrow. He shook his head. "We need to start over."

"Do we?" Patience took another bite. She looked at Henry again. "That clenchy thing you do will ruin your teeth," she said.

Henry rubbed his chin and made an effort to open his mouth. He saw the butter on Patience's upper lip and before he let himself think about it, he reached his hand out, inches from her mouth, then couldn't bring himself to touch her. With a jolt he saw his fingers tremble. Patience didn't pull away. In fact she'd closed her eyes. Shock, and something like anticipation, was all over her face.

"Help," she whispered.

Henry spun awkwardly on his heel and, forgetting completely that he'd meant to buy something at the bakery, he turned back to his office.

Patience dropped the muffin in her lap. She stared at the still-warm cake for a full minute. Then she ate it.

HENRY TOOK THE ten minutes he still had before Sally arrived to pace and thump his fist on the exam table, wrinkling the paper and setting up an ache that traveled all the way to his shoulder. He'd rowed for over an hour at first light and had been enjoying the pleasant soreness in his thighs and back. Now it just felt like pain. He couldn't imagine why Patience brought out his worst, or why he cared. It had been so long since he wanted someone to like him that he almost didn't recognize the feeling. He ripped the paper from the table and spooled out a new strip. He heard Sally click-clack through the front door and in minutes Henry smelled coffee. Grabbing the charts off his desk without even looking at the names, Henry walked out to the waiting room.

"Hey, Dr. Carlyle," Sally said handing him her mug. He waved her off and poured his own.

"Tell me about the Sparrow Sisters," he said abruptly.

"Oh, well, um." Sally shuffled the papers on her desk. "Let's see, the Sparrows are one of the founding families. They were whalers, magistrates, soldiers, doctors, vicars; you name it. Thaddeus and Honor Sparrow were the most extraordinary couple, like a storybook, and the girls were everything to them. But Honor died with Patience, and Thaddeus lost it. There were a couple of years there when we didn't think the Sisters would make it either. There used to be four of them, all with garden names like Nettie, but Marigold died. I don't think Sorrel ever got over that. There are only the three." Sally paused for breath.

"And now?" Henry said.

"They own the Sparrow Sisters Nursery on Calumet. It's pretty amazing: everything and anything grows. Even when the weather turns, the Sisters manage to produce. Even in the winter there's stuff around."

As Sally talked, Henry saw that a patient had come through the front door and was now standing uncertainly in the waiting room. He nodded at the man and held up one finger as he pulled Sally gently away from the front counter.

"What else?" he asked.

It was as Frank said: the Sparrow Sisters Nursery had quite a reputation. Sally told Henry about the Nursery that was now a landmark in the town. The plants that grew in tidy rows, the orchids that swayed delicately in the beautiful glass greenhouses, and the herbs and vegetables sown in knot gardens around the land were much in demand. Sorrel had planted a dense little Shakespeare garden as a tribute to her reading habits. The lavender, rosemary, roses and honeysuckle, clematis and pansies, creeping thyme and sage were not for sale in that garden, but Sorrel would re-create versions of it for clients whose big houses on the water needed the stamp of culture, even if their owners had little idea what their lovely gardens meant. In fact, it was the summer people who sustained the business, as they did the town. As much as the Sisters disliked the brassy, noisy women who came, checkbooks open, they knew that without them and their shiny SUVs and brand new surfboards, the Nursery and the town might well struggle.

"You wouldn't believe what the Sisters have done with the land," Sally said. "People used to talk about how much they can grow, how long they grow it. Nobody much cares anymore about their methods, just what they can buy."

The Sparrow Sisters' roses still bloomed on New Year's Day, their scent rich and warm even when snow weighed their petals closed. When customers came down the rutted road to the small eighteenth-century barn where the sisters worked, they marveled at the jasmine that twined through the split-rail fence, the perfume so intense they could feel it in their mouths. As they paid for their purchases, they wondered (vaguely, it must be said, for the people of Granite Point knew not to think too hard about the Sisters) how it was that clematis and honeysuckle climbed the barn in November and the morning glories bloomed all day. The fruit trees were so fecund that the peaches hung on the low branches, surrounded by more blossoms, apples and pears ripened in June and stayed sweet and fresh into December. Their Italian fig trees were heavy with purple teardrop fruit only weeks after they were planted. If you wanted a tomato so ripe the juice seemed to move beneath the skin, you needed only to pick up a punnet at the Nursery. In time, despite its air of enchantment, the Sparrow Sisters Nursery was considered simply a part of Granite Point. The Sisters themselves had been merely a curiosity until Patience found her gift. Then the town quite openly bragged about its not so very secret ingredients.

"You won't find anything like their stuff for miles and miles," Sally finished and moved to go back to the counter. Henry stopped her.

"No marriages, no children, none of them?" he asked and lowered his head to avoid Sally's curious gaze.

"No, I mean it's not like they're old maids or anything; they just kind of keep themselves to themselves. You've seen them," she added and circled her hand around her face. "They're hardly dogs."

"Or magicians," Henry murmured. "So Patience, she's the local faith healer." Henry's voice maintained a neutral tone, but Sally could see the skepticism in his eyes.

"Pfft! You don't need faith for Patience." Sally laughed. "She just makes people better. I don't know whether she learned it or just inherited it, but once she decided to stay, she turned a part of the Nursery into what she calls a psychic garden."

"Physic," Henry said. "A garden of remedial plants."

"Right," Sally said. "It took a while but now, the things she grows, how she puts them together, *that* could make you believe in magic."

Henry stared at Sally, his head tilted and his mouth curved up on one side.

"What?" she asked. "It's not magic, obviously."

"Have you ever used her?"

"Of course."

"Certainly not now," Henry said, pointing at Sally's enormous belly.

Sally shrugged and her face blanked.

"Sally! You're a nurse."

"Morning sickness," Sally admitted. "She fixed it."

Henry went back to his office, nearly as irritated and puzzled as he'd been standing in the Sisters' hallway. The only thing he did know, and of this he was certain: he wanted to see Patience again. He needed to know what it was she did, how she'd put such a hold on these people and, to be honest, on him.

Sally picked up the charts Henry had left on her desk: the Sparrows'.

WHILE PATIENCE ATE her muffin and steamed over Henry Carlyle, Sorrel woke Nettie and found her cool and dry, her fever long gone, her breathing easy and her chest clear. She had been so apprehensive about her sister only a few days ago that Sorrel had only reluctantly tended to the Nursery. But she saw how well Nettie was now and looked forward to the work ahead. Sorrel glanced into Patience's empty room as she headed down to the kitchen and wondered if that sister was already at work. She stood, drinking coffee and eyeing the garden. Slowly, she pushed through the screen door and took the center path. Asparagus ferns brushed against her wrists, pulling a faint shiver from her core, and she had to pause and take a breath to steady herself. She leaned over and whisked her fingers over the stiff green spears, mentally measuring how many days before she could snap them off. The asparagus grew and ripened in the same unreasonable way of all Sparrow Sisters' crops. This was her second harvest, nearly two months after the first, which itself was at least a month early. Sorrel could taste the slight metallic echo of a single spear, dripping with butter.

"Makes your pee smell." Patience stood at the kitchen door.

For the first time, Sorrel voiced her fear. "What are we going to do?" she asked, her voice disturbingly plaintive as a child's.

"Everyone's pee smells."

"No, what are we going to do when there aren't any more?"

Patience looked at Sorrel and brought her hands up. "You always have a third crop in time for the August rush."

"What will happen when the Sparrow Sisters are gone?" Sorrel said and was so surprised by the desolation she heard in her own words that she couldn't meet Patience's gaze.

Patience was so frightened by Sorrel's tone that she spoke without thought.

"Oh, for fuck's sake, Sorrel," she snapped. "Why are you asking me?"

"You sound like Dad when you swear."

"Great," Patience said. She stepped out and walked lightly over the sharp gravel. "What do you want us to do, Sorrel? Reproduce immaculately? Find a sperm donor? Or should we really adopt Rob Short's kid and rename him Sage?"

Rob Short was a widower, and his ten-year-old boy was generally agreed to be more than a little odd. His name was Matthew. The Sisters were very fond of him and let him help out at the Nursery. He could most often be found following Patience around, asking questions or humming to himself. If there were ever to be a Sparrow son, he'd do nicely—in his own odd way. And if the Sisters were being honest, they suspected they would be better parents to him than his distracted father.

Sorrel moved farther into the garden, stopping at the dahlias that were still just tender leaves and celery-pale stalks, buds like peas, nearly transparent as the sun struggled through the watery clouds.

"You know," she said, "I always imagined us with families by now. I mean, not just the Sisters to everyone."

Patience saw that Sorrel's nightgown was damp at the hem, her ratty slippers wet all the way up the toes. Her black hair was loose, the white streaks the brightest things in the garden.

"Let's go in," Patience said. "No use standing still out here. The birds will think we've put up a scarecrow."

She put her arm around Sorrel, surprised by how bony her shoulders were, how quickly her sister leaned against her. Sorrel sniffed at Patience's arm. The smell of clover was sweet and clean, and Sorrel was reassured that her sister was still full of possibility. For her part, Patience smelled the coppery tang of sadness as if it flowed straight out of Sorrel's veins.

As Patience got ready to go to the Nursery, she considered Sorrel's remark and realized that, somewhere inside herself—in that place that traps you at two in the morning when you are too disoriented to find your way out again—she too thought she might have met someone by now. She'd not really looked but while she studied biology and botany at Granite Point College, Patience had cut a wide but shallow swath through the young men at the school—students, a greenskeeper, and once an assistant professor. The only criteria she held were that each be beautiful and game. And so they were, to a man. Like the wild sweet peas that twined along the rock walls near the water, the young Patience was hungry for something to hold, if only for a season.

GPC was known for two disciplines, animal husbandry and history of music, and two stranger things to have developed side by side in a small seaside town you could not imagine. Still, the curriculum attracted some interesting male scholars— vague lute-playing boys with long hair and calloused fingers and muscled, boot-wearing ones who brought the smell of timothy and sweat into Ivy House. If Patience was careless in her conquests, she had to make up for a pretty mild high school experience after all. There hadn't been a single local boy who made her want to do more than kiss breathlessly behind the athletic fields. And when she did that, she'd found not a lover but a best friend.

True to a small town, that boy, Sam Parker, had grown up to be a fireman and EMT in the firehouse just down the road. So when Sorrel said she'd hoped that they could be more than just "The Sisters," she probably meant that at least one of the college guys who'd snuck out of Ivy House after a dreamlike time with Patience might have snuck right back in. But that was years ago now. The town had grown too small for her to quietly take a lover. Summer boys came and went and were even more cavalier than Patience, so that didn't work. And while Patience missed the release of sex, the wonderful abandon she'd felt when she ran her hands down some ridiculously handsome boy, the look on those boys' faces as she kicked her jeans into a corner, she didn't miss the way they all wanted to stay. She hated sleeping with anyone (except Nettie when Patience was little and frightened) so if she ever did "find someone," he'd better be willing to sleep in her father's old room. Whoever really wanted Patience had to want sand in his socks and dirt in his hair, bay leaves on the windowsills and thyme in his shoes. She didn't think there was anyone out there like that.

Just remembering those years made Patience's face feel hot and her lips tender. She hated the fact that Henry Carlyle's voice wouldn't leave her as she tried to recall the last boy whose whispers had filled her room. When she'd looked up at Henry that morning, the words "strong," "capable," "useful" came to mind. And, when his hand drew so close that she could feel the heat, she'd nearly leapt out of her skin—she'd almost grabbed his fingers and pulled them down to her mouth.

Patience got into the shower hoping Sorrel hadn't used up all the hot water but found that her skin was so warm that even tepid water steamed when it hit her back.

SORREL MADE SURE Nettie was settled upstairs and climbed into the pickup with Patience. They rode in silence and Patience drove a little too fast. When they turned onto the sandy road that led to the Nursery, they saw Matthew Short biking like crazy toward the greenhouses.

"Oh boy," said Sorrel.

"Missed his meds," Patience guessed.

Matty Short was what the doctors called high-functioning autistic, the town called "off," and the Sisters called friend. When he entered second grade he'd been labeled as being on the autistic spectrum, and his parents were duly reassured that he was not in any real danger. This allowed the medical community to define him and medicate him, and his father to struggle to understand him. His mother had died the year before, and every now and then Rob Short let his grief and exhaustion overtake him and lost track of his son's pills, leaving Matty to career through a day or more until one of his teachers made a call. Nobody exactly blamed Rob Short, but after a while the school and the neighbors had gotten a bit cross that he couldn't keep up with his own kid. The summer was always tough; no teacher to see the shift into darkness, no school nurse to unlock her cabinet and find the bottle with Matty's name on it.

Patience backed the jeep into the space next to the barn and jumped out with the engine left running. Sorrel reached over and turned the key before she grabbed her bag and Patience's and walked into the office.

"Hey, Matty!" Patience called to the little figure leaning over his bike, chest heaving. "Buddy?" She put her hand on his back and watched as his breathing slowed. Finally Matty looked up at her, his face red and pinched.

"I thought you were gone, that I was late," he said. "But it's you guys. You're late, you are."

"Yeah, we are," Patience said. "Nettie's had a bad cold."

"Can't you fix her?"

"Well, yes, I could. But, she went to the new doctor." Patience made a sour face.

"Is he bad?" Matty wriggled out from under Patience's hand. She was the only sister who could touch him. Actually she was the only person other than his father who could touch him. He never went rigid beneath her as he did with anyone else. He never pulled at his fingers—thumb to pinkie, thumb to pinkie—as he counted. Still, he could only take so much and now, standing with his back to the greenhouse, he was feeling a bit trapped. His anxiety was twisting up from his stomach, closing his throat and making it hard to talk. He began to whisper the names of all the plants he'd learned from Patience. The rhythm of the words calmed him as he considered the frightening prospect of a bad man in his town.

"Oh, Matty, he's good, he's fine. You know I just don't much like doctors." Patience held out her hand. "Come on, let's go see if the calendula cream is set."

Matty didn't take her hand, but he followed her toward the barn. For him things were either bad or good, as were people. He saw life through a lens that colored the world black or white, and he often asked Patience to help him choose. Patience kept talking as they walked, and Matty's shoulders loosened as her voice floated back to him.

"I'll make you some iced tea, and we'll steal Nettie's cookies," she said. "Ryder Redmond brought some over yesterday." Patience looked at Matty and smiled. "I'll let you lick the labels today, OK?"

Sorrel had a tray of seedlings out and was on her knees pressing each one into a neat hole.

"Hey, Matty," she said, shading her eyes and adding more dirt to her forehead.

"What are those?" he asked.

"They're daisies, shastas, very hardy and by July this batch will be in someone's wedding bouquet."

"They aren't poisonous?"

"No, silly, we don't grow anything like that," Patience said. "They're happy flowers and my sister's favorite." She stepped around Sorrel and into the barn. It was cool in the little building. The smell of Patience's ingredients combined to become a wash of watery green that swirled through the ceiling fan. Matty stood under it for a minute, his chin tilted up and his eyes closed. The breeze lifted his hair, and Patience had an almost overwhelming urge to brush it away from his face. But she knew how far she could go with Matty, especially when his father lost track.

Patience took a pitcher of tea out of the half fridge and poured a glass. Made from mint and comfrey leaves, it was a pale green color, clear as water. She watched Matty carefully as he swayed beneath the fan.

"Matty, do you want me to help you through this?" she asked.

He nodded and turned to her. "Please?" he said. The hollows beneath his eyes were dark as bruises, and Patience thought that Matty had probably been unwatched for days.

"OK, let's fix you, but you know that you have to tell your dad that I did, right?"

Matty nodded again, and Patience reached into the old Swedish cupboard behind her. It was tall; she had to use a stool to reach the topmost shelves. There were eight rows of narrow, deep drawers, unmarked, but Patience knew what each held. She didn't hesitate as she reached into one and pulled out a tiny vial with a dropper stop. She let three drops fall into Matty's tea and stirred it with a long silver spoon as old as Ivy House.

"Here," she said, handing the glass to Matty. "I'll get the cookies." She left Matty sitting at the counter, his legs wound around the stool, the glass to his lips. The four deep blue marbles he carried everywhere were lined up precisely in front of him like a tiny protective wall.

Sorrel was standing outside with a lithe blond woman in running clothes. She was waving her hands, and Sorrel had to step back to avoid a collision.

"I want it so big that people won't be able to see around it," she said. "Roses, peonies, that tall greeny-white stuff . . ."

"Bells of Ireland," Sorrel said softly.

"Whatever, it has to be amazing." She paused for breath. "Can you do that, Sorrel?"

"Of course she can." Patience moved into the doorway. "It'll cost you."

"Naturally," Charlotte Mayo said. "Hi, Patience. Can it be ready by the end of the day? Simon will come by."

Patience saw Sorrel blink at Simon's name.

It's not that Simon's wife was bad, as Matty would say; she didn't really know what Sorrel and her husband might have been if he hadn't given up. She could only guess at Simon's early years in Granite Point. Charlotte did know that the Sparrow Sisters were a strange but useful part of Granite Point, and right now she needed a serious flower arrangement for a party she and Simon were giving the next evening. It was the yearly Founders' Cocktails, held the last week of June, first by Simon's great-grandparents, then his grandparents and parents and now by Simon. It heralded the beginning of the season with its influx of people and cash, and the decorative centerpiece was always the original town charter, framed, propped on a rickety easel from the Historical Society and set in the large center hall of the Mayo house. Charlotte had decided to put her own stamp on the event with a grand, but still local, display, preferably large enough to hide the tatty charter. She was particularly anxious about this party for another reason: she wanted to introduce Henry Carlyle to the community. She wanted to make sure he knew who she was, what she could do for him, and what she so needed him to do for her.

Charlotte Parsons Mayo was everything a Mayo wife should be, and more. She played tennis like a pro, cooked quite well, decorated even better, and kept Simon happy and sated. Still, there were nights when he looked down at her as if she were a stranger. There were days when she looked at him with dismay. That's when Charlotte took on something else, anything, which she could do very well. What she couldn't do was conceive. And while this inability to provide a Mayo heir for the oldest of a very prominent family made her mother-in-law chilly, it positively froze Charlotte's heart. After visits with specialists from Boston to Minnesota, Charlotte was told she was idiopathically infertile. All she heard was "barren," a word that had begun to define her very soul. As she stood waiting for Sorrel to acknowledge her request, Charlotte was already rehearsing how she could get Dr. Henry Carlyle to agree to see her, to add his list of specialists to her datebook.

Dr. Higgins had been kind but firm when he spoke to her before his retirement.

"There really isn't anything we can do. You know that, Charlotte," he'd said as he tapped the file that had grown to more than two inches thick. "Modern medicine can work miracles, but I am afraid we can't make magic." She could still feel the pity that floated off him, and just remembering the look on Sally Tabor's face made her lips purse hard enough to ache.

Patience ate a cookie at the door and watched her sister carefully. Sorrel had been taking notes, and now she slipped the pad into her jeans pocket and nodded as she gestured for Charlotte to get into her car.

"It'll be ready," Sorrel said. "Really, Patience can bring it over around six."

"No, I'll send Simon. God knows he should do something for this thing. It's his party."

Charlotte drove off, her Mini bouncing over the ruts and pebbles. Sorrel didn't turn away until the little car pulled onto Calumet Landing. When she did, Patience nudged her arm.

"Patience will bring it over? Are you nuts? You know I hate that crowd."

"And now Simon will be *here*." Sorrel picked up the empty seedling trays and walked to the barn. "Either way . . ." She shrugged.

"It sucks. She is just so *Charlotte*." Patience was gearing up for a bit of a rant, and Sorrel wanted to run to the field behind the fruit trees, lie in the tall grass, and let her bitter tears water the black-eyed Susans.

Sorrel might have gotten that lecture if Matty hadn't come out of the barn.

"Why is everyone sad?" he asked. Then he paused. "Why are you angry?" he asked Patience. A completely contrary aspect of his condition was his ability to pick up on the Sisters' moods. Matty couldn't relate to his own classmates, was unable to join in games or even intuit when he was being teased. To everyone else Matty was an uncomfortable reminder of how things could go wrong—and the Sisters, they were ciphers— but to each other they were completely readable.

"We're not sad, buddy," Sorrel said. "We're just tired."

"But it's morning."

"Yes, it is," Patience said. "And there is a crap ton to do. Let's check the hollyhocks."

The rest of the day passed in a pleasant haze. Matty and Patience bent low over her plants as she picked and plucked, explaining everything she did in a soft, even voice. Matty was the only one Patience shared her secrets with. He listened with rapt attention as if the names themselves held power. As Patience listed the various ailments her plants could help, Matty almost wished he had rheumatism that called for bladderwrack or high blood pressure to be cured by skullcap. "Conjunctivitis needs eyebright," Matty repeated under his breath. "Eczema needs Chinese peony root, no bark." He had a remarkable memory and when he got home, he would transcribe all the names and uses into a black-and-white-patterned composition book he kept under his mattress. When he could (without the Sisters seeing, sometimes early or late), he snatched a petal or blossom, a leaf or seed, to paste beside the entry. Matty thought maybe he could learn to be like Patience, to save someone the way she did. He was sure that if he could, people wouldn't look away every time they saw him.

Matty seemed calmer and by lunchtime slept sweatily in the hammock strung between two pear trees at the edge of the meadow. He was boneless in the way children can be, draped over the canvas sling, his head thrown back in complete unconsciousness. Sorrel finished her planting and began work on the arrangement for Charlotte. The tallest white roses were still closed, and they could be for another day or more so Sorrel laid them in the long soapstone sink and filled it with warm water. Since everything bloomed early and long at the Sparrow Sisters Nursery, everyone had begun to count on that fact, even if they couldn't explain it. Under the Sisters' hands even the most difficult flower sat up and paid attention. Still, white roses were fiddlier than most. The peonies Charlotte wanted were nodding heavy on their stems, bowing over the edges of a tall tin bucket, blooming far past their May prime. Their blossoms were perfectly open, the scent so heady that Sorrel had to step outside for air. Honeybees had followed her into the barn, abandoning the hives Nettie kept for the flowers that spilled over the sink, for the honey that Patience stirred into teas and lotions, for the wax that she used to seal her bottles. Sorrel waved her hands to shoo them out. She tiptoed by Matty and into the field in search of bells of Ireland. Nettie had planted a long stand of them the first year the Nursery opened, and they were quickly well established. Now the tall stems were covered in electric green calyxes, the tiny white flowers at their centers only buds. They smelled faintly of mint, and Sorrel wondered if the arrangement might be positively intoxicating.

"And who will notice?" she murmured as she clipped an armload.

HENRY CARLYLE WAS bent low over his work too. A six-year-old girl had gone butt over teakettle on her bicycle and landed on her chin.

"One minute she was pedaling along like Miss Gulch and the next, wham!" Her mother was rattling away as Henry took tiny, deft stitches in her daughter's chin. He wondered what kind of mother compared her daughter to the Wicked Witch instead of Dorothy. The light from the old gooseneck lamp beside the exam table was hot on his hands; the smell of the latex gloves an acrid, powdery thing.

"They use glue at the ER in Hayward," she said, hovering too close, getting in his field. "They say it leaves less of a scar, the glue does. I'm not so sure when I look at Martin's arm. But he's driving the good car to Boston and the thought of getting on the Post Road . . ."

Henry breathed slowly and softly as he turned the little girl's chin one way and the other. Her skin was nearly transparent under the bright light. A few flecks of dried blood clung to the fine hairs on her jaw. Tears had left salty, sandy trails over her cheeks. Henry knew his sutures would not leave much of a scar at all.

"Well," he said and stripped off his gloves, "we're done now and I don't think anyone will even notice by Labor Day." He looked at the girl; she was almost sedated by the light, the anesthetic, and the shock of her fall. Her eyes were glazed, and as Henry brushed her hair away from her face, she leaned into his hand like a cat.

"Lydia, thank the doctor," Lydia's mother gathered her daughter's bike helmet and sweatshirt.

"Thank you," the little girl whispered into Henry's neck as he lifted her off the table. Her breath was warm against him, and he pressed his own cheek into her hair.

"You are entirely welcome," he said and smiled genuinely for the first time that day. Lydia gave a gappy, shaky smile and for absolutely no discernible reason, Henry felt tears prickle at the back of his eyes. He cleared his throat and ushered the two out the door, pausing to watch as they walked down the hall, Lydia swaying a bit as she held her mother's sleeve.

It was lunchtime already, the hour when Henry returned calls and tried to read his own handwriting. Sally Tabor usually got him a sandwich from Doyle's and brought it to him at his desk. It surprised him that he'd fallen into such an easy pattern in a matter of weeks. There was comfort in the routine, and Henry found himself able to go hours at a time without thinking about anything other than what was right in front of him. But as soon as a patient left his exam room, or Henry sat at his desk as he did now staring at his notes, he fell into thoughts of the strange effect this town was beginning to have. Perhaps it was the softness of the early, perfect summer that had crept up on Granite Point, blurring all the hard edges, painting every-thing in a lemony light. Or maybe it was the lovely specter of Patience Sparrow, who insisted on hovering over everything he did.

"I am a mess," he mumbled as Sally came in.

"What?" she asked.

"I'm going to clean up this mess," Henry said.

He waited until Sally left him before picking up the phone. Then he made three calls to check on patients, one to the lab to push a blood test, and one to the storage facility in Watertown to have his books sent on to Baker's Way. Finally, he called the Sparrow Sisters. He wanted to check on Nettie, and Henry wasn't sure whether he hoped that Patience would answer or that she wouldn't. She didn't.

"Oh, Dr. Carlyle," Nettie piped when he identified himself. "How nice of you to call."

"Nothing nice about it," he said and put his forehead down on his desk. "I mean, Nettie, that it's my job to be sure you're feeling better."

"Well I am. Much," she answered. "My sisters are at the Nursery, and I am sitting in the sun feeling grateful we have you." If Henry could see Nettie, he would have seen her slap her palm to her own forehead. Both of them sounded as silly as they felt, and the conversation was short. Nettie put the phone down on the grass next to her, and Henry hung his up with a bit of a slam. Nettie suspected Dr. Carlyle was trying too hard. Henry would agree. He needed to get out of his office.

"Oh, you should go down to the harbor," Sally said when she saw him in the hall. "It's beautiful out there."

The village green was the oldest in the country, lush and inviting with a gazebo at its center. Wisteria climbed the pillars all the way to the shingled roof. The Sparrow Sisters had planted it after Hurricane Bill tore away the original vines. Now, in only a few years, the cinnamon-scented purple blossoms tumbled over the entire building, the twisty branches braided themselves along the eaves. The Catholic church, Our Lady Star of the Sea, stood at one end of the green and the First Episcopal Church at the other. Henry cut across the lawn toward the harbor without a look at either. He was following his nose. The breeze off the water was heavy with salt, and as he neared the docks and day boats, the fish was so fresh it simply smelled of the sea. Gulls circled the boats, their cries as cutting as the wail of a newborn.

Henry paused to watch a man unloading lobsters. He was tall and broad through his chest, his legs long below stained, wet shorts. His biceps were the size of hams and lines framed his eyes; a map of hard work, early mornings, and sun. Dark blond hair stood out from his head in briny spikes. He swore as the lobster he was holding clamped a claw down on his thumb. The rubber band meant to hold the claw closed shot clear off across the dock. The lobster hung on as the man twisted at it, and Henry could see blood well up at the base of the guy's thumb. Henry walked over quickly and took his elbow just as he managed to yank the lobster off.

"Let me look," Henry said, suddenly eager for a purpose.

"It's fine," the fisherman growled as he held his bleeding hand away from his catch.

"Seriously, you need to clean that." Henry turned the man's hand over so he could see the thumb now covered with dark blood.

"Ben Avellar," the man said, moving his wounded right hand as if to shake, which only dripped blood on Henry's shirt-sleeve. "Oh, shit. Sorry, man," Ben said.

"No problem. I'm Henry Carlyle. I'm a doctor. Come back to the office and I'll clean this up for you. Maybe a stitch or some of that terrific glue," Henry said, thinking of the little girl.

"Really, it's no big deal. Besides, I've got to ice these first." Ben looked at his boat. "I can't leave them."

"OK, I'll help you. That hand should be elevated." Henry pulled Ben over to the edge of the dock. "Here, swish it around in the salt water and then I can wrap it in a towel or some-thing."

Ben looked at Henry with his eyebrows raised nearly into his baseball cap. Then he bent down and grabbed the hose from his boat. "I think I'll use this. The harbor water is a little oily."

As Henry began shoveling ice, his shoulders stretching the

back of his shirt in a satisfying way, a couple of guys from other boats offered their help, snickering at Ben as he fumbled the lobsters with his left hand. He was unsteady on the deck of his boat, the *Jenny Joy*. Henry wondered if Jenny was Ben's wife.

"Leave it, Ben," said one of the fishermen. "We'll do it."

"If I'm missing one bug!" Ben gave up, lifting his swaddled hand, the tip of his middle finger visible. The men laughed.

Henry and Ben walked back to the office. The sun was hot on Henry's neck and he was embarrassed about the whole dirty-water blunder. He was sure that Ben thought he was a privileged landlubber boob. The gulls seemed almost threatening as they fought for scraps on the docks.

"So, you're the new guy," Ben said.

"I guess I am," Henry answered. "It's been weeks. Why am I still so interesting?"

"Not a whole lot to talk about until the summer people come." He gestured to Henry's leg. "But people'll talk about what they got. How'd you do that?"

Henry realized he hadn't thought about his leg once while he shoveled the ice, and now it twanged with every step.

"Skiing," he said, his lie coming easily.

"Bullshit," Ben said back. "You're no skier."

"How do you know that?"

"You're too regular. I don't know, not fancy like the Mayos, say. They ski."

"You're right, I am definitely not fancy." Henry laughed at the word.

"And you're not going to tell me either."

"Right again, not worth talking about, even if the summer people aren't here yet."

Henry opened the office door for Ben, and four pairs of eyes—three patients and Sally— looked up. He'd agreed to take walk-ins two afternoons a week. They'd have to wait. He hustled Ben back to the exam room, gesturing for his nurse to follow.

Sally pulled a suture kit out of the cabinet and swung the metal tray close to Henry. Ben sat back on the exam table; his eyes followed Henry and Sally as if he'd never seen either of them before. Henry wondered if Ben had ever been in a doctor's office for anything more than a check-up, if that. He pulled the lamp over and spread Ben's hand out on the white paper. As he carefully unwrapped the towel, it stuck to the ragged edges of the cut and Ben jerked.

"Sorry," Henry said and looked at Sally. They could both see that the dirty gash was not the real problem. Ben's thumb was broken, and it amazed Henry that a lobster had been able to do so much damage, even more that Ben had carried on working for nearly half an hour. The pain had to be stunning.

Sally looked up at Ben. "Claw?"

"Yeah, a real mother." Ben's face had paled since he sat down, and Henry could see his pulse beating erratically in his throat, sweat standing out on his cheeks.

"Sally, please call—"

"I'm on it." Sally was already at the desk.

"Who're you calling?" Ben was leaning crookedly against the wall, his eyes closed.

"The EMTs," Henry said as he began to clean the cut. "This is broken, Ben. I don't want to mess around with it."

"Oh, shit," Ben murmured. "What about the boat?"

"I'll make sure the boat's OK," Sally said. "I'll call the guys, get you to Hayward. They'll take it from there."

Henry debrided the wound, the saline turning pink and then a deeper red as Ben's blood continued to flow. Ben had begun to shiver so Henry grabbed a thin cotton blanket and threw it over his shoulders. The smell of alcohol was thick in the room.

They heard the ambulance pull up, no siren only a quick "whoop-whoop" as it came to a stop. In less than a minute Henry's exam room was filled with more big men. Ben was surrounded, and Henry had to roll out of the way on his stool. He felt small and superfluous as the EMTs dropped their bags and pulled out their own stethoscopes.

"What do we have?" said one.

"Lobster versus Ben," Henry said, and the guys laughed. Henry stood, his triage instincts making his speech clipped and fast. "First phalanx is broken, thenar is torn." The EMTs nodded. "He's a little shocky. Keep the cuff on him and start an IV, saline, and five of morphine for pain."

"Oh no," said Ben. "Patience would kill me."

For a second Henry could have sworn he heard his own heart stutter.

"Why is that?" he asked as he carefully looked at anything but Ben.

"Because she got me to detox last month and I promised her I wouldn't screw it up."

"You're an addict?" Henry was honestly surprised. He might have guessed alcohol but not drugs. And, while he was at it, Patience was detoxing addicts?

"Not that kind of detox, Doc," Ben was almost laughing as he slid awkwardly off the table. One EMT grabbed his elbow as his knees buckled and his eyes rolled. Henry lunged for his other arm and pulled him upright.

"Thanks," Ben whispered. They hustled him out as Sally held the door, turning sideways to squeeze her belly away from the grinning men.

"It's a girl, Sally," the EMT said.

"Sam Parker, just because you delivered Willa May's baby does not make you an expert."

"Ask Dr. Carlyle," he called as he got in the rig.

The patients in the waiting room were already planning their dinner-table stories and taking bets on Sally.

Henry sat for a moment before he called in his next appointment. He willed the adrenaline to dissipate, ashamed that something as mundane as a broken thumb could make him miss a city ER. But that wasn't exactly it. As Henry gathered the bloody gauze and alcohol wipes and threw them in the bin, he had to admit that what he missed in that moment was the field hospital where he'd spent fifteen months, where he'd saved more men than he'd lost, the place that had nearly broken him. Henry shook his head as he shoved the last of the detritus into the garbage. "It's done now," he said under his breath.

PATIENCE LEFT SORREL to finish the Mayo arrangement and drove Matty and his bike home. They were both sunburned, and Patience wondered if Rob would give her trouble or not even notice. She lifted the bike over the tailgate and let Matty wheel it to the garage.

"Come on, I'll walk you in," she said holding out her hand.

Matty didn't take it, but he moved closer to her as they went around to the back door.

"Rob, your soldier's home from the wars," Patience called as she pushed the screen open.

"He's still at the store," Matty said as he went to the fridge. He took out a carton of milk and carefully poured a glass. "He won't be back until after six." Rob Short worked at the hardware store, the one place that seemed to actually give him peace. He kept the books, and he had an encyclopedic knowledge of the inventory and took real satisfaction in every column he reconciled; in that way he and Matty were very much kin.

"Do you want me to wait?" Patience looked at Matty until he met her eye.

"Nah, I'm OK," he said, and she saw that he was.

"Right, then, just be sure you tell your dad about today, yeah? And ask him for your pill."

Matty nodded.

"In fact, where does he keep them?"

Matty pointed to a high cabinet, and Patience stood on tiptoes to open the door. She braced one knee on the counter and pushed up to see the top shelf. A line of bottles stood near the edge of it. She recognized Rob's blood pressure medicine and Matty's Doxepin. The others were sleeping pills, antacids, and aspirin. As she climbed down, banging her shin on the counter edge, Patience was relieved that the medicines were out of Matty's reach, that Rob did at least one thing to keep his kid safe.

"OK, I won't dose you, but make your dad do it tonight, please."

Patience reached to hug Matty, but he shook his head so she lightly touched his shoulder.

"Right, see you, buddy," Patience said.

"See you." Matty stood at the back door and watched Patience pull out. He finished his milk and sat at the kitchen table until his father came home. They would have a stilted conversation about their days, and Rob would grimace as Matty recited the list of plants and their uses. Neither would see that Matty found the very same comfort at the Nursery that Rob found at the store.

As Patience drove away from Matty, she decided to stop at Pete Markham's liquor store before she went back to the Nursery for Sorrel. She had a taste for a cool gin and tonic, with lime sharp on her tongue. Also, she thought she might play for time so that she didn't have to see Simon Mayo when he came to collect the flowers. She had always liked Simon; she liked him now. But she knew his history with Sorrel (or thought she did), and she felt a little angry with them both. The Mayos had a habit of taking what they wanted through the sheer gift of privilege. Patience believed that's what Simon had done with Sorrel, and that Sorrel had let him.

Patience pulled over to the curb on Main Street and was digging in her backpack for some money when Henry Carlyle saw her. She had one foot up on the truck's running board and was leaning over the bag on her knee. Her sundress was hiked up over her thigh, and her red hair fell across her face in a fiery wave that shimmered as she rummaged. Henry considered slipping away, but he felt emboldened by the lobster episode. Besides, he needed to know what the hell Ben Avellar had been talking about. He approached from the front of the truck, noting the bumper stickers that were obviously used as much to cover the rust spots as to voice an opinion: EAT LOCAL, and GPC: SING IF YOU LIKE COWS.

"Hello," Henry said. Patience's head jerked up at the sound of his voice. She turned toward him and hit her cheek against the truck's wing mirror.

"Ow, damn it!" Patience barked.

"Oh, God, I'm so sorry," Henry said as he reached for her. He came around the hood with his hand out and was surprised when Patience stilled. Henry tilted her head and brushed his thumb over the rising bruise. "You should probably ice this."

"Then it's a good thing I was going into Pete's for some

gin," Patience said. She looked at Henry's eyes. They were blue or gray and turned slightly down at the corners. Maybe those lashes weren't too long after all.

"We need a do-over," she said and slung her bag onto her shoulder as she stuck out her hand. "I'm Patience Sparrow."

Henry took it. "Henry Carlyle."

"That's better," Patience said. "I'll see you around."

She walked into the liquor store, leaving the doctor on the pavement, his left hand on the truck to steady himself. As the door swung shut behind Patience, Henry realized he hadn't brought up Ben. He followed her in and found her paying for the gin, a lime, and a bag of ice.

"I wanted to ask you about . . ."

Patience cut him off.

"Nettie is fine," she said. *Enough gloating,* she thought.

"No, not Nettie, Ben Avellar."

"Is he sick too?"

"He broke his thumb this afternoon," Henry said. "He'll need surgery."

"I'll tell Nettie." Patience was lost.

Nettie and Ben had been in the same class all through school. He occasionally came out to the Nursery to deal with big projects: moving trees, building the split-rail fence and the willow trellis where the cutting sweet peas grew, digging the small pond at the edge of the wildflower meadow. He was a gentle man for all his size and was as careful around the plants as the Sisters were. Patience didn't know that Ben had stayed with

Nettie after he finished filling Thaddeus Sparrow's grave. He'd watched her, alone at the top of the hill, leaning against her mother's headstone, crying. No one knew that on the day she'd buried her father, Ben discovered that he had feelings for Nettie. He climbed the hill to sit with her, leaving his shovel behind so that she wouldn't think of him only as the gravedigger. Ben had given her his bandanna to blow her nose and helped her to her feet when she finished crying. It was too strange to talk about that day the longer they left it, so he and Nettie had simply gone on as they had before, buying each other's goods and services, nodding to each other on the street, shaking hands at church. So, of course, Patience couldn't make a connection between them, and Henry Carlyle had no reason to.

Henry was shaking his head. "This isn't about Nettie, or not directly. I tried to give Ben something for the pain, but he refused. He said you'd detoxed him."

"Oh," Patience said. "Oh, I get it." She picked up the gin and ice and tried to walk around Henry, who didn't get anything and hadn't moved.

"Ben decided to clean up his act," she said as she stopped in front of Henry. He could see the nimbus of light around her from the door and for a moment he could hardly focus.

"He'd been feeling kind of lurgy so I put together some stuff to, you know, wash him out." Patience scooped her hand through the air.

"Lurgy? You have a cure for lurgy?" Henry blurted.

"More like some teas and a lot of water."

Ben had followed Patience's instructions to the letter even though he'd come to her hoping to find a way to ask Nettie out. Patience suspected that Ben was in her barn because he was in love with someone. She could taste it in the air around him. But he didn't ask for help with love.

"And it worked?" Henry asked. "Your remedy?"

"Don't sound so skeptical," Patience said.

"Is lurgy a real ailment?" Henry asked as Patience stepped around him.

Patience turned at the door, one foot already out. Henry saw heat rising from the pavement behind her and vaguely acknowledged that it was well and truly summer.

"You know, I don't appreciate your jokes. This town has gotten along perfectly well with my help now and then. I've been just fine without you."

If Sorrel had heard how sharp Patience's voice turned, she might have slapped her. As it was, Henry was the one who looked like he'd been hit. His cheeks reddened and his hands curled into fists, not to hit back but to keep himself from reaching out to grab Patience. He couldn't believe how suddenly angry she was. Only hours before he'd felt slightly heroic as he worked over Ben; he'd felt accepted. Now it was as if he'd been repelled.

The two stared at each other for a minute. Patience caught Pete's eye over Henry's shoulder. He was staring too. She banged out of the door before Henry could see how much she regretted her outburst. She wanted to drive away so she didn't have to examine why she'd said, "I've been just fine without you" to a man she didn't know.

"Juniper," Pete sniffed. "She's wicked mad, but it'll pass."

Henry inhaled and realized that Pete was right. The air was rich with the smell of pine, crisp and fresh but somehow sweet. Gin, it smelled of gin, and for a second Henry thought that maybe Patience had dropped her package.

"Funny thing about Patience Sparrow," Pete said. "It's like she's part of that Nursery, she smells of it and when her moods change, so does her smell. Once she gives you a remedy, she's connected to you so"—he sniffed again—"sometimes we guess at how *she's* feeling."

"Oh, come on," Henry groaned. But he remembered the scent of chamomile in his waiting room, the eucalyptus at Nettie's throat, the aroma that rested on the air in front of Ivy House.

"You'll find out if you last," Pete said.

Henry ran out the door. Patience was sitting in her truck, her head back on the seat, eyes closed, an ice cube to her cheek. If she responded to her own gift, Patience would have prescribed arnica and comfrey-root tincture and a cool bath. But she had never reacted to a single remedy. Not even when she needed one.

When Henry came up to her window, he was so relieved she was still there that he laughed.

"What now?" Patience asked. She didn't open her eyes or turn her head.

"I came to apologize," Henry said. "Although, to be fair, I don't know why."

"Maybe because all you've done is judge me. You raise your eyebrow at me. You think I don't get that?"

Henry brought his hand to his face. "It's not raised now."

Patience opened her eyes. "Give it a second."

"Listen," Henry said, putting his hand on the door. "I don't mean to come off like an asshole." Now Patience raised an eyebrow. "I've had a day, well, it's been a long one."

"Yeah? Me, too." Patience sat up. "Are we done?"

"No," Henry said. "I don't think this is how we should be."

Both Henry and Patience heard the truth in his words. Neither of them acknowledged it.

"Tell me what you do. Show me why the people in this town trust you almost more than they trust me. Help *me* trust you." Henry willed his voice to settle. It sounded too low, too intimate, and he cleared his throat.

"*Almost* more?" Patience asked.

Henry shrugged and waggled his hand. "Almost," he said.

"Say I cared to explain myself, which I'm not saying I do," Patience said. "Would you want to come to the Nursery?"

"Yes." Henry held very still. What if she reconsidered? What if she bolted?

"Now?"

"Yes."

Patience held up the bottle. "There could be drinking involved."

Henry laughed. "Not for me. I'm going to see Ben at the hospital later." The thought of it, the loosening that came with a drink and some soft summer air, was enough to make Henry want to close his eyes and hold out a glass.

"That's good." Patience nodded. "I guess you really do make house calls." She gestured at the passenger door. "Well, get in, Dr. Carlyle."

"It's Henry."

"Don't make me regret this, Henry. I'm not entirely sure why I invited you in the first place."

Patience did know why and she didn't regret it, yet. For starters, she wanted to sit beside Henry Carlyle. Embracing the heat that had settled in her stomach, Patience grabbed her bag off the passenger seat and threw it onto the floor at his feet. She wanted to be next to him, she wanted to talk to him, to listen to his growly voice, watch to see if he pushed his hair off his forehead as they jounced down Calumet Landing. She wanted to get close enough to find out what Henry smelled of.

As for the doctor, he might have run after the truck if Patience hadn't invited him. He was almost sure that as they talked inside the liquor store, they'd leaned toward each other, even as she snapped at him. He was eager to see if he was right, to learn if, when he stood in her space, surrounded by her things, he might understand why he wanted her so. He needed to know if what he felt was ridiculous or returned.

Henry pressed his hands against the dashboard of the old

truck as Patience took a corner on what felt like two wheels. His right foot pushed reflexively at a phantom brake pedal.

"Is it far?" he asked. He hadn't been carsick since he stopped riding in military jeeps. He swallowed several times.

"Almost there." Patience steered one-handed, her left arm out the window, her fingers spread in the breeze. She looked at Henry. "Are you all right?"

"Fine," Henry said and swallowed again. "You have a very personal driving style."

"Yeah, my sisters taught me." She made a sharp left. "We're here."

They bumped down the road and pulled up in a slide of sand. Simon Mayo's car was parked in front of the office, and Patience decided she'd box him in so he'd have to ask her to be able to leave. *Sorrel's right, I am a bitch,* she thought.

Henry climbed out and was hit with such a wall of scent that he staggered, his bad leg giving under him. He felt transported, empty and full at the same time, as the smell of clover and rue, peony and Russian sage fell over him. He didn't know the names of all the smells, or why they made him feel so unsteady. He was embarrassed by his graceless lurch and kept his head down, hoping that Patience was already in the little barn. Henry didn't want her to see him like that, defined by his weakness.

But Patience had seen. She'd turned her head at the sound of the truck door and caught Henry's stumble. She winced with him and whispered, "Poppy, valerian, St. John's wort."

Henry followed Patience into the barn. The sun was beginning to set a hot orange behind the building, and when he stepped inside, it was dark and cool. If anything, the smells were even more intense. He looked around. It was a peaceful place: the long soapstone sink—clean now—Patience's table covered with at least a dozen small bottles, a stack of labels and an open notebook, the deep drift of petals, leaves, and stems on the floor. The tableau was as close and compelling as a Dutch still life.

Sorrel was standing at the high counter, the arrangement in front of her just as Charlotte had requested, only more beautiful than she could ever imagine. Simon stood on the other side, and neither of them could see the other through the flowers. Patience came up behind him.

"Wow, Sorrel."

Simon turned around and saw Henry at the door.

"Doctor," he said, smiling.

"Lawyer," Henry said, smiling back.

"Indian Chief," the Sisters finished.

It took Henry a second to get the joke. Standing just behind Patience in the shadowy room had disoriented him. He wasn't sure if he was smelling Patience, her hair curling up at the nape of her neck, dirt and sand sprayed up the back of her calves, or only the flowers. Henry had seen how Patience's back straightened when she saw Simon Mayo, and he was reminded of how Simon's voice had flattened when he asked Henry about his house call to the Sisters. He was sure that Simon Mayo was married; he was certain the party invitation he'd received had come from Simon and his wife. Then, when he saw how Simon's eyes searched for Sorrel, Henry was ashamed at his relief. He didn't know what he'd do if this blond charmer looked at Patience that way. All these thoughts and ludicrous mental gyrations ran through Henry in the time it took him to laugh at a lame joke.

"So, Simon," Patience said, "you going to fit that in the back of the Merc?"

When Patience pulled up, Henry had been in the throes of minor terror and nausea, but he now realized that the silver blur on his right had been a Mercedes convertible.

"I am, P," Simon came around the counter and held out his arms. Sorrel's face was a study in conflict. For a moment she thought Simon was going to embrace her, but he reached for the arrangement and hoisted it up. "Someone get the door," he said as he sidled away. "Am I going to knock anything?"

Henry pushed the door open and eased back from the flowers. "You're fine," he said.

Simon nestled the big glass cylinder into the back seat and came around to the front. The car looked like some kind of parade float.

"Patience?" he asked, pointing at her truck.

"Oh, am I in your way?" she asked.

"Cute, P," Simon said. He turned to Henry. "The Sisters all pretend they don't like me, but I know better." Simon opened his car door, keeping his eyes on Patience's truck.

Patience swung into the cab, scattering sand and clamshells beside the sports car as she backed up. Her bumper came a bit too close to the Mercedes, and she grinned at Simon's face.

"You'd better drive slowly, Simon, or the whole thing'll be nothing but stems by the time you get home," Sorrel said. She stood at the barn door, her arms crossed over her chest. Simon looked back at her with a nod. Henry saw that his eyes strayed to her bare feet. A smile twitched the corner of his mouth as he climbed in.

"You know, Sisters, you are both welcome at the party, and then you could see this thing in situ," he said and looked at Henry. "The Sparrows are founders too. We invite them every year, and they never show."

Patience snorted as she climbed out of the truck and came to stand beside Henry.

"Seriously, Patience, why don't you accompany the good doctor? We haven't had nearly enough gossip lately."

Henry waved his hand at Patience. "You don't have to do that."

He couldn't imagine how he could concentrate on the names and faces of current and possible patients if this woman stood beside him. Even now, he could feel her warmth; smell the hay-like scent of her sweat. He wondered if that was a good sign, the sweetness beneath the heat.

"I'll think about it," Patience said. Sorrel's eyes snapped to her sister. Simon drove off, and the three of them stood in silence listening to the evening settle.

"As if Charlotte Mayo would be caught dead socializing with the Sparrow Sisters," Sorrel finally said, her voice low.

"Ha," Patience said. "As if you would be caught dead mingling in the Mayo house."

Sorrel frowned, and Patience felt guilty

"Sorrel, I'm showing Dr. Carlyle around," Patience said in a voice that dared her sister to ask any questions. But Sorrel was already turning back to the barn, separating the strands of her heavy braid until her black and white hair fell across her back in a fan.

"I get the feeling that your sister and Simon have a history," Henry said as he followed Patience into the reclaimed pasture. It was divided into dozens of plantings—gardens—each with a distinct character. Henry felt as if he were moving through the rooms of a great house.

"Well, they *should* have a history. Sorrel is stubborn and Simon is stupid. He's not so bad, not like his father, for instance. He was a real ass. Pushed his kids until one of them, Simon's brother Howard, fell. He dropped out of school, went to L.A., took up cooking, and never came back. That is worse than insanity to the Mayos." Patience turned to Henry. "That was the year before Simon came home from Harvard with Charlotte. I guess he was afraid to push his father back."

Patience walked through the rows of young box and round containers of chartreuse oakleaf hydrangeas. Henry followed, wondering at the billowing mounds of white and purple lilac and drifts of pale cherry blossoms and clusters of ripe cherries, although he didn't know enough to question how they were all blooming and fruiting together. Patience gestured to the greenhouses. "Come on," she said. Henry kept his eyes away from how the light played through her dress, limning her slim hips as she walked. He watched the clear sky, the nearly full moon that was just visible against the deepening blue.

"Granite Point is a very small place," Patience said. "I mean, I went to kindergarten with two firemen and at least three cops, and to high school with the head of the EMS. We are all tangled up with one another. Ben Avellar, for instance; he and Nettie graduated the same year. The minister, John Hathaway, grew up here and then went to England to study. He came back with a wife, and half the women in town had their hearts broken."

"And Sorrel and Simon?" Henry stood in the aisle between a long parade of flats full of small deep-pink ruffled flowers.

"Sorrel never talks about it, but I guess they could have been more than best friends. I don't really need Sorrel to tell me what's happening, or Simon either, for that matter." Patience pushed her index finger deep into the soil of one of the flats. She felt that it was perfectly wet and brushed the dirt from her hand. "When Simon gets anywhere near Sorrel, the air changes around them, and I can feel how sorry they both are. How, oh, I don't know"—Patience tilted her head—"thwarted, I guess."

"Why hasn't Sorrel found someone else? Or why don't they try to be with each other?" Henry asked. The thought of living within blocks of someone you wanted was unimaginable to him. Except that as he looked at Patience, her hair in a jumble at her neck, her arms tanned and freckled, Henry thought maybe he could imagine it.

"Let me tell you something about Granite Point," she said. "This is a town with a very long memory and a very wide Puritan streak. Besides, there has never been a Mayo divorce, and there never will be."

"And that's true even now, in the twenty-first century?" To Henry, Patience's description was at best picturesque and at worst mean.

"Yes, now," Patience said. "Very little changes in Granite Point, not the important stuff, anyway. So, Simon's wife, Charlotte, is . . ." Patience paused, brushed her hand across the tops of the flowers. "Well, Sorrel is here, and Charlotte is with Simon in the big Mayo house on the harbor." The smell of warm cinnamon and clove drifted out from under Patience's fingertips.

"And you are with Nettie and Sorrel."

"Yes, we're the last of the Sparrows." Patience heard Sorrel's voice in her words and she frowned. She pointed at the flats. "These are dianthus, pinks, they're called—a kind of carnation, highly scented." She walked down the row and toward the door. Henry stood for a moment and let the smell of the pinks, sweet and soft, drift around him. He felt light-headed and strangely content. Henry finally moved when he saw that Patience was holding the door open at the end of the greenhouse.

Patience led Henry all through the whole Nursery, explaining how the plants were organized. When they got to the largest knot garden, the smell flowed around it, hovered over it. Henry thought he could actually see a layer of hazy green floating inches above the intricate patterns. Patience wove her way through it, reciting the names of the plants so musically that Henry felt nearly hypnotized. Threads of mist curled in her wake.

"Mallow, acanthus, germander, marjoram, calendula, viola, lady's mantle, shepherd's purse, valerian," Patience murmured. She plucked at the hedges that marked the formal design and rubbed blue-green leaves between her fingers, bruising them, releasing an acrid but oddly appealing scent.

"I use everything in this garden," she said. "The smallest flowers serve a purpose, the sharpest thorns work in their way."

They wandered through the tallest flowers in the cutting gardens.

"Delphinium, salvia, snapdragon, monkshood, foxglove," she recited.

"Do you use all of these as well?" Henry asked.

"Well, salvia is a hallucinogen, and foxglove is digitalis, so no, not really," she answered. "They are mostly for decoration."

"Digitalis? That's digoxin. It's used to treat arrhythmia," he said. "Heart medicine," he added.

"Yeah, I know that," Patience said. "Clearly I don't use it on people, Sorrel's arrangements only." She flicked a finger at the foxglove, making the blossoms shudder, and several earwigs tumbled out. "I found these in the wildflower meadow some years ago and transplanted them. The legend is that Elizabeth Howard, one of our ancestors, planted them in the seventeenth century. This was her land then."

"Surely that's not possible?" Henry asked.

"Who knows?" Patience answered. "There are a lot of impossibilities about growing things." And she began to show Henry what she meant.

While Patience was very clear about each plant, about how the sandy soil dictated much of what grew until the Sisters changed it, revealing much about the mysterious flowers and vigorous plants that covered the acres, she gave away little else about her family other than to say that they owned the Nursery together and lived comfortably off its proceeds and the Sparrow trust her father hadn't been able to touch. Henry badly wanted to learn more about the last Sparrows and why they were alone, but he heard the chill that had crept into Patience's voice as she described how they had managed to buy the land, how death had brought forth this living thing, so he held his tongue. When they walked into the wildflower meadow, he saw that she relaxed again, the planes of her face softening as she bent to cut a handful of bright blue flowers. She snapped her penknife shut and slid it into a pocket.

"Cornflowers, bachelor's buttons; one of our mother's favorites, so my sisters tell me," she said, giving him the little bouquet. Henry took it. He let his fingers brush against Patience's and looked to see if she felt the shiver that took him.

"When she died, they raised me, all three. Dad was pretty

useless, so angry and sad. Dr. Higgins couldn't help him or Marigold. When she died, we all kind of gave up on doctors."

"Is that why you make your remedies?"

"Partly," Patience said. "I do have a gift, it seems. I can read what people need, somehow. I feel exactly how to make them better. It started before I got Clarissa's book, another ancestor, the woman who built Ivy House. Once I read it, I found that I just knew how to grow things, take the ingredients and . . ." She trailed off. "You think it's all nuts, don't you?"

Henry hesitated; he had to be careful. "I don't know what it is you can do. I only know that everyone believes in you," he said. "Maybe if you gave me a chance, showed me your work . . ." Patience cocked her head and looked so hard at Henry that he felt completely disingenuous.

"I could show you how I work, too," he finished lamely.

"Yeah, right," she said.

"No, I mean it." And he did. If her mistrust of doctors was why Patience didn't like him, Henry was determined to fix it. He so wished for her to like him.

Patience made for the barn without waiting for Henry to catch up. He followed her again.

"Sally Tabor told me that you can change things, people, not just their symptoms. She said it's not faith." Henry stopped. "Is it magic, I mean not real magic, some kind of homeopathy . . . ?" He stood still, staring at Patience's back.

"I gave her ginger tea for morning sickness," Patience said. "Relief has a way of making you so grateful it just seems like magic." She turned around to face Henry. "How's Dot Avery, the arthritis?"

"She's over eighty, there's nothing much I can do besides anti-inflammatory drugs."

"See, that's where you're wrong," Patience said. "All Dot wants is to walk her dog and volunteer at the animal shelter. She's depressed because it hurts too much to do those things, and then she begins to fail even more. I can fix that part, too."

"Then why haven't you?"

"She wanted to go to you."

"So she has." Henry drew closer on the step beneath her. "Perhaps I could suggest that she see you now."

Patience wasn't sure if Henry was serious. She could smell the disinfectant that still clung to his clothes. Rubbing alcohol, ammonia, cotton wool. She saw the bloodstain on his shirt-sleeve. It all reminded her of Marigold, how she'd struggled so hard only to sink beneath the weight of her disease. Patience shivered and rubbed her eyes with the heels of her hands. To Henry she looked as young and lost as the little girl in his office that morning.

"Hey, now," Henry said. "What have I done?" He brushed his fingertips over her shoulder and reached up to stroke the bruise on her cheek.

Patience took his hand. "It's not you," she said. But it was. She let go of his hand and disappeared into the barn.

Henry felt like he'd been given another chance with Patience and was damned if he wasn't going to take it.

"Will you come with me to the party?" he called. Patience reappeared at the door. She looked so surprised that he wondered if he'd made a terrible mistake. But then she nodded. Henry let his breath out. "I don't know anyone, really. It would be nice to have a guide."

"We will be the talk of the town." Patience raised an eyebrow.

"Oh, I don't think I'm nearly interesting enough to start rumors." Henry stepped up to meet Patience in the doorway. "Now, you," he said. "You are fascinating."

PATIENCE DROVE HENRY to Baker's Way so he could get his car and head out to check on Ben Avellar. All the way she replayed the moment they had stood so close. She could still feel the doorframe against her spine as she pressed back from Henry although she'd longed to press into him. After she pulled over to the curb, Patience tucked a sprig of hyssop into Henry's shirt pocket. The camphor-like smell wasn't much better than disinfectant, but at least it came from the garden. She let her fingers linger for a moment against him, the crisp cotton of his shirt wilted by the heat. Beneath the doctor smell she could detect fresh water, wood, and man. She pressed her fingertips into him for a second before she put her hand back on the wheel. He felt the pressure acutely and held his breath. Henry climbed out of the truck and for the first time, Patience wanted to say something to him about his leg. But she didn't; she just watched him walk into the house, his hand reaching, automatically, to rub his thigh.

When she returned to the Nursery, Patience found Sorrel on the bench in the Shakespeare Garden. She joined her, and the sisters sat in silence until Sorrel couldn't stand it anymore.

"I really need you to stop hating Simon," she said. "It's not like he left me for Charlotte."

"I don't hate him," Patience said. "In fact, I'm going with Henry."

"Going with Henry?" Sorrel laughed. "Steady?"

"To the Mayo party. He asked, I said fine." Patience stood. "Come on, Nettie must be frantic with boredom."

"Nettie's often frantic," Sorrel said. "Why are you?"

"I'm nothing like frantic. I just want to get home. I've got gin to drink."

CHAPTER FOUR

Periwinkle is useful against inflammation

*H*enry drove west to Hayward with the last of the sun in his eyes. He had the windows open, and the rushing sound filled his head. It didn't block out thoughts of Patience as he'd hoped it would. He too relived the moment they had stood so close in the barn; he wanted to savor it, but all he could think was, *You are fascinating. Who says things like that?*

By the time he walked into the hospital, it was dark, a full hour later than he'd planned. He stopped at the front desk and signed in. It was the first time he'd been to Hayward Hospital since he registered for privileges. He picked up a badge and went to Ben's floor. The nurses looked up as he approached;

one glanced down at his limp, but the other was too busy staring at his face to see anything else.

"I'm here to see Ben Avellar," Henry said.

"Family?" one nurse asked.

Henry hadn't bothered with a lab coat, and he had slipped his visitor's badge into his pocket. He fished it out and showed it to the nurse. "I'm his doctor," he said.

"Well"—the nurse peered at the badge—"Dr. Carlyle, he's in room 512." She pointed as Henry thanked her and walked down the hall.

An old man, asleep, his mouth gaping, his teeth on the bedside table next to a balled-up tissue and an emesis basin, lay in the near bed. Henry tiptoed past and around the curtain where he found Ben, also asleep. His hand was on a folded pillow. It was stained brown by Betadine, wrapped in white gauze and a foam splint. Henry could see the small lump under the dressing; the wire that poked through the skin at the base of Ben's thumb. It would be some weeks before that could come out and Henry realized that Ben wouldn't be able to use the thumb until it did, and then only carefully. There was nothing careful about fishing. What happened when a lobsterman couldn't pull his traps? Henry guessed his patient was in trouble. It would soon be high season, and Ben would be without his job.

Henry took the chart off the end of the bed and read through the notes. Nothing unusual, no surprises in the blood work. He didn't know what he expected: eye of newt or horn of toad extract from Patience? Henry huffed and replaced the chart.

He went to the window and leaned his head against the cool pane. He shifted all his weight onto his good leg and sighed.

"Hey, Dr. Carlyle," Ben said. His voice was scratchy, and his mouth was so dry Henry could hear the sound his lips made as they parted.

Henry turned around and smiled. "Ben, you look well."

Ben lifted his hand. "Pretty well fucked," he said. "The surgeon told me I can't work, not for a month at least. That's the season gone."

"I know," Henry said. He brought a cup of water to Ben and held the straw while he drank. He took his stethoscope from around his neck and listened to Ben's heart. It was as steady and strong as the man himself. Never mind that he was in a hospital johnny. "There has to be someone who can run your boat."

"I guess," Ben said and squirmed up in the bed. "But summer is when I make enough to get me through. Working the cemetery, helping the Sisters, a little construction, it's not enough. Shit, even with the boat it's hard. The maintenance alone . . ."

Henry didn't know what to say. He'd never had to worry about money. He'd never had to depend on his body to make a living, and after he'd been wounded in Iraq, he knew he never would. He still missed the physicality of the field hospital but not the cold dread that settled in as soon as the warning Klaxon went off. And back in Boston, when he tried to live his old life, he remembered how he was usually the last doctor to reach an ambulance, his limp forcing him into a silly skip to keep up with the gurneys.

"Ben, give me some names. Sally and I will set up a rota of men to bait and pull your traps."

"Now why would any of the guys give up their day to help me?"

"Because it's the right thing," Henry said. "You'd do it for them."

Ben nodded. "I would," he said.

Henry took out his prescription pad and wrote down the names Ben gave him. As he did, he found himself excited by his new task. He considered going out on the boats with one of lobstermen. He pictured himself hauling the traps out of the clear cold water, measuring and weighing the lobsters, shoveling ice down the hatch. Pretty nigh impossible, he knew. When Ben sighed, Henry's own good cheer embarrassed him.

"You look happy," Ben said.

"I think I am," Henry said.

"Glad one of us is."

THE STARS WERE out by the time Henry got back to Granite Point. When he turned onto Baker's Way, the house looked forlorn, dark and unoccupied. He went around to the back to let himself in and found Patience Sparrow sitting on his little porch steps.

"Holy . . ." Henry said.

"Don't finish that," Patience warned. She had the bag from the liquor store in her lap. "I owe you a drink."

"You do?" Henry asked. He helped her up and couldn't let go of her hand.

"Well, I offered earlier and since you're all done with Ben . . . how is Ben?"

"He's worried about money. He won't be able to run the boat most of the summer."

"That's bad," Patience said. She reclaimed her hand and opened the bag. "Although, there are some guys who know him, and the firemen. We can put together enough to see Ben through."

"That's what I said," Henry reached for the lime. "I'll just go cut this up."

Patience sat back down and leaned until her vertebrae bumped the step. She'd felt like a teenager when she snuck out of the house while Nettie was cooking and hurried toward Henry's house. It was just that she thought she'd left things uneven at the nursery.

Henry came back with the lime wedges in one palm and glasses of ice in the other. He hipped the screen door open and put the glasses on the porch rail.

"Here," he said beckoning Patience over. "You know what?" he asked.

Patience shook her head.

"This is exactly what I wanted; a gin and tonic." *And you,* he thought.

"I aim to please," Patience said. *What is* with *me?* she thought.

"No you don't, that's the last thing you aim to do."

"Well, I aim to end your day with a proper cocktail then."

They stood for a minute, and Henry kept his glass close to his mouth, feeling the snap and fizz of the tonic against his lips.

"Why are you here, Henry?" Patience asked, and Henry then knew why she was on his porch.

"Ah, you're curious about the new doctor too."

"I told you my story," Patience said.

"I think not much of it." Henry took a sip of his drink.

"How about you tell me as much of yours as I did of mine."

"That seems fair." Henry gestured to the chairs. "I am thirty-three and before I came here I was in the army and before and after that I was an ER doc and before all that I went to Yale."

"And I could have gotten that from anyone in town." In fact, she had, from the bank teller over a month before.

"I graduated at twenty, was Phi Beta Kappa, and got my first match out of med school."

"Again, not what I'm looking for." Patience pulled her legs up, and Henry followed their long line over the rim of his glass.

"You want to know how I hurt my leg?" he asked.

"Only if you want to tell me."

"I don't," Henry said. He sighed and looked at the porch ceiling. "I was overseeing a vaccination program at a school near Mosul, northwest of Baghdad. There was an IED in the damn school. I'm told it could have been much worse." Henry's voice had dropped lower and lower so that by the end Patience had to lean forward to hear him.

"I'm sorry," she said.

"So." Henry looked at Patience. "You can imagine the appeal of small-town medicine. I tried the ER again, but . . ."

"It still hurts," she murmured.

"It's been a while now."

"But your leg still hurts."

"Not so much."

Patience reached to touch Henry's thigh, but he grabbed her hand.

"Don't," he said.

"Are you afraid I'll put a spell on you?" Patience tried to keep the hurt out of her voice.

"No, I don't want you to feel sorry for me. You've no idea how emasculating it is to be the object of pity." Henry stood. "I came to Granite Point to be around people who didn't know me before. I'd like to keep it that way, the not knowing me before part."

Patience understood that. She nodded at Henry, and he thought that he saw her soften a bit. She closed her eyes and turned her face away from him.

"Sometimes I think this whole town is be-spelled," she said. "Sometimes it feels like it's one of those enchanted villages the hardware store puts up in the windows at Christmas."

Henry waited quietly.

"I can see how you'd want to fit in here," Patience said. "If you go around in a little slot, doing your thing, day in, day out, then you're safe."

"Is that what you do?" Henry asked.

"Oh, God," Patience sounded almost sorry. "There is no slot for me. Don't you know? I'm not safe at all."

PATIENCE REFUSED HIS offer of another drink, but she left the gin and lime. After she'd tried to touch him, the pleasure had gone out of the air, replaced by an edgy chill. They were both relieved when she stood to go home. Henry agreed to come to Ivy House to get Patience for the party the next evening, then he watched her leave without moving, even when she turned for a last look. Henry wondered if she'd left the gin because she was coming back or giving up.

Henry poured himself another drink, but the tonic had gone flat, making it nothing more than a too-sweet punch. He tried to understand why he hadn't let Patience touch him. The pity thing did haunt him, but something told him that Patience didn't feel that way. And so, why hadn't he taken his chance when he had it? Why hadn't he let her take his leg in her hands? He could so easily have turned that exploring touch into something much better. But then he thought of the first woman he'd been with after he was back. She had actually started to cry when she saw the wound. It was still raw, the network of ugly shrapnel scars, the staple marks like tiny tracks, the deep divot over his reconstructed femur still a livid pink. The look on her face told Henry that she had crowned him some kind of tragic champion. If he hadn't been so desperate, he'd have sent her home there and then. But he hadn't. He'd closed his eyes and pulled her into his bed.

The thought of Patience reacting the same way, a mixture of pity and fascination, made Henry feel sick. Although, from what he'd seen of her, it seemed unlikely that Patience would cry over him. She'd be more likely to examine him, turning him toward the light as she probed his leg. Henry shuddered. Enough, he thought, and went inside to scare up some dinner.

Patience walked home so slowly that her stomach was growling audibly by the time she reached Sorrel waiting for her on the front steps.

"Where were you?"

"I went for a walk." Patience climbed the steps and sat down next to Sorrel. "Do you think it's a mistake going to the Mayos'?"

Sorrel tucked a strand of hair behind Patience's ear. "I think that it's a mistake to let Henry Carlyle think you're interested in him."

"Maybe I am."

"And maybe not," Sorrel said. "Please don't hurt him, Patience. Don't leave him to the pity of this town."

There was that word again.

"He would hate that," Patience acknowledged.

"So?"

"So I'm not going to get involved with him. It's a stupid party. I'll bet the only reason he's even going is to get patients."

"Not to get Patience, then?" Sorrel asked.

"Funny, Sorrel." Patience pulled her sister up and they joined Nettie in the kitchen.

"Oh, you're back." Nettie was stirring something that smelled wonderful. "I am feeling so much better and I'm starved. I didn't think I could wait."

They sat down to fresh cod soup flavored with lemongrass, cilantro, and ginger. The broth was a translucent green, and tiny flecks of red chili floated on the top. Patience tasted it first, blowing on her spoon.

"This is really good," she said.

"It's too sour." Sorrel frowned.

"It's not, it's a little too sweet," Nettie chewed a piece of firm, white cod. "Odd."

The sisters looked at Patience.

"What?" she said.

Sorrel pointed to the soup and then to Patience. "Something's happening here."

CHAPTER FIVE

*Peter's Staff is just the thing
for scorpion's sting*

The Mayo house was almost as old as Ivy House. It was white clapboard with deep green shutters and a columned porch, all set on a lawn marked by a thick stone wall that separated the house and its owners from the deep blue harbor and the boats that lay at anchor. It also kept them far away from the summer riffraff that wandered the three tidy piers. One of the original Mayo lawyers, a judge advocate, had built the house in the late eighteenth century. Since then, nearly all the Mayos had been in the law and had lived in the house. Most in the twentieth century had used it as a summer residence, but Simon's grandfather had stayed. It had the best view in town, by far. At sunset, as on the night of the party, the light off the water made the seagulls drift to a stop on the small sandy beach below the house. They turned as one to watch, none of them bothering to cry out. A white tent waited at the rear of the house, and caterers milled around setting out glasses that caught the sun in blinding flares. Soon it would be dark enough to see the Big Point lighthouse fill the sky with intermittent flashes.

Patience had spent more time than she liked to admit getting ready for the party, for Henry. She'd chosen a pale blue dress with a boat neck that exposed her collarbones in the front and her shoulder blades in the back. Patience found it hanging with several others in the cedar closet in the attic and wondered where her mother had worn it. Her neck rose, a strong, slender column, and she'd wound her hair into a low bun. Nettie wove bee balm through the auburn strands so that every time Patience moved, a lemony current swirled around her. Freckles were scattered across her chest like sand. All in all, Patience thought, not bad for a girl who usually had dirt under her nails and leaves in her hair. "You still have leaves in your hair," she said to the mirror.

Henry arrived at Ivy House early. For the first time he would see the sisters as they really were, at ease as they moved around their house. Patience came to the door, and Henry took a deep breath. She looked beautiful, and he was already trying to guess her mood by her scent; Pete's advice had taken hold in his mind. But all he smelled was the bee balm, although he certainly couldn't name that. She led him back to the kitchen. It was hard to tell who was more startled when Patience's hand stole out to take Henry's.

Sorrel was pouring lemonade into ice-filled glasses in the kitchen as Nettie added strong tea and mint. They were laughing so loudly that Henry had to clear his throat before the sisters turned to see them.

"Ah," Nettie sighed as she looked over. "You are so pretty, Patience. And Dr. Carlyle, very sharp." Nettie laughed at Henry as he pushed his hair back.

Henry was wearing gray flannels and a white shirt, the smell of starch clear in the warm kitchen. A slightly tarnished silver belt buckle caught the light as he bowed to the sisters. He held his jacket over his arm; it was too hot to put it on. His hair was wet, and Patience had to clasp her hands behind her back to keep from dashing the drops from his neck. He'd been in the sun; his cheekbones were redder than the clean-shaven face below. Henry blushed at Nettie's comment.

"You're burned," Patience said. "I'll get some salve."

"Were you at Big Point Beach?" Sorrel asked.

"Oh, no." Henry tried to focus, but he could still hear the swish of Patience's dress against her legs when she turned. "I promised Ben I'd check his boat, not that I know what to look for. He'll be discharged tomorrow, but he's sidelined for the season."

"Ben Avellar?" Nettie asked as she arranged the mint more precisely than absolutely necessary.

"Patience didn't tell you?"

Nettie shook her head.

"He broke his thumb. It was a bad break; he had surgery yesterday afternoon. He's on intravenous antibiotics to combat an infection. I'm going to pick him up in Hayward tomorrow."

"Poor Ben," Nettie murmured as she handed Henry a glass.

Patience returned and after she smoothed a dollop of thick white cream onto Henry's cheeks and nose, she took the glass from him before he'd had even a taste.

"I won't be home late," Patience said with a grimace.

Henry rubbed at his face as they walked down the porch stairs, spreading the cream into a pale mask.

"What is this? It smells awful."

Patience batted his hand away. "It's cider vinegar and some other stuff."

"I must look like a mime," Henry said.

"Just give it a minute and it'll soak in," Patience said.

He stood still outside Ivy House and waited.

"What?" Patience asked, turning back. She'd started down the walk.

"I'm giving it a minute," Henry said.

"Oh, for the love of corn." Patience put her hand out, and Henry took it.

"No, give me your hanky," she said.

"How do you know I have one?" Henry asked as he reached into his pocket.

"Men like you always have a hanky," Patience said as she

lifted the handkerchief to her mouth. She dabbed it on her tongue and began to scrub at Henry.

"Stop," he said. "Give me that." Henry finished the job and then didn't know what to do with the dirty cloth. He stuffed it into the cracked stone urn at the end of the steps to Ivy House.

"I'll be back for it later," he said to Patience. She lifted one eyebrow, and Henry hoped she couldn't see him blush beneath the sunburn.

By the time Henry and Patience arrived at the Mayos', the redness on Henry's cheeks had faded to a faint flush, and his skin was as tan as that of any local. Henry felt Patience's bare arm press against his shirtsleeve, and it was all he could do to keep walking. He wanted to turn around and take her to his apartment. He wanted to lie in his bed with her, tell her his secrets as the night air cooled them. That thought made him stop suddenly and then speed up to cover. He knew his gait was uneven, but Patience steadied him with her hand on his arm.

"What's going on in there?" Patience tapped his temple, as if she'd heard Henry's jumbled, hopeful thoughts. She saw that his eyes were the deep gray-blue of a newborn.

"We're here," Henry said as they turned onto the waterfront. And they were. The house rose above them, the seawall made of local granite, the porch steps painted a shiny gray. The front door was open, and Patience could see Sorrel's giant flowers from the sidewalk.

"Gird your loins and sharpen your tongue," she said with a wicked grin. "This will be a battle." She stepped away, putting a full three feet between them. "Let's not give the crowd anything more to talk about."

Inside a harpist played in a corner by the stairs. Patience crossed her eyes at Henry and reached for two glasses of Champagne as a summer-help waiter from the yacht club came past.

"Drink up. Think of it as anesthesia."

Henry took a sip and Patience took a gulp.

They were greeted by Charlotte Mayo who, Patience was sure, hip-checked the mayor to reach Henry.

"Dr. Carlyle!" she trilled. "And Patience," she sighed. "What a treat."

"Thank you for inviting me," Henry said as he shook Charlotte's hand.

"No, no, thank you!" Charlotte pulled Henry closer. "I have been wanting to talk to you forever."

"He's only been here since April." Patience had very little tolerance when it came to Charlotte Mayo. In general, she had little patience and even less time for the social aspect of her town. As soon as she and Henry walked through the door, Patience forgot why she had agreed to come and remembered why she never had before.

"Oh, Patience." Charlotte laughed. "You are always so literal."

"Charlotte." Patience laughed. "You are . . ." She closed her mouth.

Henry watched the women with a vague smile, so uncomfortable that he began to back away.

"Oh, no you don't," they both said when they saw him.

Henry found himself being pulled into the living room by Charlotte. He managed one panicked look at Patience before the crowd closed over him like a wave. The names and faces of the other guests ran together as Charlotte shepherded him from one group to another. He exchanged his empty glass for a full one and looked longingly at an icy tray of oysters as it whizzed past. Charlotte brought him out to the terrace overlooking the harbor, and Henry leaned against the rail in relief.

"I'm sorry to give you a full-immersion baptism but you need to know these people." Charlotte moved next to him. "Consider it the price you pay for success."

"I'm grateful," Henry said, though he considered the price a little high.

"Yes, but I wanted you alone for a moment." Charlotte put her hand on his arm. "I have a professional concern."

"I would be happy to see you in my office," Henry said. He looked at Charlotte; he could see something dark in her eyes and was unexpectedly sorry for her.

"I will make an appointment, of course," she said and then lowered her voice. "Dr. Higgins has my records, but I don't want you to dismiss me out of hand. I still have hope."

"Oh no," Henry said. "Are you ill?"

"If only." Charlotte waved her hands, and Henry leaned away from them, their nails painted a bright coral, her rings as heavy as hardware. "Simon and I want a family but . . ." she shrugged.

"I'm not a fertility specialist," Henry said.

"But you're young and new, and maybe a fresh pair of eyes?"

Henry put his hand over Charlotte's. "I'll look at your file and we'll meet."

"Thank you, Dr. Carlyle."

Patience watched Henry and Charlotte as they talked. She saw the desperation that threatened to snap Charlotte's civility like a rubber band, but she didn't know what caused it. She couldn't read her, probably because Charlotte refused to be read; some people did that, not many. For a moment Patience felt a twinge of sympathy, but when she saw Henry touch Charlotte's hand, she took a half step forward. Ridiculous really, she thought, but I'd just like to keep an eye on him. She might have managed to swerve through the crowds to rescue Henry, but that tray of oysters came by and she was distracted. She took one and a lemon, squeezing it so hard the juice stung her eye. *Fair price,* she thought as she tipped the oyster into her mouth.

It slid down her throat, with an echo of the sea, the siren song of salt and rock and dark depths.

"Oh, my God," she whispered.

"Yes?" a deep voice said in her ear.

"Sammy!" Patience nudged her shoulder against the decidedly larger one of Sam Parker, high school make-out partner, fireman, and now EMT. She could have shoved against him with all her might, and he wouldn't have shifted an inch.

"I am shocked!" Sam said. "Shocked, that you're in the house that generations of money-grubbing Mayos built."

"Well, I came on a dare." Patience kept her eye out for eavesdroppers. Then she pointed to the terrace.

"Charlotte dared you? Ooh, that would get you going." Sam looked confused as he leaned in to Patience's neck. "No, you're not feeling cranky; I smell lemon."

"It's the bee balm in my hair, and don't go sniffing around me like a dog." Patience pushed Sam back and he let her.

"So, who's the dare? You can tell me."

Sam Parker was one of Patience's best friends. Sam was the only one, other than her sisters, whom Patience let guess at her mood so openly. The rest did it when they thought she wasn't looking. Now, after more than ten years of friendship, there was little Patience could hide from Sam, little she cared to.

"See the guy standing with Charlotte?" she said, tilting her head.

"The new doctor?" Sam didn't need to search for Henry; he was tall enough to see over the throng, and Henry was tall enough to be seen. "What the hell are you doing with him?"

"I am not doing anything, like it's your business," Patience said. "He asked, I answered."

"Patience, can I just say one thing?" Sam turned her around so that her back was to the view. "Do not play with him."

"What is it with you people?" Patience grabbed a glass as a waiter skated past.

"You have not been with a guy since like a year ago," Sam said, lowering his voice. "I know this because that last one had to be talked down from a shed roof after you dumped him, and since I haven't been called out to rescue another lovesick puppy, I think it's safe to say that you're not getting any."

"Thanks, that was pretty," Patience said. "And the jumper, Tommy, Timmy? He was fragile to begin with. And high." Patience put her glass down perilously close to the lip of the table where Sorrel's flowers cascaded in a riot of scent and color and summer.

"P, if you really think you're ready to let a guy in," Sam looked around, "to want somebody more than you want things your way, don't make Henry Carlyle your test case. He is not someone to be toyed with. He's a hero, you know that, right?" Sam looked at Patience until she met his eyes.

"I know, I know, he was in the army, saving lives, wounded in action. I'm impressed, I am." Patience couldn't seem to stop herself; her voice had taken on a sharp, bitter edge even though she wanted to say that Henry Carlyle had softened her to the point of melting, that Henry made her miss him before she even knew him. And that he'd done so in the time it took most men to walk away from the challenge.

"Damn it, Patience," Sam hissed. "He saved a classroom full of kids in Iraq. Well, all but one. He would never say so, but it's true." He pulled her toward a wall and crowded her against it. "The story I hear? He ran *into* the burning building, Patience."

"You do that all the time, Sam." And he did. If Sam called Henry a hero, Patience knew she should listen.

"I was trained for it. I was a fireman for years. This guy is just a doctor. I heard he had to be pulled away before he bled out. If you screw around with him, you'll answer to me."

The air around Patience went cold, really cold. Sam watched the hair rise on his arms, thought he felt the bite of frost at his lips as he exhaled.

"Dial it back, P," he whispered.

Patience took a deep breath. "What if I like him, I mean *like him,* like him?"

Sam ran his hands over his arms. "Then prove it. Play nice."

Patience nodded and waved Sam into stepping back. "How's Abigail?" she asked.

Sam's face relaxed. "She's feeling good," he said.

"Who's going first, Sally or Abigail?"

"I don't care as long as I don't have to deliver either of them myself." Sam laughed. "One time was enough." He looked down at his wedding ring and took Patience's hand. "You deserve to be happy, Patience. You deserve to always smell of lavender and roses and lip balm."

"Bee balm, Sam."

"Right, that too." He put his thumb under her chin. "No kidding, Patience. If you have to, take your chance, but don't make Henry Carlyle pay for it."

Patience watched Sam walk away and into Abigail's arms. His wife was the only reason he was at the Mayos'. If possible, her family was even richer and more prominent where it really counted—New York. But their happily-ever-after was all down to Granite Point. Sam got what he wanted: a loving wife, a job he adored, and a baby on the way because he was brave and kind and good. Patience didn't know if she was any of those things right now, and she sure as hell couldn't think beyond finding Henry and bolting. She felt the party press in on her until the bodice of her dress felt too tight and her breath too short. And, as was often the case with Patience, her uncertainty turned to irritation, mostly with herself. She spun in a circle, trying to find Henry before she lost her nerve.

"Hey there! Is Sorrel with you?" Simon Mayo moved in front of Patience, blocking her sight line just as she thought she'd spotted Henry.

"What do you think?" she asked, swaying sideways trying to see the terrace again, trying to move away from Simon so he didn't take the brunt of her mood shift.

Simon frowned and turned to follow her gaze.

"Oh boy, Charlotte's got a live one." Simon looked back at Patience. "Wait a sec, you *did* come with the doctor?"

"Kind of," Patience said.

"Well, well." Simon was laughing. "The Sisters must have their panties in a wad right about now."

"Don't be such a frat boy."

"Oh, stop it, Patience. This could be fun. Maybe you'll finally break out. I'm happy for you. I'm sure Sorrel is. I wish I'd—" Simon held onto her by the wrist as if she could lead him out of the mistakes he'd made. Patience looked at Simon as she leaned away from his grip. She saw the regret that framed his eyes with wrinkles.

"Simon, please be careful," Patience said quietly and twisted her hand away. She walked out the front door, roughly half the guests watching her. And a good thing they were. If anyone had turned to Simon in that moment, they would have seen a man who regretted the whole damn party.

HENRY WOULDN'T REALIZE Patience was gone until she was in her own house, the smell of juniper wholly unrelated to the drink in front of her. It was tequila. The sisters took one look at Patience's face when she slammed through the door and retreated up the stairs. They could sense her intensity, and if she unsettled Simon Mayo that night, she threw a sharp splinter of caution and not a little concern into her sisters. They'd seen her irritated, peeved, angry even, but this was something else, something desperate and hungry. And although Patience's energy was turned inward, both sisters could feel the heat now rolling off their sister. Nettie wiped a drop of sweat from her temple as she pulled Sorrel down the hall.

Patience held the glass in her fist; her hand was so hot the tequila turned brown and thick as syrup. She wasn't angry with Charlotte or Henry. She knew that Charlotte had only been flirting with Henry because she needed something; that was how she got things done with men, how all the Mayo women got things done when they weren't ordering those men around. The confused look on Henry's face as he listened to Charlotte was to be expected. Patience had seen both sexes sent into a virtual fugue by the rapid-fire delivery of the Mayo wives and daughters.

Patience was angry with herself because, for the first time in years, she wanted something more than she wanted to be left alone. And that something was Henry Carlyle. She had no idea that Henry had had the very same revelation a day before. Patience wanted to know about him, to hear his stories, to watch his hands as they lifted a stethoscope, sutured a wound, transcribed his notes. She'd seen the fountain pen in his pocket; she knew his handwriting would be precise, elegant. It wasn't, of course; it was scrambled and raw, a handy metaphor for his soul. Patience listened to the rustling of her sisters as they moved around their rooms. Earlier, she'd misted each of their pillows with clary sage, knowing how it would smooth the way to sleep should she need a little privacy. Patience had been hopeful then. Now she felt bereft, purposeless.

Back on the harbor Henry wandered through the Mayo party looking for Patience. Only moments before he had locked eyes with another man, a vaguely familiar man talking to Patience, and for a second he felt the irrational clutch of jealousy. But then, Charlotte had whisked him off to another introduction and he'd lost sight of them both. When he finally broke away from his hostess, he was so exhausted and confused that he couldn't remember where Patience had been standing when he left her. Henry found himself by the front door and the harpist. He looked at the woman, her long fingers brushing lightly across the strings, and let the music fill him until he closed his eyes. When he opened them, the harpist was staring at him. She nodded and then turned her head to the front door. "That way," she mouthed, and Henry made a break for it. He was no longer confused. Henry wanted Patience. Now.

Patience was used to reading men. She always knew when a man was thinking about her and in exactly what way. She could see when one needed her help to tell him why he couldn't sleep, or slept too much, why his skin was suddenly cracked and bleeding from the salt water he'd spent his life in or how it was that he had no appetite. Just as clear was when a man came to her on a bet, to see if he was the one who would snare the Sparrow. Henry didn't fit either category, and Patience realized she hadn't the first idea why he really wanted her because it didn't occur to her that he felt exactly as she did.

"Damn it!" Patience growled and stood. She went to the screen door and braced her hands against the frame. She could see a mist settling on the plants. Night-blooming jasmine climbed the fence along the south side of the garden. The scent was soaked with desire: bare skin, tangled sheets, tears. Sweat pooled in the hollow of Patience's throat, gathered in beads along her top lip, ran in a single rivulet down her spine. She pushed the door open and stalked into the dark. Her dress was silver under the moon, her hair bronze, her skin pale as milk.

When Henry came into the house, he headed down the hall to the back door. The screen shimmered with dew. He passed the glass of tequila and paused only long enough to knock it back. It burned his tongue and slid sluggishly down his throat.

"Jesus!" he hissed and went to the sink, filled his palm with water and drank.

Patience drifted in the garden, her dress draping softly off one shoulder and her hair falling across her back like blood in the shadows. She saw his tall silhouette first as he stood at the screen. She stopped, her bare feet sparking against the gravel path. Henry saw the blue-green lights around her, his brain searching to name them. He settled on fireflies although he smelled brine and seaweed and wanted to say phosphorescence. He shook his head and went out.

"You ran away," Henry said. "I couldn't find you."

"You were with Charlotte." Patience shrugged.

"I—" Henry stopped. "Has she come to you?"

"No Mayo has ever come to me," she said.

Henry crunched onto the gravel. He smelled the jasmine and felt a surge of damp heat as Patience neared. She seemed to waver in front of him and he reached for her, certain she was about to faint or melt or something else impossible. The moment Henry touched her hand the heat lifted, the moonlight turned liquid as it fell over them both, cool and slippery.

"Is this you?" Henry asked, shivering as he pulled her toward him. "Is this us?"

Patience nodded. She laid her ear against his chest and listened as his heart sped up, slipped her arms around him and tucked her fingers under his waistband. She pressed her palms into his back. Henry sucked in a breath.

"Your hands are cold," he said. "I thought they'd be warm."

"Sometimes they are," Patience said and looked up at Henry, her chin sharp against him. She was shivering too; her hair was wet. "Come inside," she said.

"Your sisters?"

"They already know," Patience said, and Henry looked up at the windows expecting so see their faces, pale and concerned. Patience shook her head. "They will have felt the change."

Henry pulled back so he could see all of Patience. "I don't understand."

For a second he was almost frightened. Not by Patience exactly but by this place where sisters sensed each other in the dark, this town that believed a young woman could keep them well with nothing but her garden: an ordinary place where flowers bloomed long past the first frost and people sniffed the air to guess what Patience Sparrow might be feeling before they checked the weather. At that moment all Henry could smell was the lemon in Patience's hair; the bee balm had fallen away when she untangled her bun and now the strands ran with water. He dismissed his anxiety quickly because he suspected he was on the brink of something that could change him, and he knew he wanted to be changed. But then Henry feared that she must have read him, this anticipation that felt like fear. He watched Patience move away.

"No," he whispered and wrapped his hand around her forearm.

"Come, now," Patience said and pulled him toward the

screen door. When she opened it, June bugs clattered to the steps, moths fluttered up in a powdery cloud. She left wet footprints across the kitchen floor. Henry eyed the tequila bottle but remembered how it hurt. Patience stopped at the stairs, one hand on the newel post.

"Are you afraid?"

"Answer hazy, ask again later," Henry said and ran his knuckles along the pale underside of her arm.

He followed her up the dark stairs and down a hall that swam with the scent of clary sage. To Henry it just smelled of soap, but to Nettie and Sorrel it was so soothing that they had drifted into their rooms in a sudden dazed torpor. As hard as Sorrel tried, she couldn't hear Patience or Henry, she couldn't see in the dark that tugged her deeper into her bed. Her last thought before sleep was that she'd have a firm word with her sister in the morning.

Patience's room was smaller than Nettie's. There was no chaise, no bookshelves, no hope chest, dusty and empty. There was only a bed, a tall bureau, a low slipper chair covered in worn gray velvet and a pile of books beside it. The moonlight was streaming in through her open windows. The air that had cooled around her in the garden breezed past curtains covered in tiny violets and long skeins of ivy. Henry watched Patience as she lowered the windows and, still turned away from him, reached to unfasten the buttons at her back.

Henry crossed the room in three crooked steps and finished for her. He let his thumbs linger on the bones at the nape of her neck, the small whorl of hair at the base of her skull. He moved the dress down over her shoulders before he turned her to him. Henry was surprised that Patience had ceded control. She was as pliant and soft as a sleeper and for a moment Henry worried that she'd disappeared into herself, away from him, again. But she tilted her head up and pressed the length of her body against his; rising on her tiptoes so that she could reach his mouth as he bent his head to reach hers. Henry felt his belt buckle scrape along her belly. He pulled it from his trousers with a snap and dropped it to the floor.

Patience wasn't surprised at the fierce need that surged through her as soon as Henry kissed her. She spread her fingers through his hair and angled her hip into him as he took his hand away from her waist to unbutton his shirt. Henry gave up fumbling and pulled the shirt over his head. What surprised Patience was how a wash of tenderness filled her as she pressed her cheek against his chest.

That is what the night became, a tangle of ferocity and yielding for both.

It wasn't until later, as Henry had requested, that he was able to separate from Patience, to ask himself if what he saw in the garden was real and if it did indeed scare him. He watched her sleep and tried to name her scent, the taste of her that lay across his tongue, still. He wasn't sure if it was the soft white sheets beneath him that smelled of sun and summer air and wooden clothes pegs or if it was the tee shirt Patience now wore, the shirt he wanted to peel away. There was a trace of cream and

butter in his mouth and in hers. Or was it cucumber, canta-
loupe, and clover honey? Was it salt or sugar? Was her tongue
warm or cool as she kissed him? Her hands had been almost
icy in the garden, but then when she sketched the scar starting at the side of his knee, following the silvery mark up his
leg, her fingers had been hot enough to make him press his
thigh into them. His whole body warmed beneath her touch.
Henry sighed and sank back against the pillows, his hands laced
behind his head. He didn't know whether to stay or go; it was
not even midnight. Patience hadn't said a word to him, except
to tell him when she wanted more. And now she was turned
away from him in her sleep.

Henry slid carefully out of the sheets and reached for the
water on the bedside table. He was so thirsty he drank two
glasses from the pitcher as he stood naked at the window. He
realized he was starved (Henry must have watched ten trays
of hors d'oeuvres go by at the party without a single bite) and
decided that though he wouldn't leave her altogether, he had to
go down to the kitchen. Henry pulled on his pants and padded
into the hall. He expected to be stopped by Sorrel or Nettie as
he moved toward the stairs, one hand on the wall to guide him
in the dark. But he made it without incident.

Henry was bent over looking in the refrigerator, the rest of
the room black and blue with shadows when Patience came
down. She hadn't been asleep when he eased himself out of
her bed. She'd watched him as he drained the glass she'd left
him, and a second. She was afraid to sleep, afraid that he might

watch her, as she did him, which of course he had. She was more afraid to end the night. For the first time in years Patience had put something on in bed; after they made love, before she settled beside him in the chill. It was a pointless gesture. She had never been so naked in her life.

Patience watched Henry shift things around until he came up with some cold cuts and a bottle of milk.

"That was fast," she said, startling Henry into fumbling the milk and mustard against his bare stomach.

"Christ! Cold!" he yelped and dropped everything on the table.

He is something, thought Patience. Standing in her kitchen in a pair of gray flannels and nothing else, Henry Carlyle seemed too big for the room, the spindly wooden chairs around the kitchen table, the old milking stool Nettie used to reach the mixing bowls over the sink. Goose bumps had risen along his sides in the frosty air from the fridge, and his heavy hair drooped over one eye. He pushed it up and away so that he could see Patience.

"Fast?" Henry growled. "We've been up there for"—he looked at the old school clock on the wall—"a while."

"Oh, no," Patience said. "I meant yesterday we were going at each other's throats and now . . ." She shrugged.

"We're just going at it?" Henry finished for her.

"I'm not sure that's how I'd put it," she said.

"No, I wouldn't put it that way at all." Henry opened the milk and took a swallow from the bottle. "Oh, sorry," he said when he saw what he'd done. Patience reached for the milk and took a long drink. She wiped a drop from her mouth.

"You don't do this often." Henry waved his hand between them.

"Not lately."

Henry laughed and took the milk from her. He saw the tequila bottle still on the table and considered a shot. Milk might be soothing, but if he had any hope of limiting the damage he sensed was coming, he needed the liquid courage to back away now. Still, just looking at Patience made him want to pull the tee shirt off and bend her over the table. She stood rubbing one bare foot against her calf. Mosquito bites dotted her ankles. Her legs were so long that he could see the join of her thighs at her shirt hem. He saw that she wore no underpants and before he thought, he slipped his hand under the shirt until his fingers were splayed across her bottom and pulled her into him.

"What are we doing then?" he asked into her hair.

"I only meant to get to know you," Patience said, and Henry could feel her breath across his shoulder. He laughed again. The vibration in his chest traveled straight through Patience and rearranged everything in its wake. She knew that, try as she might, she wouldn't be able to put things back where they belonged.

HENRY DID STAY the night, and what's more, he spent it in Patience's room. She didn't make him leave and, with the exception of the time she got up to open the windows again, she stayed within inches of him. But when Henry opened his eyes in the morning, she was gone. He thrashed awake when he realized her side of the bed was empty. He dressed quickly, grateful that it was Sunday but horrified to see that it was after ten. If he walked home now, every churchgoer in Granite Point would see him in the clothes he'd worn to the Mayo party. He felt as exposed as a frat boy on a walk of shame. He paused to listen at the top of the stairs, hoping the smell of coffee and bacon wouldn't make his stomach rumble. Were the Sisters sitting at the table he'd so recently fallen over with Patience? *Oh, God,* he thought, *please don't let them be talking about that.* But it was silent in the hall, so Henry came halfway down the stairs just as silently and stopped when he heard a voice.

"What do you want me to say?" It was Patience. "I got drunk and brought a guy home. Not the first time, not the last."

"That's complete bullshit, and you know it," Nettie said, her voice no longer sweet or light. "Don't break this, Patience."

"For God's sake, you're being an idiot. This is the best thing that could have happened to you," Sorrel said. "Don't lump Henry in with some lobsterman."

Henry flinched so hard his head hit the wall just as Patience slammed down her mug.

"I am surprised that it took good Champagne at the Mayos to make you see what the rest of us already knew," Sorrel continued. "Do not screw up this chance, do *not* make us any more talked about than we already are."

"Stop yelling. He'll wake up and then what'll we do with him?" Patience asked.

"We'll keep him," Nettie said with a delighted laugh.

Patience pushed her chair back. "You can both just stop. I've had enough amateur analysis. I'm going to the Nursery."

Henry waited until he heard water running in the sink and the clatter of dishes before he turned around and whispered his thanks to Clarissa Sparrow for the house she built as he made for the second staircase, the formal one, at the other end of the hall. He might be willing to endure the curious eyes of near-strangers on the green, but he didn't think he could take the sympathy he would see when the Sisters looked at him. If Patience regretted what they had done last night, Henry just couldn't.

HENRY WALKED HOME trying to look as if he'd just been for a bit of a stroll in business attire. He had to rush through his shower in order to get to Ben at the hospital. Was he "the lobsterman"? he wondered as he shaved. He climbed into jeans with water still dripping down his legs and forgot to take any painkillers. He dropped his keys in the sink twice. And then he nearly forgot to lock up. On the drive to Hayward he picked apart what he'd overheard at Ivy House. Oddly, the thing that bothered him most was Patience's comment about bringing other men home. It was silly to worry about the past or the future, but Henry couldn't bear the idea that what he felt for Patience—what last night made him believe she felt for him—might be senseless.

Ben was uncharacteristically chatty on the way home. Henry

reckoned it was a reaction to the anesthesia. He'd seen patients laugh uncontrollably or cry just the same way for days after their surgery. He'd also seen some turn inward so completely that they were unrecognizable to their fellow soldiers. Ben's cheer was a perfectly good way to face his uncertain summer.

"So, I was thinking," Ben said. "Since I've got a month on my hands, literally"—he held up his thumb, which was encased in a foam mitten—"I might take this accounting course at GPC."

Henry burst into laughter.

"What?" Ben looked bewildered.

"You, hunched over a calculator," Henry said. "I'm sorry but it's not how I picture a recovering lobsterman."

"Yeah well, I noticed that Patience doesn't keep very good books. She couldn't tell me what she gave me, didn't have any kind of inventory system, and doesn't even remember who pays her what. Sorrel had to look through a bunch of old scribbles in a notebook just to see what she'd done before, and then Patience decided she wanted to give me something else anyway." Ben shifted in the small passenger seat. "You need a better car before the weather comes."

"Yeah," Henry said. "What did Patience charge you?"

"She didn't," Ben said. "I don't think she charges everyone, just the ones who can pay, and then it's usually something more like barter."

So Patience was operating as an unlicensed, well, Henry didn't know what. So he asked.

"Is she a homeopath or a nutritionist or what?"

"You know, she's just Patience Sparrow. Clarissa Sparrow was the last one to have the gift before Patience. I think there was another healer back when Granite Point was founded, back when people weren't so happy about someone with a gift."

"Tell me more," Henry said.

"About the town? I could read up, you know." Ben laughed at himself. "Not much else to do." He looked at his hand again and frowned.

"Tell me more about the Sparrow Sisters then."

Ben looked at Henry. "Why?"

"Because there is something going on with you and one of them."

Ben could not have been more surprised. "Did Nettie say something?"

"Nettie?" Henry's voice rose so improbably high that somewhere a dog was writhing. He was so relieved he couldn't help smiling.

"Oh, shit, you can't tell anyone!" Ben's voice was incapable of reaching above a gravelly growl.

"No, not at all, never, nobody!" Henry barked.

Ben kept his eyes on a completely empty road, and Henry spoke mindlessly. "I don't think I even know what you're talking about," he spluttered.

"That's crap," Ben said. "When did Patience get to you?"

HENRY FERRIED BEN home without embarrassing either of them any further. He changed his dressing and made sure Tylenol and water were within easy reach of the sofa.

"Come by tomorrow for a wound check," he said as he repacked his kit.

"I don't have insurance," Ben said. "I can't afford you."

"Okay," Henry said. "Why don't I just stop in here for lunch, off the books?"

"We're just a couple of sad-sack secret keepers, aren't we?" Ben sighed.

PATIENCE AND MATTY walked the gardens together. She held a basket over her arm; her heavy gloves were already caked with soil and mulch. Matty followed, one hand trailing the tip of each flower he passed.

"You're here early today," Patience said as she stopped to tie up a leaning delphinium.

"My dad was sleeping on the couch. I wanted to watch TV but . . ." He trailed off. "It's better here."

"I could talk to him." Patience stopped in front of a tall stand of foxglove. The deep-pink blossoms were drooping in the heat. Matty reached out to touch it.

"Don't!" Patience snapped. Matty cringed, and Patience knelt so she could look into his face.

"Foxglove," she said, holding up a finger. "Dead men's bells, witches' gloves, digitalis, whatever you call it, it's dangerous."

"I wasn't going to eat it up."

"Yuck," Patience said. "Of course you weren't. But in the right situation it can save a life."

Matty cocked his head as he looked into the hooded blossoms.

"As long as it's not too late, digitalis can fix a broken heart." Patience gestured for Matty to follow her around the plant.

"For real?" he asked as stepped into each of Patience's footsteps.

"For real, but I don't use it. Too unpredictable. These just grow on their own, even though I cut them down to nubs every spring. Stories say that they've been here for hundreds of years." Patience frowned at the hip-high flowers. "That's long enough for any plant in my garden. I think I'll dig it out. It's just trouble, attracts the wrong kind of bugs."

"But it's so pretty," Matty said.

Patience shook a stem, and several earwigs dropped out of the blooms.

"Pretty things are often the most dangerous," she said, thinking of Henry as he slept with one leg draped over hers. "Boy, that's a lesson." Patience pulled off her gloves and reached out her hand. "Right?"

Matty nodded and let Patience fold his hand into her own. "Right," he said and shook.

"Thanks for your help, bud," she said. "Let's go in. My sisters will be here soon and you have first dibs on the cookies."

HENRY DROVE TO his office and even pulled over before he swerved back out and headed for Calumet Landing. He skidded to a stop with nearly as much spraying sand as that thrown up by Patience Sparrow. He left the car door open and took the steps to the barn at a run.

Inside, Patience was sitting at the counter with a little boy. They both had their chins in their hands, and the boy's arms were so thin that his elbows looked like sailor's knots. His hair was slicked down, the comb marks and his pink scalp visible. His skin was fair to the point of translucency, and Henry found himself cataloguing what might be wrong with this fragile child.

"Henry, this is Matty Short," Patience said. "Matty, this is Henry."

Matty flicked his eyes to Henry and then to Patience.

"He's all right," she said. Matty nodded.

"Hello," he murmured without looking at Henry.

"Hello, Matty."

Henry moved slowly toward the counter. As a doctor he knew to be careful around Matty; he also felt it in his bones. He was certain that if he startled the boy, Patience would not forgive him. If Matty ran away, so would she. She already had, Henry realized.

As Henry stood opposite the two, he searched Patience's face for a sign. He'd taken a deep sniff as he came in, hoping for some kind of clue, but the barn was so filled with the air of the Nursery that whatever was happening inside Patience was lost.

He noticed a small brown bottle on the counter next to her elbow and beside that a glass of iced tea and a cookie. A sprig of lavender was baked into the cookie, and a fine dusting of sugar sparkled on top.

"That cookie looks good," Henry said.

"Don't touch. That's Matty's," Patience said as she slid it over the counter.

Henry put up his hands.

"He can have it," Matty said, his voice so thin and reedy that Henry wanted to lean in to hear him. "He's all right."

Patience raised her eyebrows, not at Matty but at Henry. "What do you know? I guess you're in with Matty."

"And you?" Henry took a bite of the cookie. It was buttery, crumbly as shortbread. He could barely taste the lavender, just the smallest whisper beneath the sugar. It was wonderful. He closed his eyes as he chewed.

"Claire Redmond, Baker's Way Bakers," Patience told him.

Henry nodded. "Unbelievable."

"I want to swing in the hammock," Matty said. "You want to talk to her." He pointed at Henry. He jumped down from the tall stool and left the barn before Henry had a chance to ask him how he knew.

Patience looked a little irritated as she watched Matty go. "He usually has a really reliable shit detector."

Henry didn't bother to reply, just came around the counter and sat on the stool next to Patience.

"I don't have the time or the patience." Henry grimaced at

the unintended pun. "I can't wait for you to decide to let me in. I want in, now."

Patience bit back a snide comment about how he'd already been in, more than once. She was surprised at how easily the real truth spilled out. "You have no idea what you're asking for," Patience said. "My sisters will tell you, the Sparrows are meant to be alone. People are random, messy. We don't like needing anyone because when we do, it never turns out well."

"That's a bit overdramatic, don't you think?" Henry asked. "If that were true, you wouldn't have spent the night with me, you wouldn't have let me"—Henry stopped at the image of pure abandonment—"into your bed at all."

"I needed to touch it," Patience whispered. This truth telling was careening out of control even if, after last night, she wasn't sure that Henry needed her or the other way around. She reached for his thigh without a thought.

"My leg?" Henry put his hand to his thigh.

"Is it hurting?" Patience asked, resigned to the rising anger she felt in the room.

Henry realized it wasn't. "I'm sitting down."

"Stand up."

Henry didn't move.

"Get up, put your weight on it."

He stood. "I'm having a good day," Henry said, shrugging.

"Are you?" Patience asked. "Does your leg have good days?"

"No," Henry admitted. "But I didn't take anything from you."

But he had. Patience had put a single drop of henbane in

the bottom of the glass and slipped burdock root and comfrey into the lemon water she kept by her bed. Henry had drunk nearly the whole thing, as she knew he would. And, of course, she had touched him. Over and over she had stroked him, her fingers so light that in his sleep he hadn't even stirred.

"Do you want me to believe you made it all better?"

"Believe what you want," Patience said. "You *are* better."

"So the only reason you slept with me was to get to my leg?"

Patience looked away. She could hear the snap of their connection breaking, could taste her own panic: sour and metallic.

"Well, fuck you, then." Henry walked to the door. He knew what he'd said was not only mean but also ludicrous.

"Wait." Patience came around the counter. Henry backed away.

"What am I, Patience, just another damaged person for your collection? Matty's not enough, you need a new project?" Henry had his back to the door, but he was awfully close to leaving and Patience began to breathe too fast. Spots swam before her eyes like the blotches after a camera flash. She leaned over and put her hands on her knees.

"Patience?" Henry said. He walked back to her. She could see his shoes and had a moment of terrible certainty that she was going to throw up on them.

"I should have had breakfast," she said, her mouth tight against the nausea.

"Come here," Henry said and drew her close, rubbing her back and urging her to unfold against him.

"Oh, God, Henry." Patience thought she might cry. "What if I *do* only want to fix you?"

"Go ahead and try. I dare you," Henry said.

Matty came to the door and saw Patience with her head bowed into Henry's chest, her arms around his waist. He'd never seen her hold a person the way she held her plants. Patience touched this man with respect and awe, as if he was her remedy. Matty knew Patience didn't ever treat herself, not even last winter when she had the same terrible stomach flu that laid half the town out for a week. It was just before Christmas, and Patience had sat at the Nursery counter in pajamas and a sweater, a cold compress on the back of her neck as she filled her bottles. She'd let Matty make the deliveries, pulling a box of her remedies behind him on his sled. No, Patience had had to fight all alone through the gripping stomach pains and sweats, her hands shaking, a fever blister marring her lip. Matty thought she'd never get better, but she did. So when he saw her fall into Henry, he thought maybe she'd finally found the cure.

What Matty saw was the blossoming of Patience Sparrow. He listened to them talk; to Patience as she spoke of her confusion, how she couldn't control how she felt about Henry and how much that irritated her, how quickly she'd given herself over. He heard Henry's rumbly laugh and it made him want to sit near enough to feel it too.

"Tell me what you're afraid of," Henry asked Patience. Matty was surprised; he didn't think Patience was afraid of anything at all.

"I don't know," Patience answered. "I'm probably afraid that you'll figure me out and decide I'm full of shit."

"Well, are you?" Henry asked.

"Some people think I am."

"And some think you make magic."

"Then they're the ones who are full of it."

Henry laughed again. He couldn't remember the last time he'd just done that, laughed without trying.

"So what've you fixed lately?" he asked.

"Oh, the usual: insomnia, acne, heartbreak, Lyme disease."

"You can cure heartbreak?"

"Sometimes all it takes is a tincture and some talk." Patience looked at Henry. "You don't want to know how I cure Lyme disease?"

"*I* can treat Lyme," Henry said. "I was told only time could mend a broken heart."

Matty sank to his haunches outside the door. He didn't know what Lyme was, but he saw the symptoms of a broken heart every day. If only his father believed in Patience the way Henry was starting to. Matty thought that if Patience fixed his dad, then his dad could fix Matty. He would ask her and if she didn't help his father, he would.

CHAPTER SIX

Comfrey is a gentle remedy
for quinsy and whooping cough

Henry came to Ben daily for about a week. He taught him how to carefully cover the wire in his thumb with thin surgical tape. As he cleaned the tiny hole and made sure Ben wasn't doing anything stupid like helping his friends haul traps, Henry heard more chapters in the Sparrow Sisters' story. It turned out that Ben Avellar had decided to become an unofficial Granite Point historian. He now knew more about the town and its denizens than the town clerk did.

"So have you made progress with Patience?" Ben asked one afternoon when he'd taken Henry to Calumet Beach to watch the tide go out. The water receded so quickly that hermit crabs were left to scuttle, panicky and confused, looking for a hidey-hole. When the tide was dead low, the blue sky and the yellow sun blended with the sand and the sea until it looked like one mirrored expanse. The water reflected the sky in the tidal pools, and dunes met the clouds where the eelgrass grew. Henry was disoriented by the sight; he felt unsure which way was up. In that uncertain moment he admitted to Ben that he had fallen hard for Patience.

"Does she feel the same?" Ben asked.

"Who can tell?" Henry said. "It could just be a summer thing to her."

"Oh, Patience doesn't do that anymore," Ben said. "She hasn't been with anybody really since just after college. At least no one has seen anything."

"An invisible lover?" Henry laughed, but it wasn't funny. If there was anybody capable of living an entire life unseen, it was Patience.

"At least Patience sees you. It's like I'm invisible to Nettie," Ben said later back at his house. He poured tomato soup into mugs with his left hand. He was getting better—more soup made it into the mug than onto the counter.

"You're not invisible, Ben. She sees you," Henry said. "I don't think she knows that you see her."

"Really?"

"The night of the Mayos' party Nettie seemed worried about you."

"Did she now?" Ben smiled. "Was I still in the hospital?"

"Yeah, I took Patience to the party."

Henry still shivered when he thought about that night. He hadn't been back to Ivy House since. But he had been with Patience nearly every night. They met at the Nursery after Sorrel and Nettie went home. Henry couldn't say what made him return there again and again but he did, as soon as Sally left the office each evening. Once they'd made love in the small orchid greenhouse. It was so humid he'd been sweating before he even touched her. They'd fallen into a raised bed of soft moss that Patience used to pot the orchids. Henry washed the deep green stains from her knees as they sat drinking cold water from the sink in the barn. A nail head had scraped down the back of her calf leaving a long thin scratch. He'd cleaned it, her leg in his lap, her toes scrabbling against his jeans while he dabbed alcohol along the wound. Patience herself had given Henry a salve to stanch the trickle of blood, the smell of yarrow and periwinkle as strange to him as the intense yearning he felt for Patience. Of course, the salve didn't work, and a tiny thread of deep red dried where it reached her ankle.

Just last night she'd finally come to him, using the back door so that she didn't have to walk through the office, wouldn't smell the medicinal fog that hung in the waiting room. He'd been dictating his notes and looked up to see her standing outside his window. She was wearing one of her mother's dresses, the skirt held out in front of her, filled with blackberries from the bush he didn't even know he had. Under her arm was a quilt, already stained purple from the berries. He'd taken her up to the little apartment, suddenly self-conscious as she trailed her fingers over his books, horrified when she moved a stack of medical journals onto the floor and found his Purple Heart, his Commendation Medal. She'd said nothing, just looked at him and slid the journals back over the small box, which had broken open in the move. She brought the quilt, strewn with violets and ivy like her curtains, and they'd gone into his little garden to eat the blackberries. Henry took her into his arms and laid her down, licking the berry juice from her throat until she giggled so hard she hit his head with her chin. And not once did she ask if his leg hurt him.

But it did. His leg hurt whenever he left her. And now, sitting with Ben at his tiny kitchen table, he felt a hot spike of pain that couldn't be ignored.

"You know the town is talking," Ben said a few days later. They were back at the beach, the ocean this time. It was a place that drew them both, Henry because the water gave him peace and Ben because he couldn't stay away from the fish he couldn't catch.

Henry had to shake his head to clear it of Patience. "The summer people are here. They'll lose interest in us by August." He sounded hopeful.

"Maybe," Ben said. "Sometimes we need a new story about the same old people."

"Terrific." Henry nodded.

"For instance," Ben said, "Granite Point was first settled in 1653 by farmers from Plymouth."

"I saw the monument."

"Yeah, well, the Sparrows were in that bunch." Ben leaned in to Henry, as if there were eavesdroppers amongst the sand-pipers. "But they weren't farmers."

"No?"

"Well, they were farmers, I guess, because everybody had to eat, but they were also the first lawyers, judges, doctors, ship-builders, and captains. The Sparrows ran the town for years. They were never challenged."

"Sally said as much." Henry wanted more. "Where are you going with this?"

"There was one power struggle, before Ivy House went up, long before Clarissa wrote her book." Ben warmed to his story, his lumpy hand waving as he talked. "George Sparrow's great-great-great-great-grandmother had a run-in with the church, 1691; that's what the inscription is for, the one on the village green. It was before she was a Sparrow. She was the center of Granite Point's very own witch hunt. I guess she and her sisters could be pretty wild, no mother, a Puritan dad. Maybe they just liked to poke at, you know, authority, but Eliza got in real trouble. There's a little section at the library about it."

Henry wasn't surprised that Patience came from a long line of "pokers." The inscription Ben pointed out was on the gazebo. Henry had never noticed it. It was hard to see beneath the wisteria dripping in swags from every corner. Something about ever innocent, Henry read.

"Two sisters and the father died of scarlet fever," Ben said.

"Practically the whole town was sick, and a lot of them died. Eliza Howard was the only survivor in her family. First the minister took her in, but she kept running away. Once they found her surrounded by stranded pilot whales near the spit. The story in the town records is that somehow Eliza got them all back into the ocean, all but one. Eventually, she was sent to live with her uncle, and that's when a whole bunch of bad luck hit the town. It was the usual stuff: failed crops, storms. In fact, the town green was a swamp for months."

"That's what you get when you mess with a witch." Henry laughed. "When will they learn?"

Ben laughed too. "I know, I'm careful never to poke a Sparrow. So Eliza was accused of witchcraft after her uncle died of scarlet fever too. She was tried right in town, but she escaped hanging; somebody paid off the judge and the minister—that's the story anyway. It hardly mattered that she was found innocent officially; the people had turned against her anyway. I'd guess being cut off from everyone she knew is what broke Eliza."

Did everyone go against her?" Henry asked.

"Maybe not, because everything went back to normal in town eventually, except that now Granite Point had its own crazy lady. Eliza built the first house—the one the Sisters use for the Nursery now—out on Calumet Landing. She was like a hermit. She planted the original gardens out there, lived through the terrible winter of 1693 on her own. The whole town was afraid of her and expected her to die alone. But Nicholas Sparrow found her and married her."

"At least there was a happy ending," Henry said.

"Yeah, and there's a kind of balance in the whole thing," Ben said. "The Sparrow Sisters Nursery is on the original land, and Patience is a healer too."

"Ah," Henry said, "the old 'there are no accidents in the universe.'" And he was right: the Sisters had turned their bitter history into a place of sweetness.

"So," Ben said, "even though there are only the three left, the Sparrow women are still pretty powerful. I mean, it's their birthright." Ben had the grace to look a little embarrassed.

"Are you telling me to be careful around Patience?"

"I think we both need to be careful around all of them. They're a package deal, and if one hurts, they all do."

Henry looked at Ben with new respect. He had gotten to the heart of the Sparrow Sisters' mystery while Henry was still trying to find his way around Granite Point.

They made an unlikely pair, Ben and Henry, as they walked the docks and checked the boat or ate dinner at Doyle's bar. Long after Ben could manage with his thumb, Henry sought out his company. Days and days went by in a smudgy haze as Henry worked and waited to be with Patience. Summer had settled over Granite Point and even with all the activity, time moved slowly. The days were long; most were sunny and hot, which made for a great start to the season. The nights could be hot too, and Henry began to regret not putting in an air conditioner, especially when he was alone in his bed. He chafed against the secret he kept. Instead of a private thrill, Henry was filled with sadness that Patience didn't want anyone to know about them, not openly anyway. He flailed and tossed, sleep just out of reach. The sheets twisted around him when he did drift off, and he woke bound into an uncomfortable coil, his body half off the mattress, the quilt Patience had left a lumpy wad under his hips.

Henry rose early, too breathless to lie flat anymore, and walked the still-quiet streets until the rest of the town began to stir. Sometimes he rowed across the calm water of Frost Fish Cove or swam out to the Laney's Pond marker and back, more than a mile. But soon the town was so busy that people spilled into the water, even at dawn. Granite Point had changed with high summer, and Henry was finding it harder to remember why he thought he could stay separate here.

Henry first noticed that the population began to swell on the weekends. The exodus from Boston and New York kicked up on Friday afternoons so that by dinnertime the sidewalks were clotted with strollers and couples pausing at every shop window, drifting toward Baker's Way Bakers as if in a dream. Everyone stayed open later now, the bookstore, the pharmacy, the coffee shop, the linen shop that made Henry want to lie down every time he passed the display. The benches outside Doyle's weren't home to many smokers anymore; customers waiting for a table had colonized them. Henry knew it was good for the town, this tide of cash and commotion, but he missed the quiet. It was good for his practice too. The people who had second homes also had second doctors. The vacationers with only two weeks to spend were damned if they'd spend them with a sick child. His appointment book was inky with ear infections, sunburns, surf rash, and stomach bugs. Because of this, it took Charlotte Mayo nearly three weeks to get a full half hour with him.

"I take it you've familiarized yourself with my file," Charlotte said when Henry didn't smile as he greeted her.

"I have, Mrs. Mayo."

"Charlotte, please," she said. "You've been to my home."

Henry sat at his desk with Charlotte. It seemed unnecessary to perform an examination. Dr. Higgins and several fertility experts had tested and treated Charlotte for all the most likely causes: fibroids, endometriosis, cystic ovaries, and hormone issues. He'd seen the reports that showed she was ovulating, that her eggs were healthy, that Simon's sperm motility wasn't a problem. In fact, there didn't really seem to *be* a problem.

"Charlotte," Henry began.

Charlotte held up her hand. "Don't," she said, and Henry heard the steel in her voice. "Don't tell me there's nothing you can do."

"There is nothing medically wrong with either of you. If you were to begin fertility treatment, IVF, for instance, I wouldn't be comfortable. Treating you with drugs designed to increase egg production when it's clear that's not the problem . . ." He trailed off. "Adoption? Surrogacy?"

"Please." Charlotte rolled her eyes. "A no-Mayo Mayo?"

Henry laughed and apologized.

"Use your imagination along with that Yale degree," Charlotte said. "I'm open to just about anything short of a witch's brew."

Henry looked at her file again. "You're forty."

"Not until Labor Day, ironically." Charlotte pointed at the file.

"Right, thirty-nine, so it's not too late. On the other hand, it's not ideal."

"If things were ideal, I would not be here."

Henry thought—surprisingly these days—before he spoke next. He didn't want to offend Charlotte Mayo; she could be helpful, and he respected her desire to have a family. But he couldn't resist pushing her just a little.

"Have you considered alternative therapies, at least to address your state of mind?" he asked. "There have been a number of studies that suggest anxiety, depression, stress can all suppress fertility."

"Fringe therapy." Charlotte had already begun to gather her things. "Next you'll recommend Patience Sparrow."

"I . . ." Henry shut his mouth when he saw Charlotte narrow her eyes at him.

"Well, there it is," she said. "I'd heard rumors, but I didn't believe them. You and Patience Sparrow." Charlotte stood. "You had better be cautious around that family. Those women have an unnatural hold over this town. What I said about witch's brew? I meant it."

She walked out without shaking Henry's hand, and he had

to rush to get the door open for her. Charlotte marched down the hall ahead of Henry and if he'd seen her face, he would have noticed the unusually furtive look that crossed it. Charlotte kept her head down, phone in hand as she left. There was no need to reveal she'd seen Patience herself some months before. What was needed, really, was a reminder to Patience Sparrow that their meeting had never taken place.

Patience came to see Henry after he closed the office, coming around the back with steps so light he was always surprised to see her. He was still bothered by Charlotte's visit that day. The witch comment had been mean-spirited. As for an unnatural hold, well, he was proof of that. He was as eager as a teenager when he heard her whistle outside his window.

Patience always arrived after dark, which was later these days, and Henry missed her in the newly empty hour. She never stayed till morning, sometimes tiptoeing out while he slept; he always slept deeply when she was beside him. That night they ate hamburgers from Doyle's. Patience brought a box of profiteroles from Baker's Way Bakers for dessert. She unwrapped the hamburgers with a profiterole already between her teeth.

"I nearly told Charlotte Mayo to come see you today," Henry said.

Patience caught the profiterole as it dropped out of her gaping mouth.

"I know," Henry said. "What was I thinking?" He took a bite of his burger.

Patience had gone very still. Henry didn't notice; he was busy shaking French fries onto a plate.

"Why would you send Charlotte to me? Since when do you refer anybody to the local witch doctor?" There was that word again. Patience picked up the profiterole and put it back in her mouth. The pastry cream oozed out onto her bottom lip, and Henry dipped his finger in for a taste.

"I never called you that, Patience, and, I didn't end up saying anything to Charlotte. I mean, I couldn't. It wouldn't be very professional."

"Gee, thanks," Patience said.

"What I meant was that since you have resolutely refused to let me see behind the Sparrow Sisters Nursery curtain, I can't very well recommend you."

"What's wrong with her anyway?" Patience was on her second profiterole, and Henry couldn't help but hope it would sweeten her.

"You know I can't tell you that," he said.

"Then I'll tell you." Patience wiped her mouth and stared at Henry.

"Are you trying to read my mind?"

"No, oh man of science." Patience laughed. "I'm thinking about Charlotte."

"I wish you were thinking about me," Henry said and reached across the counter to take Patience's hand.

"She can't get pregnant," Patience said. She let her hand stay in Henry's. His was big enough that hers disappeared beneath his fingers.

"Wow, that was weird." Henry took his hand back. "How did you do that?"

"Just a good guess. If she could, Simon would have a houseful by now. He loves kids."

"Well, that's the end of that topic," Henry said, reaching for his burger.

"It's not Charlotte's fault," Patience said.

"It's not a matter of fault, medical or not." Henry just couldn't find that physical element.

"No, it's Simon's fault. He doesn't love Charlotte, not enough," she said.

"Patience! That's a terrible thing to say."

"It's true. Simon and Sorrel have loved each other since grade school."

"Then he should have married Sorrel," Henry said with not a little irritation.

"Neither one of them could ever tell the other. They just went along, psychically bumping into each other now and then until Charlotte turned up." Patience looked angry.

"I'm sorry for all three of them," Henry said. "It must be miserable to go through your days without being able to touch the object of your affection." He reached for Patience and trailed his arm over her shoulder as he came around the counter into the kitchen. "Never to do this, for instance." Henry brought his hand under Patience's breast. "Or this," he pressed his cheek against hers.

Patience reached up and cupped his jaw. It was rough as a cat's tongue, a day's worth of dark whiskers scattered across his chin. "I don't think I've ever been the object of anyone's affection. Lust, yes, affection, hmmm."

"Well, I think it's safe to say that you affect me." Henry laughed and drew her against his hip.

"As you do me." Patience tilted her head in a little bow.

"So, what do we do for Charlotte and Simon?"

"That's easy," Patience said. "Charlotte really does love Simon. Now Simon has to love her or leave her. If he doesn't, they'll never have children and they'll never know happiness."

"Well, that's it for them then, oh, woman of the heart." Henry stifled his laugh when he saw that Patience was serious. "So it's all about true love?"

"Yes," Patience said. "True love." Her voice trailed off, and she moved away from the counter.

If Henry had known Patience better, he'd have recognized the smell of angelica that rose from her hair, a sharp dill-like scent that made his breath catch in his throat. He would have known that she was trying to shutter her heart.

"I'm not going to give up on the Mayos," Henry said. "There's an ob-gyn at Brigham and Women's who does amazing things with idiopathic infertility. Simon and Charlotte deserve a chance at a family, at that happiness you're so quick to deny them."

"The happiness you deny yourself?" Patience asked. The words flew out unbidden before she could swallow them unsaid.

"Excuse me?" Henry didn't physically pull back, but Patience felt him move beyond her reach all the same.

"The pain," she said. "It's your punishment, isn't it?" *And driving you away is mine,* she thought.

"Stop, Patience. You do *not* want to diagnose me."

"Why not? You dared me. I'm just taking that dare."

"I was daring you to be with me. I still don't know what happened when I met you; I was irrational with desire." Henry wanted to say "love," but a mixture of anger and caution prevented him from being truthful.

With what felt like enormous effort Patience waved her hands at Henry. She would not be distracted by his detour, his ability to turn her bones to water.

"I know what happened to you, what really happened at the school in Iraq."

"Is that so?" Henry asked, and his face became a mask. "If you really know what happened, you would know that you can't fix me. I should never have dared you. You shouldn't even try."

"You couldn't have saved that girl," Patience said. "I Googled you."

"You Googled me?" Henry was stunned.

"You wouldn't tell me. I needed to know what made you. So, after Sam talked to me, I read about the attack. I know the bomb was brutal. I know shrapnel is what got you." She pointed to his leg, and Henry, against his will, shifted his weight. "It was an impossible situation. *You* would have died. It was a horrible thing, but it was not your fault."

"So we're now going to dissect my service in the military and whether or not, as a doctor, a soldier, and a man, I failed." Henry was rigid with distress. Everything he'd done was designed to distance himself from that day. If he couldn't undo the death of a child, which to Henry was the greatest of tragedies, he could at least take up a life that was harmless.

"I only want to say that I understand and, if you'll let me, I can help you," Patience said. "Given the metallic content of the shrapnel, I have various remedies, I can feel what you need . . ." She stopped talking as she saw Henry's eyes harden until they glittered like Matty's marbles.

Henry walked to the door. "I think you should go now."

Patience was, foolishly, surprised that Henry was doing just what she had known he would, and quickly. For some reason, an image from her childhood came to her. She'd knocked over a beautiful ironstone pitcher that had belonged to Clarissa Sparrow. She watched as it fell and smashed to pieces on the floor, paralyzed by disbelief. Yet the pitcher had done the only thing it could under the circumstances. And so, here was Henry sending her away.

What have I done? Patience thought. *I won't let this happen.* Sometimes it really is that simple, if both people are willing. Patience was, and she reversed course and begged, her own voice so foreign to her that she almost looked over her shoulder for another woman.

"Please," she said. "I was wrong to think I know anything at all, about you or Charlotte, or war or, really, anything." Patience met Henry at the door and closed it. "I won't say another word. I will stop making you want to send me home." Patience led Henry to the couch and pushed him down.

"What are you trying to do?" Henry asked.

"I'm apologizing for my thoughtlessness, something I should have done that day at the liquor store, before I ever had the chance to hurt you." Patience pulled her shirt over her head, the camisole beneath unexpectedly lacy and feminine. It was as out of character for Patience as was her remorse.

"If this is how you apologize," Henry said as he unbuttoned his own shirt, "Pete might have called the cops that day."

Later, as Patience got dressed, Henry ate cold French fries and soggy profiteroles in his underwear. He thought that, contrary to her theory, he was as happy as he'd ever been. But, he watched Patience, slightly uneasy, trying to see if her duplicity showed on the surface. A "sorry" Patience was not real. He knew she had probably never apologized in her life and that he'd really frightened her when he asked her to leave. He also knew that she wouldn't stop trying to fix him, something he wished he'd never offered up.

Henry hadn't really wanted Patience to go home. In fact, he was desperately hoping for a way out of his own bad temper. Still, when she prodded him about his leg, it stung as if she'd taken a stick to the wound itself. He'd reacted like an injured animal, swiftly biting at the hand that had fed him everything he'd ever wanted. Then, as he'd held her in his arms, their sweat mixing with the bits of leaves and streaks of sandy soil on Patience, Henry couldn't see beyond that minute. Henry had let her seduce him instead of making her understand where the line was drawn.

Patience wouldn't meet Henry's eye. She was ashamed; she'd used her beauty, her body, to get what she wanted. *And why not?* Patience would have said once. But anything she'd wanted before Henry was usually of little consequence. Tonight she had indeed be-spelled Henry using the oldest of charms. When she'd taken him to the couch, she'd seen that he favored his leg. She wondered if it was because she'd named the wound for what it was, Henry's self-inflicted life sentence. Small price for the loss of a child: was this what Henry believed was just?

The hurt was real, the injury fresh enough that pale pink still lay beneath the silver scar. She guessed it had been little more than a year. Patience had grabbed both his legs, pulling him under her until he stopped caring where she had her hands. Now, as he moved around the kitchen, clearing the counter, opening a beer, she saw that his weight was evenly placed, strong muscle sliding easily under marred skin as he walked toward her.

Henry decided to poke Patience with a similar stick.

"Did you really want me to send you home tonight?" Henry ducked his head, trying to make Patience look at him.

"I did," she admitted. "Only because if you don't do it now, it'll hurt more later."

"Would you stop." Henry put his beer down with a clank. "The whole inscrutable Sparrow Sister with her mysterious gift, her self-destructive streak, her secrets. Enough." He laughed at the look on Patience's face. She was actually offended.

"You cannot drive me away, Patience, any more than you can leave. It's done, the spell, enchantment, whatever. I am a man of science, you're right. But this"—Henry waved his hand between them—"this is something else." He warmed to his subject. "I will not give you up. If you'll only stay to fix me, the dare is back on." He thumped his chest. "I'm yours."

Patience put her hand on his and covered his heart. "You are mine."

PATIENCE DIDN'T GO home after that and regretted it as soon as she opened her eyes the next morning. She was remarkably content spooned against Henry's stomach, but she couldn't see a thing. Patience wore contact lenses and she'd tossed them in the sink without thought after she and Henry had taken a bath together in the deep claw-foot tub. Now she was effectively blind; of course she hadn't brought her glasses—she never stayed the night. She was grateful that she hadn't driven, but the idea of walking home like this, no matter how well she knew every street in Granite Point, was more than Patience could face. She was going to need Henry's help. It was the ripple as she smacked her fist into the bed that woke him.

"What is going on?" Henry said as he sat up, taking the sheet with him.

"I can't see," Patience said.

"Christ!" Henry barked and took her face in his hands.

"No. I don't have my glasses. I didn't expect to be here."

Patience had to shove Henry's shoulder to make him stop laughing.

"So this is what it takes to get you to promenade hand in hand with me," he hooted.

"Can we drive?" Patience asked.

"Nope," Henry answered.

Henry and Patience walked to Ivy House with a stop at Baker's Way Bakers. She held his arm in an oddly formal way. Henry hummed quietly, tunelessly until Patience stepped on his foot, hard.

"This is it then," she said as Henry held the bakery door for her.

"This is what?" he asked.

"This is when the whole town gets in on the act."

"Patience, no one has the slightest interest in us."

But they did. First Ryder Redmond had to put a hand over her mouth to trap her squeal when she saw the two come in, then several smudgily familiar people stuttered as they stared and said good morning. They continued down the street, drinking coffee and sharing a cinnamon bun, Patience's squinty frown the only dark spot in Henry's life.

"This is just great," Patience growled.

"Isn't it?" Henry grinned foolishly. "Utterly great! Let's do this a lot."

"Be quiet, you overemotional oaf."

"Oaf, what a terrific word," Henry crowed. He was inexpressibly happy; Patience's hand was in the crook of his arm, her eyes had an unfocused, dreamy look that he chose to believe was happiness. He was on a stroll with his now public, nearly blind lover.

When they opened the door at Ivy House, Sorrel was standing in the hallway dangling Patience's glasses in her hand. They were tortoiseshell, old-fashioned, and thick enough that Henry understood Patience's need for help. What he didn't understand was how Sorrel knew to be waiting there.

"Oh, man," he said as Patience slipped them on. "You are a complete goob." Henry reached for her arm again, thinking that they'd crossed some kind of magical border and come out into a sunshiny state where his girlfriend was openly loving and grateful. He was wrong. Patience shook his hand off and escaped into the kitchen, leaving Henry and Sorrel in uncomfortable silence.

"Go to her," Sorrel said finally. "She's embarrassed to be seen in those clunkers."

"She's embarrassed by me," Henry said in his low voice.

"She's only embarrassed to need you." Sorrel gave Henry a little shove. "She doesn't mean to be a bully."

Patience was in the garden. Henry came up behind her. She leaned into him before he even put his arms around her waist.

"I don't know what is the matter with me," she said. "Now that I've spent a whole night with you, I am completely incapable of imagining one alone."

"And this notion of being apart compels you to be rude and snappish?" Henry rested his head on top of Patience's. He sniffed, involuntarily.

"Catnip," Patience said.

"Yes, you are," Henry murmured.

"That's not what I meant."

Henry turned Patience around. "I find myself heavily invested in . . ." He rubbed his forehead against hers, searching for a name for their collision. They weren't really dating, it wasn't an affair, but calling it love would absolutely send Patience over the edge. "This thing we're doing is extremely wonderful and important to me. I am unrecognizable to myself, in the best way," Henry said. "But I really can't bear it when you get snarly and touchy. So what do you say we just move on to the hopelessly romantic part?"

And they did. They had two perfect weeks. The weather was fine, the Sisters fed and fussed over Henry, and he spent more nights at Ivy House than he did at his own. It was as if his admission had cleared not just his heart but also his whole being. He was funny and clever; his good looks were polished by his happiness. Patients and passersby were drawn to his wisdom. He seemed to have acquired a remarkably quick and deft hand at diagnosis and repair. Strangely, his leg was truly better; whether it was time, sun, and sea, or Patience, Henry didn't particularly care, although he did notice. But, of course, Patience knew exactly what had changed him.

Everything about Henry tilted into the light. His speech

was infused with delightful sounds and his heart with unexpected softness. He woke each morning as giddy as Patience was alarmed. Ridiculous impulses overtook him regularly, and he put in a daily order at Baker's Way Bakers so that there was always a plate of cookies in his waiting room. Sally Tabor was tempted to take her boss aside and feel his forehead for fever.

Sorrel created delicate floral tributes to Henry's good fortune, and her sister's, and delivered them to his office every few days. The scent of delphinium, stock, and phlox obliterated the antiseptic haze. His patients appeared endearing in their minor illnesses, and Henry even took greater care with his charts, earning him a jar of beach plum jelly from Sally. He had only one patient who required more than minimal attention and that brought him to tears, even though it was an elderly man who was clearly in the last stages of his life and needed only to be eased. The fact that Patience was already on the case and had not only given him remedies to see the man through but had made sure he was settled into hospice care made Henry thoroughly useless with love.

The only wavelet in this lovely tide of romance came when Henry fell unexpectedly ill. Even then, it was a weekend and as he lay feverish and faintly despairing, Patience nursed him with remarkable good humor, given her general impatience with ill men. Too often they became whiny boys, but with Henry she found her concern was a gentle, coddling thing. She offered him several of her own remedies, but Henry, in a voice that had moved from a low grumble to a raspy whisper, turned her down. He allowed her to bathe him with cooling witch hazel when his temperature rose to 102 and to keep water and aspirin by his bed. She watched him as he slept fitfully and flinched when he murmured, "I'm so sorry" into the night. He never knew that the agrimony she tucked under his pillow finally sent him into a dreamless, healing sleep. By Sunday afternoon his fever had broken, and Patience took him to the Outer Beach to let him paddle in the unseasonably warm ocean water. She was of the opinion that there was very little that salt water couldn't cure. And she was right. As they climbed under clean sheets that night, Henry turned to her with a vigor that belied how sick he'd been, and she laughed as he held her against his chest. He awoke the next morning reborn, and Patience found she could barely remember how unsettled she'd been watching him suffer.

One Friday Ben Avellar brought Henry three huge lobsters, courtesy of his helpers. Henry took them to Ivy House, dragging Ben, a nervous wreck, beside him. Nettie hauled out a giant steamer and served the lobsters whole along with asparagus from the garden.

"Asparagus in July!" Henry marveled, earning him a dazzling smile from Sorrel and an eye roll from Patience.

Nettie insisted that Ben stay, and they all sat around the kitchen table until Ben began to yawn.

Every night Henry and Patience made love furiously, silently down the hall from the Sisters, or tumbled across the furniture in his apartment. Henry couldn't believe he was so very lucky.

Henry stared at his beloved beneath him and watched for signs that she felt as he did. He was becoming fairly sure of her; she hadn't pulled one of her attempts to make him change his mind since "the profiterole disaster," as he came to think of it. Nor did she bring up his injury. When she touched him, it was everywhere, her hands leaving a trail of heat so satisfying that Henry groaned and Patience had to hush him.

Sometimes when they kissed he peeked to see if Patience had her eyes open. Henry was of the belief that if you did, then you weren't really in the moment, you didn't care enough. He was grateful that hers were shut tight. When she tilted her chin up, her lips parted, her head pressed into the pillow as Henry moved over her, *he* was unwilling even to blink.

For her part Patience felt as if she were holding a soap bubble in her hand. She glided through her day intent on keeping this shiny, temporary, beautiful, perfect thing intact. This in itself was unusual. Patience was adept at snatching misery from the tender jaws of joy. If Henry had metaphorically salted his wound to remind himself of his failure, Patience did the opposite. She refused to examine her luck too closely. She held herself as still as she could, intent on not popping the damn bubble.

Finally Patience decided that if she was ever to release that fragile thing and grab what was now clearly something worth holding on to, she needed to let Henry in as he'd demanded. So one evening she took him to the Nursery to let him see her chest of remedies. She hoped that once he was back in the midst of her—honestly—very appealing world, he might be less likely to leave it. In that, she was so much like her sisters. Plus, Patience thought she might just slip him a little something to ensure that he couldn't forget her. As it happened, she didn't need to, and she never had the chance.

Henry was reminded that this was how their relationship had started, Patience showing him the instruments of her gift, and he felt it was an encouraging development. Ben came along with his new, if untested, inventory skills. It was the perfect opportunity for him to begin cataloguing just what it was that Patience kept in her stores. Together they sat at the counter and drank an inexplicably delicious tea: it was sweet, sour, bitter, and salty all at once and utterly irresistible. Both men took one sip and forgot why, exactly, they were there at all. Patience described what she made and how she used each remedy. There was no explaining how she knew what was really wrong underneath the symptoms. Ben took notes in handwriting that suffered from his broken thumb.

"Whatever it is I do, it's as natural to me as breathing," Patience said as Henry sifted through the leaves and petals on the counter. He lifted the tiny vials to the light and marveled at their pure, clean colors.

"Now, Ben here." Patience patted his big shoulder. "He's been holding onto love forever."

Ben blushed so hard Henry thought he might explode like an overfilled tick.

"I wish you wouldn't do that," Ben said.

"Then tell her, Ben. Don't wait until she's gone," Patience scolded.

"Is Nettie leaving?" Ben sat up straight.

"So it *is* Nettie!" Patience crowed.

"Oh, for God's sake, I can't believe this!" Ben said and put his head in his hands. "Please just talk about someone else."

"OK, let's take Matty," Patience said as she picked up one of the bottles. She smiled at Henry, and he felt like they were a team, a feeling that made him smile back.

"Yes, tell me about Matty," Henry said.

"He's autistic, on the milder spectrum. It's the anxiety that really gets to him; no ten-year-old should be such a mess. Anyway, his father hasn't been able to keep up since his wife died, so Matty doesn't get his meds regularly and he doesn't get the attention he needs."

"That's dangerous," Henry said and tore a piece of paper from Ben's pad. "Give me the dad's name and I'll call him. I can stop in now and then or get some neighbors to pitch in."

"Well, that would work if Rob Short weren't a son of a bitch," Patience said, irritated that such a simple solution was not available to Matty. "Even though I know he never got over his wife's death, I still blame him. Anyway, I can usually get Matty through the bad patches."

Henry put his pen down and took a deep breath. He didn't want to challenge Patience, and certainly not in front of Ben, who was already shifting his stool away. It's true there was a gathering in the air, a slight vibration that Ben noticed and

Henry, unfortunately, did not. Confident that his love was palpable in the slant of his shoulders as he leaned toward Patience, sure that their budding relationship was still painted in the rosy glow of newness, Henry decided to be honest. He miscalculated.

"You can't just medicate this child at will, Patience," he said. "And what's more, I've seen him. He's incredibly fragile. I don't think he's well on a number of levels. If he's on Dr. Higgins's books, I can intervene. Let me deal with this."

And just like that, the hopelessly romantic part was over.

Ben watched Patience's face close down; he felt the chill settle in the air and looked out, expecting rain clouds. All he saw was the wisteria so greenly muscular that it threatened to snake straight through the windows. She gathered up her bottles, powders, plants, and pots and began shoving them back in the drawers in a rush. Henry looked at Ben and made a face.

"Patience, sweetheart," he said. It was the first time he'd used any endearment. He was careful not to give her too much overt affection; she could be as skittish as Matty. It stopped Patience in her tracks.

"What are you doing?" she hissed.

"I'm trying to help Matty and cut you off at the wig-out pass." Henry attempted a smile; it was stillborn when he felt the cold leap off Patience like a blow.

"Well, you suck at it," Patience said. "I am perilously close to a wig-out." She'd snarled on the last words.

"Look, you don't expect me to stand back and let you treat

a potentially sick child without some kind of *conventional*"— Henry emphasized the word—"medical participation?"

"You know, I told you this already," Patience said. "This town was just fine before you rolled up."

"If that were true, we wouldn't be so worried about Matty right now," Henry said softly.

Patience stared at him, opened her mouth, and shut it just as quickly. Henry thought maybe he saw affection flit across her face before she walked away.

"Okay, then," Ben said and stood. "I should probably get a move on."

"You can't leave without me," Henry said. "I drove."

"Right, right." Ben sat back down.

Patience turned in the open door. "At this moment I am enormously angry at you, Henry Carlyle. Mostly, I'm afraid that you are right, that I've fucked up." She took a deep breath, and Henry hoped she would come back to him and settle down. But she didn't.

"I need some time to reflect and drink and recover my bad attitude," she said and left. The men heard her truck start up with a roar.

"You've really mellowed her," Ben said. "She could have, like, cursed you with, you know, one of these." He picked up a bundle of an unnamed spiky herb.

Henry put his head on the tall counter. The last two weeks had gone by in a lovely swoon, and now he felt the dizzy-ingly empty space where Patience had just been. His voice was hollow when he said, "Ben, I am seized with love for that woman."

There was nothing for them to do but go to Doyle's for a beer.

PATIENCE DROVE HOME. *Have I learned nothing?* she thought. *Must I spoil everything?* By the time she got to Ivy House, she was shivering so hard that she bruised her elbow on the gear-shift.

Nettie was in the kitchen with a glass of wine and a bowl of fresh peas.

She looked up and after a quick assessment that involved sniffing said, "Can you take it back?"

"Take what back?" Patience said disingenuously.

"Whatever you've done."

"Henry questioned how we take care of Matty."

"We?" Nettie asked.

"Me, then. Henry doesn't think it's safe for me to help Matty." Patience took Nettie's wine and drank it down. "I'm terrified that he's right so I snapped at him and left him with Ben at the Nursery."

"Well, they won't stay there long," Nettie said. "Ben will take Henry somewhere bright and noisy to get his mind off you."

"Great, everyone in Doyle's can watch him get drunk and assume I've driven him to it."

"You have, but Henry won't get drunk at Doyle's. He'll wait till he gets home. And, if you really cared what the people of this town think, you wouldn't be you, if you know what I mean." Nettie took her glass back and rinsed it out. "Please try to just *not* be you for a little while."

Patience stayed in the kitchen and drank the rest of the wine, which, as it turned out, was more than enough to give her a colossal headache the next morning. She limped through the day on nothing more than Coca-Cola, cursing her petulance and her inability to be served by her own remedies. A little milk thistle could have done her a world of good. Even in her state, she turned Henry's concerns over in her mind until, when Matty showed up just before three, Patience had come to the decision that Henry was indeed right. She couldn't just go around dosing a little boy with hops flower and valerian, passiflora, vinca, and green tea when she agreed with Henry that there was something else terribly wrong with Matty. And if she was being honest, she'd known Matty was struggling since May but she couldn't feel what it was and she feared that he might need more than she could give him.

PATIENCE WATCHED THE little boy as he helped Sorrel deadhead coneflowers and gather the blossoms for echinacea powder. His hands were so thin that his fingers looked like bone. The sun was very hot as it poured over the meadow, and Sorrel was sweating. Matty's neck was red at the top of his tee shirt.

"It's too hot out here for Matty," Patience called. "I'm taking him home."

As they drove, she tried to explain why she wouldn't be helping him anymore.

"I think it's safer all around if you and Henry and your dad make a plan," she said.

"I thought you liked helping me?" Matty hunched against the truck door. He held a small pot of butter lettuce between his knees.

"I love helping you, I do," Patience said. "But Henry thinks it would be better if he helped your dad keep track of your medicine. Then you won't need my help."

"I am sad," Matty said. "Maybe my heart is broken."

Patience pulled the truck over, and Matty's head bumped against the seat.

"Listen to me," she said. "I care about you and if your heart ever breaks, I'll fix it, right?"

"Does that mean I can't come to the Nursery anymore?" Matty's voice was so thready and light that Patience had to lean in to hear him.

"No, no!" she said. "You can always come to the Nursery. I wouldn't know what to do if you stopped. I need you, Matty."

Patience dropped Matty off. She didn't walk him in because she wanted to talk to Henry first, or wanted him to talk to Rob Short first. She had been reluctant to see Matty go, and he'd let her brush her hand over his head, hot and damp with sweat. She'd resisted the urge to pull him toward her.

Patience was exhausted by her hangover, thirsty, achy, and soon to be snarly again. She would talk to Henry the next day;

everything would be so much easier if she just waited and took a breath. As she backed out, she saw Matty standing at the window watching her.

IN THE KITCHEN Matty drank water from the sink. He splashed some on his face; it was flushed with heat and dirt, and sand stuck to his neck. His hair lay limp against his scalp. He didn't think he'd ever been so tired. Still, he wanted to write down everything he'd learned that morning because he wasn't sure if he would ever go back to the Sparrow Sisters Nursery. He was afraid to believe Patience really meant it when she said she needed him. In fact, he wasn't sure that he wanted to go back. Matty didn't often feel angry anymore, not since his mother died. She'd taken all his anger and, it seemed, all his energy with her. Certainly she had emptied Rob of anything like happiness. Perhaps Annie Short killed herself because she couldn't fix her son. It was as stupid a reason as any. Matty knew that reason, he didn't need to be told, and when his mother left him, Matty felt guilty. Now a tiny ember of anger did set up in his chest. Matty was angry that he couldn't seem to hold onto anyone he cared about, or they couldn't hold onto him.

Matty shouldered the drawstring bag he packed each day and climbed the stairs, trailing one hand along the wall. He left a faint green smudge in a long stripe behind him. In his room he knelt beside his neatly made bed and fished under the mattress for his notebook. It was cooler in his room; he'd lowered the shades when he left that morning. Matty was the careful son of a careless father. Patience had given him bundles of thyme to put on the windowsills, and the room was lightly scented, as shadowed and secret as a glade. Matty settled at the little table that had belonged to his mother when she was as happy as Matty would never be again. He spread out the notebook and began to transcribe from memory all the things he had been taught each day.

"Cat's claw for arthritis," he wrote, his fingers gripping the pen so tightly they were white beneath the nails. "Alfalfa is for prosperity but will thin the blood, celandine is a liver tonic and good for escape, dandelion leaf and root will call spirits and grant wishes, foxglove will mend a broken heart."

Matty put his pen down. He wasn't sure that he'd gotten everything right, that he'd remembered all the bits Patience told him about the plants. He dug into his bag and pulled out an entire dandelion, roots dusty with earth, a limp clump of alfalfa, several lemony-yellow celandine flowers, and four squashed foxglove spears and a handkerchief full of the leaves. He picked this up between two fingers, wary of Patience's warning. Foxglove could save your life or not, Matty thought. That made no sense. Perhaps he'd heard wrong. Nevertheless, it was part of his homemade textbook. He wrote "Eliza Howard" next to the foxglove description. He wondered how a flower could be as old as the town. He'd begun collecting the flowers as soon as Patience told him how powerful they could be, careful to stay out of sight when he tucked the overly pink blossoms into his bag. He'd grabbed a tall stalk so quickly one day that he brought home several earwigs. Now he took the petals off of each plant and pressed them between sheets of waxed paper. Then he slipped the lumpy leaves between the pages of one of the four dictionaries he kept in his room, licking his index finger neatly as he turned each leaf. He'd gotten the dictionaries at the church tag sale, carrying them home one by one across the village green. He heard the nice ladies chuckle as he went back and forth over the next hour, but he didn't laugh with them. Each cost no more than a dollar because they were so out of date as to be nearly useless. But not to Matty: he read the dictionaries, that was true, but he also hid things in them. He liked to put the plants he learned about in alphabetical order in the pages. By now, two of the heavy books were buckling with the mass of flowers and seeds, the pages wavy and gray with soil. The clary sage, purple and feathery, he put beneath his pillow. Even though he was too tired to eat, Matty knew that he would have terrible dreams that would wake him in a breathless sweat. So he put his faith in Patience once again and hoped the faint scent coming through the pillow would be enough to save him this night. He looked at the clock by his bed. Somehow hours had gone by without his noticing. It was seven, still light. Matty decided to eat something after all. But when he got down to the kitchen, he found that all he wanted was the cookies Patience had packed for him. He poured a glass of milk and ate two of them, lavender sprigs as well, and licked the sugar off his fingers.

SALLY TABOR WENT into labor on that last day of July, two days after Henry's fight with Patience, the afternoon Patience made her decision about Matty and drove off still mourning her inability to "fix him." Henry didn't know that she'd told Matty because they hadn't spoken in that time, and Henry had descended into a gray funk that extended to the office. Sally, for one, was on the verge of calling Patience to get them both back on track. "For heaven's sake," she murmured as Henry sighed behind her at the files. She stomped to the exam room.

Sally had stayed late to organize the office. She was stacking the doctor's charts on his desk, hoping he'd get to them over the weekend because her contractions had been marching (gently at first) through her since noon. Sally wasn't due until early August, but now she knew she wouldn't be in on Monday. She needed to make sure the office ran smoothly while she was on maternity leave. Her water broke just behind Henry's chair, trickling down her legs into a pink puddle. Swearing, she grabbed a handful of paper towels from over his sink and was squatting down, wiping the floor when Henry came in with two bottles of water. He thought he'd power through some paperwork before giving in to his crippling need for Patience.

"What happened?" he asked and then noticed the streaks of blood on the towels.

"Give me your hand, Sally," he said. "Let me see you."

"Sorry about this," Sally grunted as she stood, lifting her belly with one hand as she rose.

"Please," Henry said. He took her elbow and led her to the exam table. "Just sit and I'll call your husband."

"He's in Hingham on a job." Warren Tabor was a contractor, and he worked the whole region. "I'll call. If he hears your voice, he'll panic."

"We've got time," Henry said. "You talk to him and then I'll drive you to Hayward. We'll be there in twenty-five minutes."

"Actually, we were planning a home birth with Dr. May."

"Willa May, the fertility expert?" Henry gaped. He knew her work and had met her once when he was in Boston, and he was surprised she was local. Dr. May was an obstetrician who spent part of the year in Granite Point but had made a name for herself in Boston. She was the only other doctor in town when she was in her house on the Heights. Women loved her because she was so capable and because Sam Parker had delivered the doctor's own baby in a mad dash when her labor moved too fast to get her to the hospital. That made her one of them no matter how much time she spent in the city.

"Home birth?" Henry couldn't imagine anything more terrifying.

"See, this is why I never told you," Sally said and called Warren. Henry could hear his staccato, alarmed voice through the phone. Next she called Dr. May who, to Henry's horror, was in fact at Brigham and Women's in Boston. She promised to get in the car that minute. It was a summer Friday. It could be hours before Willa made it.

"Well," Henry said. "First baby, it'll be fine."

"It's my third," Sally said.

"Jesus!" Henry groaned. "Anything else you haven't told me?"

"I assumed you knew, small town and all." Sally's face twisted as a contraction took her. She was silent, and Henry thought he might just have to swear since she wouldn't.

"OK, Sally, let's think for a second," Henry said, trying to decide how to override his nurse's birth plan and just throw her in his car and go. He pulled out a stack of lap pads and moved to put them on the table under her. Sally held up one finger. She looked distinctly nauseated. "This is way too fast," Henry thought.

Henry went to the sink and washed his hands. He rolled up his sleeves and tucked his tie into his shirt. It had been more than two years since he'd delivered a baby. That one had been in the ER with full access to equipment and experts. He still remembered how quickly bad things could happen. If he was lucky, he could get the EMS here in time. All he needed was one look to determine how far Sally had gone.

"I should do an internal," Henry said as he turned around, and both of them winced. "I'm sorry."

"We should call Patience Sparrow?" Sally was out of breath, and her statement came out as a question.

"Seriously?" Henry spoke without thought and was glad Patience wasn't already there to hear him. "I mean, fine, but can I ask what she's going to do for you?"

"She was with me the last two times. She's very calming."

"That is not the word I'd use these days," Henry said as he

dialed Patience. When she answered, she didn't bother to ask why Henry was involved.

"On my way," she said and hung up.

Sally was being very brave. She tried to run Henry through what she'd set up for her absence, the name and number of the temp she'd hired to begin the first week in August, the schedule for supply deliveries. But when she started to get off the table to point out the files, Sally finally made some noise.

"All right, that's it," Henry said as he stood behind Sally's hunched form. He rubbed the heel of his hand along the base of her back.

"Oh, boy," Sally whispered, and Henry saw a tear hit her hand on her knee. It was now clear how short time really was. He gave her a shot of Demerol in her hip and hoped he hadn't left it too late. Twice he moved to call the EMS and twice Sally asked for a minute. By the time Patience arrived, Henry knew he was in way too deep.

"You're going to beat Abigail," Patience said as she headed for the sink.

When Henry met her at the front door, she put her hand on his chest and smiled. He was elated by the simple gesture and felt, in that moment, that he could do anything. And then he wondered if it was Patience who made him feel that way or the instantly refreshing, briny breeze that followed her in.

"Don't tell Sam I'm on deck," Sally said.

"He'll find out when he comes to get you," Henry said, and Sally saw that he'd nearly resigned himself to the delivery. "I am a little concerned that you're sprinting along here." He looked at his watch. "It's only been twenty minutes since your water broke, and the contractions are right on top of each other."

"Actually, they've been kind of piddling along since lunch." Sally looked at Patience and shrugged. A fleeting but profound sense of well-being rolled through her as the injection took the edge off the pain.

"For God's sake, Sally," Henry said. "Warren's definitely going to miss this. I shouldn't have given you Demerol so close to delivery."

"Terrific," Sally said through gritted teeth.

"You don't need drugs, Sally," Patience whispered in her ear.

"Shut up!" Henry snapped. "You, get her undressed," Henry ordered Patience with a sharply pointed finger.

"Did you do this on purpose, Sally?" Patience asked with Henry out of the room.

"No, I seriously thought I had more time. Then I couldn't stand the thought of Sam delivering me in the back of his ambulance bouncing down Route 6." Sally managed a chuckle. "I could never look him in the face again," she said.

"He'd never look at *just* your face again," Patience said rather hysterically. "Of course now you've got Henry around all day."

"Yeah, I didn't think this through completely." Sally closed her eyes. "And," she said, "can you guys settle whatever it is and get on with things? The doctor's been a wreck for two days."

This was oddly pleasing to Patience.

Henry rummaged around in the supply room and found the stirrups. He had always found them vaguely torturous in appearance, but often useful in the event. He pulled his button-down and tie off and mentally waved good-bye to his nice white undershirt. Back with the women he shook his head and muttered the whole time he set up the table and positioned Sally's feet. He was about to launch a little lecture about having a back-up birth plan and taking a longer view of things when he thought he smelled something, a clean yet remarkably soothing scent that felt like cool water and shade. His anger faded, and, as a bonus, his sinuses cleared. He looked at Patience, who was standing by Sally, stroking her face and neck with a damp cloth. Two small bottles were tucked into Patience's shirt pocket.

"Bay laurel," she said. "And blessed thistle, for her milk." Henry opened his mouth to remind Patience of her purely supportive role, but he looked at Sally and paused. Her gaze had gone soft and blank, her eyes half closed and for a minute he thought she'd drifted off. She was clearly in as calm a state as was possible given the circumstances. Then the next contraction hit, and she screwed up her face and blew short, harsh breaths into the quiet. Henry waited for the pain to pass and moved to her feet.

"Now hold as still as you can. I'll be quick and then we'll deliver this baby together." Henry pulled on gloves and lifted Sally's gown. He looked over her knees at Patience and grinned.

He felt positively heroic as he prepared to bring a new life into the world. *Really,* he thought, *how could she resist him?*

Seventeen minutes later, Katherine Chapman Tabor was born. Five minutes after Henry cleaned everyone up and gave Sally a pair of his own pajama pants to wear, Sam and his partner arrived. Patience led him back to the exam room, and the look on Sam's face when he saw Sally and her daughter was priceless. Henry laughed so hard, mostly out of relief, that he had to put his head down for a minute.

Sam recovered enough to do his job in the gentle, efficient manner that had attracted Patience to him in the first place. He got mother and baby out and into the ambulance without once asking for his bets to be paid. He had been right after all. It was a girl. Patience and Henry were left standing in the sudden quiet of the waiting room and, to Henry's surprise, Patience was the first to speak.

"I have given a lot of thought to what you said, and I told Matty that you would be taking care of him from now on."

"Oh, well." Henry wasn't sure if her conciliatory demeanor was hiding a bit of a seethe or if Patience really had come to some kind of peace with his brand of healing. He pulled her into a fierce hug before she could stop him. "Have you talked to his father?" he asked as he breathed deep into her hair. He wanted to be sure that she was serious about this.

"No, I think a doctor should do it." Patience pressed against Henry. "It would be better coming from you, a capable, useful professional."

"Which makes you what?" Henry asked.

"I am a capable, useful, extraordinarily insightful savant," she said and placed a hand on his hip. His tee shirt was untucked. All manner of fluids had stained the front near his waist. "Really," said Patience, "this shirt has got to come off."

"If you think that I can forget you left me for fifty whole hours by distracting me with an artfully placed caress . . ." Henry trailed off, his voice muffled beneath his shirt. "As you so rightly pointed out, I am a professional, and this is my office. I am not a cheap date," he continued as he pulled Patience's shirttails from her jeans. More than anything Henry wanted to scoop Patience up and thunder, carefully because the pain in his leg had been building for two days, up the stairs to his apartment. But he needed to talk, to dissolve the wall that went up every time he spoke to Patience about her work.

"As lovely as it would be to forget everything but you"— Henry rubbed his thumbs over Patience's collarbones, and she shivered—"we have to figure out how to work without stepping on each other's toes. I couldn't stand another day like the last ones."

"You're right," Patience said, and Henry cursed.

"What?" she said.

"I was counting on you to feel so guilty you'd take me to bed again. I find that a most pleasing way to work out our differences."

They went back to the exam room. Henry pulled his shirt back on and threw his undershirt in the hazardous waste bin. They cleaned up together. As they did, Henry asked Patience how she treated Matty; they hadn't gotten to the specifics that day in the Nursery. He went through Sally's meticulous filing system and found Matty's records, only to realize that a doctor hadn't seen him since Higgins retired. His prescriptions had run out, and he hadn't been treated by any kind of therapist as far as Henry could tell.

"Matty's probably got no meds at all by now. If Dr. Higgins wasn't attending to him," Henry said, waving the file folder at Patience, "who was?"

"I guess me," she said and slumped as she acknowledged how let down Matty had really been. "I just assumed his prescriptions were filled. Mostly I nudge his dad to keep up with his Doxepin, but when he doesn't, if Matty's with me, I use my remedies. I taught him some self-calming exercises."

"Have you tried those on yourself?" Henry asked.

"No, but I have a few ideas for you," she said and rolled her stool into Henry's chair.

"Pay attention," he said. "Tell me the combination again."

Henry jotted down the names of the ingredients in Patience's prescriptions for Matty.

"You do know it's a fine line you're walking with your work?" Henry asked. "It's not a hobby or a curiosity when a whole town comes to you for help."

"The whole town doesn't come to me," Patience said. "In fact, most of the men have always been a little wary of me altogether. And," she added, "as for a curiosity, that's me all right, but my work didn't start out that way."

And it hadn't. Patience remembered the day she had found the recipe book. She was only seventeen and, not surprisingly, was awfully tired of her older sisters the year before she started college. Where better to hide out than the attic on a chilly November afternoon? Patience planned to raid her mother's wardrobe, which had for some reason escaped Thaddeus's grief-fueled rage. Everything from silk trousers so fine they felt like water running through her fingers, to bulky sweaters to the sundresses she would wear years later, to dried-out Wellington boots, were stored as if waiting for Honor to come back. Behind both Honor's leftovers and the girls' still-stored winter coats and snow pants was the real Sparrow legacy.

You would think such a treasure as an early nineteenth-century notebook would have been kept safe and sound but, like so much of the Sparrow history, it had been stacked up with other stories: ledgers from the whaling fleet, several—no doubt valuable—pieces of scrimshaw, a straw boater that called out for a punter, and a sailor's valentine that fell to pieces in Patience's hands, scattering shells and sharp shell fragments across the wide plank floor. The book itself was wound round with a faded blue grosgrain ribbon as wide as the boater's hatband. It was at the back of the cedar closet, and Patience might never have even seen it if she hadn't gone looking for her mother's kitten heel satin pumps. She had a mind to wear them with her ripped jeans, a combination that would have been terrific had she found the shoes. In the end, Patience sat on the floor leafing through the recipe book until Sorrel found her.

The Sisters agreed that the book was to be kept secret from Mrs. Bartlet, who was nearly as likely to snoop as Patience, and from the town until they figured out exactly what it said. It was Patience who managed to decipher the faded brown ink, who learned that Clarissa Sparrow had compiled all the remedies she knew in one place. Those remedies were culled from the nearly unreadable notes left by Eliza Howard, the witch of Granite Point. The original Howard book was lost to history and Clarissa's edition was twice as long. Had the Sisters known about the author at the start, they might not have been so eager to make the book their own (or maybe they would). As it was, it took Patience nearly three years to read and copy out Clarissa and Eliza's recipe book after classes. She studied botany at GPC using the book as an extracurricular text. She pored over seed catalogues and arcane websites compiling both the information and eventually the actual seeds to begin to replicate her ancestor's remedies. In all that time Patience kept the book hidden, just as Matty kept his book hidden, just as Clarissa and Eliza had kept their skills hidden until needed. Then, once Patience had finished her work, she took the book to the historical society, along with the scrimshaw, and gave it to the town, where it sat beside glass net buoys, slightly moldy baskets, faded photos of the old duck farm on the post road, and all the other ephemera that drew very few tourists away from the beach. But the essence, the real guts of the book, stayed with Patience. It would become her book as she added to it, rewrote parts, and learned how to gather the past and the present together.

"WHAT HAPPENED TO Matty's mother?" Henry asked.

"She died when Matty was nine." Patience shook her head. "That's not totally true. She killed herself. It was before anyone really knew what was going on with him; he acted out, ran away. Once made it halfway to Hayward. Sam picked him up on the post road in a nearly catatonic state."

"Do not tell me she committed suicide over Matty," Henry said.

Patience only tipped her head. "No note, so no answer to that. I think she was heartbroken over her inability to fix her son. Rob sort of shut down, and Matty still pays the price."

"It's hard to force an unwilling or unable patient to make appointments, let alone keep them. And with a minor . . ." Henry looked at Patience. "Can I just say this? Where was everybody in this precious town?" He was surprised at his anger and then it felt good, hot and muscular and righteous somehow. "I mean, really, all of your 'we're a village, we're all in this together' shit." Henry stopped. "Sorry."

"No, you're not wrong," Patience said, as ashamed as Henry was angry. "We all enjoyed clucking away at Rob, throwing in some help now and then, but we never made a bit of difference. Here's the thing, Rob was—is—an outsider. He's not from here; his wife was but then she died. It made it all too easy to discount him and Matty in some way."

"An inlander," Henry said.

"Yeah—no—what?" Patience asked.

Henry explained about his first night at Doyle's and how it

was made clear to him that he would be an outsider for, well, forever.

"That's probably true," Patience agreed. "But I suppose I could vouch for you."

Henry couldn't tell if she was being serious.

"So what are we going to do about Matty?" Henry asked.

"We? I thought you didn't trust me to keep caring for him."

"I do trust you," Henry said. "The way you see what's wrong at the heart of someone. I may not understand what you do, but I am certain that your diagnostic skills are as good as mine. Tell me what you see in Matty, beneath the autism."

"Really, you want my take?"

"You know him best."

"All right. After you said you thought he was sick, I began to think about it. He's too thin, his skin is so pale, and there are times when he isn't really 'there' if you know what I mean." Patience thought a minute. "Lately, when he's with me, he almost always sleeps for a couple hours in the afternoon. It's like he can't stay conscious. He's never hungry, except for sweets, and he complains he's dizzy, though he calls it seasick."

Henry nodded. "And?"

"And Matty seems to know there's something wrong."

"Kids on his level of the spectrum know that they're different, that their behaviors are causing stress to themselves and their parents," Henry said. "You say Matty is very bright. I'm sure that he senses what's going on."

Patience agreed. But what she felt from him was more. It

was as if he was letting go, drifting away from her, from everything. Henry and Patience saw the same thing in Matty: he was becoming so transparent and light that he was in danger of being swept away for good. They just had different ideas on how to tether him.

"He has such faith in me," Patience said. "He really believed I could make him better, and I'm not sure anymore."

Henry looked at his notes. "I think it's time to bring Matty in, find out what's causing the fatigue and weight loss. I would like to reinstate his treatment with me. I'll speak with Rob Short on Monday." Henry sounded certain, completely equipped to make good where Patience couldn't: he would make Matty better. Henry pulled Patience toward him on her stool. "I will take care of Matty for you, Patience, I promise."

PATIENCE WAS BOTH too tired and too invigorated to go home so she ended up in the apartment. The birth had filled her with awe, naturally. And Henry's performance, the calm way he'd gone about the business of bringing forth life, had all but undone her. She'd stood next to Sally and watched the top of Henry's head as he worked. She noticed that he had more gray in the heavy hair that fell over his forehead and felt certain she'd caused it. When he'd stood abruptly and slung the stirrups out of their posts, she jumped. "Grab her legs," he'd barked. "Those things are medieval."

Patience shivered and nestled closer to Henry in the bed. She was astonished by how pleasant it was to be happy, how strangely freeing it was to depend on someone else for something as enormous as that happiness. She decided that she would, as Nettie had suggested weeks ago, keep Henry Carlyle.

The next morning they both woke early. The sun sloped in through the windows and Patience could tell it was going to be hot. She considered taking Henry to the Outermost Beach after she went home to change. Or maybe they could go to see Sally and the baby. She wriggled in anticipation.

Patience was again without her glasses. But Henry had cleverly squirted some saline into a cup for her the night before, and her lenses floated lazily in it on the bedside table. She popped them in as Henry made coffee so that when Sam Parker called, she could see his name on her phone and smiled. When he told her that Matty Short was dead, the phone broke open where she dropped it.

CHAPTER SEVEN

Agrimony is most soothing for stomach upset in children

*T*he night that Patience and Henry found their way to a plan for Matty, Sam ferried Sally and Katherine to the hospital in Hayward. It had taken well over two hours to get back to the firehouse after the pick-up at Henry's office and the hospital check-in. There was traffic both ways and paperwork of the most annoying sort, particularly because Henry Carlyle had scrawled his notes in an unreadable smear. Then, both Sally's husband, Warren, and Dr. May peppered him with questions he couldn't answer. He'd directed them to call Dr. Carlyle until Sally, who was by now settled in her bed with her baby at her breast, told everyone to just shut up.

"I think Dr. Carlyle is busy this evening," she said and raised her eyebrows at Sam.

"Oh." Sam got it. "Yeah, he was with someone when I left." He was still smiling when he got back in the rig with his partner. Of course, he'd called his wife, Abigail, to tell her about Sally and to suggest that, from what he'd seen, this Dr. Carlyle was the one to call in an emergency.

It was about 5:30 A.M. when Sam's unit got the call about Matty. Sam was as deep into sleep as you could be at six-foot-four in a bunk bed. Rob Short dialed 911 when he found his son slumped over the kitchen table. He was cold as ice, he told the operator; someone had to come right away. Rob was crying, and he didn't stop until Sam's partner got a sedative into him. Even then, he sat in the kitchen doorway and hiccupped. Police cars and a second ambulance pulled up within minutes, and the room filled with people. Poor Matty stayed where he was on the floor, where Rob had tried to revive him even as he felt the coldness seeping out of Matty and into him. The boy was surrounded now by gloves and stethoscopes and ripped packaging, the braided kitchen rug pushed up against the sink. It was apparent to everyone that he was dead and had been for some time. No one could move him again until the authorities came. Sam felt sick; he turned his head, not because the scene was grotesque, although it was, but because he was sure he felt his heart clawing up his throat. When the coroner arrived, he cleared out everyone but Sam. Dr. Clayton gestured with a gloved hand, and Rob Short was led into the living room by two policemen who sat with him while Matty's body was loaded onto a gurney. Sam couldn't believe how light he was as he lifted him. When the coroner OK'd the transfer, Sam had nearly thrown the body because he'd been so surprised by its lack of substance. He cradled Matty for a moment before he put him on the open body bag. Maybe it was because Abigail was pregnant or because he'd checked Sally's newborn only hours before, but Dr. Clayton had to say Sam's name twice before he heard him. He had to tell Sam to put the boy down because Sam couldn't seem to uncurl his arms.

Child Services was called, and Sam looked in on Rob Short before he left the house. Two cops and a tired woman questioned a completely incoherent man. Rob had begun crying again, and Sam thought he heard him say "Patience Sparrow" and wondered if the man knew how much she loved Matty. A part of him wanted to tell them to shove off, to let this man who now had nothing and no one just be for a moment. But Sam remembered how often Matty had been left to fend for himself in all sorts of ways. If Patience hadn't taken an interest . . . Sam stopped with one foot in the rig, unused IV bags and tubing still in his hand. He looked at his watch; somehow it was already eight o'clock. His shift was over in thirty minutes. Crap, he should be with Patience; she must be frantic after his call. He made his excuses and sent his partner back with the ambulance while he ran to Ivy House.

Sorrel answered the door; she was dressed but Sam could see Nettie in the hall, still in her nightgown.

"Sam?" Sorrel said. Her face began to pale when she registered his state, his uniform askew, the sweat on his brow.

"Where's Patience?" Sam asked.

"She's with Henry. What's happened?"

"It's Matty." Sam watched Nettie as she sank against the banister, her hand to her heart.

By the time Sam got to Henry's, Patience had stopped throwing up. For twenty minutes Henry held her hair as she hunched over the toilet, retching until he thought her ribs would crack. She kept apologizing, and he kept telling her he'd seen it all. He'd had to help her to his couch, her knees marked by the bathroom tiles, her face so pale the veins beneath were as clear and blue as thread. She'd cried the whole time, gasping for breath, her forehead pressed against the toilet rim. Now Patience sat in his Yale sweatshirt and scrubs, her legs pulled up to her chin.

Just after Henry led Sam into the apartment, there was another knock at the door. It was the police chief. Nettie had gotten dressed, and she and Sorrel were about to follow Sam in their car when Chief Kelsey arrived at Ivy House. He gave them a ride over to Henry's. It was a crowded apartment by nine o'clock.

Patience curled on the couch. A brutal shiver took her every few moments as Henry knelt at her feet, trying to convince Patience to let him sedate her. Chief Kelsey sat down next to her and shook his head at Henry.

"Patience?" he asked. "Do you think you can talk about Matty for a minute?" His voice was gentle, and he moved to put his hand on her arm, but she shuddered so hard it was batted away. She nodded.

"Let's start with what you know about the boy."

At that Patience drew herself up. Henry thought he could hear her spine clicking into a solid rod. Sorrel felt the snap of anger as Patience turned to the chief.

"Shouldn't you be talking to his doctor?" Patience asked.

"We would," Kelsey said. "But"—he looked at Henry—"he was a Higgins patient. Did Rob bring him in to you, Dr. Carlyle?"

"No," Henry said. "As a matter of fact, I was planning to see Rob Short on Monday to make a care plan. Matty hadn't been seen by anyone for the last months. His meds must surely have run out." He clasped Patience's hand. "We both felt that Matty's recent symptoms were troubling."

"Well, now," the chief said and looked at Henry and Patience's linked hands. "This is the thing. Rob Short seems to think that Patience and his son were close. He's got an idea that she might know something about . . ." Kelsey trailed off. "His wife died in that kitchen too. You can't blame the man for trying to make sense of it."

Henry couldn't take it. He stood so quickly that Kelsey's neck cricked as he followed him.

"What Patience knows about this little boy is that his father was incompetent and that he needed a doctor's care, and that's my job."

Chief Kelsey stood too, and both men leaned toward each

other slightly, unwittingly setting the adversarial tenor that would ultimately poison the town.

EVERYONE WAS STANDING except for Patience. Her sisters exchanged frightened looks, and the chief felt the cold as it crept through the room. He stuttered a bit over his next words. "If you think of anything that could help us, Patience . . . ," he said and walked out with Henry on his heels.

"Patience?" Sam leaned over the couch. "He's gone."

"Henry?" Patience whispered. All she could think was that Henry had left her, and why not? She couldn't even keep Matty safe long enough for Henry to help him.

Sam moved so he could see Patience's face and when he did, he looked at Nettie in alarm. "Jesus, Nettie," he said.

"Henry will be right back." Nettie came to sit by her sister. "Come home," she said. Nettie didn't recognize this Patience either, and Sorrel was so shaken that she stayed by the door.

"I want to wait for Henry," Patience said and drew a shuddering breath. "I think I need Henry."

Henry was still with the chief. He was being questioned in a far less gentle manner.

"What was he doing with the Sparrow girls? Why did Matty hang around the Nursery?" he asked.

"The Sisters were the only ones who didn't treat him like the village idiot." *Which is a position that's open to you,* Henry thought. "Why are you singling out Patience?" he snapped.

"Because Rob had some crazy talk about Matty and what

he called his 'good' days and they were all with Patience. The 'bad' ones were all with him. He claims that Matty was turned against him by the Sisters." The chief stopped. "He's so jumbled up he thinks Patience hypnotized Matty or something. He didn't get his own kid. It's like he's angry at Patience, jealous of the Sisters."

"That's just sick," Henry said and felt a quiver of dread.

Kelsey hung his head. "Rob has nothing left. I don't know what he's going to do now."

Henry looked at the chief. He could see that the boy's death had affected him. He felt sorry for him, for everyone involved. He suspected that somehow Rob Short would end up being at the center of this tragedy. Of course, had he been at the center of Matty's life, there wouldn't be a tragedy at all. Now a careless father was looking to be absolved, or to lay the blame elsewhere. This made Henry furious.

"If Matty's good days were because of Patience, we should all be grateful and be done," Henry said.

"Dr. Carlyle, this is far from done." Chief Kelsey got into his cruiser and pulled out. Henry saw that a few people had drifted down from the bakery to see what was going on. He wondered how much they already knew.

PATIENCE HAD HER eyes closed when Henry came up. She twisted around searching for him as soon as she heard his steps. He sat on the coffee table in front of her. Nettie brought over a cup of ginger tea.

"She always does this," she said to Henry. He looked at her blankly. "She gets sick when she's really upset."

Henry nodded. Vaguely he hoped she didn't vomit every time she cried because there was an ocean of tears ahead.

"Patience, Rob Short thinks you might know something about why, or how, I guess, Matty died," he said. "I have to tell you this now because the police are going to later."

"What did he die of?" Patience asked. Henry looked up at Sam.

"They don't know, P," Sam said.

"Was he alone?" she whispered.

"Rob found him. I was first on the scene." Sam didn't know how much to tell her, but she made the decision for him when she asked. Sam told her how he'd found Matty at the kitchen table, how broken up Rob was. "There was nothing I could do for him," Sam said. "It was too late; he must have died some- time in the night."

"At the kitchen table?" Patience's voice rose, and Henry took her shaking knees in his hands. "Where the fuck was Rob?"

"He fell asleep at the store, P." Sam stood. "I've got to go file my report." He turned to Henry. "Take care of her, okay?"

It took both Sorrel and Nettie to get Patience off the couch and into Henry's car. They announced that she'd do better at Ivy House, away from the prying eyes of the town. When they walked out the front door onto Baker's Way, Henry tried to shield her from passersby, which only tripped Patience up. Henry caught her as she went to one knee, scooped her into his arms, and angled her into the backseat with Nettie. Sorrel sat beside him, her back not even touching the seat. He wondered if she was angry with him until she reached a hand out and patted his arm.

"She'll come out of this," Sorrel whispered. "Patience hasn't fallen apart since Marigold. She just needs to digest it all."

Henry thought "digest" was an odd word to apply to a woman who had just thrown up hard enough to burst a blood vessel in her right eye. Patience looked so wounded that he had to check himself from running his hands over her, looking for injury. He would have carried her up the stairs to her room had Nettie not stopped him.

"She's home now, Henry. Come back later."

Henry watched the Sisters climb the wide porch steps. Three heads bowed into each other, arms laced around Patience, feet moving in unison, a closed circle. After her desperate need for him, Patience had simply left him behind. Unexpectedly, he remembered the first time he'd seen them, in church on Easter Sunday. He'd told himself a story as he watched them laugh together. It was not this story.

Ben was waiting for Henry in front of his house. He had two coffees and a bag from Baker's Way Bakers. They walked around to the back porch and sat in silence for a full minute.

"Man, what a mess," Ben said. "Everybody's talking about Matty, but no one knows anything. I figured Patience might've fallen apart, and you might need this." He held up the coffee. "What the hell happened?"

Henry told him what he knew. Ben covered his eyes as Henry described the scene of Matty's death; he nodded when Henry said he needed to know how it happened so that he could reassure Patience.

"You should call the coroner," Ben said. "I mean, you're kind of Matty's doctor, right?" But Henry shook his head.

"I've really got no claim on Matty, certainly not now." He pounded his fist on his thigh and winced. "If I'd gone to Patience before . . ." He turned to Ben. "I was planning to take Matty on; Patience and I discussed it last night, in fact. We both felt there was something really wrong. Who knows what I might have discovered if I'd examined him?"

"Then you should talk to Sam Parker alone. If he found Matty, he'll have to be involved in the investigation. He'll know stuff we can't."

Henry got to his feet, ready to go to the firehouse.

"Not now, Henry," Ben said. "It'll look bad."

"Why?"

"Because everyone knows Chief Kelsey was here this morning. They just aren't sure why. If you go tearing off to see Sam, there'll be all kinds of talk, more talk. That won't help anyone."

So Henry stayed home, the hot summer day spooling out before him, a ribbon of pain. Ben, released from the wire in his thumb, could at least go to the beach or work around his boat. Henry felt insulted by such a perfect summer day and sat in a sweaty slump on his porch, wondering what everybody else was doing, infuriated that no one seemed to need him. He was still confident that any antagonism building around Patience would disperse as quickly as it came up. As soon as she settled, Patience would see that he could guide her safely through her despair, her hand in his.

AFTER THE SISTERS had put Patience to bed upstairs, Sorrel drove out to the Nursery to make sure the big white gate was locked. It was, as always. It was just that she didn't want to linger at Ivy House. It was too cold there and Patience hadn't stopped shivering, even after Nettie piled three eiderdowns over her. By noon it was 82 degrees at the Nursery, yet Ivy House was still so cold that when Sam walked in, Nettie took him straight out to the garden. He looked terrible, short on sleep and ill from what he'd seen and heard already. If Patience saw him, Nettie thought, she'd have just the thing for Sam. But of course, Patience wasn't in the garden where she belonged. And she was completely incapable of helping anyone, including herself. The only reason Patience wasn't still throwing up was because Henry had finally gotten some Compazine into her before she left his apartment—that and because her stomach muscles had simply worn out.

The Sisters and the three men on the edges of their lives weren't the only ones interested in what was happening to Patience. News had spread outward from the bakery like a still puddle hiding a bit of broken glass. On the surface everyone was concerned about Rob Short, devastated by little Matty's death, distressed by Patience's collapse. But beneath there was a frisson of dark excitement, the thrill that comes with actually knowing someone at the center of a drama. Already the chief's visit had gossiped into an interrogation, and Henry's careful transfer of Patience to the car had twisted into a staggering, drugged parade. By lunchtime, Pete Markham stood in front of his liquor store, chin tilted toward the sky. He was not the only Granite Point resident who was scenting the air, waiting for a clue to Patience's state.

When Henry couldn't stand to be in his own skin anymore, he showered and walked to Ivy House only to find Sam Parker already there, sprawled in the shade of the crab apple tree in the center of the garden. The scent of the tissue-thin blossoms was as strong as Henry's longing for Patience. Henry went up to check on Patience, to read her as she did her clients. As soon as he checked on her, sure that she wasn't dehydrated (he'd brought an IV kit and banana bag just in case), he planned to track Rob Short down wherever he had ended up and sift through what had happened. Someone had to tell Rob to leave Patience out of his wholesale blame game.

Patience was so small and flat beneath the covers that Henry turned back to look for her downstairs. But then she sat up, her eyes wild with horror, and he knew she woke to recall what had happened, new again. He came to her side, afraid to touch her because she was so disoriented. The still gray room was cold and airless, the curtains drawn, a glass of water swirling with dust on the bedside table. It was nothing like the room

Henry had shared with Patience. The sweat cooled on his skin as he stood beside the bed until he too shivered.

Once she could focus, Patience put her arms out to Henry and he realized how frightened he'd been, how terrified she still was. He leaned down and pulled her into his chest. She was freezing; he could feel it straight through his shirt. And her thighs pressed so hard against his jeans that Henry had to fight to keep from pushing her back so he could rub the cold away. Without thinking he put his hand to the pulse at her neck and felt its rapid tap against his fingers. He moved it down until it rested over her heart, stroked her side. Her ribs were apparent under his palm; he was certain they hadn't been so the night before. Patience was reduced by Matty's death. Henry let her hold onto him for some minutes, her fingers pulling at the back of his tee shirt until the neck line left a mark on his throat. Finally, she loosened her grip.

"I'm sorry about this morning," Patience said into Henry's chest. "I am a barfer by nature." She laughed a little, and Henry heard her teeth chatter.

"I got that," he said. "I think you need to control the nausea before you get up again. In fact, I'd like you to stay put until I'm sure you're not going to barf again. Will you do that?"

"No," she said and let him go. "I need to clean up." She swayed once on the way into the bathroom. But the look she gave Henry shut his mouth before he could scold her.

Henry left Patience to shower. He dared to think that maybe, as horrible as everything was, things might turn out fine after all. Surely he could be of use in the days ahead; he could console her, that much he knew. He remembered how he himself had behaved in the hospital in Germany. The pain was terrible, but it was the memory of his failure that made him irrational with agony. It was the image of the girl's face, blood pooling in her ears, her eyes first pleading and then empty, that turned his days into waking nightmares.

After the second surgery he'd completely shut down. He'd taken the painkillers with silent acceptance. If he hadn't been a doctor, he was sure the standard psych evaluation would have been marked not just unfit for service but also most likely to explode like the bomb that had taken him out. But as soon as he could walk with nothing more than a cane, Henry was on the ward at the VA hospital and then back to Mass General with an honorable discharge. Henry felt sick himself at the thought of those first weeks. He resolved that, if nothing else, he was uniquely fit for helping Patience through the worst of it. It simply never occurred to him that anything more could happen.

While Ivy House gathered her wounded close, Sorrel stood in the Nursery shed and looked at Patience's cupboard. She turned her back and rinsed out her little harvest, but she couldn't ignore the dread that nudged at her shoulders. Sorrel ran her fingers over the unmarked drawers, pulled one open, sifted through the labels on the counter. What did Patience make, really? She thought. How did she know what was wrong, how to make it right? What if *Patience* was wrong?

Sorrel drove back from the Nursery with a basket full of let-tuce, nasturtiums, broccoli rabe, and radishes. She carried with her the insistent seeds of doubt.

Nettie lined Sam and Henry up in the shady part of the garden and brought them glasses of tea and an ice-filled bowl of cherries. When Ben appeared at the back door, Nettie went nearly airborne with surprise. Patience came just behind him and served to deflate Nettie's excitement so that she looked merely welcoming instead of incandescent with delight. Ben opened the screen and held Patience's elbow as she took the three steps carefully. No one had ever seen Patience move so gingerly. Henry leapt to his feet and bent in an awkward, crouchy stance as he tried to check her reddened eye and sniff her breath for ketosis. Patience tapped his head lightly as she passed him.

"Would you stop," she said and folded shakily onto the cool grass beneath the crab apple tree. Nettie handed her a glass of pale mint tea and Henry couldn't see a reason to argue with any of it. Patience rested her head on Nettie's lap, Ben sat next to Nettie, Sorrel cleaned the vegetables in the kitchen sink, Sam tied up the clematis, and Henry perched uselessly on the kneeler the Sisters used to weed. From the outside this tableau might have looked charming, like nursery children scattered about a summer lawn, resting before the next game took them scampering around the flowerbeds.

"I wanted to hydrate you properly," Henry said to Patience with as much authority as he could muster on her turf. "I brought an IV kit . . ." He trailed off weakly as the women grimaced. "But you seem to be in good hands." It was ridiculous that Henry felt put off by the Sisters, but he did. The fact that Sam and Ben were so comfortable, so slotted in at Ivy House, really bugged him. How did that happen, exactly? Everyone turned to Sam when Henry suggested an IV, as if they needed the paramedic's input. Henry was irked enough to consider leaving. But he didn't because he needed Sam too.

"Could I talk to you for a minute?" Henry asked Sam. The two men went back into the house, which had warmed considerably since the morning. Sam waved his hand through the air in the kitchen and looked at Sorrel standing at the sink. They both nodded.

"Patience is better," Sam said.

Henry nodded too though he couldn't think why. "What happened, Sam?"

"Fuck if I know," Sam said. "It was awful. Matty was at the kitchen table." He shook his head as if to clear it of the image. "He'd been there all night, I guess."

"Could you tell what the cause was?" Henry asked. "Was he beaten?"

"No, no, nothing like that," Sam answered. "We'll have to wait for the postmortem but if I had to guess, I'd say some kind of anaphylactic reaction."

"Swelling, rash, petechial hemorrhage?" Henry drew closer to Sam and lowered his voice. "Was there anything on the table with him, food, drink, meds?"

Sorrel looked up from the sink. "What are you asking, Henry?"

"I'm asking if Matty had a reaction to something he ate or drank," Henry said.

"Or something Patience gave him?" Sorrel bowed her head. "You're asking if Patience did this."

Until Sorrel spoke, Henry could almost convince himself that he didn't consider Patience a factor in Matty's death. After she gave voice to his fear, there was no point denying it. Sorrel's seeds of doubt had just been watered. Right then he knew that, in fact, things could get worse.

"Sorrel, the police have already come. They'll be back, and that's what they'll ask too," Henry said.

"Patience would never hurt Matty," Sorrel said.

"Don't you think I know that?" Henry said. "I would rather hear it from Patience now than in front of Chief Kelsey."

"There's not a person in Granite Point who would accuse Patience of such a thing!" Sorrel's voice rose. "Whatever Patience's unusual abilities are, everyone knows she only uses them to help."

"Henry's not saying she did anything to harm Matty," Sam said. "But we have to be realistic. The minute Rob Short brought Patience up, she got in the middle of this thing."

"Do you think she knows that?" Sorrel asked.

Henry and Sam looked at each other.

"I think there's very little Patience doesn't know," Sam said.

Sorrel made a salad from the Nursery produce, and Henry

got out cold cuts and a loaf of bread from Baker's Way. Claire Redmond had left it on the Sisters' porch that morning as if she knew they needed simple sustenance. He helped Sorrel carry the tray out to the garden. Patience was still in Nettie's lap, but she was crying again, and Ben looked uncomfortable and felt worse. Henry knew that one look at food, and Patience would be sick again. He pulled her to her feet and led her back inside.

It was stuffy and hot in Patience's room. Again, nothing like the place where Henry had spent hours in the weeks before Matty's death. He peeled Patience's shorts off and left her in her underpants. She was as limp and compliant as an exhausted child. She stood, weeping silently as he pulled back her covers.

"This is my fault," she said, and Henry turned around to look at her. She wiped her nose with the palm of her hand. "I did this."

"You did not," Henry said and held out his hand. "Come here."

Patience walked the few steps to him, and he saw that there were bruises along her ribs, as if she had been battered from the inside, her grief fighting to get out.

"Jesus, Patience," he said as he took her into his arms. She was shivering again even though the air around them was heavy with heat. He felt her breasts press against his shirt, the nipples tight as if she were freezing. She was.

"I'm sorry," she said. "I can't seem to stop crying."

Henry settled her in the bed and lay alongside her on top of the covers.

"Why do you blame yourself?" he asked.

"Because if I'd listened to you the first time, you could have saved Matty." She began to weep in earnest. "I promised I'd take care of him."

"None of this is your fault," Henry said as he stroked her hair away from her teary face. "Whatever happened to Matty—and we'll find out from the police—it had nothing to do with you."

Patience twitched at the word "police." "I should talk to Rob," she said.

"No, you shouldn't," Henry snapped. "You should stay away from him and everything else to do with this terrible thing."

Patience finally drifted off to sleep, one hand fisted under her chin. Henry left Ivy House with a promise to return in the evening. Sam had already gone home, and Ben and Nettie were still in the garden. Only Sorrel said good-bye, and as she watched Henry leave, she felt a sudden shiver herself and wondered if he should come back at all.

Down at Clear Lake that afternoon, Henry slid his shell carefully off the roof of the car and carried it over his head to the water. He had to thread his way through the children who clustered like birds on the shoreline. Balancing the shell at the end of the worn wooden boat ramp, Henry settled in with one oar out to steady him. He rowed gently around the teenagers who bobbed in clumps in the deep water. They splashed each other and laughed and jostled closely in a game designed purely to allow the boys to graze the girls' bodies with their own.

Henry didn't notice the silence that fell over the mothers as he walked by. On any other Saturday the women might have paused in their conversations to appreciate the doctor's long tan torso as he carried his boat. They might have sucked in a breath as his scarred thigh passed close enough to touch. But today they closed their mouths over the urge to ask him what had gone on in Rob Short's kitchen, what had happened to Patience that had turned her into something more than the local adept and less than a member of their community.

Henry rowed until he reached the far side of Clear Lake. He was as light and graceful as a mayfly skimming the surface, his wake merely a ripple, thin as a knife's edge. There were no houses there, only an abandoned, rickety float left from the boys' camp that had closed in the seventies. Wedging the shell with an oar against it, he pulled himself up the gap-toothed ladder and lay down on the hot wood. He was still stunned by how quickly everything had gone wrong. One minute Henry had stood on the threshold of happiness for the first time in his life, really, and the next he was surrounded by rubble and destruction. It brought to mind, reluctantly, the day he'd been wounded, the crush of children laughing and shoving as he held a fistful of American candy over his head, a reward for their bravery in the face of syringes. And a moment later, there was the slam of pressurized air and the feeling of gritty concrete under his cheek. A tangle of bodies and blood and dust. Nothing but chaos and pain and fear, the bitter taste of airborne plaster, melting plastic, the hideous smell of burning flesh.

Henry sat up and got to his feet. He looked down at the wet print he'd left behind and thought of the chalk outline at a murder scene. *That's it,* he thought, *this feels exactly like a senseless crime.* And then he shuddered. *What if it was?*

He rowed back, nodding at the women on the shore, at the tourists, pale and spongy under their umbrellas. He caught a toddler by the arm as she pitched forward over her own bucket. He slid the shell back onto his car and got in, his leg now quivering painfully against the towel on the front seat.

IT WOULD BE their last simple evening together but one, Patience and Henry. The heat remained, an unwelcome guest, overstaying dreadfully as the clock slid toward nine. Nettie and Sorrel sat at the kitchen table with their sister as Henry cleared the mostly full plates. Cold lemony chicken, baby greens in a sweet balsamic dressing, the last of Claire Redmond's bread all tumbled into the garbage. The only thing anyone finished was the wine, and Henry already felt a headache lurking in his left temple. He drank everyone's leftover water as he loaded the dishwasher, willing one of the sisters to speak. But it was as if Matty's death had taken their voices, and none of the women could make their way through the close air to relieve the silence. Henry was desperate to reconnect with Patience. Selfishly, he thought about making love to her even though he could see that she was as fragile and desiccated by her tears as the seaweed that lined the beach, as distant as the horizon. He wanted to take her upstairs and spread her naked on the bed, cover every inch of her with his hands, smooth away the frost of salt left by her weeping.

In fact, he did bring her to her room. He sat on the slipper chair while she brushed her teeth. He even toed off his loafers, hoping his bare feet would be a signal to Patience that he wanted to stay. She came out of the bathroom in a pair of boxer shorts; his, he realized with a hopeful shock, and Henry tried to remember when he'd left them. But Patience crawled into bed and turned away. He went to her and rubbed her back for a moment, waiting for her to turn and invite him in. She didn't, so Henry bent to kiss her neck, his lips warm against her cold skin, and left. The Sisters barely looked up as he passed through the kitchen on his way out. Henry felt adrift, cut loose from the only mooring he had in the town.

ROB SHORT'S HOUSE was hot and close. His windows were shut and cloudy with dust as he sat in the living room staring at the fireplace he hadn't cleaned out since early May. He wondered if he should open the windows, if only to clear the room of his own body odor, but the thought of fresh air actually made Rob shiver. It had been three days since he found Matty in the kitchen, two days since he'd last been outside, one day since he'd shut all the windows and pulled the shades. In a town where more than a few people didn't lock their doors unless they were leaving Granite Point altogether, Rob Short had put the chain across his. He didn't know if he was keeping something in or out. He did know that the looks he got when he walked to Pete's liquor store were not of sympathy but of dismay.

He had slept very little in the days since he lost Matty. Lost Matty, that's how Rob thought of the death. Annie left him when she took the pills, now Matty had gone, poisoned, Rob was certain, by those Sisters. That wasn't his first idea and of course, he had no real reason to believe it but, given enough time alone, enough liquor and cigarettes (the last things Rob bought on the last day he left his house), enough sadness that so easily distills into anger and then spills over into blame looking for a target, and Rob had no trouble settling on Patience Sparrow. He'd seen the two of them more than once in town, coming out of the bakery, eating popsicles from the drugstore, unloading luscious window boxes for the Main Street shops. Matty hadn't even looked up, this Rob remembered, but Patience had given him a wave and Matty a nudge that Rob was sure now was just laden with judgment. At the time he'd been guiltily grateful that Matty had something to do, someone to be with, as he hurried back into the hardware store and took his place in the little office on the second floor. He'd promised himself that as soon as he cleared the books, adjusted the purchase orders, stopped missing Annie so, he'd find more time for Matty. And Matty would want less time with Patience.

Now, if there was any reason to leave his house, Rob thought, it just might be to make that Sparrow girl face him, see what a truly broken heart looks like. In fact, the more Rob thought about Patience Sparrow and the way the people in town, especially the women—the flighty girls and the solid moms—respected her, needed her, the angrier he became. He'd come to Granite Point with his new wife; he'd agreed to move to Annie's hometown because he loved her that much and yet he was an outsider. More than fifteen years on and he still felt the curtness of the nods, the cool edge to Matty's teacher's voice, saw the way people looked at him after Annie died, as if he might be a bit poisonous himself.

Rob Short was not yet drunk, but he was in an unreasonable state. He wanted kindness, compassion, pity, even from this town, but no one had come to him, not a single pan of brownies, Pyrex dish of noodle casserole, or fish pie had been left on his doorstep. Nobody had heard him cry or patted his shoulder as he sobbed into closed fists. Clearly Rob Short was outside the sealed circle of Granite Point, no matter how long he lived here or how much he needed to belong. And so, before he let himself think any further, before his anger and resentment dissipated, Rob unchained his front door and headed straight for the Nursery.

THE SANDY LITTLE parking lot already had a few cars scattered so Rob left his at the gate. As he made for the barn where the Sisters worked, his pace picked up, as did his pulse. He unclenched his fists and wiped them on his pants. By the time he stood at the steps, his hands were shaking.

"I know what you did," Rob said.

The Sisters were ringing up four gallon buckets of sedum, their rubbery leaves green and pillowy. Sorrel turned first, then Nettie, and last Patience, who really wasn't helping at all, just leaning against the worktable as if she couldn't stand on her own. The three women looked at Rob for a long moment, long enough that the small gathering of customers stepped back and looked at Rob too. It took most of them a moment to recognize him. It took Patience only seconds.

"I know what you did," Rob said again. "I know you hurt my boy and here you are"—he waved at the Nursery, his voice rising—"growing your, your . . ." He trailed off and looked at the people who'd gathered. There was a mother with a baby in a sling across her hip and her husband, who held a bunch of cosmos in his hand, two hearty landscapers who'd come to get the thistle only the Sisters could grow, and Dot Avery, who held in her string bag a carefully wrapped burnet plant for her summer salads. A tourist who had only come to take pictures of the Shakespeare garden so his wife could plant one of her own held up his phone. Behind him the news editor of the *Granite Point Clarion* stood with the red wagon he had been about to fill with on-sale peonies. Ambrose Smith really wished he'd brought his phone; this could be news.

Rob collected himself. Patience pushed off from the table and came to the top of the steps, the sun turning her hair to embers.

"What is it, Rob?" she asked. "What have I grown here that has done anything but make our lives better?"

"You killed Matty," Rob spat. "You poisoned him with one of your concoctions. My boy is dead, and you just go on as if nothing's wrong. Well, *you're* wrong," he shouted. "You're the something wrong here!"

Sorrel put her hand on Patience's arm while Nettie tried to shepherd the customers back to their purchases. But Patience wouldn't stay. She took the steps at a run, and Rob backed away.

"I loved Matty," she said. "We all did. If you're so sure I could hurt him with one of my concoctions," she spat, "then you'd best leave here before I do something to you!"

There was a collective murmur, and then Nettie hissed, "Excellent, Patience! Now you've done it."

It was in that moment that Granite Point began to think about the Sparrow Sisters and their nursery in a very different way. As Rob Short stalked back to his car, there was a palpable shift in the air; whether it was Patience gathering her anger or simply the sun slipping behind the thunderheads that had stacked up in what seemed like minutes, it didn't much matter. The gossip would circulate, and the men in town would begin to wonder what exactly their wives kept in the small blue bottles in the pantry. Those men would ponder if they hadn't better keep their women a little closer.

Poor Rob Short nearly ran to his car. Patience moved back inside, neatly stepping on Sorrel's foot.

"For God's sake, Patience," Sorrel snapped out of pain and fear. "What the hell were you thinking engaging that man?"

"We should have left her at home," Nettie whispered. "You've just made things so much worse, Patience."

Patience put her head down on the worktable while the shaken customers paid up and scurried away. It would take mere hours before the idle chatter swelled and turned ugly, racketing from house to house and shop to shop until it reached Chief Kelsey.

CHAPTER EIGHT

Sweetgrass makes a strong tincture for hayfever

It was an overcast Wednesday morning, the first bad weather since July fifth. Granite Point was as gray and chilly as its namesake. Chief Kelsey and his deputy stood on the steps of Ivy House and straightened their already tidy uniforms in a bid to put off their next move. The chief had gone to early Mass, and his wife had watched him change into his work clothes with barely disguised dismay. The deputy picked him up in an unmarked sedan and they drove in silence, the dispatch radio turned off.

Patience answered the door. She was wearing a pale blue cotton sweater over her jeans; her hair was wet and heavy against her long neck. Sorrel stood at the top of the stairs, and Nettie lingered halfway down the hall from the kitchen. Before the chief spoke, he looked up at Sorrel and winced. Sorrel descended, and both women drew together behind their sister.

"It's Rob Short," the chief said. "He came to the station."

Sorrel and Nettie exchanged looks, and Patience shook her head.

"I'm afraid that when he came to the Nursery, I got a little angry," Patience said. "He accused me of poisoning Matty."

"See, that's the problem," Kelsey said. "Once the accusation is out there, once the whispers start . . ." He shrugged. "It's better if we try to nip this thing in the bud."

The sisters winced, and the chief tried a smile.

"Can we head over to the Nursery and have a look?" he asked.

"Do I have a choice?" Patience asked.

"Of course you do. This isn't a search; it's just a look-see before anyone gets it into their heads to start messing around."

"As in one of us has something to hide?" Sorrel asked.

"Please, Sorrel," Kelsey said, holding up his hands. "Why don't you all come?"

Patience looked at her sisters. "We'll come," she said.

The policemen walked through the gardens, touching plants with questions, and the Sisters answered them. They stopped at the compost pile at the edge of the wildflower meadow. It was steaming slightly, and the chief nodded approvingly.

"This must be your secret," he said. "I mean, the secret to your stuff, the flowers and vegetables." Kelsey had stumbled over his comment. After all, he was there to find secrets.

The Sisters trailed after the men; Nettie walked ahead of Patience, a trug in her hand, and Sorrel carried the bamboo rake she'd picked up at the compost heap. Officer Fancy stayed beside Sorrel. Everyone stopped in front of Patience's largest herb bed. To Kelsey they looked like a tableau: villagers with monster and pitchfork.

"Can you point out the plants used for Matty?" Kelsey asked.

Patience stepped carefully between the rows and put her hand on a plant.

"Passiflora," she said, stroking the heavy flowers, their petals spiky and their stamens rearing out of the deep-purple centers. A huge bee dropped down until it hovered at her fingertips. She didn't move, but Chief Kelsey stood back.

"I'm allergic," he said and felt for the EpiPen in his pocket.

Patience flicked at the bee with her nail. It swerved away. Patience moved on. "Valerian." She turned to Nettie and held out her hand. Nettie put a small pair of secateurs into her palm. Patience snipped at the valerian, and went back for the passi-flora. Then she knelt down to cut away a small sample from a low-growing flowering plant. "Madagascar periwinkle." She handed the plants to the chief, who passed them on to his silent deputy. Several more times Patience bent and clipped until the officer had eight clear evidence bags in his arms.

"You know how to use all of these?" Chief Kelsey asked.

"I do," Patience answered. "And before you ask, some of them can be toxic in the wrong amounts."

"Patience!" Sorrel snapped.

The chief held up his hand. "I appreciate your cooperation." He took Patience's elbow as she stepped out of the garden; box leaves and dill clung to her sleeves. "I need to see your work space," he said.

Officer Fancy led the way back to the shed. "Oh look," he said. "Monkshood."

"You're right, Martin," said Sorrel. "It's only grown for arrangements, like the foxglove. Patience won't touch the stuff."

The Sisters stood in a line as Kelsey and his deputy, who had, in fact, gone to elementary school with Patience, began rummaging. Chief Kelsey asked Patience what things were as he pulled each drawer out, cleared a space on the counter, and organized the bottles and packets alphabetically. He checked his notepad as he looked at the names on the labels. Finally he swept four items—distillations of Matty's remedies—into his hand and sealed them each into separate evidence bags. He stripped off his gloves and waved Officer Fancy out the door.

"I have to take these to the lab," Kelsey said. "If they can rule out your remedies, we can all move on."

"I never made a secret of helping Matty," Patience said. "I only did it because Rob didn't."

Kelsey nodded. "He knows that, somewhere, he does."

"So why aren't you looking for the real cause?" Nettie said in a voice more suited to Sorrel.

"We are." Chief Kelsey left.

The women stood in the shed looking at the mess. It wasn't that the two policemen had ripped through the place; it was that no one but the Sisters had ever touched the surfaces, the ball of twine, the row of scissors over the sink. To Patience it all felt contaminated. She expected to be able to see handprints, as if a black light had been used to show up bacteria. And that's how it was now. Her world was poisoned.

The Sparrow Sisters Nursery was open that day. It had to be. Weekends often saved the quiet weeks, even in summer but the Sisters couldn't take a chance with another empty till. It was bad enough that two days had been lost to Patience's grief. And that the town noticed. Sorrel and Nettie tried to convince their sister to go home; she looked wrung out and felt worse. Her bloodshot eye had paled to an unsettling pink, so she wore sunglasses to hide it as well as the puffy purple shadows across her cheeks. She made her way to the greenhouses after the three of them cleaned up the shed. The sun still hid behind low clouds; it would rain later. She walked past the Kousa dogwoods, their blossoms already so limp with humidity that they no longer resembled a blood-tipped cross but more a victim of crucifixion, petals bowed in defeat. The snapdragons struggled, the weight of the moisture in the cupped flowers so heavy their mouths gaped and tiny gnats drowned in them.

When Patience was wrapped up in a problem, she wasn't always terribly welcoming to customers. On this day her sisters were certain she could easily drive them off, so they were relieved when she drifted away. They might have been less so if they had seen her lie down under the Meyer lemon tree in the farthest greenhouse. They would have been very worried had they seen the wrinkled lemons that fell, already gray with mold, around her.

Henry Carlyle invited Sam over for coffee. He knew that Sam had a line on how Patience worked, something Henry could not yet claim. The doctor was eager to find his role again after Matty's death and Patience's collapse. He was no longer the capable professional nor the lover who had blurred her edges until Patience was soft with pleasure. He certainly could not claim to be her best friend. That was something he'd hoped to become over the warm weeks. Henry had dared to picture a life with Patience beyond summer. He had a vivid vision of them through the seasons, the peaks of Thanksgiving and Christmas, the valleys of February and March, the long lazy plateaus of September and October. He'd jinxed everything by imagining a year from now, when three hundred plus days had filtered their messy meeting into a fond, distant memory.

Now the two men stood at Henry's kitchen counter, their coffee gone cold, the muffins from Baker's Way Bakers untouched. They faced the kitchen as if waiting to be served at a bar.

"So, have you seen her today?" Henry asked.

Sam shook his head. "Chief Kelsey called last night. He says I should keep away for a day or two. He's had a look around the Nursery, took some samples."

"This is beginning to sound ominous," Henry said. "They've got to be doing a tox screen."

"Yeah, and they're looking for Patience's stuff."

"For God's sake." Henry stood and poured out his coffee. "Half this town is full of her stuff."

"True, but half this town did not just drop dead."

Sam and Henry knew that they shouldn't be seen together outside of work either, which made Henry feel particularly alone. Ben had gone out on a charter boat for some extra cash. That left exactly one person who might be glad to see him: Patience. But when Henry called Ivy House, no one answered, and Patience no longer had a cell phone. It didn't occur to him that she'd be at the Nursery, although it should have. In Henry's mind Patience was as alone as he. She was still incapacitated, hobbled in the aftermath. He didn't realize that being around her plants was the very thing for that. He didn't yet know that those plants were already failing her.

Finally, Henry left the apartment vaguely exhausted by his uselessness. He went to see Sally Tabor and her new baby. *Nothing better than a days-old infant to settle existential anxiety,* he thought. He drove over after picking out a cashmere baby blanket at the linen shop. He knew he was spending too much, but when he noticed that the other customers fell silent as the proprietor (and a patient) greeted him, Henry simply paid for the thing he held in his hands and left. Any sweetness he had begun to take from living in a small town turned sour. His hand trembled as he signed his name, making it more illegible than ever.

Sally answered the door. She grabbed his arm and pulled him into the house before he said a word. Henry handed her the blanket in an overly festooned gift bag, and she patted him in thanks.

"Here," she said, handing him another cup of coffee. "Sit, talk, you look like hell."

Sally knew everything, how the police had been to the Nursery before nine in the morning, how word of Rob Short's confrontation had gone round, how the husbands and boyfriends were asking their partners a lot of questions about Patience Sparrow. Henry tried to stand, wanting to go to Patience, to keep her from all the ugliness, but Sally pushed him down.

"Leave it. Just stay here for a minute," she said. "You can't run off every time Patience riles up the town."

Henry fell back against the sofa and closed his eyes. He heard the uniquely stomach-dropping sound of the new baby crying through the monitor on the coffee table and felt the cushion shift as Sally got up to go to her daughter. He listened as her voice softened, the cooing and rustling as she lifted Katherine into her arms.

"You did this."

Henry opened one eye to see a jammy face inches from his own.

"You made that baby," the little boy said as he put a sticky hand on Henry's knee and shoved, hard.

"Technically I just delivered . . ." Henry stopped. "Hello," he said. "You must be . . ." He realized he didn't know who this kid might be since he didn't know there were any other Tabor kids until the last one arrived.

"I'm Declan, and now I'm not the baby anymore." Declan frowned as Henry peeled his hand away.

"Well, you're a big brother, which is much more interesting."

"No it's not."

"Sure it is," Henry said. "You can teach Katherine all the important stuff."

"Like?"

"Tree climbing, baseball, fishing, taking out the garbage." Henry thought he'd never sounded so inane.

"I'd rather put *her* in the garbage." Declan ran out of the room.

Sally came back with the baby, and Henry smiled. It was awfully hard to be out of sorts around a baby. Sally handed her off to him without hesitation, and Henry protested that he hadn't washed up.

"Oh, quit," Sally said. "You think she's not going to eat a little dirt around here?"

Henry brought the baby's head to his nose and inhaled.

"I know." Sally smiled. "Best smell in the world."

"What's going to happen now?" Henry asked.

"You don't mean after Katherine spits up on your shoulder, right."

Henry looked at Sally. She was exhausted, he could see that, but it was the kind of tired that came from something good, it was the sum of something, not the terrible emptiness that defined Patience now. Loss only looked like exhaustion.

"So, according to"—Sally chuckled—"you know I want to say scuttlebutt"—she adjusted her gaping shirt—"the news is that Kelsey himself went to the Nursery, which could be a good thing."

"Or?" Henry shifted the baby to his shoulder and rubbed her back in small circles, just as he had with Patience. He was rewarded with a breathy, milky burp.

"Or it could be that this is getting ugly."

"It's already ugly, Sally. Matty's dead, and Patience blames herself."

"Right, but when Rob Short blames her and the police listen, then it's really ugly." Sally took the baby and called out. Warren came in from the kitchen and gently gathered Katherine. Before retreating, he thanked Henry with tears in his eyes for delivering his wife.

"He is such a softy," Sally said. "He wanted to come see you after we got home, but then . . ." She shrugged.

"What if the police question you?" Henry asked.

"I'll tell them the truth. Patience has helped me through more than just pregnancies. She's treated most of Granite Point; I think she's treated some of the guys on the force. Who do you think could throw the first stone?"

As it turned out, any number of people had stones in their pockets.

THE AUTOPSY ON Matty Short was conducted in Hayward. The results showed that Matty's heart had simply stopped, a fact the medical examiner was hesitant to accept. How could an otherwise healthy heart have broken? The toxicology report wouldn't come through for some days. Chief Kelsey interviewed Henry, and Matty's patient file was taken away. Even though he hadn't treated the boy, Henry Carlyle was the doctor of record. He so wished that he had been the doctor in fact. Sam was questioned again to determine exactly what he saw when he arrived at the Short house. Rob Short was visited at his home where he was found drunk and disoriented in the kitchen where Matty died. He continued to insist that Patience had poisoned his son even after he was reassured that his statement was already on file and told that this kind of talk wouldn't help the investigation. He followed the policemen around until they got to Matty's room. He couldn't bring himself to go in and looked away as the two men sifted through the clothes in the bureau and the books and papers on his little table. It never occurred to any of them to look under his mattress.

And finally, the chief interviewed Patience at Ivy House. Minute by minute he walked her through Matty's last day. Halfway through her recitation, Simon Mayo flew through the front door shaking rain from his hair.

"Not another word, Patience," he barked. "Joe, you know better," he said as he stood behind Patience's chair.

"I'm merely trying to establish what Matty's movements

were the day before his death," Kelsey said. "None of us want to be having this talk."

"Then you won't be bothered if I end it right now." Simon gestured for Kelsey to stand. "Let me see you out."

As soon as the two men were gone, Sorrel rounded on Nettie.

"Did you call Simon?"

"I did," Nettie said with uncharacteristic snap.

Simon came back in before Sorrel could lash out again.

"Right, that was the last time you are alone with anyone from the police." He turned to the Sisters. "The last time any of you do anything without me."

"Jesus, Simon, we're not criminals," Patience said.

"And let's keep it that way." Simon took a pad out of the briefcase he'd slung onto the sofa. "Start at the beginning, Patience."

An hour later they'd moved to the kitchen. It was dusk, and four bent heads were reflected in the back door. Pages covered the table, and a bottle of Scotch sat at Simon's elbow. He'd had one drink and felt as unsettled as if he'd had too many. On the surface there was nothing in Patience's statement that should trouble him, but he'd felt the shift in town since Matty's death. Simon knew that it didn't matter who was telling the truth, just who told it best. One look at the inscription on the band shell was enough to remind everyone in Granite Point how long it had been since panic seized the town, and how fast it had nearly destroyed it. If there was to be another witch hunt, it certainly had a strong start.

"I've arranged for you to make a formal statement tomorrow at the station. That's why we're nailing it down now," Simon said.

"If I could just talk to Rob Short properly, tell him how sorry I am?" Patience asked.

"No!" Simon nearly shouted. "Never apologize. It's an admission of guilt."

"But I'm not guilty of anything, am I?" Patience was picking at her nails. They were disturbingly clean. She hadn't worked in the soil since Matty died.

"Of course you aren't guilty, Patience," Sorrel said. She turned to Simon. "No matter what this one says."

At that Nettie returned from her brief sojourn into confidence and began to flutter.

"I had to call him, Sorrel," she said. "I mean who else do we know? Mr. Gibson?"

"Mr. Gibson would have been fine," Sorrel said.

"Isn't he drifting away from the dock a little, Sorrel? I saw him at the library talking to an umbrella handle." Nettie leaned into the table until her chin hovered over the bowl of plums at its center. "Simon Mayo is the best lawyer in this town."

"The entire Southern New England region, actually," Simon said. "I have a plaque."

Sorrel snorted and put her head in her hands. "Fine."

Patience took a sip of Scotch. She didn't even feel it in her mouth or her throat. It seemed chilling instead of warming. Everyone was gathered at the table to take care of her, as if she were a difficult child who needed to be handled carefully. She hadn't been handled in years, and it saddened her. She should have been angry, but she just couldn't gin up the energy.

A strangely festive air had settled over Sorrel and Nettie. They were relieved to have a lawyer on board, and it made them punchy. But Patience couldn't join in. Matty was dead, she was rattled by the Nursery search, and she hadn't seen Henry since Saturday night. She couldn't help but think that he suspected her too.

But Henry *had* tried to see Patience: first on Sunday when he called the empty house and then on Monday evening when he stopped by after his last appointment. He didn't know that Patience was asleep in the back garden then. She was lying on the grass covered in a thin, nearly white mist that gathered in her eyelashes and brows, the weave of her tee shirt and the delicate hairs on her arms. Henry would never have imagined that scene as he stood at the front door in the fine rain that replaced the storm and now seemed to have been falling all day. He'd turned away and driven home only moments before the Sisters came back from the Nursery. The to-ing and fro-ing was amusing, worthy of a French farce had anyone been in the mood.

On that Wednesday, the day after Chief Kelsey came to Ivy House, around the time that Simon Mayo rode to the rescue, the very moment that Patience sat bemoaning Henry's disappearance, he was at the hospice in Hayward. His oldest patient, Walter Gatmore, who had lingered at the doorway for almost a week, stepped through it into death at last. His sons and daughters-in-law were with him, and Henry was grateful that he was too. Still, he felt no more than an usher: new life in, old out. As he listened to the last agonal breaths of a man who was so loved by his silent family, Henry wondered if Patience couldn't have eased the way for them all. And this scared him as he thought of how Matty had trusted Patience to ease his pain.

The rain stopped long enough on Thursday for the Sisters to get to the police station in a dry state. Simon drove, and as much as he begged them to stay behind, Sorrel and Nettie insisted on going along. It was far too much of an acknowledgment of how worried they were for Simon's comfort, and he managed to convince them to wait in the car. From the backseat of the dark sedan Simon had borrowed from his mother (the little Mercedes would have been thoroughly inappropriate), Sorrel and Nettie had a perfect view of the slow trickle of the curious as news spread that Patience Sparrow was in the station. They slunk lower and lower in the hour her statement took to be entered into the system, for Chief Kelsey to confirm every detail and for Simon to clarify it. By the time Simon led their sister out, he scanned the street wondering where Nettie and Sorrel were. Patience looked at the small crowd and met each person's eye as she fumbled to open her door. She smiled at Annica Martel, owner of the linen shop, who stood holding several packages to post, and she waved at Thomas Shea, who struggled to hold on to his bicycle as people jostled for a better look. It was ridiculous. Several of them were customers at the Nursery. More than one of them had sought Patience's help. Yet all of them watched Patience with something that looked very much like fear.

Simon took the Sisters directly to the Nursery. He left them clustered around Patience on the steps of the shed. When he pulled into his own driveway, Charlotte was unloading groceries. She turned and frowned at the old sedan.

"Ah, Ford Fairlane," she said. "Preferred by undercover cops in 1975 and your mother."

"Hello, darling," Simon kissed Charlotte's cheek. "I'm switching back to the Merc, car of lawyers in mid-life crises."

"Is that what this is, Simon," Charlotte asked as she handed him a bag, "this crusade on behalf of the Sisters?"

"No, it's the right thing to do."

"Is it?" Charlotte asked.

Simon followed his wife into the kitchen. "I only ask because Granite Point seems to be doing that nasty small-town thing."

"What's that?" Simon asked, but he already knew.

"The whole whispering, rumormongering, schadenfreude thing," Charlotte said as she opened the fridge, taking out a bottle of leftover Founders' party wine.

Simon pointed at the wine. "If you want to get pregnant . . ."

She pinned Simon with a tired look. "We both know where that project stands."

"Charlotte," Simon took the bottle and placed it on the counter. He put his hand on Charlotte's arm.

"Don't feel sorry for me," she said. "Your client is the one who's about to take a fall. Please do not go down with her."

AT THE NURSERY the first thing the Sisters noticed was the morning glories, or rather, the lack of them. It was past ten but the Sparrow Sisters' morning glories bloomed all day, so blue they were nearly purple. Today every blossom was closed, clenched tight like a furled umbrella.

"Goddamned rain," Patience said as she walked into the shed. She hadn't been back since the search, but the Sisters had made sure that all her supplies were re-ordered in their drawers and shelves. She ran her fingers over the logbook Ben Avellar had left for her and flipped it open to the last entry. "Rosemary for remembrance," it said. Ha, thought Patience, like there's anything worth remembering about this week.

Nettie and Sorrel busied themselves sorting invoices until there really was nothing to do but go outside in the heavy air and weed the gardens. Patience watched them, their backs bent over the task, Nettie's hair a damp halo of near transparency and Sorrel's shirtsleeves rolled up over her strong arms. A rubber bucket began to fill with muddy bits. Sorrel pushed it along with her foot as Nettie pulled it with her hand. Once the sight might have made Patience melancholy: the solitary nature of her sisters at work. Today, as she stood at the shed door, Patience was grateful that the two were tied to one another. More though, she was so, so sorry that they would need to be.

EVERYTHING HAD GONE so intensely green in Granite Point that the vegetation looked menacing as if Triffids had come to claim the town and its people. Henry had taken a walk, mostly to get away from Sally's temporary nurse replacement who was so eager he'd followed Henry down the hall to the very door of the bathroom before he caught himself and scurried back to the front desk. The gazebo offered Henry shelter from the temperature that rose along with the humidity. The sun had come out, but it was too hot to be anything but painful. By afternoon the drops of water covering every plant would heat to boiling, burning the tender leaves with ragged holes.

Henry sat on the damp bench and ate a tuna sandwich from the Dock, the snack bar on the harbor. He'd looked for Ben, but since his thumb was on the mend, Henry didn't see his friend as much. He was back fishing most days. After Matty's death everyone Henry cared about had drawn together and then scattered. He missed them all. He resolved to go to Patience that evening even if he had to climb the apple tree outside her window. That picture made Henry smile, and he stood to go back and race through his afternoon patients, to get ready for her. He brushed away a ropey wisteria vine that hung over the gazebo opening. It was limp, and the flowers—usually rich with a scent not so sweet as lilac or so sharp as freesia—were gray and slick. Henry lifted his fingers and saw that they were smeared with slime. The vine itself had collapsed under his touch, and he had to shake his whole arm to release it.

He looked around for something to wipe his hand and settled, furtively, on the upright of the gazebo. Henry examined the rest of the wisteria, a particularly robust specimen planted by the Sisters when they started the Nursery and replanted after Hurricane Bill. Over the years it had climbed to cover the small building with a heady scent and outrageously large purple blossoms. Now it clung to the lattice and draped over the walls, borne up only by the woody twisted trunks that snaked out of the ground at the foundation. There wasn't a healthy inch of it left; even Henry could see that. He sniffed at the rot that still stuck to his hand. *Clearly the near constant rain had done something to it,* he thought. Another reason to see Patience. She would want to know, and she would know what to do. Henry rocked back to see the roofline and read the inscription that ran along it: INNOCENT SHE WAS AND SHALL EVER BE.

"If you say so," he muttered as he crossed the green thinking about Ben's story, about Eliza Howard, the first Sparrow healer, the last Sparrow witch.

BY THE TIME the doctor dictated his final notes, tidied the apartment, shaved, and filled his ice trays (Henry had an improbably vigorous hope that Patience would wish to stay with him), it was nearly seven and all he could think of was a gin and tonic with the woman he loved. The tang of juniper and lime seemed to have already washed over his tongue so that he kept swallowing as he drove to Ivy House. He might have walked but, just in case Patience was in the kind of hurry he felt, he wanted a quick getaway. Henry suspected that she needed to get out of Ivy House, to leave behind the cloying care of her sisters. They both needed to fall upon each other in his bed. What is it about men, he thought? Why do we react to death with fervent desire, an extreme affirmation of our existence as we grapple a woman into our arms? Well, that was it, really, he supposed: a declaration of life.

Henry knocked on the big black door, waited a moment, and then went in. He followed the tick of the clock into the kitchen and found it empty and clean, the white sink blinding in the slanting sun. It was hot and as much as Henry had wanted gin, he now craved water. He took a glass off the draining board and filled it, leaning against the sink as he looked out at the garden. He reckoned the Sisters would be home soon; they'd see his car out front and know he'd come for Patience. He could wait.

It was cooler under the apple tree, and Henry was glad he'd moved out of the kitchen. He looked at his watch; after seven and still no Sisters. He'd never known them to go out to dinner, but then, what did he really know about the Sparrows? That rankled, both the lack of knowledge and the idea that they might be out enjoying a meal while he sat hungry, cranky, and sweaty in their garden.

It was Patience who found him. She stood over Henry's sleeping form and resisted the urge to brush his hair out of his eyes. She knew his neck would hurt when he woke; it was cricked so that his chin rested just above his collarbone. She wondered how he could sleep in such an awkward position, how he could sleep in her garden at all.

Henry did wake with a stiff neck. As soon as he lifted his head, he clapped his hand to it and grunted. Patience laughed and squatted down beside him.

"I thought I'd lost you again," Henry said as he blinked up at her.

"That would be careless." Patience held out her hand, and Henry made a show of pulling himself up with a dramatic groan.

"I can't seem to be in the same place with you," he said and gathered her into his arms.

"Come back with me. We'll be careless and forgetful together."

"I'm afraid that's how I got here to begin with," Patience said and turned toward the house. "Are you hungry?" she asked.

Patience made Henry an omelet. She plucked herbs from the garden and chopped a tomato into perfect cubes as he sat at the kitchen table drinking a beer. Patience wasn't hungry, hadn't been for days, but there was comfort in providing for Henry. She hadn't done anything for anyone lately. She was tired of being cared for, being coddled by her sisters as she tried to accept Matty's death. It amazed her that she could say those words, if only in her head. The image of Matty collapsed over himself had almost ceased to make her sick. Almost.

Henry watched Patience as she moved around the kitchen. He leaned back in his chair as she slipped behind him, let his head brush against her hip when she bent to lay his place. When she put his plate before him, he took a bite and closed his eyes with an open-mouthed groan.

"If food be the music of love," Patience said.

"I think you've got that backward," Henry said through a full mouth, his hand held to his lips.

"Really?" Patience smiled.

Henry ate everything, wiping a bit of bread across his plate, picking up the last of the lettuce with his fingers. He wanted to just go on consuming, not food perhaps but the quiet in the kitchen, the cooling shadows that crept through the garden, mostly the long muscles that wrapped around Patience's bare shoulders as she reached up to put away a mixing bowl. He stood and came behind her, felt her give in to him as she came down off her toes.

"Please let me stay," he said.

Patience shook her head and then nodded. "Maybe just for a while."

Henry was so relieved he was light-headed. *I will take what I can get of this woman,* he thought. *When this is over, I will have all of her.*

Henry didn't ask where the Sisters were; Patience would have told him to be quiet if they were near. He never tired of following her down the long hall, the scent of her as he walked behind her. His heart skittered at every step until when they got to her room, he backed her into the bed with graceless urgency. She pulled his shirt over his head and pressed her cheek against his chest. Henry had to raise her by her shoulders to get her to look at him. He sat her on the end of the bed and she put her hands on his hips. When she ran one down over his thigh, he let her. In that moment Henry didn't care what her purpose was. He was aware enough to realize that Patience wanted to reach inside him; she was back to trying to fix him and that was fine. If she pulled every broken bit out of him, straight through his skin, he would not even cry out.

In the end it was Henry who left. Patience didn't need to ask him; he felt her withdraw as a heavy fog moved in from the water, swaddling the house in cold silence. The temperature dropped so fast that Henry felt the scatter of goose bumps as they rose on Patience's arm where it lay across his stomach. He slid out from under her and pulled on his clothes. Patience watched him, and when he bent to kiss her goodnight, she raised her hand in a languid wave. Henry grabbed it for a final squeeze and placed it over her breast before he tiptoed down the stairs. Patience curled into the dark and let her tears fall. She felt the sharp tug of homesickness.

CHAPTER NINE

*Foxglove is not for
the reckless or careless collector*

The medical examiner from Hayward brought the toxicology results to Chief Kelsey by hand. He could have emailed them and sent the text copy with his seal overnight, but Dr. Wilkinson was bored, or perhaps more to the point, he wanted to be in on the action. It was rare to catch a case like this; a child's heart did simply stop now and then, but never had he seen a report like this. Digitalis—the doctor still couldn't believe the level in the kid's blood. He would have had to take more than a few sublingual tabs to hit this toxicity. *He must have gotten into someone's digoxin,* he thought.

"Grandpa should have kept his meds out of reach," Dr. Wilkinson said as he handed over his report.

"There is no grandpa and what meds?" Chief Kelsey replied.

"This boy died of an overdose of digitalis, heart medication. Someone must have been taking it in the house."

"Matty only had his father," Kelsey said. "As far as I know, his heart is fine; it's his liver I'd worry about." He thumbed through the pages of the report. "What am I looking at?" he asked.

"Toxic levels of digitalis in the kid's blood and tissues. It's hard to know if it built up over days or was administered in one go."

"Wait, administered?" Kelsey asked.

"Well, taken then," Dr. Wilkinson said. "Though why a little boy would search out this medication and eat a bunch of bitter little pills is beyond me. Of course, in pediatric cases it's usually given in a syrup, so maybe he took some from a friend."

"Matty didn't have any friends, not kids that is," the chief said. "He spent most all his time with the Sisters and their plant nursery." An ugly thought was settling into Chief Kelsey's mind.

"What is digoxin made of?" he asked.

"It's as old as the hills, folk medicine originally," Dr. Wilkinson said. "Comes from the foxglove plant; that's still the only real source for the cardiac glycoside."

"Oh, shit," said Chief Kelsey.

THE CHIEF PUT the report into a desk drawer and locked it. First he'd stop home for a bite with his wife. Pamela could always steady him. Then he was going to have to get a sample of Patience's foxglove. He wished Sorrel had never pointed out the plant. More than that, he wished he'd never heard her say how poisonous it was.

"What am I going to do?" he asked his wife.

"Joe," Pam said as she sat down at the kitchen table with him. "You know there is an explanation for this that has nothing to do with Patience. There isn't one reason on earth that anything she grows, anything she treats us with, hurt Matty."

"Yeah, maybe, but three of the herbs she admits to using on him showed up in Matty's blood, those and the digitalis. I saw the plants, Pam."

"Admits?" Pam leaned in until her face was level with Joe's bowed head. "Jesus, Joe, you sound like you want to arrest her!"

"I don't want to arrest anybody," he said. "I just want this thing over. I want Rob Short to get help. I want everybody to stop talking about Patience like she's some kind of wicked witch. What I really want," he sighed, "is to get the hell out of Granite Point before we become the next scandal at the supermarket checkout."

"Well, it's probably too late for that, dear," Pam said. "That busybody Ambrose Smith wrote a piece in the *Clarion* claiming Patience threatened to curse Rob Short that day he came to the Nursery."

"Curse? Please, what is wrong with this town?"

"Maybe he wrote poison or hex or something. Doesn't matter, you know how people are. Now he's connected Eliza Howard and Patience Sparrow. He's dug up the old stories, and you're about to give them real wings."

THE *CLARION* STORY did indeed give rumors wings. Ambrose Smith felt duty-bound to report the confrontation between Patience and Rob. He—not unreasonably Ambrose would assure anyone who asked—felt compelled to quote Rob's accusation that Patience had poisoned his boy and Patience's shouted threat to "do something" to Rob too. What that something was fascinated *Clarion* readers. The fact that Patience had visited the police station with Simon Mayo certainly looked damning. Soon enough the talk turned from "what a tragedy" to "that Patience Sparrow was always a little off." If Ambrose Smith didn't have a tape recorder with him, it was no trouble for that nameless tourist to share the shaky video he shot with his phone.

In the same thoughtless way that Pamela Kelsey tossed around the words "hex" and "curse," so the video flew around. First it made the rounds in town, then its flight widened and a game of Chinese whispers began to take shape. Telephones rang, beer drinkers at Doyle's nodded when anyone asked, "Did you see . . . ?" The words "threaten" and "nasty" started following Patience's name. The bank manager came home at lunch and rummaged around the kitchen looking for Sparrow remedies. When his wife walked in, he got a little shouty.

This is what transpired in other kitchens, on other porches and during dinner as husbands and fathers questioned their wives about what the hell they'd been giving the family all this time. And the women shouted right back, defending their healer, their friend Patience Sparrow. It did no good.

In Hayward the county prosecutor Paul Hutchins watched the video on the *Clarion*'s website, then he Googled Patience Sparrow to see what came up. The first hit was the video, over and over, from YouTube to Salem's Plot, the website his wife sent to him. She called it "Witchy-Poo.com" and made fun of small-town superstitions. He couldn't imagine where she'd heard of the ridiculous thing because he didn't know that Linda Hutchins had driven to see Patience six months before when their baby was so colicky his mother wanted to leave him in a basket at the church. Eager-beaver prosecutor Hutchins didn't know that the sudden peace and quiet that swept through their house was all due to Patience. What he did know was that this Granite Point scandal could *be* something . . . and his chance to be something, too.

Well, he'd just have to head down to the seaside and have a bit of a day trip. If nothing else, Paul Hutchins thought, I'll bring home some lobster for dinner.

THERE ARE ALL sorts of regulations about accusing someone of a crime. There are laws and statutes and personal rights and just plain old common sense and courtesy. Somewhere between Matty's death and the video of the scene at the Nursery all those rules and any shred of civility collapsed. Maybe it was because the weather had been so dodgy, and locals and tourists were tiring of jigsaw puzzles, napping, reading, and the one movie theater. Or it could have been a result of the arguments simmering in so many households, the face-off that seemed to pit one part of the town against the other on the subject of Patience's guilt or innocence, her healing abilities or her rather questionable behavior over the years. When Paul Hutchins arrived that muggy morning to speak with Chief Kelsey, even he felt the tension; he didn't need to scent the air to know that this town was straining to live up to the pretty postcards for sale in the drugstore.

KELSEY AND HUTCHINS sat down over coffee at Baker's Way Bakers. A mistake since no one recognized the guy in the suit with the chief and everyone started positing theories.

"I'm not going to mess around with a grand jury," Hutchins said. "We just need a complaint to get a warrant to bring her in. File an affidavit that states this Sparrow woman's role in the Short kid's death. All you have to do is show probable cause then boom, catch, question, and maybe, maybe release," Hutchins whispered. "That's the way to go for now. You follow the rules; you demonstrate that you take the crime seriously; you get to be the good guy."

"Christ, you think I'm going to be the good guy? Besides, I did question her," Kelsey said. "With the tox report in I can go back to ask about digitalis, but that's about it." The horrible thing was that the chief knew that one more visit to Ivy House was unavoidable, and it wouldn't be a chat this time. Hutchins's presence had kicked the investigation up.

"You have to establish that she grows the stuff, that she knows how dangerous it is, that the little boy could have easily gotten hold of it on her watch. This isn't some cozy little town mystery anymore, chief. This could be a murder investigation, if only because the silly girl got caught threatening the boy's father."

"She didn't threaten him, for God's sake. She was pissed off and hurting. They both were, are."

"It was a stupid admission of culpability whether Patience Sparrow meant it or not."

Chief Kelsey used his thumb to dab up the rest of the muffin crumbs on his plate. Even in his state he couldn't leave Claire's baked goods alone. He pointed at Hutchins's cookie.

"You going to eat that?" he asked.

"Listen, Kelsey," Hutchins said as he pushed the cookie over. "Do not let this blow up in your face. Get out in front. I want this case to be handled right. We can get her in on the father's accusations. I can talk with Rob Short to make a formal complaint to me, convince him to work with us on this."

"All I wanted was to ask her about the digitalis," Kelsey said. "There is no way I think she poisoned the kid."

"I don't care what you think. I only care what the law says." Hutchins hunched in close. "If she knew this kid was a mess, if she even suspected he was a danger to himself, or, say she thought he'd be better dead than with the useless dad, or if she told him that digitalis was poisonous, or if she didn't but knew he could get some, we might be able to get her on negligent manslaughter. You file the complaint, I'll get the warrant."

"We don't even know for sure that's where the stuff came from, the Nursery, I mean," Kelsey said with no conviction. "Why is this so important to you, counselor? What's your angle?"

"Look, I'm just doing my job. Don't make me get someone in here to do yours."

Hutchins followed the chief back to the station and took down the affidavit himself. He felt only a tiny bit remorseful about being so forceful with the guy. But now he could get the mournful dad on board.

CHAPTER TEN

Rue is a reliable remedy for nervous nightmare

*P*atience Sparrow," Chief Kelsey said, his words formal, his voice shaking, "you are under arrest for negligent manslaughter in the death of Matthew Short."

Patience didn't hear her Miranda warning although she stood calmly as the chief had to read it off a little card—that's how infrequently anything really bad happened in Granite Point. It was early, and the Sisters were still vague with sleep. Patience's mind had already flown off in search of comfort. In her head she was at the Nursery, wandering amidst her plants, pressing labels to her bottles, pinching flowers from their stems. The two policemen actually smelled basil and lavender as they led

Patience down Ivy House's steps to the car. The deputy thought he tasted mint as he licked his lips and gently bowed Patience's head to get her into the backseat. Even Chief Kelsey detected the scent of tarragon rising from her wrists as he snapped the handcuffs shut.

He'd been advised by the prosecutor to follow the book. "You don't want any holes in this," Hutchins had said. Kelsey and the deputy flinched at the metallic click, but their quarry was as still as water. Patience Sparrow was gone long before the car pulled away from Ivy House.

It was Sorrel who called Simon Mayo this time. Nettie called Ben, and Ben called Henry. Simon was at the house before the Sisters were dressed; he wanted to see them before he went to Patience. He sat in the kitchen, drinking coffee he made himself, and waited. True to form, Nettie was more than a little frantic, and Sorrel sat so stiffly in her chair that Simon was afraid to put a mug into her hand, afraid she'd splinter into pieces.

"Listen," he said. "I'm going to head to the station as soon as I make sure you guys are all right. You're both to stay by the phone, but don't talk to anyone but me." He looked from one sister to the other. "Are you hearing me?" They nodded.

"I will get Patience out and home." Simon left his cup on the table, and the Sisters heard his Mercedes pull away with a screech.

Chief Kelsey sat at his desk with his own cup of coffee. He refused to look down the hall toward the holding tank. He refused to think of Patience as he'd left her, sitting on the metal shelf that served as a bench and a bunk, her hands clasped so tightly her knuckles bulged white against her freckles. She'd come to the door of Ivy House barefoot. The chief hadn't noticed that she'd come along to the station that way. He found a pair of socks in his bottom desk drawer (*Why do I have socks?* he thought) and tossed them through the bars when she didn't respond to his voice. He didn't want her to be barefoot in the cell; he could only imagine the Sisters' reaction to that. And now he looked at the arrest report on his computer screen, the cursor blinking beside her name: Impatiens Sparrow. None of the Sisters had middle names; it was enough that their first names were so remarkable.

Simon Mayo slammed through the front door of the police station with such force that even Patience raised her head in her cell. Chief Kelsey looked up expecting the Sisters; he thought their anger must be a flammable thing by now. But it was Simon who was so furious he'd ignored his untucked shirt, the whiskers on his jaw. Normally Simon was hyper aware of his appearance as if starched shirts, Hermès ties, and knife-creased trousers somehow mitigated the fact that he was, indeed, a country lawyer. But today he was like a half-open drawer spilling haste, distress, and yes, fury.

"Christ, Joe!" he said. "What the hell is going on?"

"It looks like something at the Nursery could be behind the boy's death." Chief Kelsey wanted to whisper, but he forced himself to speak with confidence, the last thing he felt.

"How did you get a warrant so fast?" Simon asked.

"Rob Short filed a complaint. I swore an affidavit."

"You?" Simon was shocked. "You know Patience. This is extreme, Joe!"

"There is enough evidence: the foxglove, the fact that Matty spent so much time around her, her blowup with Rob Short. County got into it. We had to bring her in."

Hot shame washed over the chief. What had happened at that coffee shop? Did that ferret of a prosecutor railroad him?

"I want her out," Simon said.

"Not till tomorrow, bail."

"You really charged her?" Simon was aghast.

"Negligent manslaughter," he said, as if unintentional death made Matty less dead, Patience less arrested.

"Good God, Chief, you can't honestly think she gave him a poisonous plant? You can't believe she'd ever let him near one! She's treated your wife, your granddaughter Sarah. Remember her hornet sting?" Simon's face went slack with disbelief. "This charge can't stand. Let me see her."

The chief gestured toward the two cells. "Let's go," he said.

He led Simon down the hall and unlocked the cell door. Patience was where he'd left her; feet still bare, the socks in a ball on the floor. Simon shot him a look that was, frankly, one Joe Kelsey felt he deserved. The case was far from airtight. He could blame Rob Short for starting it with his stink, and he did. Then the damn video, and the shit spread around about a town that let some delusional Wiccan wannabe get away with murder. Chief Kelsey had to do something, or Hutchins would have. He'd rather it be his circus, but he wanted to have some small hand in protecting Patience.

If Patience had turned inward and still when they came for her, she was absolutely present now. Her skin looked as gray as the walls, her hair as stringy and limp as the mop that stood in a corner just outside the cell. She shook in erratic bursts. It was a wonder she hadn't thrown up.

Simon waited until Kelsey left before he knelt down in front of Patience and gently rolled the socks over her cold feet.

"P," he said. "I'll get you out of this, but you must do everything I tell you, okay?"

He got no response. Simon sat down beside her on the hard shelf. *Shit,* he thought, *this is really bad.* Thunder moved over the building, and Simon heard the first slap of another storm throw itself against the windows. Patience didn't raise her eyes until he told her she'd be in overnight. At that she gave him such a desperate look that Simon clutched her hands, and she let him. He turned them over to see that her fingertips were stained, her nails black, not with soil but with ink. For Simon this was the moment he truly committed.

"They think I hurt Matty," she said. Patience couldn't bring herself to say "killed." "I thought I did, too, at first." Simon shushed her.

"You can't ever say that, you can't think it," he hissed. "You must stay absolutely silent when I am not with you."

Patience nodded and pulled her feet up, floppy in the huge socks and heartrendingly childlike.

"Now, tell me what you know. Tell me what you can't tell anyone else." Simon took out his pad.

"I don't know anything," Patience said. "We loved Matty. He was so happy with us." She pushed her hair behind her ears. "Henry was going to take Matty on. He was going to fix everything."

"I think we should leave that aside for now," Simon said. "Let's look at you. Why would Rob single you out? Why is he so sure you hurt Matty?"

Patience flinched. "When his father didn't take care, I did," she said. "I gave him remedies. I did. That's no secret." She looked up at Simon. "It's the foxglove, that's what Chief Kelsey keeps asking about. Is this my fault?" she asked.

"No!" Simon said. "You've done nothing wrong. There are plenty of dangers in this world, plenty of ways for kids to get hurt. You will be exonerated. This"—he waved his arms around the cell—"all of this is because Rob knows he neglected Matty. He's terrified and guilty as hell that he couldn't look after his own child. And Kelsey's been hypnotized by that ADA from Hayward."

Patience put her head down on her knees. Simon saw a tear drop onto her sock and nearly groaned.

"Matty took care of his father, you know," she said. "He was always asking me for something to mend his broken heart."

"Rob Short hasn't been the same since his wife died, and that's sad but it is no excuse for ignoring Matty or accusing you."

"I want to go home," she whispered.

"And you will." Simon squeezed her hands. "I promise."

"Don't let my sisters see me here," she said.

Simon nodded and stood. "I'm going back to them now. Everything will be fine. I'll be here first thing tomorrow," he said and called out for Chief Kelsey.

Patience lay against the wall and listened to the men talk as they left her. They were arguing about the wisdom of keeping her in the cell. The chief actually admitted that he worried about the effect her arrest might have on, as he said, "You know, things." She couldn't hear how Simon responded. She was surprised that he'd come to her, and she was so thankful that she smiled for the first time since she was arrested.

The rain got harder and harder, the wind kicked up, and before Chief Kelsey came back with a bottle of water and a sandwich for Patience, the hundred-year-old elm in front of the post office had pulled straight out of the ground, its roots heaving the sidewalk into the air with an audible, chilling crack.

THE SISTERS, BEN, and Henry had gathered in the kitchen again. Sorrel had to close the back door to keep the water out. Already the gravel paths swam in a blurry ribbon through the garden. Sorrel worried vaguely about the dahlias, and Nettie might have gone out to cut the cilantro before it was flattened, but the storm frightened her. It was nearly dark at three o'clock, and Ben had twice touched Nettie's shoulder to settle her as the lightning flashed white against the windows. Her neck and chest were covered with angry red blotches. Ben so wanted to lay his hand against one to soothe her. Instead, he laced his fingers behind his back and waited.

Simon didn't bother to knock and came straight through to the kitchen. When he saw Sorrel, he took her in his arms. Henry saw how her neck, long like Patience's, curved until her forehead rested on Simon's shoulder. They stepped apart, and Simon held up his hands as if he expected a flurry of questions.

"Okay, she's in until tomorrow."

Nettie gasped, and Ben leaned toward her, his hands still clasped.

"I know, it's bad, for everyone, but this is a crap charge, I told the chief that, and I'll get it dismissed before it gets to a grand jury or anyone even says the word trial."

"You've just said it," Sorrel murmured. She stood with her back against the tall cupboard that Clarissa had originally used for her remedies. It smelled of white pepper and lavender, crocus stamens and dry mustard. Simon and Sorrel looked at each other and, even Ben could see that whatever they might have meant to each other, whatever they were now, Sorrel trusted Simon. Henry had to trust him, too. There was absolutely nothing he could do for Patience. He still felt disoriented from Ben's call telling him Patience was gone, from his inability to get to her. He'd wanted to go to the police department and demand that his love be brought to him. He imagined Patience in a cell, trembling with cold. For some reason, he pictured her in his boxers, already suffering from scurvy or rickets. His fingers curled into fists at the thought of her vulnerability. Henry acknowledged that even his thoughts were useless.

"There is nothing to do except bring Patience some clothing," Simon said.

Oh, God, Henry thought, *she* is *in my boxers.*

"She's got no shoes, and a pair of sweatpants would keep her warmer than her jeans."

Sorrel looked at Henry: his groan had been too loud.

"I'll bring them," he said.

"No!" Sorrel snapped. "She belongs to us." Ben and Henry gaped at her, but Simon shook his head.

"Henry should do that," he said. "It'll be good for the town to see that her boyfriend—a doctor—hasn't abandoned her."

Everyone began talking at once. Ben offered to go with Henry, Sorrel complained that Henry wasn't family, Simon told Ben no, and finally, Nettie gave a piercing whistle through her fingers. Only Sorrel didn't flinch.

"All of you stop," Nettie said. "We are going to follow Simon's instructions to the letter. If he says jump, we say how high."

Ben and Sorrel laughed weakly and nodded.

"So, I'll get Patience's things, and Simon and Henry can drive over." Nettie walked to the back stairs and turned. "I think you're both safe out there," she said pointing at the rain, "but the rest of the town had better watch out."

It was a vicious storm, but Henry didn't care; he was too eager to see Patience. Nettie had packed Patience's clothes and something to read—*The Compleat Herb Book*. Henry thought she should have a complete fiction book instead. The book never made it into the cell anyway. Sorrel snatched it with a pointed look and tossed it back on the hall table. Simon led the way in his car, and they pulled into the small parking lot behind the police station, an equally small brick building with the town seal over the door: a schooner flanked by two mermaids. Henry remembered how charming he'd thought it was when Patience pointed it out, explaining that Granite Point had such a long record of fishermen coming home safe that in 1827 the mermaids had been added to the seal. Some years later, George Sparrow would be lost at sea. Now the mermaids leered at him ferociously as if to say, *We've claimed her, good luck getting her back.*

Patience looked as unhealthy as anything to Henry. Even when she was cross and obstinate, there was always something nourishing about her. But here was a woman who had pressed herself so tightly into the corner where the metal bunk met the wall that she looked like rags.

Simon waited a few yards down the hall with the chief, who had examined the clothes as if they were themselves a threat, before he passed them back to Henry. Kelsey allowed Henry into the cell only because the police chief was starting to worry about getting home in the weather, concerned that if Patience got agitated, he'd be stuck at the station or knocked out by a falling branch. He wanted to settle Patience before he passed her on to his deputy. He understood that Henry could do that.

Henry sat beside Patience, and she moved the clothes onto her lap.

"This is a really big mistake," she said, loud enough for the men in the hall to lift their heads. Henry heard an echo of the old Patience and put his arm around her shoulder, drawing her closer. He stuck his nose into her hair and realized it was wet, as if all her tears had gathered there.

Patience stripped her jeans off and wriggled into the sweats. She pulled her heavy hair into the elastic Nettie had wound around her brush. She looked at Henry. "I don't have my glasses," she said.

"I do." Henry pulled them out of his shirt pocket. He reached into his pants pocket and produced a toothbrush, toothpaste, and her contact lens case.

"Oh," Patience said as she folded her hand over his. "You are wonderful."

"I am," Henry agreed. "And I'm right here no matter what happens."

But then Chief Kelsey came back and told Henry to leave. Henry held Patience's hand and nodded witlessly, trying to communicate that everything would be all right. He and Simon changed places, and Henry followed Kelsey out to the office. There were two other officers at desks, and both looked up when Henry appeared.

"Take his statement," the chief said to one of them.

As they asked Henry where he'd been the night Matty died, if Patience had been with him the entire time, if he had ever seen her give Matty any of her remedies, Henry began to realize how very much trouble Patience was in. Because, although he hadn't seen the remedies pass from Patience to Matty, had in fact never seen Patience dose anybody—even during Sally's labor Henry couldn't say he'd watched Patience administer anything—Henry knew she had given both of them something. She never hid that fact. *What does that mean?* he thought. *Am I a suspect, too? An accessory?* But then he thought that in order to be those things, Patience had to be guilty, and Henry swallowed the bile at the back of his throat.

Simon came through some minutes into Henry's interview and gave both the officer and the chief such a poisonous look that Joe Kelsey pulled up a chair and gestured for Simon to sit.

"Clearly you want to be in on this," he said as Simon dropped his briefcase and sat.

"Clearly you thought I didn't need to be," Simon said. "There is absolutely nothing in this whole procedure that feels right, Joe, and you know it."

After that the questions were not so disturbing, more nonspecific and less dangerous to Patience. If nothing else, everyone now knew that Patience had spent that night in Henry's bed. Within minutes Simon had Henry by the arm and was leading him out of the building. Every step Henry took away from Patience sickened him.

"They will try to connect you two through Patience's work,

make it seem as if you helped her," Simon said. "I want to make sure they can't. That will only make her look as if her moves were intentional. You need to tell me everything."

Henry admitted that he hadn't really credited Patience's remedies, not until he began to fall in love. By the time that happened, he believed everything she did was extraordinary whether it involved a salve made from cider vinegar, dark green drops from passiflora, or the way she curved her hand around his neck when she reached up to kiss him.

"That's good, that's fine," Simon said. "If you thought the stuff was harmless, if she didn't ask you about conventional medicine, as a doctor or colleague, it goes a long way to show-ing that she couldn't have poisoned Matty."

Henry thought about how they'd planned to be colleagues to save Matty, but he said nothing.

"My God, Simon, how is this happening?" Henry leaned on the hood of his car and bent over until his head hung. He noticed the rain dripping off his hair, onto his hands; he was soaked, and he didn't care. A few shoppers wandered the side-walks looking to buy something to make the wet day worth-while. Henry's display qualified.

Simon nudged Henry's leg with his own. "Stand up," he said. "I don't want them to see you upset."

A cluster of three or four people had paused to watch as Henry fell apart. He thought he recognized a patient, and the older man was definitely the cantankerous guy who ran the news shop. Henry straightened up and shook Simon's hand.

"Thank you," he said. "Will you come for her tomorrow?"

"Yes," Simon said and headed for his own car. "I'll bring her to Ivy House as soon as possible, but I suggest you wait till the evening to see her. She'll need to be on her own with the Sisters. They'll know what to do."

"I have patients," Henry said. "I can't, I don't know . . . what about Sam? He's good for her, could he . . . ?"

"Sam cannot be involved," Simon interrupted. "He was first on the scene. He can't get near Patience now."

So there it was. Henry and the Sisters were in charge of Patience. And Simon. Henry was certain that the lawyer had taken on a burnished look with his new responsibility; his eyes seemed brighter, more alert and aware, ready to ply his trade and save them all.

In the event, there was no one who could save Patience from her own town.

IT HAD BEEN a remarkably dry summer before Matty died so at first Granite Point welcomed the rain. It turned the greensward lush and fragrant as it rolled along in an unconscious echo of Big Point Bay beyond the harbor. But rain was one thing, the persistent deluge quite another. Small deep ponds had settled around the town green, and large ragged strips of lawn had buckled and shrugged, turning up at the edges so that the dark soil was exposed. Earthworms struggled to release themselves from the thick mud only to drop into the water and drown. Henry had forgotten to tell Patience about the wisteria, so no red flags had been raised with the Sisters, but the piles of rotting vines and flowers around the gazebo had already started the talk.

The storm that came in as Patience was charged and herded into the little jail finally blew out to sea after a full day of punishment. It was strangely quiet on the morning of her appearance before the magistrate judge. Brackish water lingered at every street corner, and leaves stuck to the roads and footpaths, making them treacherous and sending cars and people skidding in frantic pinwheels around town. The sky was low and gray, as bruised and damaged as Patience. A new front threatened before the day was out. The whole town smelled of salt-water muck. The elm that had been torn out of the ground still lay across the road; one of Kelsey's deputies had to direct traffic with white gloves and a paddle. He was humiliated and anxious to get back to real work so he could watch Patience Sparrow fight for bail. You never know—there could be real excitement and here he'd be, kicking shattered branches and muddy roots to the curb.

As it turned out, the judge who had issued her arrest warrant (with Paul Hutchins's encouragement) had left on vacation after doing so. It was summer, after all, his assistant pointed out. What she didn't add was that the judge's wife had heard about his action. Being an occasional and satisfied Sparrow customer, she threatened him with various unpleasant consequences if he presided over the bail hearing or anything else to do with the Sisters. A locum tenens was called in to hear the charges and set bail, or not. Simon Mayo didn't know whether to be pleased or concerned by the upheaval as he stood with Chief Kelsey waiting for Patience to change into the clothes he had brought her. Maybe a judge unfamiliar with the brewing gossip would be more likely to see how impossible the charge was.

The Sisters had insisted on coming, but they didn't go back to see Patience. They sat together on the bench facing the little bullpen. Ben Avellar sat with them, and both he and Nettie found their hands straying toward each other until, by the third time, Ben just grabbed Nettie's and set their clasped fists between them.

Simon brought Patience out. She was neatly dressed in fresh linen trousers and a white long-sleeved shirt. Thanks to Henry, her teeth were brushed, her lenses in, and she'd pulled her hair back into a low coil. Sorrel and Nettie stood in silence. Sorrel handed Patience a pair of sunglasses to cover her still-injured eye, and Ben followed Simon to the door. They were headed for the courthouse. Only Simon and Ben could see the crowd that had gathered outside. For God's sake, Simon thought, don't these people have to be at the beach or something? But of course, it was an ugly day and the tourists and locals alike had drifted into town in search of distraction. They found it. As the little group moved out to the chief's car, Kelsey gestured for a couple of patrolmen to make a path. Patience looked at the sunglasses in her hand and then at Sorrel.

"I don't know," Sorrel said. "They seemed like the thing this morning."

Patience shook her head. "This is completely ridiculous," she said. They stood at the door for a moment longer, looking at the milling crowd. "I mean, no one really thinks I could hurt anybody, never Matty, right?" There were nods all around. "So I'm not worried, and you shouldn't be either." Everyone, including Patience, smiled hideously.

"That's my Patience," Simon said. "Pay no attention to these assholes, and we'll be in and out in no time. There is no way the new judge will uphold the arrest."

With that everyone felt hopeful and, as if they were chained at the ankle, Patience, Chief Kelsey, and Simon shuffled to the car. At first, Patience thought she was being cheered, and she almost laughed. *Really,* she thought, *people have way too much time on their hands in this town.* But then she got a look at the face of a man standing just behind the officer nearest the car. His eyes were narrowed and his mouth turned down in a thin peel. *Has he ever been to the Nursery, has someone he loves come to me?* Patience wondered. *Is he local?* But then she was in the car, and Joe Kelsey was reminding her to stand up straight and make eye contact with the judge.

"Why are you doing this?" she asked.

Kelsey had to twist around in the front seat to answer. "I'm only doing my job, and while the evidence may point to your plants, Patience, none of us feels good about our part."

"So you don't believe I had anything to do with this horrible thing, but you arrested me anyway?" Patience asked. "You have to know how much I cared about Matty." The little bravado she'd scared up had been spent on her sisters. She felt fresh tears coming, but with the handcuffs on she could only tilt her head back to keep them away.

"I have to follow all the steps. You're in the system. It's out of my hands now."

The Granite Point courthouse was four blocks on, past the middle school and the A&P. The only reason the town even had a courthouse—in this case only a large high-ceilinged room that smelled like a schoolroom and a suite of offices in the town hall—was because Granite Point had briefly been the county seat. Hayward outstripped Granite Point, but the little harbor town kept the court apparatus and now it would see its first activity other than traffic or real estate disputes and civil marriages or uncivil divorces since the late nineteenth century. The little clump of ghouls had no trouble following the police car through town and now stood in almost identical order in front of the town hall. Chief Kelsey, being a husband and father and sick about all this, felt for his passenger. He directed the car around to the back so that Patience ended up meeting her destiny by way of a driver's ed class. Kelsey threw his rain jacket over her hands as she stumbled past four surprised teenagers and her old chemistry teacher.

Chief Kelsey removed the cuffs as soon as Patience was in the courtroom. Because she was the only defendant appearing that day, the judge was already staring at her from the bench. Judge Adams hadn't expected the folding chairs behind the attorneys' tables to be occupied, but word had spread, and there was a shifting clot of people just behind the defendant's family. The Sparrow Sisters—he never could keep the girls straight, certainly not the twins. Well, here they were; he would have to keep them straight today.

Henry had closed his office for the afternoon, disconcerting his temp and feeding the rumor mill with the finest grist, heartbreak. Now he sat beside Ben and tried not to look worried. The audience shifted and murmured as Patience was led in. This interested the old man with the gavel, and he banged it energetically.

Thomas Adams was semiretired. He had lived all his life in the twenty-two-mile area around Hayward. This was the stretch that included the ocean beach at Granite Point, the bay beaches abutting Old Hayward, and the farms that lay along the railroad tracks. Although he went to law school in Cambridge (one never said Harvard—that would be boastful), Judge Adams returned to his hometown of Wewanett and worked his way through both the system and his family until he could retire. Now he filled in for the three judges in the area in the summer months. He told his wife it was because crime doesn't take a holiday, but really it was because he was overwhelmed by the tide of grandchildren that filled the house from June until Labor Day. Being called to Granite Point should have been a pleasant diversion, not for the defendant or the victim, but for Thomas Adams as he recalled his own summers in the ocean so near. But the weather was foul, and he'd had to ask for a second cup of coffee to wake him. The rain was just too soporific as it drummed down on the flat roof.

Judge Adams looked at Patience Sparrow. There was a story to her, more than the one unfolding now, but he couldn't quite recall it. Perhaps his wife would remember; she still kept up with local families. He opened the folder on the bench, glanced at the charges, and every breath of sleep went right out of him: negligent manslaughter, a child. If this woman killed her child in some wanton manner, he really would be embarrassed by small-town life. He read further. What kind of woman was this? A practitioner of what: remedies, herbs, and tinctures? And, as he saw now, she was the youngest Sparrow. Yes, this was the trouble, no mother to raise her, that much he knew about Patience. He scanned the room. The two lawyers looked at him and then at each other. Judge Adams watched the people who had stopped their day to sit in his courtroom. He narrowed his eyes to look at Patience. She swallowed a gasp. She was frightened of Judge Adams.

It had been years since the judge had seen something this serious, never mind the preliminary hearing to come. He scanned the papers again as the woman and her lawyer stood uncertainly. Whatever this thing turned out to be, there was no way in hell he'd find an impartial jury should it go to trial. It seemed like half the town was crowded into the courtroom; the other half was probably leaning across counters and car hoods talking about it. This would have to be his judgment, his ruling, his reading of the law, and his conscience as he considered whether Patience Sparrow should face a grand jury.

The county prosecutor cleared his throat once, twice, and finally the judge looked up.

"Your Honor, the charge is negligent manslaughter." He raised his voice on the word "manslaughter." "The community is troubled, and rightly so, by the suspect's access to the Sparrow Sisters Nursery and its contents. She is, by the very nature of the charge, a danger to the community. We ask that you deny bail."

Patience looked at Simon, who put his hand on her arm.

"And you?" Judge Adams said to the defense.

"Your Honor, I am Simon Mayo, attorney for the defendant. This is not a capital charge, and Patience Sparrow has lived in Granite Point, as have I, all her life. She has a business, not some secret garden, sisters who depend on her, she is certainly not a flight risk, and since we will enter a plea of not guilty . . ." He stopped. "In fact, we haven't had a chance to plead."

"You're a Mayo," Judge Adams said. "I went to law school with your father."

"Oh," Simon said, "I see." But he couldn't see if this was a good or a bad thing. What if they'd hated each other at Harvard? One on law review, the other denied? One got the girl, the other a broken heart?

"How do you plead?" Judge Adams turned his gaze on Patience. His eyes were sharp and clear. He would not be easy to charm.

"Not guilty, Your Honor," she whispered.

"Again," he snapped, and Patience said it again.

"Back to bail, sir," Hutchins said. "We are talking about the death of a child here. This may be a small town, but it is mere hours from a major airport."

"Come on," Simon said. "I'd be surprised if she had a passport."

Patience frowned. "I do, actually," she said quietly. "Sorrel made me get one." Simon went still, resisting the urge to kick her foot under the table.

"Your Honor, please," Simon continued. "There is no evidence of any value, no motive, only a regretful, neglectful father who has focused his guilty grief on the only good thing in his son's life. If there is any crime here, it is the father's."

"Objection!" the prosecutor snapped. "This is not about Robert Short."

"Quiet," Judge Adams said. "As for evidence, that remains to be seen." He steepled his hands and looked over them at the Sisters. He noticed that the chairs had now completely filled with people. Rows of faces were turned to him: expectant, alight with excitement.

"I will set bail at two hundred thousand dollars." There was a ripple of amazement from the observers. The Sisters were stunned by the amount, the prosecutor pleased. Simon Mayo just shook his head.

"If Miss Sparrow is as humble as you say, counselor, that number is beyond her bank account, and she will remain in custody." Judge Adams turned to the prosecutor. "If Mr. Short is as devastated by his son's death as *you* say, Mr. Hutchins, why is he not in this room fighting for justice?"

Paul Hutchins stuttered as he tried to think of a way to spin Rob Short's drunken absence. "Mr. Short is ill," he said at last. "He has been unable to leave his house practically since the murder."

"Objection!" shouted Simon. "The charge is not murder."

"You can't object to Mr. Hutchins answering my direct question, Mr. Mayo." Judge Adams nodded to the policeman who served as the occasional bailiff.

Patience was led away again. Shock turned her face pale and mask-like. To the spectators she looked unmoved. She eased into the car as gently as she could. She felt skinned by the judge as he eyed her with contempt. Now even Chief Kelsey couldn't meet her gaze. He was stunned too; he didn't believe Patience was guilty, not really, and he had naturally assumed that the judge would take one look at Rob Short and toss the whole thing out. But Rob Short wasn't there. Which left Patience in front of a near stranger who had no reason at all to believe in her.

ALL THE WAY home the Sisters argued with Simon about how to pay the bail.

"We'll use Ivy House," Sorrel said, and Nettie agreed.

"No," Simon said. "You can't, it's your home."

"Patience isn't going to flee, Simon," Sorrel said. "Besides, do you have a better idea? A secret Mayo fund for the wrongly accused, perhaps?"

Simon just shook his head.

"I can't put the money up," he said. "It would be a conflict of interest down the line."

"What about the Nursery?" Nettie asked.

"How much is it worth?" Simon asked Sorrel.

"Not very much as a business without us, but the land . . ." She trailed off.

"None of this should matter," Nettie said. "We do what we have to and find the money. Patience is innocent. This will all be over, and we'll go back to the way we were."

"Oh, Nettie." Sorrel sighed.

When they pulled up at Ivy House, Ben was pacing the sidewalk.

"They're searching Henry's place," he said before Simon turned off the engine.

"How can they do that?" Nettie asked.

"The judge must have issued a warrant, given that Henry's the only doctor in town, Matty's doctor of record. You'll be next," Simon said as he opened Sorrel's door. "Is there anything I need to know?"

Sorrel frowned. "How can you ask that?"

Nevertheless, the Sisters led Simon into Patience's room. He looked around at the bed, neatly made by Nettie, the stack of books by her chair, and the sundress hanging on the back of the door. He walked down the hall to the bathroom but stopped at the door to Sorrel's room. He drew in a breath when he saw her nightgown draped across the foot of her bed, her hairbrush on top of that. In the bathroom he opened the medicine cabinet and shifted the items around. Simon didn't know what he was looking for, and he hoped he wouldn't find it. He stood with his hands on the sink until he heard Ben call his name.

"Simon," Ben yelled from the foot of the stairs, "they're here."

It was Nettie's turn to feel sick. Three policemen split up, two downstairs and one up. The officer squeezed by Sorrel awkwardly, and she stared him down.

"Who's out catching bad guys?" Sorrel growled, and Simon shook his head. "Oh, sorry, I mean who's directing traffic?" she asked.

Ben followed the cop through the living room, the formal dining room—which was so seldom used it was as dusty as Nettie ever let anything get in Ivy House—the library that Thaddeus Sparrow had filled with travel books and several antique globes. He had hoped to convince the Sisters to leave Granite Point, find another place to call home, another way to live. In the end all the library did was give Marigold a place to die, her sisters somewhere to grieve.

Officer Fancy came into the kitchen. Ben started to get nervous as the policeman reached for the tall cupboard door. Of course, he told himself, there was nothing in *that* cupboard, and the one at the Nursery had already been searched. Still, as Ben watched the man open it, watched how the smells that came out affected the young cop, saw the slight flutter of his lashes as he inhaled, Ben was relieved. He could tell that whatever was in the cupboard—and truthfully, it was nothing more than the ingredients the Sisters used every day as they fed one another—it was enough to distract the cop. Martin Fancy closed the door and turned toward the garden, his mind still less than present. If Ben had asked him what he was thinking as he drifted to the screen door and paused with his hand splayed against it, Martin would have told him that the smell of cumin and coriander seed reminded him of his grandmother and the gentle curry she made whenever he or his brothers caught cold. He and Patience had always gotten along, even way back in grade school. It was the warmth of that memory that had made him close his eyes as he searched the cupboard shelves for some item that looked out of place. He couldn't see a thing; he didn't want to.

Henry Carlyle had not been quite so polite when the chief handed him a search warrant. He seethed as the same policemen had scattered through his apartment. The office had already been covered when Chief Kelsey took away Matty Short's records. Such a small place, and the three additional men made it feel like a clown car; they spilled out of one small room after another until, in Henry's bedroom, one of them lifted up the quilt Patience had left him and stood still for a moment, his eyes slightly glazed as he looked out the window. Henry remembered how he and Patience had fallen asleep on that quilt in the backyard, a bowl of blackberries turned over between them, dark juice staining their lips and fingertips.

"Hey!" Henry said and reached for the quilt. "Come on."

"I'm sorry, doctor, but this is what a search entails." This from a cop who Henry had seen only the week before for a virulent stomach bug he'd caught from his toddler. He'd actually held his crew-cut head as he heaved into a basin in his office. Now this same guy was holding Henry's bed linen, touching things Patience had touched, kneeling on places where Patience had lain in his arms.

The cop put the quilt back on the bed and said, "It could use a clean."

Now it can, thought Henry. Now everything is dirty.

After they rummaged through his kitchen and made a record of his pain meds, gave him a respectful nod when they found his medals, Henry was left alone. He picked up for a while, but was suddenly so exhausted that he lay down on his bed and pulled the quilt around him. The storms had left the air heavy and wet. Henry was chilled now that he'd changed out of his courtroom suit. He thought he might actually be able to sleep, a state that had eluded him for days now. He closed his eyes, knowing he should be doing something to help Patience, but he couldn't come up with a thing, nor could he come up with the energy. Pain simmered beneath the skin on his leg and there was a constant cramp in his calf from his limp. Henry rolled over until he was on Patience's side of the bed and swore in frustration.

Henry decided that he needed to get out; at least his office would be free of Patience memories. He'd already rescheduled patients for the day, and he knew the temp would be in a lather over the mud the policemen had left in the waiting room. If he couldn't be with her, he might as well work. Henry unwrapped the quilt and sat up. *I can't wash this,* he thought. *It still smells of Patience.* And it did, as clean and fresh as her skin when Henry pressed his face into her shoulder. Henry rubbed the fabric between his fingers. The ivy ran along in loopy tangles, and the violets were scattered across the surface in a purple wave. *Like her curtains,* he thought, and drew it closer. The deep green of the leaves seemed almost three-dimensional, picked out as they were by tiny hand stitches, and the purple petals felt silky beneath his fingers. He'd always assumed that the coverlet was old, an heirloom from Sparrow ancestors, a grandmother or an aunt whose hopes for the girls seemed foolish now. But he realized that it wasn't so; it was new, it had to be. The cotton lawn was too white, too pristine to have been used well over the years. He saw that the quilt was filled with padding and something else, herbs or plants. They released their scent as he folded and unfolded it, slid under his hands until they were crushed and bled pale green through the white cotton. The flowers stitched into it were new, too. Or more correctly, as Henry finally saw, they were real, as fresh as the day they bloomed. Henry shivered and dropped the quilt onto his bed. Dirt crunched underfoot as he walked out of the bedroom, mud was smeared across his fingertips, and pollen feathered his chin. He was unsteady as he went downstairs, his bad leg giving under him with each step. And then he took off at a dead painful run.

"WHAT HAS SHE done to me?" Henry shouted. He'd come through the door without knocking, through Ivy House without stopping, past Simon bent over his briefcase in the front hall. His hands were fisted at his sides, and he stumbled as his leg finally gave way completely. Grabbing the back of a kitchen chair, Henry nearly went down, but Nettie snagged his arm. He shook her off as he regained his footing.

"Leave it!" he snapped, and Nettie stepped back with a soft cry.

"Henry, you need to calm down," Sorrel said and moved toward him.

"Don't touch me," Henry said. "I can't stand it." He dropped into the chair. "What the hell are you people?"

Simon came into the kitchen. He walked to the sink and poured a glass of Scotch. It seemed to be the only thing he got right lately. He handed it to Henry, who gulped it without expression. He held his glass out to Simon, who poured again.

"Now," Simon said. "Tell me what just happened."

"The quilt, it's full of something, the violets . . . I don't know." Henry stopped and ran his hand through his hair until it stood up. Nettie thought he looked like a boy and had to stifle the urge to hold him. Henry fell into a chair, put his elbows on the table, and rested his forehead in his palms. "Patience tricked me, didn't she?"

"No, Henry!" Nettie came around the table and knelt next to Henry. "Patience loves you."

"And I love her," Henry said and looked at Nettie. "But is it real?"

"Of course it is," Sorrel answered. "A Sparrow doesn't fall lightly." She looked at Simon. "She would never hurt you, Henry. Patience knows better."

"Then what has she done to me?"

"Nothing," Simon said. "Patience has no power over you, Henry. She has no mysterious potions, no incantations. Whatever her healing gift is, it is firmly of this plane." He rolled his eyes. "I cannot believe I'm saying this to a doctor. That quilt has no more magic than the innate properties of the herbs she sewed into it, the hands that took each stitch."

"That's just it, though," Henry said. "The things she makes, they *do* work."

Everyone nodded, and Nettie thought that maybe Henry had come through his crisis safely. At the very least, he finally understood what Patience could do for him.

"Then they can backfire, too," he said.

Sorrel and Nettie exchanged a confused look.

"Her remedies, if they have power, can heal or harm." Henry slammed his hands on the table. "Don't you get it? Even if there are no poisons in her stores, there are poisonous doses. Patience could have hurt Matty. She didn't mean to, but she was reckless, after all, and now he's dead."

No one moved. Henry was breathing hard, and Simon noticed with the detachment of shock that Nettie's hands were shaking and Sorrel was crying. He didn't think he'd ever seen Sorrel shed a single tear. Not even when Marigold died.

"Shut up, Henry," Simon said. "This stays in Ivy House."

"How can you be so callous?" Henry asked.

"Matty is dead. I am certain that Patience had nothing to do with it, and if you are not so sure, then you can either keep your doubts to yourself or get out."

"I can't," Henry said.

"You can't be quiet?" Simon wondered what he was going to do now.

"I can't betray Patience."

Now Simon wanted a drink and as he poured it, he acknowledged how reckless *he* was, how precarious his position had just become. But there was no going back. If he couldn't give Sorrel his love, he could at least return her sister.

"Well then," Simon said, "We're all in this together."

PATIENCE FELT THE real change begin as she sat in the holding cell and suspected that she had started it. She wasn't angry when the judge set bail so impossibly high. She wasn't angry when Annica, the linen lady, watched her leave the courthouse and deliberately dropped a bottle from the Sparrow Sisters Nursery to the ground. It shattered, and the scent of alfalfa, strong as Annica's disgust, drifted up from the sidewalk. Patience didn't get angry until she heard Chief Kelsey order his men to search Henry's apartment. Her belly clenched at the thought of the little haven she'd made for herself there, and she clamped her teeth together so fast and hard she bit her tongue. Blood filled her mouth and she stood to spit into the small sink in the corner.

Self-control was a near thing as Patience wrapped her hands around the bars and shouted for Chief Kelsey. When he came to her, his eyes liquid with regret, Patience let the air out of her fury.

"I want a blanket," she said. "Can I have a blanket?"

Chief Kelsey stayed his hand as it reached to pat Patience's knuckles and nodded. It had gotten cold in the cells, and he walked back to the office with an honest purpose for the first time. He called his wife.

"We need a few things," he said.

Pamela Kelsey drove over to the department in the station wagon that had belonged to her parents. She had filled the back with a duvet and pillow, two paperback novels she hoped Patience would not have time to read, flip-flops, shampoo, and a proper towel. She brought two thermoses of soup, a packet of oyster crackers, a bottle of seltzer water, and a chocolate bar. Pamela piled it all into a laundry basket and carried it to her husband's office. He blinked in surprise when she thumped her load down on his desk.

"I've brought you some soup," she said, and Chief Kelsey smiled. "Everything else is for Patience Sparrow."

And that is when the first of the women took a stand. But it was too late. It would take a lot more than soup and pillows to stop the rising panic. It would take more than one woman to turn the tide that already threatened to sweep Patience away. She would not go alone.

Patience was thrown when the chief came back to her with his wife's care package. He opened the door to her cell and came in without closing it. *Really,* he thought, *where's she going to go?* The rain had begun again, only now hail was mixed in with it, and one of his men had already informed him of a cracked windshield and a dented mailbox. The candlelight vigil for Matty organized by some fool group from the Methodist church in Old Hayward was rushed off its well-heeled feet when a street drain backed up and bathed them all ankle deep in a brown, gritty paste. It looked remarkably like shit to the two officers who were dispatched to keep watch. When they came back to the station, Chief Kelsey thought they smelled like shit too.

Rob Short stood at his kitchen window watching the church group disband. They left behind their placards and signs that had less to do with Christian kindness and more to do with some kind of anti-pagan crusade. He thought they resembled a bunch of cats kicking their feet and shaking their legs as if they had scotch tape on their paws. It's not that he didn't want the attention for Matty, the covered dishes that started appearing after Patience was arrested. A few of the guys from the hardware store had come by to bring him beer and cigarettes, drink his bourbon, and tell him how Patience Sparrow had gotten hauled off. Rob felt a little uncomfortable as the men reveled in her downfall. He wondered if maybe things were getting out of hand when his friends told him they had a plan to trash the Nursery.

"A few phone calls, Rob, and we've gotten a boatload of guys ready to show those Sparrows their kind of gardening is not welcome in Granite Point."

After the men left, Rob went back to watching the rain-washed street. He hadn't bothered to turn on any lights; all he needed was the bulb in the fridge when he opened it to get another beer. He turned away and went to sit at the kitchen table, careful not to choose Matty's chair. He sat there every night. Was it mourning or penance? He didn't bother to distinguish between the two or to even note the ritual: a beer, a bottle of bourbon, and cigarettes. Until Matty died he hadn't smoked in fifteen years, hadn't had a drink in over ten, not since Annie told him she was pregnant. He'd done it for her, then for his son, and now there was no one to care what he did. Rob really did believe that Matty died because Patience Sparrow gave him something that, instead of getting him through the day, plain old got him. He knew it was his fault that Matty needed an outsider's help, but he didn't care anymore. His anger and grief had overflowed, like that sewage, and now it was spreading through the town. It had been so easy to let the prosecutor take over. He seemed so sure that Patience was guilty of something. Rob couldn't remember all the legal terms; he'd been halfway to the bottom of a bottle by then. Anyway, they took his complaint, the chief, the lawyer, and a court stenographer, right there in his kitchen. He didn't have to leave, but he did take the empties out to the trash.

As numb as Rob Short worked to be, even he felt the changes around him. Something was happening, or rather, something had stopped happening since Patience was arrested. Granite Point seemed deflated by her incarceration. The buzzy hum of summer was missing, and vacationers and locals alike felt as if there was less oxygen in their air. The dogs that could usually be found snoozing on porches were more often huddled under their houses, terrified by the thunder, soaked by the rain. When the sun came out, it was so hot that everyone felt like ants trapped under a magnifying glass. The children who might have been experimenting with that magnifying glass dropped their bikes and scooters on the sidewalk and stayed inside, not just because of the weather and not just because their mothers pulled them closer, but because they were anxious, although they would never have been able to name the feeling. Instead they complained of sore throats and tummy aches, infected mosquito bites and lingering rashes.

Henry Carlyle put *his* anxiety into his work, and although there were a few cancellations, his office too had never been busier. Most of the summer folk didn't know he was connected to the hubbub at the police station; they had no idea that the longest-standing prisoner (now at forty-eight hours and counting) had spent her happiest moments in his bed. They dragged their children and spouses into his exam room with all the irritation their ruined vacations called forth. The migraine headaches, swimmer's ear, and infant colds weren't enough to distract Henry. He felt Patience's nearness and his inability to be with her acutely. His nerves were frayed by his realization of how thoroughly she had affected the people in the town. The fact that her remedies were genuine should have been satisfying to Henry. He should have been thinking about how they could team up like a couple of medical superheroes. He teetered on the edge of making the connection between Granite Point's suddenly disastrous summer season and Patience's situation. But the idea that a town was as much a living, breathing entity as any of its residents, the understanding that that town could fall ill just like one of his patients, eluded Henry. He might have asked Patience what was going on, and she might have been able to tell him. Instead, he was filled with a terrible certainty that if he did go to Patience, she would take one look at his face and turn him away forever. This was something he did not think he could take, even as he allowed himself the agony of imagining her dosing Matty with poison.

The day he galloped over to confront the Sisters, Henry drank too much. The third Scotch he let Simon pour burned a hangover into him while he was still a little drunk, and he had to ask the lawyer to drive him home. The Sisters stood in such silence as Henry limped out of Ivy House that he felt pressure in his ears. His leg sang with pain. He took a Vicodin, and drank glass after glass of water standing in his bathroom. It was not enough to sedate him, but enough to make him groggy and unfocused so that the afternoon was murky with every sort of pain.

Sorrel, who had sometimes suspected that Henry had fallen

in love with the idea of Patience, now wondered if he was about to destroy the reality of her. She and Nettie went back to the Nursery in search of the property paperwork. If it was down to them to make bail, they needed to do it fast. There was no telling how bad things could get if Patience stayed in jail. Clouds hung like anvils in the sky over the town. Already the Nursery was changing. Patience's gardens were trampled by a flood of the curious who'd started coming the day after the Clarion article and the video release. The police had been more careful in their search than the visitors taking pictures of plants they couldn't name. No one bought any remedies—that would be foolhardy and besides, the sisters had locked the cupboard and put away all of Patience's bits and bobs. But the customers almost all came away with bouquets from the farm stand, tomatoes, arugula, and zucchini, pots of coneflowers and dahlias, flats of creeping phlox, anemones, dwarf marigolds, and zinnias. The Sparrow Sisters Nursery was bringing in cash, and the Sisters had to split up to look after the crowds. It wouldn't last.

Nettie finally found the deed to the land (it was back at Ivy House in the library), the last quarterly tax filing, and the mortgage they had taken out on Ivy House the year they bought the Nursery. She put the papers into a manila envelope. She and Sorrel closed up and took everything to Simon's office. His assistant, an older woman who had begun her career at Mr. Mayo Sr.'s elbow, greeted them. Her mouth was a thin, pale line, and when she held out her hand for the envelope, she was careful not to touch Nettie's. Sorrel surprised herself by staying silent. She didn't even ask where Simon was although both Sisters were desperate to get things moving.

As it turned out, the Nursery would not be the thing to save anybody. The little burst of business in the early days after Matty's death only served to call attention to the Sparrows. By the time the Sisters arrived the morning after they agreed to use the Nursery as bond, not only had someone taken a bolt cutter to the gate locks, they had run over the herb gardens with what looked like a tractor. Entire years-old stands of sage and rosemary were torn out by the roots, the creeping thyme was flattened and muddied, and the box hedges that marked each area like walls were snapped at ground level. Sorrel and Nettie were so shocked they couldn't even cry, although they both felt the loss like a death. Sorrel turned in a circle, trying to understand what she was seeing. Nettie was the one who finally spoke.

"Patience can't know about this," she said, and Sorrel nodded. "I cannot believe people are such shits," she added.

"Those shits are the very same people who came to her for help," Sorrel said.

"I wonder if they're the same shits who shopped here yesterday," Nettie said.

The Sisters spent the day trying to save what they could. The little cart on the road had been turned over, and the honesty box was smashed but not emptied. Dollar bills had blown against the stone wall along the road like notes left at a memorial. For now, both women thought, the Nursery was just that. It was no longer a living thing at all.

Simon Mayo found Sorrel and Nettie sitting in the shed. He'd seen the overturned cart and the ruined plants, but he just couldn't believe that the damage was deliberate. One look at the women, and he had to face facts. The very physicality of the destruction spoke to him of men, and he suspected that the husbands and boyfriends, the fathers, not the mothers, were responsible. He was right. The women in town were horrified when they heard about the Nursery. They had spent the week listening to their husbands bluster yet they had never guessed they would turn to vandalism. Most of the women stood up for themselves and for Patience, and they all hid their remedies where they knew the men would never look: in the linen closet, at the bottom of the laundry hamper, behind packets and canned goods in their pantries, in the glove box of the family minivan. They spoke to each other in whispers about how fragile everything was with Patience in trouble.

Simon didn't have good news. He hadn't yet arranged bail. There was no standing bondsman; he was in Hayward, and one town banker made it clear no one wanted to deal with the Sparrows. As Simon and the Sisters met each other across the counter, all three were bereft in every way. When Simon's cell phone rang, they all jumped.

Simon listened in silence and then gave his location.

"That was Charlotte," he said. "She's coming over here."

Sorrel frowned, and Nettie asked why.

Simon shook his head. "She wouldn't say, just that she wanted to see all of us."

It was not yet four o'clock, but the sky was so low that it felt like dusk. Charlotte had her headlights on, and they swept through the room, making Sorrel realize she should turn on the lights too.

Charlotte walked in with her usual purpose. Nettie shrank away; she couldn't help herself.

"Right," Charlotte said and plopped her bag on the counter. "I'm taking over here." She fished around for a minute before coming up with a cashier's check and handing it to Simon.

"Bail," she said and looked at the Sisters. "Patience can be out tonight if you hurry."

Here was another woman, and the most unexpected, to take Patience's side. If Charlotte surprised the Sisters, she stunned Simon. It wasn't the money, although she certainly had enough of her own to spend as she chose; it was the fact that Charlotte Parsons Mayo chose the Sparrow Sisters. She could easily have stood back as Simon did his job; she could even have made it clear that she did not agree with him. Instead, she not only took sides, she took a stand.

"I won't let this ridiculous little town repeat its own history," she said. "There is no need for Granite Point to become some late night comic's joke. I won't watch any woman be victimized, and I will definitely do what I can to stop this deranged witch hunt." Charlotte reached across the counter and took her husband's hand.

"We are all counting on you, Simon. If you ever loved Sorrel, save her sister." Charlotte turned and left the shed, her little car humming as it sped up the sandy drive and back to town.

Simon stared at the check for all of thirty seconds before he too left. He wanted to get everything settled before nightfall. Mostly he wanted to get out of the Nursery without looking at Sorrel and before he started to cry. He almost made it. The Sisters politely turned their heads when he swallowed a sob.

Independently, quietly, subtly the women of Granite Point were marshaling their strength. It would be necessary for them to bind that strength together before the town tore itself apart.

SORREL AND NETTIE locked the shed and drove home in silence. There was nothing to say, really. Charlotte had said it all. Granite Point was convulsing around them, foaming at the mouth with the nastiness that had survived over three hundred years. During the Salem witch trials, the town's spasm of keeping up with the Joneses should have worn itself out on Eliza Howard. But she would become a Sparrow, so when Patience was arrested it didn't take much for the town to absorb the symmetry of the moment. Really, it was just too good to pass up, although there was no satisfaction in the death of a child. It was obvious to everyone that Patience's ingredients had to go. The vandals could have saved their energy; the Nursery would begin to truly fail the next day.

Sorrel went home to Ivy House to wait for Patience, and Nettie whipped through the supermarket with the idea that dinner should be a comforting, healing thing. Simon went to the police station, and he and Chief Kelsey presented the check to the court clerk, who filed all the necessary paperwork while the two men stood over her. Cash was a beautiful thing, Simon thought. They both fairly ran back to the station, and Patience was in Simon's car within the hour. No one called Henry to tell him the news.

"Please take me to the Nursery," Patience said.

Simon slowed the car. "Patience, that's the last place you should be seen. As your lawyer I cannot condone this and should take you straight home."

"It is home."

"There's been some trouble, P," Simon said. "You might want to wait till your sisters are with you."

But Patience didn't want to wait. She needed to be around the plants, hopeful that they could soothe her now. Although Simon warned her, she was unprepared for the devastation. After she asked him to collect her in an hour, Patience climbed over the gate. Ben and Simon had wrapped a heavy chain around it (the same one Ben had used to drag the oldest of the yews out of the ground after it had been nearly felled by some-one's axe). He couldn't do anything else to help the Sisters, so the big lobsterman had shut the Nursery off from the town.

Patience could now see how broken it was. The beds that had escaped the fear that swept across Granite Point along with the rain were no healthier. As Patience walked between them, she saw that disease was spreading. Rose petals were brown with rot, the new buds black on their stems. Only the thorns were green: acid, poisonous green dripping with clear liquid. She knelt at a raised bed planted with cucumbers and radishes. Shriveled thumb-sized cucumbers ended in wilted, twisted blossoms. When Patience pulled on a radish clump, the leaves powdered in her hand and the roots ended in foul-smelling knobs. Darkness spread with the disease, and Patience began to cry. It was a low, howling sound that hurt as it left her chest. She barely made it to the meadow before she fell to the ground. Beneath her the grass was sharp as needles, blood spotted her clothes, tiny cuts covered her legs, her arms, the soft skin on her hips. All around her the ground hardened, and the black-eyed Susans rattled and cracked on their stems. The cornflowers curled up into gray balls before they sagged into the dirt.

Henry wouldn't find her for some thirty minutes. Ben told him Patience was out on bail, and when Henry made known his intention to go to Ivy House, to confront her about what was torturing him, Ben stopped him.

"Don't do that. You'll kill her," he said. "Please don't hurt her anymore. We can't take it."

Henry was surprised at the intensity of Ben's words. He had no idea Ben was so affected, and he told him so.

"Not me, all of us," Ben said. "Can't you see what's happening here?"

But Henry just couldn't. The man of science was back. He felt distant from himself, as if the Henry of the last weeks was nothing more than a dream instead of a memory. He had come to measure his life in the before-and-after of his wound, the death of a little girl in his arms. Now he found that he'd crossed yet another line. There was the Henry who tasted happiness in the blood and bone of Patience, and now there was the one who looked at his hands, certain he could see the blood and bone of Matty Short. If Patience coiled in hot, tearful agony as she measured her culpability in herbs and flowers, Henry had become cold and rigid with the knowledge that he'd watched, unmoving, as calamity had gathered.

But there was something else Henry Carlyle could not stop: the pull he felt from Patience. It was as subtle as the green tendrils of the sweet peas she'd planted along his porch, and just as insistent. Ben left, holding his scarred hand up in warning, but Henry was already gathering his keys, shoving his feet into his sneakers, pulling a sweatshirt over his head. He didn't think as he drove off and ended up at Calumet Landing; perhaps Patience was calling to him. One breath and he knew she was somewhere near. He climbed over the fence and bit down on a groan when pain burned its way up his leg as he landed on the other side. He followed the sandy drive in near darkness, the only light the small fixture on the shed. As Henry turned toward the greenhouses, looking for Patience, he acknowledged that he had no idea what he was doing.

Henry passed through the gardens. There was a rank smell, and he heard as well as felt the insects crunching under his feet. He didn't need to go into the greenhouse to see that the orchids were dying, papery and nearly transparent. They leaned against the glass like drunken debutantes. He swung away, his hand to his mouth, and started toward the wildflower field. He noticed the buzz of crickets and the rumble of the bullfrogs in the duckweed around the pond, the absolute silence that surrounded their insistent drone. There was something very wrong, and Henry forced himself to stop and listen beneath the noise and the silence. That's when he heard Patience sobbing. He followed the sound, his head turned as if that would help him track her. And it did because he found her before she took her next gulping breath. Henry nearly fell over her. Stumbling back to avoid crushing her, he went down hard on his knees beside her.

"Shit," Henry growled as he caught himself with both hands on Patience's arm. She stopped crying and looked up at him. He was frowning, and sweat stood out on his lip. Henry was in pain and Patience longed to help him, but now she was afraid of her own gift.

"I'm so sorry," he said as he shifted back on his heels. He put one hand down and wobbled before giving up and landing on his ass. "Jesus, we're a mess," he said.

Patience sat up and put her hand out to Henry. He found he couldn't refuse her. As much as his leg hurt, as gritty as his bones felt as they rubbed against each other with every step, he wanted only to gather her up and carry her out of this poisonous place. Henry took her hand and they dragged each other closer, the grass scraping sharply against their thighs.

"What is that?" Henry asked as he pulled his torn pant leg

around for a look. "Has someone thrown a bottle?" Could the town have turned that ugly? He turned Patience's hand palm up and saw that the heel of it was speckled with blood. "What's happened to you?"

"It's the ground, it's gone sharp, the grass has died, everything's died," Patience said. "I've killed it all."

He looked around at the dead and dying. "You haven't done this any more than you killed Matty." If he had said those words before, he believed them now. Watching Patience weep, Henry let go of every sliver of anger. "Whatever is happening in these gardens, it's because you were taken away from them."

Patience laughed weakly. "Oh dear," she said, "I'm in jail a couple of days and you go all mystical on me." Henry dropped his head. "Wait till I tell my sisters," Patience said, and she brushed at the blood drying on her hand.

"Oh, I think they've heard enough from me already," Henry said. "Let me take you home."

"Yes, let's go away," Patience said as if Henry could transport her.

They stood together and with her arm through Henry's, Patience walked lightly over the gravel and the hundreds of insects that fluttered or spun or flapped at her feet, each of them helpless to stop the end. Henry was unnerved by the bugs and tried his best to step around them. But for every one he missed, another fell onto the path with a snapping, clapping sound. He pulled a little harder on Patience's arm, but she'd paused and was leaning over a tall clump of pink flowers.

"What's happened to those?" Henry asked.

"Nothing. That's just it," Patience said. "It's the foxglove plants. They're alive. I'd planned to pull them out before Matty because they're full of earwigs, pretty toxic, and I never used them. I never did believe all the Eliza Howard stories so why keep them around? Now I never want to see them again. Still, these"— she stopped short of touching them—"these are perfectly fine, which is all wrong. I should bag them before they screw up the soil."

"I think that ship has sailed, Patience. This place is a graveyard." Henry pulled Patience again. "Please, let's get out of here. We need to talk."

"This is all we have. I've got to try to save it." She gestured at the gardens. "Maybe I should stay."

"You know what? This is the part where you have no choice," Henry said. "I almost lost you this week. Then I almost threw you away. I won't do that again." He lunged at Patience and picked her up. She offered no resistance, and Henry limped toward the gate.

"You really don't have to do this," Patience said as he ducked under a willow tree whose long branches bowed too deep, their leaves already lacy and yellow.

"Yeah, well, I may have to put you down in a sec." Henry grimaced. "Okay, now, actually," he said as he lowered Patience. He rubbed at his thigh and swore. "Whatever you did to me, you need to do it again," he said.

Patience put her hand over his as he rubbed. "How bad is it?"

"Very." Henry hated saying so, but the absence of pain for even those few weeks had spoiled him. He put his head down and bent at the waist, breathing slowly as the pain swelled and faded in waves. He saw stars and swallowed the saliva that gathered in his mouth along with the nausea.

"Poor Henry," Patience murmured. This time she led him and helped him to sit on the shed steps. The door was locked, and the new dead bolt was shiny even in the dusk.

"I'd get something for you if I could," Patience said and tilted her head to the door.

Henry fished around in his pocket until he came up with a linty Vicodin. "This'll do," he said and swallowed it dry. "Have you seen your sisters yet?"

"No, I came here."

"Then I should tell you that I kind of blew up at them the other day." Henry put his hands on his knee and pressed down. Sometimes he could shift the pain around a little. Not tonight. "If I accept your ability, Patience, then I have to accept that you could have hurt Matty."

Patience nodded. "That's what I've said from the beginning. I haven't hidden anything."

"That quilt you left with me. I thought it was just an old blanket."

"It was. I upgraded it."

"That's what I mean," Henry said. "The herbs, the flowers, your touch . . ." He trailed off.

"I was only trying to help," Patience said and carefully

placed her hand on Henry's leg. He felt the warmth under her palm and inhaled. He tried to maintain a professional distance, to analyze what was happening as the heat traveled into his hip and down to his thigh. He felt the pain retreat, a cool wave replacing the heat, a softening of the muscle and nerve beneath her hand. Finally, Henry let go and in a moment of near grace he arched into Patience with a deep sigh.

They both heard a car pull over on the other side of the gate. The door closed with a thunk, and Simon called to Patience. She stood and offered her hand to Henry; he felt light with relief and overtaken by the possibility that Patience could make his life easy again. Or that this was the last easy moment either one would have. He rose and pulled her to him, sliding his hands around her waist.

"How I wish I could do this to you," he whispered into her hair.

"You do," she said and slipped away.

Patience went back to Ivy House with Simon, and Henry climbed over the gate again, this time with ease, and drove home to his empty apartment. When he arrived, he collapsed on his bed, pulling Patience's quilt over him, and fell into a heavy sleep: deep and painless for the first time in days. His shoes left a trail of split carapaces on the stairs. His pants, piled at the foot of the bed, were gray with torn spider webs, and in his hair dried pollen made him sneeze in his dreams.

CHAPTER ELEVEN

*Evening primrose is most successful
in treating liver torpor*

A murder of crows."

Pete stood behind his liquor store, a box cutter in his hand, a pile of empty wine cases at his feet, and beyond him, some twenty dead birds.

"No one would murder crows." His son toed one of the corpses.

"That's what a flock of crows is called," Pete said. "A murder."

Down at the harbor, Ben Avellar stepped over coiled lines to squat at the edge of the dock. Dead fish floated around the *Jenny Joy* in a silvery wake; alewives, washed from their freshwater breeding grounds. Yet not a single boat had come in with a catch. Lobster traps, still baited, were hauled up light and empty. The day boats came home heavy with frustration, not fish. If the men didn't say anything to each other, it was because they all thought the same thing: Sparrows. If they didn't blame them, exactly, they certainly knew Sister trouble when they saw it.

Before the boats went out each day, the men gave a quick pat to the painted tin mermaid hammered into the side of the harbormaster's cabin. Her features had long ago been rubbed away by so many fingers. They were a superstitious lot, fishermen, and it was an easy thing to drop a hand to the figure as they headed out. Now, as they stood in small clumps around their boats, they felt uneasy. Had any of these men been to the Nursery the day Patience got out? Had any of them pulled out a plant with the same vigor needed to haul in a full net? Hard to know. They were a silent bunch too. Should they fault the Sisters, just Patience, or themselves, for the bad luck that lapped at them all like a red tide? One thing was certain, all of them—each and every fisherman, dockworker, fish shack cook—couldn't shake the persistent anxiety that curled in their bellies and burned in their throats.

Ben left his boat and drove into town. He parked halfway between Ivy House and Henry's office and walked to the green. The grass was spongy beneath his feet, waterlogged and flooded in places. The mud gathered along the footpath across the green and seeped into the streets, a thick current of salty muck that belonged far from town. He picked his way along the brick sidewalks, now slick with feathery seaweed, and came to the town hall. His heavy boots left sloppy prints across the lobby. Ben nodded at the clerk who stood behind the counter stuffing envelopes.

"It's nasty out there," she said when she saw Ben's feet.

"Yeah, the season's pretty well screwed now," he said.

Ben asked for the town records from the summer of 1691, the year Eliza Howard was arrested. He didn't really know what he was looking for, but he found it anyway. And it did not surprise him. He took copies from the outdated microfiche and drove his car to Ivy House, the folder clamped between his legs.

When Ben tossed the papers on the kitchen table, Sorrel and Nettie looked on blankly. Patience was still upstairs; she hadn't left her room much since the night she came home. She'd played with the dinner Nettie made, drank endless glasses of water, and never even glanced out at the garden.

"You know that whole history-repeats-itself thing?" Ben asked. He handed Nettie a page. "Well, here we go again."

It didn't take long to read the full story of Eliza Howard. Nettie and Sorrel had always known it, of course. After all, the Sisters had read Clarissa's book, read her references to Eliza's gift and the trouble it caused her, the formulas Clarissa carefully transcribed and edited, which Patience copied over. Then they hid it because they knew how it might seem to some. Giving it to the museum was a way of preserving it should Patience need it again, of hiding it in plain sight. But seeing that then, as now, Granite Point had turned against one of its own as quickly as the tide turns froze the Sisters where they stood. There was no going back; events would play out, as they must, as they had over three hundred years before. They could only hope that, in the end, Patience would be saved too.

CHAPTER TWELVE

Tansy may allay spasms

Granite Point had always been such a clean and tidy town. Consistently stoic. Used to taking care of its business quickly and with little fuss. And despite the bizarre weather and general feeling of unease that filled every hour of the day and night, Granite Point did what it was good at and got Patience Sparrow's preliminary hearing running in the allotted time. The Sisters took comfort in the fact that Judge Adams hadn't called for a grand jury the first time on the strength of the prosecutor's zeal. The town was grateful the case hadn't been taken to Hayward. That drive was a real pain during the season. Although with the rain paused and temperatures hovering in the high eighties, the air conditioning at the big courthouse might have been worth the traffic, and certainly nobody wanted to miss this spectacle.

Testimony began on a day so hot that finches and blue jays shared the same puddles, butterflies fell from the dogwoods into dusty piles, and chipmunks lay exposed and panting in the shade of the salt-seared privet. In the courtroom the curious and the complicit—it was impossible to tell which was which— gathered beneath the ceiling fans. Judge Adams was already sweating under his black robe. For the first time he lamented working the summer and thought with regret about his wife, whom he'd left standing on their porch that morning, a glass of icy lemonade in her hand. He looked down at the list of witnesses—there weren't many—and banged his gavel. He hoped that the opening arguments would be brief but, given the crowd before him and the Boston news van out front, he guessed he was in for a performance.

The Weather Channel had sent a reporter in a windbreaker out earlier that week to cover the tight pod of storms that had settled over Granite Point. His cameraman stalked the fishing boats and took close-ups of the mud that lined the streets, the knotted clematis and thorny roses along the increasingly moldy picket fences. He missed the pilot whale that washed ashore early one morning at the Outermost Beach. The beach patrol rolled the carcass beyond the low dunes and buried it. Before nightfall, someone had stacked stones over the grave, shaped them into the outline of a whale and stuck a small white cross deep into the sand. Pictures of toppled headstones in the tiny old graveyard, their bases pulled free of the porous earth, had even made it into the *Boston Globe*. The Granite Point Tourist Information booth was shuttered after the woman who ran it came down with such a bad case of poison ivy that Henry had her hospitalized. Chief Kelsey sent a gloved deputy over to remove all the pamphlets she'd touched, now curling at their edges with toxic oil.

Judge Adams pressed his bottled water against his neck and called the court to order again. As he listened to the prosecutor outline his case against Patience Sparrow, he looked at the defendant in her neat skirt and blouse and recalled that he had, in fact, known her mother, if only through his wife. He remembered her wedding because his wife had wanted to go, but he was on a case, not yet a judge but already pointlessly ambitious. Just last night she'd recalled the sad circumstances of the death of Honor Sparrow. Now the motherless daughters were sitting before him, and he wished he hadn't listened to his wife's story, wished he didn't see loss in each of the women's faces.

Simon Mayo rose and began to speak. Judge Adams refocused. He needed to pay attention, to determine whether all this talk about Patience Sparrow and her remedies was the story of a murder or just a story.

Both lawyers spoke of the central role the Sparrow Sisters played in Granite Point. Paul Hutchins painted a picture of bitter, lonely women whose only pleasure came in winding themselves through the lives of the people of the town, tight and invasive as the ivy on their house. He spoke of Patience as if she stood before an ancient grimoire, mixing and dosing with abandon, heedless of the damage she was inflicting. Ben Avellar, who sat beside Nettie, felt his hands fist as the prosecutor looked at the Sisters and sneered, dismissing them, heaping disrespect on them until Sorrel and her sister bent their heads in shame. When it was Simon's turn, he spoke of the Sisters with respect. The story was the same: the Nursery that fed and adorned the town, the women who remade the land with their own hands, a healer who maintained the delicate balance between well and sick, sadness and contentment. Simon tried to put the Sisters firmly in the light, to banish the shadows that Paul Hutchins had drawn over them all.

And this was just the beginning.

Simon had never been so nervous. He too had the list of prosecution witnesses. Henry Carlyle's name stood out from a short column of Granite Point residents and a medical expert from the city. The coroner's report stated the cause of death, coronary arrest. It was as mysterious and unsatisfying as could be. Matty's body still lay in the Hayward morgue. Rob Short could not come to a decision about where to bury him: with his mother in Meacham or close to him in Granite Point.

Poor Matty, Simon thought. He'd been taken apart in the last days and there were still no answers. What would be left to bury? What was left of Patience now, of Granite Point? Matty's death had poisoned an entire town. And yet, the proof of Patience's innocence was right in front of him. There were no harmful levels of any of the herbs Patience had given Matty, so as Simon paged through his notes, he tried to imagine what the medical expert would present. He couldn't begin to imagine what Henry would be asked.

Robert Short sat beside the prosecutor. He was newly shaven, his Adam's apple scraped raw by the razor. His hands lay on the table like dead things, limp and pale. He kept his eyes to the front of the room, though not on the judge. They were blood-shot and blank, and one knee bobbed rapidly. Nettie could not keep her gaze away from him. She could not believe that such a little man was capable of so much destruction. Finally she closed her eyes to try to listen to the atmosphere in the court-room. If Matty's father was silent, the murmur and shift behind her told Nettie that everyone else couldn't wait to talk. The gossip would spread quickly, as venomous as the blight that destroyed the Nursery. She was surprised to hear that the au-dience was divided equally between men and women. Didn't these people have jobs, children, lives?

Sorrel looked for Henry. He'd been a fixture each evening as the Sisters tried to maintain some kind of routine. The days leading up to the hearing crawled by, perhaps because every-body was trapped by the poor weather and even poorer moods. But when Henry was with Patience, everyone settled. It was strangely changeable weather, even for New England. There wasn't one person in town who hadn't been caught dressed poorly: a sweater when the thermometer spiked to ninety-seven, flips-flops that slipped and slid over a sudden sheen of sleet. Sometimes there was a break in the near blinding rain or a breeze that lifted a wave of stifling heat, a flash of sun to warm the cold that draped over the town when no one was paying attention.

When those breaks happened, the Sisters rushed outside to pick vegetables and flowers or just stand for a few minutes in the fresh air of the Ivy House garden. It was barely marred by the troubles that afflicted the Nursery and the town. Certainly it rained and heat wavered over the asparagus ferns when it was cold enough for the Sisters to wear socks to bed. True, the jasmine had stopped blooming, and there were no more sugar snaps, but these were part of the natural order of things, an order that had never before placed itself over the Sparrow Sisters' gardens. Still, the dahlias were as tall as Nettie, the blossoms as big as sunflowers, their colors so deep they looked like velvet. Sorrel had to pick them twice a day to keep them from falling under their own weight. As it was, the flowers crowded together until they formed a solid block of red and pink in the dusk.

The Sisters' patterns reasserted themselves. They turned the radio up and listened to banal, addictive pop songs as they changed the linens and swept sand from the broad floorboards, cleared mud from the cracks between the porch steps. Nettie and Sorrel prepared dinner after one or the other went to the market. After dinner had been eaten, dishes washed and put away, Henry sat with Patience. If it was raining, they stayed in the kitchen and the Sisters left them. If it was not too hot, they sat outside. Each night that Henry sat at their table, he felt more tightly bound to the women. As he stood at the sink, rinsing glasses and handing them off to Nettie, he never wanted to leave. He couldn't take the chance of imagining his life in this house, but he couldn't help himself when the fragile peace set roots in him. If they could just get through this ludicrous trial, surely they could start afresh. But, of course, that would be impossible. Patience had, in her way, turned against Granite Point. It was generally agreed that all the nasty natural events had started at the very moment Patience was arrested. So it was no surprise that the town, in all its nearly genetic superstition, turned on Patience, on all the Sisters. As the first hearing day approached, news had traveled beyond the harbor town so that the nation was creeping in slowly, closer and closer to Patience.

Witnesses were lined up on both sides of the aisle. The day after Paul Hutchins told Matty's father he had to sit beside him for however long the hearing took, Rob Short stopped drinking. He still smoked. As his head cleared, he became more and more anxious. He wondered if this was how Matty had felt all the time, this certainty that everything was about to go terribly wrong. It wasn't that he didn't still blame Patience somehow; it's just that now there didn't seem to be any point to the thing. Matty was gone, Rob wasn't going anywhere, and half the women in the town looked at him with distaste now that he was back at the hardware store. He stopped covering the till for anyone at lunch and stayed in his tiny office with his ledgers.

Rob thought about the witnesses that would be called, the narrowed eyes he'd have to meet in the courthouse. He wondered if the Sisters might actually spit at him or something worse. Did he think that they could actually put a hex on him, curse him, be-spell him? No, not really, not now that he was sober and the anger had burned remorse into his heart as it left him. But Rob Short could still be frightened.

SIMON HAD WARNED Henry not to tell Patience about his subpoena, but Henry couldn't keep secrets from her, not anymore. She'd looked at him with such regret that he'd mistaken it for pity.

"Don't worry about me," he said. "I have nothing to say."

"But you will have to tell the truth," Patience said. She put her hand on his chest. "I am so sorry."

"I'm not," Henry said and brought her hand to his cheek. "I hate to think what would have happened to me without you. You are the only thing I have ever wanted to keep."

And now, on the second day of the hearing, Henry sat in the old courtroom. He'd picked at his cuticles until they bled. He had to use his handkerchief to stanch the blood and remembered the night he let Patience plaster his face with her sticky salve, how he'd wiped it away with the handkerchief she was so sure he had, the one he went back for hoping he would see her again. The witness chair was hard, and he shifted as the pain in his leg returned with an almost electric shock. His back was beginning to seize up from the strain, and he felt as useless as he had in the VA hospital.

Henry hadn't come during the first day of the trial. Simon

instructed him to keep to his regular schedule, to go about his business quietly. He knew he couldn't have borne to listen to Sam Parker describe what he'd found when he came barreling into Rob Short's kitchen. He couldn't watch Patience as she heard, for the first time, how Matty's blood had pooled in his face and arms because he had died with his head cradled in them. He knew that it would destroy her to know that Matty had been dead for hours before he was found. Henry knew that every single detail the police saw and every action they took would be stated and dissected in the courtroom. So Henry stayed away and saw to his patients, some of whom hesitated before they asked, "How are you?" as if he might actually tell them.

Henry had already seen Matty's autopsy record; Sam snuck him a look at it just before the trial started. It held nothing to condemn Patience exactly; the levels of the herbs in his system were of no consequence, good or bad. As Henry ran over the stomach contents, he couldn't stop the shudder that went through him; there was a partially digested sprig of lavender. And yet, almost nothing else. It was true, Matty was frail, but it looked like he hadn't eaten anything but that cookie for some twelve hours. It was the digitalis that made Matty's heart stop, and that was more than enough to bring them all here.

"You are a medical doctor, is that right?" The young prosecutor—his name was something Hutchins—Henry hadn't listened—was talking, and Henry tried to appear professional and unaffected by the sight of Patience in a long-sleeved dress.

She was the only person not sweating in the close courtroom. Henry nodded before he remembered he had to speak out loud for the record.

"I am," Henry said. His voice was deep but soft.

"And you are a U.S. Army captain?"

"I was." Again Henry's voice rumbled, but this time he had to clear his throat. He dreaded where this Hutchins asshole was taking him.

"Yes, you were honorably discharged some seventeen months ago." Hutchins looked at the papers on the table in front of him, and Henry looked at them too. The room was small enough that he could see the U.S. Army seal on the letterhead.

"You were wounded, spent nearly four months in a VA hospital. You still walk with a limp."

Judge Adams looked down to Henry's legs and then back at Hutchins.

"I am hoping that this is going somewhere of interest, counselor," he said.

"Dr. Carlyle, do you walk with a limp? Do you still suffer pain from your wound?"

Henry cleared his throat again. "Sometimes," he murmured.

"You take medication for this pain. Vicodin, an opiate, is that right?"

"Yes."

"Does it help?"

"Sometimes," Henry said again.

"But not much." Hutchins moved closer to the stand.

"No, not always."

"Do you consider yourself an addict, Dr. Carlyle?"

"Objection," Simon Mayo snapped.

"Rephrase," Hutchins said. "Your prescriptions are filled regularly. Is that right?"

"Yes."

"Have you considered other methods to deal with your pain?"

"Yes, of course," Henry said. "I have spent months in physical therapy. I still work at it."

"You've been seen rowing, something that sounds painful for your wound."

"Rowing stretches both the semimembranosus and gastrocnemius muscles, and yes, that is painful." Henry liked the confused look on Hutchins's face and nearly smiled.

"Did you seek help from Patience Sparrow?" Hutchins turned to look at the courtroom even before the audience broke into whispers. Then he almost smiled. *These people are so predictable,* he thought, and he felt his nerves lie still completely, replaced by the thrill of the chase. He knew where he was going; the witness couldn't. He turned back to Henry.

"Dr. Carlyle?" Hutchins pressed.

"I did not go to Patience for help," Henry answered.

"You are under oath, sir."

Simon had been half out of his chair before the judge spoke and now he stood, uncertain what he wanted to say.

"Mr. Mayo?" Judge Adams said.

"I object," Simon said. "Asked and answered."

"Sustained."

"Fine," Hutchins said. "Did you receive treatment from Patience Sparrow?"

Henry stared at Simon, willing him to stop the prosecutor, to stop Henry himself. But Simon refused to meet his eye. Patience looked at Henry and nodded.

"Yes," he said. The room erupted, and this time Judge Adams rapped his gavel so hard his papers jumped. Hutchins had to raise his voice.

"And did this treatment work?" Silence replaced the babble as every person in the room looked at Henry and waited. "Did Patience Sparrow relieve your pain?"

Henry never took his eyes off Patience. "Yes," he answered and smiled.

"So, as a medical doctor you are saying you found Patience Sparrow's remedies to have real power?"

Henry's smile faded as he saw the trap too late. The very same logic he'd used when he shouted at the Sisters now twisted his words into something very close to a conviction.

"No, that's . . ." he stuttered. "Patience has done only good in this town. Her gift is for healing." He looked around. "How many of you have been to her?" he asked. "How many of you have begged her for help, for a remedy to soothe you, to mend a broken heart, ease your baby's colic, soften hands roughened by nets?"

Hutchins let him talk.

"For God's sake, it could be the placebo effect. They're just herbal remedies, the very same you could buy in any . . ." Henry stopped. What was done was done, and Patience had dropped her head nearly to the tabletop.

"Not really, not Patience Sparrow's concoctions, those are not available in any shop but hers," Hutchins said with a triumphant look around the room. "Real remedies, the ones you *can* buy in a drugstore, are made in large licensed facilities, to professional standards. These elixirs were made by an untrained amateur in a broken-down shed on Calumet Landing. These potions were stirred up in the very same place poisonous plants are grown."

"Objection!" Simon was up.

"Withdrawn," Hutchins said. "Dr. Carlyle, is it true that you were wounded while carrying out a vaccination program in an Iraqi school?"

Henry could hardly speak, but he managed a yes as he tried to guess how badly he'd hurt Patience's chances.

"And you and your fellow soldiers were able to save the children?"

Again Henry said yes. He couldn't care less what Hutchins asked him now.

"But not all of the them. You couldn't save one nine-year-old girl." Hutchins stepped back and looked at the eager audience again. Not only the parents in the room were shaken by his words. Judge Adams was inches from telling the prosecutor to knock it off, but he was curious to hear his point.

This time, when Henry nodded, Hutchins didn't have to remind him to speak up.

"She was hit by shrapnel from the bomb. Her injuries were too extensive. I couldn't do anything for her."

"You were hit by shrapnel, too, Dr. Carlyle. Yet you went into the school and dragged children to safety. You and your men saved nearly twenty children."

Henry didn't bother to answer. He kept his eyes on his hands. He didn't hear the murmurs of admiration that ran through the courtroom.

Paul Hutchins kept talking. His voice became a buzz in Henry's ears.

"You fought against the medics who were trying to save you. You fought so hard that you nearly bled to death. You had to be physically pulled from the girl. You gave no thought to yourself, and now you are crippled."

Henry didn't need any reminder of that day. He dragged his failure around with him just as he pulled his injured leg behind him. Or had, until he found Patience. The word "crippled" did remind him that he hadn't been man enough to save Matty or Patience. And that's all Paul Hutchins needed.

"Your point, counselor?" Judge Adams asked.

"My point is this." The prosecutor warmed to his performance, his voice filling the courtroom, one arm spread toward Henry, the other to Patience. "Dr. Carlyle acknowledges that Patience Sparrow's remedies work. Why, he considers himself proof! He must know that they are as capable of harm as they are of good. Is it any wonder that Dr. Carlyle refuses to believe that Patience Sparrow's careless hobby killed Matthew Short? If he does, if he accepts her guilt, then he will be the witness to another child's death. Matty died because Henry Carlyle couldn't stop his lover from poisoning him."

"Objection!" Simon was frantic. Sweat flew off his face as he whipped around to look at the gabbling crowd behind him.

"Your language is a bit inflammatory, Mr. Hutchins," Judge Adams said.

"I am trying to establish that Dr. Carlyle's judgment may be impaired by the tragedy he suffered in Iraq. What he saw there"—Hutchins pointed at Henry—"has blinded him to what he saw here." He pointed to Patience. "This medical doctor should have recognized the danger when he saw her with another child, also destined to die."

"Henry Carlyle is not under investigation here, Mr. Hutchins," Judge Adams said. "Still, as he is Matty Short's physician of record, I will have this record show that he did not act in the best interest of his patient."

Oh fuck, Henry thought, it's over. I've done what no amount of blood or stroke of a scalpel could. I've condemned Patience. He refused to let his face show anything more than it already had. He slowed his breathing until he was sure his hand wouldn't shake when he brought it up to push his hair away. Simon and the prosecutor were standing in front of the judge. Their fierce whispers weren't loud enough for him to understand, and there was nothing for him to do but sit and stare at the top of Patience's head. She was looking at her own hands; Henry knew they were shaking because all of her was shaking. Her hair had slipped from its knot and fell over her shoulders, tangled, dull in the fluorescent light. Finally she raised her eyes. She had given up; it was clear from the way she smiled at him. It wasn't the smile he saw when she showed him the Nursery or the one when he slipped her dress from her shoulders. It was forgiveness, and Henry knew he didn't deserve it.

JUDGE ADAMS CALLED a recess, and Ben saw one woman race out of the courtroom before anyone else. As soon as he steered the Sisters into the hall, he ran to the steps. The woman was on her phone, one hand over her free ear. Ben couldn't hear the words, but something told him to wait. She stopped talking and turned, her eyes lighting up as soon as she saw him.

"You're with the Sparrows, aren't you?" she asked.

Ben didn't respond. Instead he walked toward her and watched as her bright interest changed to suspicion, and she backed away until he had to grab her arm to keep her from toppling down the stairs.

"Hey," she said and tried to shake him off.

"You would have fallen," Ben said.

"I'm fine." The woman shifted her heavy bag. "So?"

"You're a reporter." It wasn't a question.

"This is an interesting story," she said and stuck her hand out. "I'm Emily Winston. 'Emily's Evidence'?" She waited, her head tipped back so she could see Ben's face as recognition dawned. Nothing.

"Why are you in such a hurry?" Ben asked.

"Oh, come on," Emily said. "This is too good: seaside village in the grip of hysteria, lovers torn apart by a murder. It's great stuff."

"There was no murder," Ben growled, and Emily Winston, star reporter, got a little nervous. *This guy is huge,* she thought as her hand strayed to her phone. If she called 911, would police come pouring out of the police station down the road, or were they closer, still milling around the courtroom?

"Listen," she said, "this is news. There hasn't been a witch hunt like this since . . ."

"Eliza Howard," Ben said.

"Who?"

Great, Ben thought, *I've just made everything more interesting.*

"Patience is no witch," he said. "Leave us alone. Now." He turned and left Emily standing in the heat, the sweat on her back cooling as she realized just how serious the man was.

Of course there was no way she'd leave this town or the Sparrow Sisters alone, and by the next morning her new piece ran on her blog and was then plastered all over the Internet by religious nutbars, feminist supporters, and gossip sites. The attention earned spots for two more satellite vans in front of the Granite Point Town Hall.

It hadn't taken Emily more than an hour to get what she needed out of the library after the salty guy confronted her, less than that to rough out a great piece connecting Eliza Howard and Patience Sparrow. As she stood at the copier, organizing the story of the first witch hunt and building up the story of the second, a woman came over.

"Did Ben Avellar send you?" she asked.

"Who's that?" Emily asked and shoved the papers into her bag.

"He's a friend of the Sisters, a lobsterman, but no one's doing much fishing these days." The woman shrugged. "Ben did a bit of digging around just before the hearing. I thought maybe he was helping you."

So that's who Cap'n Birdseye is, Emily thought. She talked with the woman for a few more minutes before swinging her bag over her shoulder. She walked out into the heat and decided she'd have to hunt down this Ben Avellar, even if he scared her with his burly brawn and grump. Obviously, he had the inside track on the Sparrows.

Emily had already spent two days in Granite Point dividing her time between the courtroom and the town, walking its narrow streets, listening to conversations in the little bakery that even she could not resist. She was tired of the ever-changing weather (none of it good), the heat that sapped her of her characteristic drive and the wall of cold fog that crawled in at night, sending her back to her motel room near the high school. The rain soaked everything into soup and made everyone touchy and itchy under their damp clothes.

She was unnerved by the foxes that wandered into the

streets, tongues hanging, making cars spin to a stop, horns blaring. At the docks she saw fishermen reduced to sitting on empty lobster traps, playing cards, smoking, and, lately, drinking. She'd watched a family pack up, boogie boards and beach towels thrown hastily over suitcases in the back of their SUV. They were leaving early, the father said. There was no reason to stay with the weather so bad. The persistent red tide had closed most of the restaurants that depended on lobsters, scallops, and clams. The greenhead flies, usually gone by the first full moon of July, were bolder than usual, their bites becoming infected within hours. What was there to stay for, the mother had said as she loaded her children into the car. Might as well go back to the city. Emily wanted to go back too. She wanted to drink cold white wine and sit in front of her air conditioner. But, drawn to the story of the Sparrows, determined to see where it took her, she didn't leave.

Emily drove out to the Sparrow Sisters Nursery and stared at the locked gate and closely woven willow fences in frustration. Police tape was loosely strewn across the entrance, hardly enough to keep anyone out but enough to send Emily off. She went to Ivy House and knocked on the door as dusk was falling. The door was answered not by a Sparrow but by the doctor. Emily thought for a moment that someone was ill, but then she remembered his appearance that morning and wondered if Patience Sparrow had forgiven him his damning testimony. Henry stood, his whole body filling the doorway as if he thought she was going to rush him. As soon as Emily identified herself, she saw his jaw pop, and a muscle began to tic next to his eye.

"Go away," he snarled and slammed the door.

And she did, but only as far as the Nursery again. This time, she looked both ways before she ducked under the tape, climbed over the gate, and skidded down the sandy drive. What she saw was as chilling as any of the angry whispers she'd heard from the men milling around in the back of the courthouse. Everything was dead, some plants were ripped out, others were furry with mold, drooping under the weight of it. She walked between the rows, careful not to touch anything. She batted away insects and spat at the gnats that flew at her lips. She put her hand against the orchid house glass and peered in. The downy moss that had once cradled Patience and Henry was dry and cracked, yellow in the last of the light.

Emily knew nothing about plants, but she could guess that this was not the nursery that the police officer had described at the trial. It was certainly not the one she'd heard about from people she'd interviewed. The woman at the library described a heavenly place, lush as Eden, full to bursting with useful beauty. She had whispered (not just because she was in a library) that the Sparrow Sisters Nursery was an enchanted place and admitted that more than one woman in Granite Point had found her heart's desire through Patience, and not a few more had let her patch them up when they didn't. *Now that's a story,* Emily thought as she pulled out a flashlight. She swung it in a circle, feeling only a little foolish, and more than a little nervous as the dead and dying threw shadows on each other. It was as if everything had been rendered in black and white, all color leeched away by God knew what. But then she saw a blaze of bright pink, another of purple, and she followed the beam to a stand of tall flowers. The top of the hooded blossoms swayed above her hip. She reached to touch one but instead she took out her phone and snapped pictures. Not exactly above-the-fold stuff, but it did make for an interesting contrast: the living among the dead. She'd have to find out the name of the flower. And when she did, learning that it was foxglove, the very plant at the heart of the trial, Emily knew she had a real story. She was able to upload her blog by nine o'clock and return the *New York Times* call minutes later.

WHEN HENRY RESUMED his testimony the next day, the rain was so loud against the tall windows that a microphone had been set up next to the witness chair. This made Henry have to lean in every time he answered, putting him off balance as he braced his thigh against the chair. Paul Hutchins began the session by asking him questions about what he saw Patience do with Matty.

"She let him come to the Nursery any day he wished," Henry said. "She made him feel like a regular kid, at least for a while."

Rob Short flinched when he heard that. He rubbed his hands over his face; he'd forgotten to shave and now was beginning to look like the Rob Short the town had come to know.

"Did you ever see the defendant feed him anything, give him one of her remedies?"

Henry was certain in his answer. "No," he said firmly. "All I ever saw him eat was a cookie from Baker's Way"—he paused—"wait, I ate that cookie," he said.

The audience laughed and the judge glared.

"So Matthew Short never consumed anything in your presence?"

"No."

"What did Patience Sparrow give you, Dr. Carlyle?"

"She didn't give me anything," Henry said. *Did she?* he thought.

"Yet you said that she relieved your pain."

"Yes." Henry remembered her touch and hoped he wouldn't have to describe the coverlet. Even now he couldn't explain it, the way the violets stayed soft as silk, fresh as paint. He still couldn't sleep without it. He still dreamt only of Patience.

"How?" Paul Hutchins stepped back, sharing the stage with everyone. "If you are so sure that she didn't give you one of her remedies, how did she take your pain away?"

"I don't know," Henry said, and he didn't, not really.

"Right, you don't know if she slipped something into a drink or a bit of food." Hutchins was fairly strutting now, and Henry wanted to leap out of his chair at him.

"Listen to me." Henry gritted his teeth. "Patience did not try to trick me or sneak anything into me. She did not lie to me about her abilities, she never promised me anything she couldn't give. I am a doctor. I can't explain what happens in my science, why one person lives and another dies. How one woman has three perfect children and another is barren. I don't know why I can't fix someone and Patience can."

Charlotte Mayo stood in the back of the courtroom. She had been staring at the back of Sorrel Sparrow's head, wondering if she'd released her husband to be with the oldest sister. When Henry's voice dropped into a growl, she started listening again and recognized herself in his words. She looked at Patience, who was turned slightly in her chair, facing her husband and Rob Short across the aisle. In the set of Patience's neck Charlotte saw defeat, and in that moment she didn't think she could bear it. She knew the Sparrow Sisters (or certainly one sister) were the very things that had always kept Simon separate from her. But now she didn't want to see them so broken. It seemed as if everyone in the town had broken with them. It wasn't just the terrible weather, the fishermen painting houses in their salty jeans, the tourists who took one look at the blighted elms along Main Street and turned around, their RVs and boat trailers swerving as they left. People were biting and angry. The men came home with their hands already outstretched for a drink, the women sat at their counters staring at their groceries as if they'd forgotten how to feed their families. Granite Point was failing; the Sparrow Sisters Nursery was only the first sign.

Charlotte slipped out of the court and ran to the bathroom, her heels clicking so loudly in the empty hall that inside the room Sorrel turned her head at the sound. Cold water settled

Charlotte's stomach, but just in case she sat on the ratty bench by the door. She put her head down on her knees and waited, thinking about what she needed to do. Simon now spent more time at Ivy House than he ever had when he longed openly for Sorrel. They hardly ever spoke of anything but the case anymore. The last time Charlotte and Simon had made love was after the Founders' party. There was a desperate quality to Simon that night and as she clung to him, Charlotte knew that he was already far away. She also knew that she loved him, she cared if he was happy, more than she did herself, which surprised her. The day before she had gone to Patience Sparrow, driving her mother-in-law's car, her hair under a baseball cap. They met at the gates, out of sight. Charlotte needed her help, and that was something she could never tell Simon. And, even after bringing Patience's remedies home, she couldn't yet bring herself to slip them into Simon's water, for that's what Patience told her to do. Charlotte hid the three blue bottles behind her face creams so disturbed by her own actions her hands shook. When she consulted Dr. Carlyle some weeks after, she dismissed Patience with a defensive sneer. What else could she do? She'd sworn Patience to secrecy. Charlotte still believed in the established order of things; she'd always believed in keeping secrets.

Charlotte Mayo stood up and dug her phone out of her bag. She walked out of the town hall as she started texting.

Simon began his cross-examination of Henry Carlyle with an apology.

"I know this is hard for you, Dr. Carlyle," he said. "You are a physician and a soldier, and we are asking you to testify to something none of us can even define."

Henry nodded. He saw that Simon had sweated through his suit jacket.

"Do you believe that Patience Sparrow is capable of harming anyone?"

"No," Henry said.

The night before, Henry had made his own apologies. He had offered to fall to his knees in the front hall when he arrived at Ivy House and had gotten the first laugh in days out of the Sisters. He didn't know why or how they could find anything funny about his testimony that morning. Agony still rolled through him every time he thought of how thoroughly he'd exposed Patience. But as she pulled him into the kitchen, her finger hooked through his belt loop, Patience just said, "Hush."

So now, as he stared at Simon Mayo, Henry was determined to earn the forgiveness Patience promised him.

"Can you tell us what you discussed with Patience Sparrow the day before Matthew Short's death?"

"Patience wanted me to take Matty on as a patient. She was concerned that he hadn't been supervised since Dr. Higgins retired."

"And what about his father? Why wasn't he involved in Matty's care?"

"Objection," Paul Hutchins said. "Rob Short is not on trial here."

Judge Adams looked at Rob Short. *That man is a mess,* he thought. *Who's to say if he even knew where his kid was?*

"Overruled," Judge Adams said. "I wish to know how Matthew's care was administered."

Henry looked at Simon, who nodded.

"As far as I could tell, Matty did not take his medication as prescribed."

"How could you tell this?"

"He was alternately agitated or lethargic, and his symptoms were consistent with irregular dosage of both his anti-anxiety and anti-OCD meds." Henry paused. "As you can see from his patient file, his prescriptions were, in fact, not kept up-to-date. I had not yet seen him in my office. I can only testify to his behavior when I saw him at the Nursery."

"But you agreed to talk to Rob Short about taking over Matty's treatment?"

"Yes, at Patience's urging."

"Do you know why Matthew Short came to the Nursery every day?"

"He had nowhere else to go."

Henry and Simon looked at Rob Short along with everyone in the room.

"What is your relationship to Patience Sparrow?" Simon spoke only after he was sure everyone had time to despise Rob Short a little.

"I love her."

Henry surprised Simon. He'd expected Henry to say what

they'd discussed, that their mutual concern for Matty had brought them together. Simon had to scramble for another question, and he had the time as Judge Adams warned the whisperers into silence.

"Was Patience still treating Matthew Short?"

"No, she stopped two days before his death."

"Why did she stop?"

"She said she was concerned that Matty was ill, that his condition was more complicated, more serious than she could handle." That's not helpful, Henry thought as he saw Hutchins scribbling away on his pad.

"In other words," Simon continued, "Patience Sparrow refused to do anything to harm Matthew Short."

"Objection, hearsay."

"Sustained." Judge Adams nodded at Simon.

"Did she continue to treat you formally with her plant remedies?"

"No. I never asked her for a specific remedy."

Patience looked at her hands and wondered if it was perjury if you didn't know you were lying.

"If you had asked her, would she have made a remedy for you?"

"Yes, she wanted to."

"But you refused?"

"Look, I know exactly what Patience did to me. For the first time since I was wounded, I was happy. Maybe that's what it took to take the pain away." He looked at the judge. "If that is the kind of witchcraft she does, the magic Patience Sparrow makes, then I am begging you to leave her to make it."

Every person who had ever been treated by Patience held a breath as they listened to Henry. As one, they let it go, and it was as if a sweet breeze swept through. Even Rob Short felt it and closed his eyes, leaning his head against the back of his chair. He didn't open them until Judge Adams called for order although the room was as silent as if it had been emptied. Rob thought he knew what it felt like to be loved like that; he was almost certain that Matty's mother had made him hold his breath because he was too amazed to take the next one. In that moment, Rob Short began to doubt.

As Paul Hutchins had his final pass at Henry Carlyle, he began to feel the change around him. The chairs had cleared during the last recess; now only a few people scattered the back of the room. Rob Short was huddled behind the prosecution table as if he was cold instead of sweating. When court was called for the day, Paul Hutchins left as soon as the judge did, before Simon and the Sisters rose from their seats. Henry watched Hutchins go as he stood drinking cup after cup of water from the cooler beside the men's room. He gave Henry a curt nod before he realized he'd left Rob Short behind. God knows what the man might say. *That's it,* he thought, *I've lost the edge here. There'll be no call to indict Patience Sparrow now. I won't be riding any of this to a bigger, better place.*

Nettie Sparrow picked a newspaper off a bench and held it over her head as she and her sisters ducked out of the town hall and into the rain. Henry and Simon followed them. Ben was waiting for everyone at Ivy House. Patience felt claustrophobic, the people she cared about pressing into her. She almost wished for the solitude of the little jail.

Everyone smelled like wet dog as they peeled off their layers. Simon looked completely wrung out, even though his face ran with water. Nettie tossed the sodden newspaper onto the hall table and moved into the kitchen. Patience picked it up; it would stain with its damp.

"Don't read any of that," Ben said and held out his hand.

"Why?" she asked and looked at the paper. "Has the *New York Times* hauled out their burning stake too?"

"It's that blogger from the courthouse, Emily Winston," Ben said. "She's all over this."

Patience looked down the page until she read the byline. When she saw the picture of the digitalis, she held it up to Sorrel.

"This is from the Nursery," she said. "How did she get this?"

"Well, obviously she was out there." Nettie took the paper back into the kitchen with her. She read quickly through the first paragraphs until the room filled up. Nettie shoved the newspaper under the sink and turned to the cupboards. Ben came to stand beside her.

"Can I help?" he asked.

Nettie let him come out to the garden with her. No one could face hot food so she picked lettuce and cucumbers, scarlet radishes and nasturtium blossoms, and placed them in the basket Ben held. Nettie bent to pinch off some basil and sat on the edge of the bed to reach in for tomatoes. Ben watched her, the basket like a toy in his big hands.

"I think we should talk to her," he said. Nettie looked up at him. The rain had stopped and everything, including Ben, was steaming in the sudden sunlight.

"She's been digging around. Maybe she knows something."

"Oh, Ben," Nettie said. "What could she find to help Patience?"

"She played the Eliza Howard connection for good in her piece. She wrote how Granite Point has a history of accusing the wrong people, going a little nuts, collective hysteria stuff."

"Well, people have certainly gone nuts this time," Nettie said. She accepted Ben's help standing, and they walked back in together, her shoulder barely touching his arm.

They were the only residents of Granite Point who would be eating local produce. For several acres in each direction, the rain and alternating cold and heat had all but destroyed every crop: corn, lettuce, peppers, and zucchini, melons, peaches, rhubarb, and potatoes. If anyone believed in curses, and right about now they did, Granite Point was under one. And while Charlotte discovered that all the women she contacted figured that Patience was at the center of the bad luck, she also found that none of them really blamed her.

Sally Tabor was the first person to put words to the theory that the town needed to get behind Patience before she was indicted. Who knew what could happen if a grand jury was called? Charlotte met her for coffee in Sally's kitchen. Claire from the bakery; Marni Sanborne, the vet; and Fiona Hathaway, the Episcopal minister's wife, joined them. Had Charlotte been a pearl-clutching sort, she might have reached for hers. Instead she said, "What the hell?"

"Why are you so surprised?" Sally asked. "You've lived here long enough to see how central the Sparrows are to us all. We all know you've been calling around your circle. Well, here is ours. Let's put this together."

They agreed that yes, Patience was innocent of any wrongdoing and that it was, for the most part, the men in Granite Point who were whipping up anti-Sparrow feelings. All of them, and all the women they knew, continued to take their remedies and smooth their creams over their chapped hands, rub salve into their children's scrapes, drink tea as clean and green as grass. They made sure their husbands and grown sons drank their coffee only from the thermoses or mugs they carefully dosed and wore undershirts washed in Patience's berberine solution. They argued in furious whispers when those same men dared to bad-mouth the Sparrows, and they kept each other's confidences as they always had. What they needed now was a critical mass. As their remedy stocks dwindled and their babies stopped sleeping through the night, their toddlers stomped cranky and obstinate through their kitchens, their teenagers lay exhausted and weepy in their rooms, and their husbands turned away from them in their beds, the women of

Granite Point found the strength to make themselves heard. Charlotte Mayo made sure of that.

Simon was on his way out of Ivy House when his wife came to the door. They stood facing each other in the hall when Sorrel walked in.

"Oh, Charlotte," she said. "Would you like to stay for dinner?"

"I was just leaving," Simon said and moved to take Charlotte's elbow.

"Yes, I would very much like that, Sorrel," Charlotte said and left Simon open-mouthed at the door.

Charlotte entered the kitchen as if she wasn't terrified of everything the Sparrow Sisters meant to her. She smiled as if she didn't care that Patience held her secrets and Sorrel her husband's heart.

"I've been thinking about how I can help you, Patience," she said.

"You've already paid my bail," Patience said and reached for Henry's hand.

"Yes, well, that's just money. I'm here to offer more." Charlotte looked around at the people in the kitchen. *Here's a family,* she thought. *These people belong to each other, even if they have chosen to be together. They love one another no matter what it costs. I want this,* she thought and nodded firmly.

Charlotte took out her phone and scrolled through a list of contacts before she held it up to show Patience, the names still spinning by.

"These women are willing to support you," she said. "They

know what I have only just realized: you are at the heart of this town, Patience. Without you, and your sisters, Granite Point is failing. We all know this is true." She looked around the room and settled on Simon. "Now we convince the judge."

"The judge couldn't care less where Patience fits in this town, Charlotte," Simon said. "I need to prove that she didn't kill Matty."

"That's where you're wrong," Charlotte said. "Judge Adams grew up out here. I've been watching him, and I am betting that somewhere in his story there is a Sparrow. When we find that connection, then he will care about Patience and this town, and he won't need proof that Patience did nothing to Matty. He'll simply know it."

"And I know how to do that," Nettie said and reached under the sink. She unfolded the newspaper and pointed at the picture of the digitalis. "Emily Winston."

Patience stared at the *New York Times,* her head to one side as everyone else in the room began talking at once. She walked toward Nettie and took the paper, holding it closer to her face.

"There's a marble here," she said.

"Matty's marble?" Sorrel asked and reached for the paper. Below the eerie, shadowy blossoms, at the base of their still-green stems, there was a dark blue marble, no bigger than a Sparrow Sisters' blueberry, which is to say about the size of a gumball. If you didn't know what it was, you'd never see it at all. It was lying in a clump of drying mud, partially covered with fallen leaves. But to the Sisters it was terribly clear.

"Oh, Matty," Patience whispered and sat down at the table. Henry stepped to her side.

"I'm not getting this," Charlotte said as she sat next to Patience. She swallowed and rubbed her palm over her forehead. "May I have some water?" she asked in a thin voice.

Simon filled a glass at the sink and gave it to Charlotte. Henry turned so he could see her face and took her wrist gently between his fingers.

"This heat is hideous," Charlotte said.

Patience put her hand on Charlotte's shoulder and then reached to take a sip of her water.

"Yes, I'm sorry," she said. Charlotte looked at Patience. She saw that she was diminished by the last weeks. Her hair was more brown than red, her freckles as stark as pepper. She wondered which one of them felt worse.

Patience listened to the talk around her. At first she understood it. They were trying to make a plan with Charlotte, something about the women of Granite Point coming together to signal her innocence, something else about getting the reporter to write another story. Then Patience lost focus. She didn't hear them because there was something she was trying to grab. It was as if everyone was saying the same word over and over until it became nothing but a collection of meaningless sounds. The one thing she needed to understand was just out of reach.

"So what are we going to do?" Charlotte asked. "Who will call this Emily Winston?"

"I will," Nettie said.

"Wait a minute," Simon said. "What are we doing, who are we calling?"

In a startling display of solidarity Charlotte and Nettie and Sorrel all groaned.

"Keep up, Simon," Sorrel said. "Emily Winston writes the 'Emily's Evidence' blog, her piece is in the *Times* today because she's been in court every day this week. She's digging around, she's following Patience, and much as I don't like it, Ben and Nettie are right. This woman could help change what's happening."

Henry watched Patience. Her eyes jittered between her sisters, and she kept shaking her head as if to clear it. As everyone gathered around the table, filling the salad bowl with lettuce, squeezing lemon over the leaves, slicing hard garlicky sausages and cold steak, tearing basil, pouring icy white wine, Henry thought that as horrible as the situation was, he'd never felt so safe. If Charlotte saw a family, Henry saw a team, and for the first time, he thought that maybe this team was going to win. Except that Patience was still missing. When he placed a glass of wine in her hand, she finally looked away from her sisters.

"I think I need to go to the Nursery," she said.

Henry squatted down next to her. "Can't it wait until the morning?"

Patience thought for a moment. She let her fingers drift over Henry's where they gripped the edge of the table. His nails were bitten, his cuticles ragged. She nodded and stood. Charlotte reached for her wine, but Patience slid it away. Charlotte looked at her and then drank from her water. Patience pulled out a drawer beside the sink and brought a small tube over to Henry.

"This will soothe you," she said as she smoothed the cream over his fingertips. It smelled of mint and witch hazel.

"There," Charlotte said. "This is what I'm talking about. People need to see what Patience does, not what they imagine she does." She turned to Nettie. "Call the reporter," she said and handed her the phone.

CHAPTER THIRTEEN

Clove is a most stimulating and carminative aromatic

H ere's what I see," Emily Winston said.

Henry had taken up a spot at the sink in the crowded kitchen. *This is so peculiar,* he thought. The reporter sat at the Sparrows' kitchen table, a glass of wine in her hand and a notepad dark with ink at her elbow. Simon leaned against the tall cupboard; Nettie, Sorrel, and Ben sat across from Emily with Patience and Charlotte to either side. Emily couldn't keep her eyes off Patience, as if she could see the truth beneath her skin. What she could see was Patience's remarkable beauty, the fragile bones that made her hands look like birds as they fluttered over the table.

"Rob Short is wavering." Emily took a drink of her wine and reached out to pop a cherry tomato into her mouth. "It was obvious this morning when you"—she pointed at Henry—"were testifying."

"What did I say?" Henry asked.

"You begged for Patience. It was clear that you love her, and I think that Matty's father saw that he'd already lost, saw *what* he lost, I think." Emily slapped the table for emphasis. "Besides, the evidence against Patience leaves room for doubt, and Hutchins knows it. That doesn't mean Rob Short can't sue you, but he really doesn't look up to that, does he?"

"If that's what you got from the session, why didn't Hutchins jump on the opportunity put the grieving father on the stand, save what he could of the case?" Simon asked.

"Didn't you see him tear out of the courtroom? He couldn't wait to shake that man." Emily looked at Simon. "You know it too. If Hutchins succeeds in getting Patience Sparrow in front of a jury, which by the way is the only way he'll get anywhere with this judge, it will be solely because you guys fail her. And if he gets her that far, then she'll be moved to Hayward where she's as good as convicted because she'll have already been tried in the court of public opinion."

Everyone stared at the reporter.

"What? Do you think people are any kinder or gentler in the real world than they are here in 'Story Town'? If Judge Grumpy Adams is having a hard time believing Patience Sparrow isn't the wicked witch, good luck in the big leagues."

"Then why are we asking you for help?" Henry asked. "You think we're such idiots, we can't win for losing, why bother to offer your help?"

"Because it's not just the judge you need to win over, it's the town. And that's something I'm good at."

Patience opened her mouth, but Emily stopped her, putting her hand up.

"In the four days I've been here I have been soaked by rain, fried by the sun, bitten raw by mosquitoes, seen little kids sitting on their porches like old ladies, dogs lying down in the middle of Main Street, and a hermit crab scuttling over a gravestone miles from the ocean." She looked at the Sisters. "Am I right? Is this town seizing under some kind of guilty conscience?"

"Something like that," Ben said.

Emily Winston dug in her bag and came up with all the research she'd done on Eliza Howard. She sifted through the damp copies until she found what she wanted.

"Here," she said. "Eliza Howard was accused of witchcraft, falsely, obviously. The whole town began to fail and people were frightened, just like now." She began to read. "'Granite Point is a forgotten place. Never have so many elements gone so horribly wrong. With Eliza Howard in the dock, the summer is lost and anything good with it.'" That's testimony from the court records at the Howard trial." She put her papers on the table.

"So, three hundred years later, and none of you can see the

parallels, the story here?" Emily said, looking up at Henry. "I'm not about helping you. I'm a reporter, and this is a good story. If, as a result of my digging, Patience Sparrow finds justice, or Rob Short gets revenge, then I'll report that too." She stood. "I have a call to make."

Emily was going to tell her editor (the editor of the *Times,* yes!) that she was in with the Sparrows. She would turn this column into a headline in less than a day, into a TV piece soon after, a book contract, HBO series, who knows. *You gotta love small-town scandal,* she thought.

WHAT SHE SAID was true: the town was indeed spasming, completely undone by its own history. Just the other day Chief Kelsey had reached into his pocket to pay Claire for his coffee and come up with a handful of tiny mussel shells, wet and sandy. Paul Hutchins returned to his car to find it freckled with plover shit. He tried to scrub it off, but it was baked on hard by the heat that had swept in while he was in court. When he dipped his handkerchief into the old trough kept filled by the village improvement society, he found it running over with seawater, three skipjacks swimming in circles against the stone sides. Judge Adams's wife came to town on a whim to collect her husband one early evening. She parked behind the courthouse and opened the glove box to get a wet wipe; it was so hot, her mascara had run. She brought her hand out filled with deep-purple viola petals. She closed her eyes and remembered

Honor Sparrow, her best friend all through school. Sandra Adams cried.

Emily Winston may have given a name to the strangeness gripping Granite Point, but most people already believed in it. Everyone watched Emily leave, gawping like carp, wondering if this was a good or bad thing they'd gotten themselves into. For Patience, it was clear: it was good for the journalist and it wouldn't change what was happening to Patience. She understood Emily Winston: here was a woman who went after what she wanted, and although she preferred not to run anyone over on the way, sometimes she had to. Also, Emily Winston was a loner, something Patience certainly understood. Although she couldn't quite remember why now.

Patience gazed around the kitchen at the people who loved her—the ones who had to, her sisters, the one who chose to, Henry, and the ones who had gotten dragged along: Simon, Charlotte, and Ben. She thought that maybe everything that had happened in the last weeks might almost be worth it if she could keep these people. But Patience knew that if she was convicted, they would be lost to her in the most physical way. If she was released, would any of this odd little family ever forgive her for pulling them into the dark with her? Losing looked all kinds of ways to Patience.

"Is this woman for real?" Sorrel asked. It was late and she was tired. There was something slightly predatory about Emily Winston, and Sorrel wasn't entirely sure she trusted her.

"I believe that if this case gets a lot of light, people will begin to see that whether or not Emily is for real, Patience is." Ben finished one of the longer sentences he'd ever spoken and smiled at Nettie.

"Well," Patience said. "Thank you."

Sorrel was indeed physically tired, as was everyone in the kitchen. No one was sleeping properly; they all either startled awake in the night, woke before dawn, or tossed among alternately hot or cold sheets for hours before falling, flailing really, into troubled dreams. But Sorrel was more than tired; the unfamiliar feeling of fondness and respect she'd developed toward Charlotte Mayo exhausted her. Then she was surprised that over the weeks she'd watched Simon defend Patience, Sorrel had come to realize that she did love Simon, just not in the way she had once been so certain of. She felt the absence of that tiny torch with a sensation of lightness in her chest. As everyone else marked out the next steps, Sorrel watched Charlotte watch her husband and knew that, if nothing else, those two had found their way home.

So it was decided that the following day, after court, Patience and Emily would go to the Nursery together. Emily would profile Patience, and the tide of public opinion and the power of a fascinated nation would naturally raise her up beyond the reach of even Judge Adams. That is not what happened.

First, Henry stayed the night at Ivy House. It still amazed him that there wasn't some sort of rule about a prosecution witness sleeping with the accused person so, as if he were a school child and Simon his teacher, Henry avoided making eye contact with him as Patience took his hand to lead him up the stairs, grateful for every step they took toward her room and each other. And if the kitchen was the site of multiple epiphanies that evening, it was the small gray bedroom that woke in Patience the answer to Matty's death.

Just after midnight Patience sat up with a certainty that made the air turn cold around her. The moon was high and for the first time in days the sky was clear so that her room was as light as midday under it. Henry turned restlessly in his sleep but did not wake. She saw that his hair had gotten so long that it fell over his eyes in a dark mass. His arm was thrown above him as if he was warding something off. *Me,* she thought, and pulled on her clothes. When she got into the truck, she put it in reverse and coasted down the driveway and onto the street before she started the engine.

It was so simple, obvious really, now that she thought about it. The only living thing left in the Nursery was why Matty was dead, and although she hadn't mixed up an elixir of poisonous digitalis, she might as well have. She was sure of that. By the time she stood in front of the cluster of foxglove, it was bathed in ice crystals as well as moonlight. Patience bent to retrieve the blue marble and remembered the day she'd told Matty that this plant, this last of the Sparrow Sisters' flowers, could fix a broken heart. Matty, being Matty, had taken that to be true, literally. And, although Patience might have thought of a scenario whereby he'd give it to his father, whose heart had broken in so many ways, somehow Matty took it himself. Patience pulled off her sweatshirt, wrapped it around her hands and began yanking the plants out of the ground. She didn't give a thought to the evidence they still represented or to the trouble she might be pulling out of the ground right along with them. All Patience thought was to rid the Nursery of the poison. Her sweatshirt became coated in dirt and stained with a sticky white sap that leaked out of the stems. As soon as she touched the foxglove, it wilted beneath her hand, the blossoms closed in and browned. Fog rose from the ground and wrapped around her legs in ribbons of silver and pale blue. The bitter scent of dandelion and black elder hung in the air. Her arms were soon covered with long streaks of red blisters, as if she'd been stung by jellyfish. The welts rose visibly as she gathered the rotting foxglove and carried it toward the shed. Patience dumped it in a pile on the sandy driveway. She snapped her fingers against each other, wiped them down her pants to rub away bits of soil and stalk.

Patience walked over to the shed and fell to her knees beside the step. She bent at her waist; to anyone watching she looked like a pilgrim seeking absolution at a shrine. Except that Patience was sweeping her right hand and arm back and forth under the step until she found the box. If she'd thought about it, under a single step, open to the elements on both sides and right under her sisters' noses was not an ideal place to hide anything. But when Patience started smoking in college, she slid her cigarettes into a baggie and threw them under the steps because she knew she always had an excuse to come to the Nursery. Later, when her collection of random bits of family treasure grew, she put everything in her father's small lockbox, joined by the cigarettes. Eventually, Patience quit smoking, although she kept a pack in the box for emergencies. She hadn't had an emergency in nearly a year so she hadn't opened the box.

Now Patience turned the key that she kept in the truck and opened it. She took out her mother's lighter, the one she'd used through college. It was short and brown, wrapped in a kind of faux leather. Honor's initials were engraved on a tiny silver plaque on the front: H. J. F. Honor Jane Fairfield. The Sisters sometimes thought they should have called the nursery Fairfield. The lighter still worked because Patience kept the fluid topped up. She left the box on the step and went to stand in front of the foxglove, flicking the flint wheel over and over until the sound was so sharp and fast the crickets silenced themselves to listen.

The moon was bright white and cast shadows as inky and dark as the nights had been all month. As soon as Rob Short started walking down the drive, Patience recognized him. She pocketed the lighter and stood as still as any startled animal. When Rob drew close enough to speak, he did.

"Don't burn that," he said, his voice scratchy from disuse. "Whatever it is, they'll see the smoke and think something's wrong."

"Something *is* wrong," Patience said. "You said I'm wrong."

"I know." Rob rubbed his hand over his jaw. There was a stain on his shirtfront and he smelled like undone laundry. "I don't . . ." he started. "I wish . . ." He reached into his pocket and for a ridiculous second Patience thought he was going to pull out a gun. But it was only his cigarettes. He shook one up and offered it to Patience. He had to lean over the foxglove pile. It was an oddly courtly gesture, the bow, the offer. Patience took the cigarette and used her mother's lighter and tossed it to Rob. The smoke climbed down her throat with complete and satisfying familiarity, and she remembered why she'd quit in the first place. They stood staring and smoking for a minute or so before Rob spoke again.

"I know you didn't mean to kill my boy," he said. Patience opened her mouth. "No. I'm saying I don't think you hurt him at all." Rob walked over to the step and sat, and Patience followed.

"We probably aren't supposed to be talking to each other," Patience said. Her voice was so light with relief it was barely audible. Hearing Rob Short say he knew she was innocent was almost better than hearing Judge Adams say it.

"I don't give a shit about the rules," Rob said. In the moonlight his jaw was so jagged it looked as if it hurt. "Matty was born like he was. I know that too. His mother thought it was her fault, that she'd done something to make him sick. When it got so bad that last year, she once said she thought that she ought to let Matty go if he was so determined to leave." Rob lit another cigarette. "Of course, she was the one who left." He turned to Patience. "Everyone thinks she didn't leave a note, but she did. She asked me to remember her as better than she was." Rob wiped at his nose. "Do you think anybody will do that for me?"

Patience lifted her hand to touch Rob, but he waved it away.

"I don't deserve your touch," he said. Patience looked at him in surprise.

"Oh, yes," he said. "I know what you can do. I know that you helped Matty and that, if I let you, you could help me."

"Why won't you let me?"

"Because, as I said, I don't deserve it."

"Everyone deserves to be happy, to be well," Patience said and knew that Rob Short had probably not been either since his wife died.

"Well, that hardly seems true after what I did to you," Rob said.

"You didn't do it," Patience said. "You weren't thinking straight, and then the police and the prosecutor, they were all so eager, then the town got in on it." She shook her head. "The tragedy is Matty, but this place seems to have forgotten that."

Rob ground his cigarette out. "Well, I can help remind them. I can tell them how easy I made it for Matty to get lost, make sure you're not lost too." He walked back to the foxglove. "Why were you burning this?"

"Because I agree it's what killed Matty. He must have come back to the Nursery alone so he could take some. He believed it could cure a broken heart. But it broke his." Patience expected Rob to react, shout or cry or at least gape at her. But he only nodded.

"Matty tried to tell me about all the things he learned here, but I couldn't make sense of them. Maybe he didn't either. I guess that's as good a theory as any."

"The coroner said his heart just stopped." Patience pointed at the pile of flowers that had now begun to smell very bad. "Foxglove can do that to a person."

"Oh, lots of things can do that," Rob said. "I've been walking around for a year with a heart that doesn't work."

"That's what I mean." Patience came around to stand next to Rob. "Matty thought it was medicine for heartbreak, not heart trouble." As she said it, she realized how sad it really was that a little boy had to worry about anyone's broken heart.

"When I found Matty, I couldn't move. I just stood there looking at him." Rob rubbed his face again. "He was at the table, in the kitchen. His head was on his arms, and I thought he'd fallen asleep, like I had at the store. When I felt his cheek, I knew."

Rob began to cry silently, convulsively, and Patience wanted so badly to touch him that she made fists with her hands behind her back. Her body leaned toward him, and the scent of fresh lavender and lovage flowed around them both.

"I thought about his mother and how she'd chosen to leave us, and I thought for a second that Matty had done the same. I couldn't imagine what could make him so sad that he'd want to do what his mom did." Rob wiped his eyes with the back of his hand and lit another cigarette. He'd stopped offering them to Patience.

"I quit smoking when I met Annie," Rob said. "I quit drinking when she got pregnant."

Patience didn't know what to say to that. Clearly Rob Short had been drinking almost constantly since Matty died. Somehow, she'd always imagined Rob as a drinker. Maybe it was all the times Matty told her his dad was asleep on the sofa, or out with friends. The truth was that Rob slept on the sofa because he couldn't bear to be in the bed he had shared with Annie, the bed where he'd found her. And when he was out with friends, he wasn't. He was sitting in the office at the back of his hardware store, staring at the account books and drinking cup after cup of coffee. Once, when Patience brought Matty home from the Nursery, Rob watched them as he stood in the shadows down the street. He saw how his son let her touch him, how he smiled at something Patience said. Rob couldn't remember the last smile he'd gotten from Matty.

"You should put new gates up," Rob said. "Anyone could get in and take stuff. I could get you a real lock, put it up tomorrow, get some wood for a proper swing gate."

"Don't bother, there's nothing left to take," Patience said and waved her arm. Even in the dark it was clear that everything was dead or dying. Before, there had been so many plants of varying heights covering the land that it looked like breakers rolling in to shore. Now a thin layer of mist settled over the still, flattened landscape.

"It's a shame," Rob said. "Everything gone, everything dead. It's a goddamn shame." Of course he didn't mean the Nursery, not really.

"Well, there's nothing to do about it now," Patience said. "Let's go home." She left the foxglove where it was and shoved the box back under the step. She'd forgotten that Rob had her mother's lighter.

"What's in that box?" Rob asked.

"Stuff that belonged to my sister Marigold, my mother, a letter my dad wrote to me when I was born, memories, Matty's marble."

"A blue one?" Rob asked.

Patience nodded. She'd slipped it into the box when she went for the lighter.

"Oh, God, how did I lose him?" Rob put his head in his hands, and Patience saw Matty. Finally, she touched him, putting her hand on his back. She felt his tears ebb, the muscles relax as he took a last, heaving breath. She smelled the anger and regret leave him, a sweet and sour smell like lemons left too long in a bowl. His grief stayed, smoky and dark, as did hers, but that was right, so she just stroked the top of his shoulder once more before she put her hands in her lap.

"I'm going to call Hutchins in the morning, tell him to stop the hearing," Rob said, his voice hollow in the circle of his arms.

Patience almost laughed. "Rob, you can't stop this. You didn't start it, not by yourself."

"What are we going to do then?" he asked.

"See it through."

"When it's over," Rob said, "I'm leaving Granite Point. I never really belonged here anyway."

Patience looked at him. He was as tired as she was and as desperate to disappear somehow, to start over as if nothing had happened.

"Rob, you can't leave," she said. "You do belong here because Matty belonged here." She swept her hand around the Nursery. "He was happy here. You could be too."

"You think?" Rob asked. "Do you think anybody can forgive me?"

"Well," said Patience, "let's wait and see if anybody can forgive me."

"I forgive you, Patience," Rob said. "I thank you for what you gave Matty."

"Thank you," Patience whispered.

As they turned to walk back to the gate, Rob slowed his step and, making sure Patience had her eyes forward, he flicked the lighter and threw it over his shoulder. The foxglove was smoldering by the time they got to their cars.

WHEN ROB TURNED off onto Main Street, he flashed his headlights at the Nursery truck. Patience shivered with the oddest feeling of anticipation, but she wasn't cold. She felt her bones moving under her skin as she swung her legs out of the cab. Her fingertips tingled and buzzed as she opened the back door.

She tiptoed upstairs and slipped under the sheets, her bare feet leaving a trail of bruised clover and ground ivy. Henry stirred and turned to her, his body so warm that steam rose from the damp sheets, and they dried as she watched his chest rise and fall in the moonlight. She slid her hands around his waist and pulled herself closer until her chin bumped on his collarbone and Henry woke with a gasp.

"Were you gone?" he asked.

"I was, but only for a little while," Patience said. "I went to the Nursery. Rob Short was there."

"Jesus Christ!" Henry sat up. "Did he go after you?"

"God, no." Patience curled into Henry so that her voice was muffled when she told him what had happened. Her breath blew against him and as she talked, he felt heat rising into his throat. By the time she finished, Henry was covered in a sheen of sweat. He smelled of chervil and yarrow as if he too had been to the Nursery.

"I can't even think about what he might have done to you, how things might have been very different tonight, how angry Simon and Charlotte would be that you squandered the help they've given you," Henry said. He lifted Patience's head and gently pushed her back so that he could see her face. "Do you understand how dangerous Rob Short is?"

"He's not," Patience said. "He never really was." She lay down and pulled Henry with her.

Henry slipped his arms around Patience. He wanted to make

love to her, but he was overtaken by lethargy. He closed his eyes and as he drifted away into a dream about the woman next to him, he heard Patience say something, but it was already too late for him to understand the words.

"Charlotte is pregnant," she murmured.

CHAPTER FOURTEEN

Eglantine needs only a rain shower to bring out its full sweetness

The air was clean and fresh as Patience dressed for court. Henry had snuck out as soon as the sun rose and she felt, for the first time in a long time, that he was not where he belonged. Patience listened to her sisters down the hall. She heard Nettie laugh and Sorrel shush her. But, Patience thought, it was fine to laugh this morning. Whatever was about to happen, it was too late for any of them to stop it: not by being quiet or serious or even hopeful. But Patience did feel hopeful. She had only wished for Rob Short's forgiveness, but she had gotten much more at the Nursery. Even knowing that Matty had gone there in secret, taking what he thought could fix him, knowing that somehow it was still her fault, Patience knew that whatever came next, it would be what she had coming. So her hope was of the kind that held in it an idea of ending, of finishing this terrible time.

Simon Mayo had already left the big house on the harbor. He was at his desk in his office reading Emily Winston's piece in the paper, then scrolling through the comments on the website and wondering who these people were who had the time to have an opinion of a small-town trial. He was amazed at how many strangers gave a damn about Patience Sparrow. It took him several minutes to realize that over three-quarters of the comments were from Granite Point residents, mostly women whom Charlotte had rallied. Infant colic, eczema, straying husbands, invisible lovers, migraines, insomnia, bitter blood, unfulfilled desire, infertility, longing, heartburn, and heartache. Woman after woman told her story. And Patience Sparrow was at the center of them all. *Well,* he thought, *this is something.*

Charlotte was on her computer, too. She was feeling quite satisfied when she wasn't fighting nausea; never had heading so many committees been so useful. Charlotte took a sip of her tea. She figured her nerves were shot by the last few days; her hands trembled around her cup, and she swallowed acidy threads as they coiled in her mouth. Sitting in the Sparrow Sisters' kitchen, watching how Sorrel moved with unconscious grace, the way Simon easily anticipated those movements, handing Sorrel a bowl, wiping the breadknife and putting it away in a drawer he knew, had not been as easy as it looked, and Charlotte was drained. She did not yet know what Patience had whispered to Henry.

Henry was drained, too. He'd scheduled evening hours and several early morning appointments on the days he'd been in court, and he was already bent over his exam table giving a surly teenager a test for chlamydia. His testimony was finished, but after last night there was no way he'd not be in the room today. By nine he was finished and left the office to his temp. He walked to the town hall without hunching under rain or wiping sweat from his neck. It was pleasant, warm, sunny, and lovely, really. This fact was so surprising to the town that anyone who was able, and some who weren't, had come outside. As Henry walked, he saw things that surprised him: Claire Redmond came to the Bakery door to smile at him and blow a kiss off her floury fingertips; Pete looked up from the moldy window box he was emptying to salute Henry; and a man he recognized as the same one he'd treated for hives shook his hand and whispered, "It will all be fine now." When he reached the doors to the courtroom, the bailiff leaned in and Henry nearly flinched.

"You have a bit of shaving cream on your ear," he said and opened the door.

Henry swiped at his face and blinked. The room was filled again, only now it was nearly all women. Old and young, beautiful and marked by loss, angry and determined, women in the folding chairs, lined up against the wall, handbags and backpacks clasped in their laps, parked at their feet. There was a murmur as Henry searched for a seat. He saw Patience's back, straight in her chair, and Simon, who was turned in his seat to look at Charlotte sitting beside the Sisters. There was tenderness on Simon's face, and gratitude as he waggled his fingers at his wife. There was a rustling as the women in the last row shifted until an empty seat appeared at Henry's side. He sat, and the woman next to him patted his hand where it gripped his knee.

"Dr. Carlyle," she greeted him, and he saw that it was Sally Tabor. He knew what it took for her to leave an infant at home, and Henry's eyes grew hot with unshed tears.

Judge Adams came in through the door from the town offices. His black robe swished around his calves as he climbed the single step to the bench and the bailiff called for order. Everyone stood, and the judge waved his hand without looking up. When he did, he saw his wife. She was halfway back and gave him such a sunny smile that he smiled too, at which point the entire room filled with twitching mouths. Judge Adams cleared his throat and banged his gavel with intent.

"Settle down," he said to a mostly settled room.

He swung his gaze to the prosecutor and Rob Short. Neither looked well. Matty's father had bathed and shaved, but he'd grown so thin that his skin was pulled tight against his cheeks, and he was as pale as paper. Paul Hutchins had caught

Rob's case of nerves and was jiggling his ankle under the table so fast it was a blur.

"Mr. Hutchins?" Judge Adams asked. "Where are we?"

"I beg your pardon?" Hutchins said. He worried that the old judge had lost track of the hearing.

"You wish to recall the medical examiner?"

"Oh, yes," Hutchins said. "The prosecution recalls Dr. Wilkinson."

The M.E. walked to the stand and was reminded that he was still under oath.

"Would you please refresh our memories of your findings in the death of Matthew Short?"

Henry watched as Patience's shoulders sagged. Simon picked up his pen and fiddled with his pad. He had known Wilkinson was coming back up, but he didn't know why and that made him jumpy. He wanted to leap to his feet and shout "objection" just to get one in.

"Matthew Short died of cardiac arrest, coronary failure, to be more precise," the doctor said. "Digitalis toxicity, as stated."

"And what is digitalis?" Hutchins had stepped from behind the desk and buttoned his jacket.

"Well, as I said, it is derived from the foxglove plant. Death by toxicity is usually related to arrhythmia."

"Get to it," the judge barked. "We've heard this."

"I'm trying," Hutchins almost whined.

"Can you posit a theory as to how Matthew Short's body reached toxicity levels?" he said to the witness.

"I could posit any number of theories: a congenital problem heretofore undiagnosed, kidney disease, severe dehydration, an illness that put such a strain on the boy that a small amount of digitalis might . . ." He trailed off.

"And did your autopsy find any of these diseases?"

"No."

"Being given this poison, administered a significant dose of it, is that a theory you could posit?"

Simon stood. Every woman in the courtroom hissed. The sound was startling; their breaths released a chill that fell over the judge. He found his wife's eyes as she whispered, "Shame." *On me?* Judge Adams wondered and shivered under his robes.

"There is no evidence of purposeful administration," Wilkinson said and looked at Patience. "None."

"Accidental?" Hutchins asked.

"Well, clearly ingestion is unexplained. Digitalis was not found in the home."

"Yes, but foxglove, could Matty have eaten foxglove inadvertently?"

"Maybe, but it is unpleasant tasting at best, and he would have to get hold of more than a petal or two."

"Yes, he would, thank you," Hutchins said with a bit of his former bravado.

The doctor left the stand, and Paul Hutchins turned toward Patience Sparrow. He was going to call her; he knew it would cause a fuss, he knew there'd be a recess, a chambers meeting, but he also knew he had to get her up there in the end. She'd admit she grew foxglove, and she'd admit that Matty spent all his time with her in that spooky nursery. The prosecutor was beginning to think things were going his way again. He was as unprepared as anyone when Matty's father stood.

"Judge, I want to speak," Rob said. "I have something to show you." He held a worn black-and-white composition book; its pages were lumpy and crinkled. His face was empty, calm.

"Oh, for God's sake," Judge Adams growled. "Control this man, counselor."

"I have no idea what's going on," Hutchins said, turning in a half circle.

Simon rose to object, but Patience grabbed a handful of his jacket.

Rob looked at Patience, and she nodded. Judge Adams looked at them both.

"Fine," he said and waved his hand at Rob Short.

"Matty is gone. There is nothing we can do to change that, no trial, no conviction. There is no justice to find in this room," he said and turned to take in all the women, the scattering of sheepish men. They tilted their heads at him, some nodding, some frowning in sadness.

"This was his book," Rob said. "He hid it under his mattress, he hid it from me, from Patience Sparrow."

"Your Honor, this is not on the evidence list," Simon said.

There had been a raft of bits and pieces from Matty's room

in evidence: his last two marbles, the contents of his backpack, a collection of snow globes, chewing gum wrapper chains, and, of course, the dictionaries filled with pressed flowers and herbs. Matty was a magpie, drawn to shiny things, special things, things no one else quite saw. But the composition book, so carefully tucked away in his bed, was never uncovered in the search.

"Have you seen this?" Judge Adams asked Paul Hutchins.

"No," he answered.

"You, Miss Sparrow?"

"No," Patience said.

"It's full of stuff about the plants, and it's full of the plants he pressed in the big books," Rob said. He turned one of the pages and dried leaves fell to the floor. "Belladonna good for fevers and nights terrors," he read.

"Actually, belladonna can cause night terrors," Patience said softly.

"Blood root," Rob Short continued, "for asthma and the expectant."

"Expectorant," Patience whispered.

"See, that's just it," Rob said. "Matty had this whole note-book that was not right at all." He turned to Patience. "He listened to your words, and maybe he tried to make his own remedy from something he shouldn't have."

The room hummed, and Judge Adams narrowed his eyes.

"Look, look at this." Rob held the book wide in front of the judge and then turned to show the spectators as if they were bidding on something. "This is foxglove! Four stems of it over these pages, flowers, leaves, even bits of dirt! Here's his writing, here's what he thought it could do for someone: Can fix a broken heart if you get it just right."

"You can call it coronary failure or a cardiac episode, but what really happened was Matty died of a broken heart, maybe because he thought he could cure mine." Rob Short blinked back tears, and a soft sob echoed from Sally Tabor. "And I'm not saying it's all my fault, but I am saying it wasn't Patience Sparrow's at all. Leave it be, leave her be now." Rob sat down.

Judge Adams raised his gavel ready to slam everyone into silence, but there was no need. Faces, bright and attentive, were turned to him. Even Paul Hutchins looked eager for an end.

"Counselors, approach," he said.

When the men stood before him, Simon with a hand on the bench as if he needed help staying upright, Judge Adams spoke. He made no effort to keep his voice down.

"This is over," he said. "It should never have begun." He shot a look at Chief Kelsey, who, other than the direct participants, was the only other man in the room. "I know it, you know it, and Mr. Short has been wise and gracious enough to declare it so." He brushed Simon's hand off his bench. "Now, get back."

"If, when I address this chamber, there is one sound out of any of you," Judge Adams warned, "I will reconsider everything I am about to say."

The room was so still that birdsong floated in through the open windows, and several people turned sharply, realizing that the air had been silent for weeks.

"I am dismissing this case and everyone in this courtroom, something I should have done on the very first day of this misbegotten hearing. You, Mr. Hutchins, have shown me no probable cause as to the commission of a crime, nor as to the accused's role in it." He stopped to be sure his instructions had been followed, that the audience was quiet. "Mr. Short, I suspect that you were swept up in this hysteria and that your grief made you irresponsible with your accusations. I am relieved that you came to your senses before it was too late."

"Patience Sparrow, go away. Go back to your plants, pick your flowers, and make your magic, but keep your methods to yourself. This court will not call you again."

Judge Adams snatched his gavel and brought it down.

Not surprisingly, Emily Winston was the first out of the room. *Twenty-four hours after I got into it,* she thought smugly. *One day and it's all over. There's a movie in this.* She slipped down the town hall steps, waving at the network producer who was standing in the shade of the satellite truck. She saw Ben Avellar pacing on the sidewalk at the foot of the stairs.

"Hey, where were you?" Emily asked.

"I couldn't take it anymore," Ben said. "Besides, it was nearly all women in there."

"Yeah, that's pretty weird. I guess Patience's got real girl power."

Ben looked at Emily with such naked panic that she realized she hadn't told him what had happened.

"It was dismissed," she said. "The case, it's done, she's free to go."

Ben stumbled as his legs gave under him, and he grabbed the wooden banister that ran along the wheelchair ramp. He swung half down before he hauled himself up again.

"Okay, then," Emily said. "I guess that's good news."

Ben couldn't speak.

"Well, I still want that interview with the witch," Emily said firmly. "My story's not finished."

Ben was still trying to find the strength to climb the steps when the entire courtroom came pouring out the doors. He scanned the crowd for Nettie, for Sorrel. He knew he looked more than a little crazed as he talked himself forward, step by step, whispering, "Excuse me" and "Please, please," as he swam upstream. Nettie found him and pulled him back into the hall.

"It's over," she said and wrapped her hands around Ben's big biceps. "You're shaking!"

"I'm a wreck," Ben said and drew Nettie in until she was safe against him. He picked her up and pulled her out of the flow of people. Nettie pushed down on his arms and tilted her head until she could kiss him square on the lips.

Patience and Henry were alone in the courtroom. Simon and Sorrel had walked out with Charlotte. After Judge Adams's declaration, Rob Short was led from the room by the bailiff who couldn't wait to get back to Patience about his psoriasis. Now Patience stood in front of Henry. He couldn't stop smiling, and she put her finger against the tiny half-moon scar at the corner of his mouth. She remembered how she had run her tongue over it the first time she kissed him. Henry could not believe his luck: that he'd found Patience at all and then that she wanted him and now that he had gotten her back. They didn't speak for long moments, not just because the birds were singing again and were terribly loud.

SORREL LOOKED AROUND the Nursery. Under the sunlight, in the sweet cacophony of birdsong, the soft air that seemed hardly to have any weight at all, the damage was beyond imagining. In the middle of the driveway, just in front of the shed there was a still-smoking black mess. Sorrel bent to see if she recognized the plants—she knew that much: it was definitely a pile of burned vegetation.

"Haven't they done enough?" Sorrel whispered. She picked up a broken, thorny rose cane and poked. The smell was pungent and choking, and she turned away and dropped the stick. "Jesus," she said and went for a shovel.

Charlotte had left Simon on the town hall steps talking to Emily Winston and a cluster of reporters. The sight of several television cameras privately thrilled her. This could only be good for Simon's practice, she'd thought. Take that, Papa Mayo.

She'd had to wait, her Mini growling, for the parking lot to clear enough for her to leave. By the time she found herself on Calumet Landing, it was obvious that she meant to go to the Nursery. She smelled the burning foxglove as she turned in.

Sorrel was shoveling sand over everything so that, after it cooled, she could dump it into the pickup and take it away. Charlotte pulled up, and Sorrel stood the shovel at her side and stared.

"Hi," Charlotte said as she climbed out.

"Thank you, Charlotte. You saved us all today." Sorrel thought both their voices sounded thin, too high and uncertain in the quiet.

"Saved?" Charlotte shook her head. She didn't feel particularly saved. "What is that?" she asked, pointing at the foxglove.

"Probably a final love note from the vandals who trashed the Nursery." Sorrel twirled the shovel between her palms.

"Vandals?" Charlotte asked. "More like an angry mob. This place is a disaster." She looked out over the damage. "Boy, the guys are going to regret this once Patience gets back on track. Maybe she should just curse all the men and be done."

"Oh, I have no doubt that if she could, she would," Sorrel said. "But in case you didn't get the subtext today, Patience is incapable of harm."

"I got it, Sorrel," Charlotte started to snap but backed off. "I always got that about Patience."

Charlotte held her hand out. "Give me that," she said. Sorrel gave her the shovel and went for another. Together they tamped down the foxglove. Together they went into the shed and sat across the unused counter.

"You love Simon," Charlotte said.

"I did," Sorrel agreed. "But that was long ago, and we're different people now."

"Not so different. Simon still loves you. He never stopped."

"Oh, Charlotte, that's not true." Sorrel meant what she said. If she and Simon really loved each other, they would have found themselves beyond the playground.

"Don't be patronizing. Simon looks at you as if you're water in the desert. He looks at me as if he's waiting for me to change."

"You have changed!" Sorrel said. "Look what you did for Patience. But more, Simon has changed."

Charlotte turned and walked out the shed door. Suddenly she just couldn't stand another minute of being the noble Charlotte. She wanted to be the sharp Charlotte, the stiff, cool, numb one who only a few weeks ago would have been willing to spend the rest of her marriage with a man who didn't want her just because she hated failure. She'd almost convinced herself that she didn't want him either. But then she'd seen Simon as he took on Patience Sparrow. She'd seen him fill in the sketchy outlines of his own fine character. He became the real Simon who made the Sparrows feel safe in a way she never let him do for her.

Charlotte took a step and her sandal snapped. She stumbled and found Sorrel at her elbow. She kicked the shoe off and the other one too and stood in her bare feet on the cooling sand.

"Fuck!" she growled. "God Dammit!" she screamed into the sky. Starlings, larks, and mockingbirds startled up from the tupelo trees ringing the Nursery.

Sorrel began to laugh and as her voice rose, the birds returned and settled back into the trees, their song louder even than Charlotte's shout.

EPILOGUE

*I*t would be late August before anyone really registered that the Sparrow Sisters Nursery looked as if the lost summer had never happened. Roses climbed the shed, entwined with dark purple clematis, leaves as glossy as satin. There were no thorns. Patience's cupboard was overflowing with remedies, and the little barn was often crowded with seekers. The half acre of meadow was wild with cosmos and lupine, coreopsis, and sweet William. Basil, thyme, coriander, and broad leaf parsley grew in billowing clouds of green; the smell so fresh your mouth watered and you began to plan the next meal. Cucumbers spilled out of the raised beds, fighting for space with the peas and beans, lettuce, tomatoes, and bright yellow peppers.

The cart was righted out by the road and was soon bowed under glass jars and tin pails of sunflowers, zinnias, dahlias, and salvia. Pears, apples, and out-of-season apricots sat in balsa wood baskets in the shade, and watermelons, some with pink flesh, some with yellow, all sweet and seedless, lined the willow fence. Rob Short had indeed replaced the gate and lock, but there was no need. There was not a single soul in Granite Point who would dare to push the Sparrows.

The town recovered, too. Although the wisteria had to be replanted again on the town green, and the lobsters were neither so big nor so plentiful as in other years, and the painted mermaid was rubbed paper thin by all the fishermen. Chief Kelsey took his family on vacation to California.

When Charlotte went to see Henry Carlyle, uneasy over her lethargy and lack of appetite, he needed only the briefest look to say the whispered words he hadn't heard the first time they were spoken. Charlotte called Patience before she even got home, and Patience, of course, pretended to be as surprised as Charlotte. Simon burst into tears in front of his secretary.

Nettie and Ben went to see Matty's grave late one afternoon when the sun was already beginning to lower too early. They held hands as they stood before the tangle of lobelia and alyssum that softened the raw soil. After she watered the flowers, Nettie reached up to cup Ben's jaw and kissed him.

Patience and Henry found in each other the balm they didn't even know they needed. What began for them both in a flurry of heat and sweat, an irresistible tide of passion and want, shifted into gentleness. When Patience stroked Henry's leg, he hardly noticed anymore. The tighter she held him, the closer he pulled her. If there was magic to be found, that was it.

And Sorrel? That is a story for another time . . .

ACKNOWLEDGMENTS

I want to thank Grub Street in Boston for encouraging writers to create and discuss their work with generous, like-minded people in a clean, well-lighted place. In particular, novelist and teacher Sophie Powell gave me the wings and the courage to share *The Sparrow Sisters* for the very first time and for that I am so very grateful. My agent, Faye Bender, showed me that my voice had beauty and worth and that there was indeed someone out there willing to listen. Brave editor Lucia Macro was the someone who heard that voice and gave it the shape and strength needed to really sing out. Much gratitude to my small and dedicated writers' group for hard truths and gentle guidance. Finally, thank you to David, who isn't the least bit surprised that this dream has come true for me.

About the author

2 Meet Ellen Herrick

About the book

3 Reading Group Discussion
Questions

Insights,
Interviews
& More . . .

Meet Ellen Herrick

© Susan Lapides

ELLEN HERRICK was a publishing professional in New York City until she and her husband moved to London for a brief stint; they returned nearly twenty years later with three children (her own, it must be said). She now divides her time between Cambridge, Massachusetts, and a small town on Cape Cod very much like Granite Point. ∾

Reading Group Discussion Questions

1. What do you think is the meaning of the first line in *The Sparrow Sisters*: "All stories are true, some of them actually happened." Do you think, for instance, that it is a reference to the story that is about to be told?

2. *The Sparrow Sisters* is set in a New England seaside village, Granite Point. Why are we often attracted to stories about small-town life?

3. Living a simple life in a small town is seductive. Yet, Granite Point becomes very complicated as it turns on Patience Sparrow. Is that particular to small towns?

4. The three sisters in this novel each play a role in their family and at the Nursery. Discuss each role and how they complement each other and sometimes conflict with each other.

5. How does the author create the tension that exists between Patience and Henry? How does she create it differently between Sorrel and Charlotte, Simon and Sorrel, Nettie and Ben?

6. *The Sparrow Sisters* has an old-fashioned feel. In fact, in the early pages it could almost be set many, many years in the past. Do you think this timeless effect makes it easier for the reader to believe the magical realism aspects? ▶

Reading Group Discussion Questions
(continued)

7. There are a handful of vivid characters that inform *The Sparrow Sisters* even though they are dead. How does the author make those characters real and relevant to the sisters and to the reader?

8. The author paints both a realistic picture of Granite Point and its residents and a fairy-tale one. What elements and senses and words does she use to make her word pictures so vivid? Which of the senses she employs is most appealing to you?

9. Why do you think Henry Carlyle and Patience Sparrow are attracted to each other when they so clearly have very different views on healing?

10. Do you believe that Eliza Howard and Clarissa Sparrow were really witches? Do you believe that Patience Sparrow is a witch?

11. Do you think Rob Short will stay in Granite Point?

12. Do you feel hopeful for Sorrel?

13. Do you believe in magic? ◟